The Cajuns

a novel

Gus Weill

Simon & Schuster
New York • London • Toronto • Sydney

SIMON & SCHUSTER
Rockefeller Center
1230 Avenue of the Americas
New York, NY 10020

SIMON & SCHUSTER and colophon are registered trademarks
of Simon & Schuster, Inc.

For information about special discounts for bulk purchases,
please contact Simon & Schuster Special Sales:
1-800-456-6798 or business@simonandschuster.com

Designed by Paul Dippolito

Manufactured in the United States of America

10   9   8   7   6   5   4   3   2   1

Library of Congress Cataloging-in-Publication Data

Weill, Gus.
    The Cajuns : a novel / Gus Weill.
        p. cm.
        1. City and town life--Fiction. 2. Louisiana--Fiction. 3. Cajuns--
Fiction. I. Title.

PS3573.E388C34 2004
813'.54--dc22
                                                    2004042819

ISBN 0-7432-4979-8

Chuck Adams, Editor
When the young tenor Enrico Caruso auditioned for
Giacomo Puccini, Puccini said, "God has sent you to me."

James Carville
Whose idea this book was. "It's the Cajuns, stupid!"

Gus Weill, son; and Gus Solomon Weill, grandson
Thus, do we endure.

Ray Sara Weill Weil, sister
You still got it, Tonsi!

Theodore (Ted) L. Jones
Georgia boy. Louisiana man. Friend always.

John McGregor
I cannot think of a legitimate reason.

Marie and Roland Laurent
Allons à Lafayette.

We came

We saw

and

We surrendered

to

The good times

—Karrell Ardoin

The Cajuns

1956

Three days before the end of the school year, Bob Boudreaux, Sheriff of Richelieu Parish, Louisiana, walked down a short flight of steps at the rear of the courthouse where his gray unmarked Ford was parked, got in, turned on the ignition, and backed out onto St. Peter Street.

The cruiser was immaculate, kept that way by Herman "Thank You Please" Washington, the trustee who was by far the Sheriff's most dependable employee.

Bob Boudreaux was a neat compact man, not quite six feet tall, who by midsummer would look Spanish. He wore khaki shirt and trousers over polished brown boots. A simple star-shaped, gold badge that read SHERIFF was pinned to his shirt pocket. His black hair was neatly parted, and you could see his scalp; white was beginning to show above his small ears.

His gray eyes peered out from beneath narrow upper lids, shielding thoughts turned inward. His nose lay flat against his face, broken in a long ago fight and ill set by the late Dr. Prudhomme.

The mouth was a straight line, like something drawn on the ground with a stick. The lips were all but nonexistent.

He turned on the radio as he drove onto Main Street, where telephone poles were festooned with fading pink and gray circulars, old promises from the last campaign. Promises for rural people who wanted to believe. Promise: Drainage ditches are kept clean and open at all times. Promise: Grass is cut monthly in ditches and on roadsides. Promise: Garbage is collected weekly.

All these candidates had lost. People stayed with the tried and the true, Sheriff Bob Boudreaux thought, whatever tried and true meant.

He had been elected by trickery and reelected without opposition, and thought, I am tried but am I true? In some ways, he reasoned, in some ways.

Then he quickly put the thought behind him. What point would be served? What in hell was truth but a sore he kept picking at? He thought of BeBe and with guilt turned on the radio to make that thought go away as well.

He saw Na Na Duhon spinning records, standing in the plate glass window of his radio station, CAJN. Na Na's bow tie bobbed as he sent sweet nothings to his De De: "Daddy's gonna bring home some good ice cream for his De De." Play the music, Na Na, for God's sake play the music! Mean people said, Why didn't Na Na send sweet nothings over the air to his little papoon at Misty's Paradise Inn, huh?

Na Na saw the Sheriff, gave a big wave, then shot him the finger. Boudreaux stared back, face expressionless. Na Na threw back his head and laughed. No way to get a rise out of Bob Boudreaux!

For sure. Music at last. Thank you Jesus. Thought of BeBe now gone.

The only Roman numerals in Richelieu were on the face of the clock on the First National Bank, stuck at 4:00, like Main Street's single stoplight—stuck on red. There was something comforting about it. Always 4:00, always red. Old-timers leaned against the bank, dressed in Tuf-Nut coveralls, brogans, white socks, cash from their Social Security checks in their pockets. Most were tenant farmers too old to work the land, thrown out of the shacks they had raised their children in, spent a productive lifetime in. That was the catch: you had to be productive.

Big Shot Fontenot exited the bank, high-stepping it to Savoy's Pool Room for one final bourrée game before the wake. Funny how men walked, Boudreaux thought. Big Shot walked like he owned the earth—which he just about did. Along with the Senator. The Senator made him think of BeBe. Bad. He was saved again by Father Brother-in-law's soothing voice caressing God via the Rosary, which he recited every afternoon on CAJN.

"Hail Mary full of grace . . ."

Having the Rosary in the background seemed somehow appropriate while going past Hurphy Perrault's law offices, the best looking building on Main. All white brick and glass, like an alien spaceship amid the plain wooden fronts of almost everything else. Hurphy was attorney for the diocese, district attorney for the parish. Hurphy would be left the Bishop's ring upon his death and was the only Knight of St. Gregory in all of Richelieu. Hurphy had a clubfoot, but no one noticed it because Hurphy was also very rich. "He got it coming out the ass," was the way Bad Ass Thibodeaux, the town drunk, described him, and everyone nodded. Bad Ass certainly had a way of putting things. Drunk or sober, although his sobriety was really only a memory.

Bobby drove past Moe Weiss's Notions and Tobacco. Camel cigarettes, Gillette Blue Blades, Vitalis, Keep Moving Cigars.

Doc Alcide Mouton's redbrick clinic was next, the red light on outside the emergency entrance.

Coon's—Since 1900. Already filled with bourrée players and Jax beer drinkers, slapping their cards down on the table like a fusillade of pistol shots! Catfish François stirring the courtbouillon or gumbo or sauce piquant of the day in his big black pot. Drink, play cards, shoot the shit. Coon Soileau should have been a wealthy man, but he was his own best customer and always lost.

The Sheriff rolled past Hot Dog Hebert's Bakery, scent of donuts and cream puffs and fresh French loaves filling the air like perfume. Hot Dog admitted, "It don' taste good as it smells," a puzzle he had never solved. "Like a virgin's pussy," Hot Dog liked to brag. No one argued.

Past Tooky "Best Rates in Town" Trahan's Insurance. Maryland Casualty, Travelers, and Aetna—he had them all. Blessed Mother in the window, smiling like Tooky had got her a good policy, and a cross over the door. Tooky did a big church business and believed in advertising.

Past Possum Aucoin's Barbershop. Possum asleep in his own chair, the *Gazette* over his face to keep the sun out. Gossip slept in Richelieu. Rumor took a snooze.

"Blessed art thou amongst women . . ."

Watch Out Naquin's Funeral Parlor came into view, one of Watch Out's coloreds out front polishing the black hearse. The Sheriff smiled, though his lips barely moved. Watch Out swore to one and all at One Lung Savoy's poolroom (in defense of a direct accusation by Possum Aucoin) that he absolutely "my han' to Gawd!" made the colored boy get out of the room when he embalmed a white lady. Further, Watch Out declared, "I believe in states' rights firs', las', and always!" His mean-spirited listeners snickered. They weren't so sure. Possum had previously stated that the colored boy was Watch Out's son. He was known to prefer black women. Watch Out was forced to take another oath.

"Our Father, who art in Heaven . . ."

Slowly past Richelieu High School, where Cap'n Eddie, the crossing guard, waiting for the buses that would take the children home, offered a salute which the Sheriff did not return. One of these days real soon he was going to have to do something about Eddie Sonnier, Purple Heart or not. Enough is enough, he thought and tapped his steering wheel in frustration. He dreaded the inevitable.

"Blessed art thou among women . . ." Father Brother-in-law was reciting the Rosary at an accelerated pace. He too had to get to Ti Boy's wake.

Poor little Ti Boy, an image of him scooting by on his bicycle, the *Gazette* bag dancing side to side on his handlebars.

Bobby thought, The last time I attended a child's wake it was Hot Dog Hebert's son. The kid couldn't leave his daddy's donuts alone, ate thirty-six of them for breakfast, died of obesity. Took twelve pallbearers. Watch Out Naquin, who'd embalmed him, said the lad weighed in at three hundred pounds. Bobby was unable to eat donuts thereafter, though he still loved their smell.

Father Brother-in-law's final "amen" came as Bobby pulled into Prejean's Esso for a fill-up. President Prejean himself tanked him up. "It's a sad day," President said as he halfheartedly wiped at the window with a dirty cloth. "It looks worse," Bobby muttered, but President paid him no mind. Prejean's mama had named him President so that no matter what, people would have to address her pride and joy as President. It was a self-fulfilling prophecy, as Prejean was in his fourth term as President of the Rotary, Richelieu's only civic club, though it boasted at least eleven Catholic organizations (Sodality of the Blessed Virgin, Catholic Daughters of America, Ladies Altar Guild, Society of the Little Sisters of the Poor, Knights of Columbus, et cetera, et cetera.) No one could say exactly why they voted for Prejean. It had to be the name, Bobby thought as he drove away. Rumor was that Prejean was thinking of running for public office, maybe Mayor, bad news for Big Head Arceneaux, who was both Mayor and Richelieu's only midget. Big Head told the boys at Possum Aucoin's barbershop, "He's gon' find out there's a hell of a difference in being Mayor and being President." Hurphy Perrault offered what he thought he'd heard President's campaign slogan would be: "It takes a big man for a big job." The Mayor, who stood just over four feet tall, said he didn't think that was a damn bit funny and stormed from the barbershop, laughter following him out the door. Hurphy innocently asked, "What the hell's he mad about?" And got some more laughter.

One of the last shops on Main Street was Maybelle's Beauty Parlor. Slogan: "A little corner of Paris in Richelieu." Maybelle actually went to Paris every other year to keep up with the latest in styles. The *Gazette* followed up on these exotic visits every time with a front-page interview in which Maybelle gave very little away about those new styles. "They're both fascinating and unique" was the most she'd say. But it stimulated her business so much that men even sneaked into the shop at night (by appointment) so that they could be up to date on hairstyles. The radio station owner, Na Na Duhon, was one of her customers for sure. "That and a twenty-dollar bill is how he keeps his little papoon," Possum Aucoin said, not liking the competition one darn bit. Possum also suggested that Maybelle didn't go to Paris at all but slipped away to her sister's in neighboring Port Arthur, Texas. "That's her Paris," he said, giving the whole world the finger. Bobby Boudreaux's BeBe went to Maybelle's religiously every week, and honestly he couldn't tell much difference, even with a Paris style. BeBe loved her bangs.

The Sheriff was now out into the country.

The sun was a big neon peach. The heavens were pink and blue like a rainbow had tipped over, spilling color everyplace. He slowed to let an armadillo cross the blacktopped road. All the roads leading to the Senator's land were blacktopped. Thank you, Governor. Thank you, Baton Rouge.

To his left was a coulee where colored kids played. He turned on his siren and they laughed, and he waved at them and they waved back. To his right were the endless rows of cotton—it looked good, green, healthy. He shook his head. That very field would look like snow-laden earth when the cotton bloomed.

BeBe saying, in his head, One day that'll all be ours, like she was compensating him for what was missing in their life, though neither could say exactly what that was. But something was. Like an empty room in a house. Mysterious and sad. He shook these thoughts away as he realized he'd left the siren on and self-consciously turned it off.

A white egret fed at the coulee's side, balanced perfectly on reedlike legs. Overhead a crow. So much life. So damn much life!

Accordion and fiddle music was playing on the radio, the singer saying that the trouble was his girlfriend didn't understand him. He mournfully asked, Why? Singer and song offered no answers. The question became monotonous and somehow burdensome, and Bobby turned off the radio. Now there was the silence, another kind of burden. He felt alone and could not have said why.

Aristede and Marie Brouliette farmed twenty acres of the Senator's good cotton land, something they had done with the help of their late son, Ti Boy. From this, they picked two or three bales of cotton a year. They stayed in debt, and though the Senator never pressed them, was in fact generous about advancing them money on which to subsist, they were as trapped as a nutria in one of those traps in the swamp. They knew this and accepted it. They were the third generation to farm someone else's land.

Their house rested on cinder blocks and was covered in fake brick material, and it tilted ever so slightly to the right like it was trying to catch a breeze. There was, of course, no wind, just heat and afternoon rains, and the cottonwoods that flanked the screen door were still.

Beulah the milk cow munched grass nearby.

On the tiny front porch was a swing. On the side of the house toward the rear was a privy, a much used path leading to it.

Leaning against the side of the house was Ti Boy's bike. A J. C. Higgins. It had once been red. The seat was beginning to rot. On the handlebars was slung the *Gazette* bag. That very year Ti Boy had been named Carrier of the Year. His photo had been on the front page of the newspaper, receiving from Zeke Daigle a certificate for a suit from Harmon's Department Store in Lafayette, which advertised in the *Gazette*. Ti Boy had a big grin, and Zeke had a hand on his shoulder. Zeke was quoted as saying, "That Ti Boy is definitely going places."

Well he sure was. Into six feet of rich soil.

The yard was filled with cars that Chief Deputy Slo' Down Angelle helped park. He had saved two spots nearest the house for the Senator and the Sheriff. Bad Ass Thibodeaux, plastered as usual, argued that he had as much right to a good parking spot as "those big shots." That he had no car was not mentioned.

Slo' Down paid him no mind. He arrested Bad Ass once a week, and they were good friends. "Why you so bad?" Slo' Down asked, and Bad Ass answered, "Thass jist my ways." Slo' Down nodded. That made good sense.

Bobby stepped from his car. He walked almost stiffly, as though in lockstep with invisible troops. He did not greet Slo' Down, who didn't expect it anyway but who considered Bobby to be one strange man, a man who had gotten his job by a trick, without which he would be as common as the rest of them.

Inside the house, the room was filled with whispers shattered by a booming baritone voice. Mayor Big Head Arceneaux was holding court, compensating for his lack of stature with a voice that seemed to come from a megaphone. He was talking about World War II, primarily errors made by Ike. He said the name like they'd gone to West Point together.

Strangers to Richelieu wondered how Big Head had ever gotten elected Mayor. Attorney Hurphy Perrault offered, "What the hell you want us to do with him? Would you hire him?"

Tooky Trahan once said while getting a shave at Possum's barbershop that he wished someone would get Big Head on an elevator and fart on him. That broke the boys up. There were several volunteers but limited elevators in Richelieu.

Chicken and sausage gumbo, made by Catfish François himself, was bubbling in the kitchen, and everybody would have a bowl or two with some of Hot Dog Hebert's French bread. BeBe had sent over a big earthenware bowl of potato salad, which everybody acknowledged she made better than anyone else in the parish. A lot of celery.

The Sheriff approached Marie and Aristede, who huddled together in silence. She wore black and would wear only that color for a year. Bobby shook hands with Aristede and slipped him a folded hundred-dollar bill to help pay for the funeral. He kissed Marie on the cheek. Their hands were callused from all the cotton picking. Bobby thought, Where they really need calluses is around their hearts. He said, "I'm sorry." There wasn't anything else to say. Aristede nodded. Marie eyed the Sheriff steadily. "We don' understand . . ."

"No," he said. Who would? Understand what?

Suddenly the whispering stopped, even Big Head grew silent. Father Justin Gaspard, Father Brother-in-law, entered the room and made his way to the Brouliettes.

He was a beautiful man, there was no other way to describe him. He was like one of those gold-haired angels in paintings—grown-up but losing none of the spiritual glory. Perhaps it was the hair, gold ringlets over his eyes and about his neck. His eyes were clear blue, like the most perfect sky, and his lips sensuous and somehow sad. He was a big man, perfectly proportioned, with huge shoulders coming down to a slender, almost female waist. Everyone in Richelieu knew for sure he could have been a movie star. But no, for as long as they could remember, the Senator's son had wanted to be a priest. Which was a kind of miracle in itself, him being the son of Papoot.

He opened his arms, and the bereaved couple entered his embrace, people finding shelter in a storm.

In a soft, musical voice filled with passion, he said, "Ti Boy is here with us now."

Everyone in the room leaned forward to see for themselves. Looking down at the parents whom he encircled, Father Justin Gaspard said, "Our Lord and Savior Jesus Christ has him by the hand and both are smiling. He's come home to his Father."

Now those assembled made the sign of the cross. Bobby did this self-consciously, a voice inside telling him, You're doing it because everybody's doing it. It was true. A man who loses God somehow loses himself. Didn't want to even think about it. What's going on in me? he wondered.

The group followed Father Gaspard and the Brouliettes into the other room, where a small coffin nestled on sawhorses. Another child stood there, Attorney Hurphy Perrault's son Li'l Hurphy, who along with Ti Boy served as altar boy. The child seemed stunned; he bit down on his lip. His mother, Anita, dressed in a smart black cocktail dress and with her hair just done at Maybelle's—maybe a Paris fashion—patted his shoulder. Hurphy, dressed in a tux and wearing a plumed hat, which was his Knights of St. Gregory uniform, couldn't help but think that his family resembled the Holy Family.

Bobby's eyes caught those of Moe Weiss, who wore a little black skullcap. His pants were baggy, and there were shoes that could be slippers on his feet. A none-too-clean white dress shirt with an old necktie and a blue sweater, in that heat! He held his hands down in front of him, locked together. He was about seventy years of age but looked eighty. The bags under his eyes seemed carved into his sallow face. His features appeared to be losing their padding, and his nose was increasingly hooked.

One Lung Savoy coughed, as he always did. He claimed to have lost a lung in the war, but Barber Possum Aucoin said to anyone who'd listen, and everyone would listen—his bullshit was so much better than his haircuts—"How could he lose it in Fort Benning, Georgia? Now, Cap'n Eddie Sonnier, that was a real hero!" And they laughed. The hero was known to give little boys a quarter to look at their weenies, though he never asked to touch.

The screen door opened, and Senator Glenn "Papoot" Gaspard with his daughter, Clara, the Sheriff's BeBe, entered. There was something electric about his entrance, like a storm had moved in without warning. Bobby often wondered how his father-in-law did it. Dominate. Everything. Everybody. And not obnoxiously. He just did.

"Sorry we late, sorry we late," he said, moving through the crowd, BeBe bringing up the rear with another bowl of potato salad in her fat hands. Papoot looked like some kind of unbelievably newfangled train, one that could travel a thousand miles an hour. Sweet BeBe looked like his caboose.

Papoot managed to shake every hand as he moved among and through people, stopping to kiss the ladies on the cheek. He watched as BeBe held her face up for a kiss from her husband, which he dutifully gave. Something's up, and it's not good, he thought. It didn't shock him. He'd suspected it for a long time and knew that one day soon he'd have to do something about it. It had to be okay. He adored his daughter and had some affection for Bobby Boudreaux. It was gon' to take some mending for sure. How, he had no idea. But he'd do it. That he knew for sure.

Papoot reached into his coat pocket, took out an envelope, and presented it to the Brouliettes.

Mayor Big Head Arceneaux, who tried unsuccessfully to whisper, but whose voice carried for a quarter of a mile, said, "I bet it's a hundred bucks." Big Shot Fontenot, who'd already given the couple a hundred, said, "More than that." Big Head whistled like he was calling hunting dogs, but he was only expressing wonder at such generosity. It was known that the Senator had paid for the funeral because Undertaker Watch Out Naquin asked him, "Was everything satisfactory?" The Senator, who gave compliments like other men breathed, replied, "Wonderful like everything you do, Watch Out."

Watch Out was pleased, even though the Senator had demanded and gotten a 40 percent discount. "The Brouliettes ain't got nothin'," the Senator had said, and Watch Out had thought, But you do. The Senator knew what he was thinking and gave his famous laugh. "Hee, hee!"

Father Gaspard said, "Let us pray," and everybody but Moe Weiss got down on his and her knees. Tooky Trahan was first to hit the floor. He felt that he sold insurance by leading, plus help from his little "close the deal" emblem in his wallet: a tiny speck of St. Theresa's pelvic bone, given to him by some unnamed Cardinal in charge of the Vatican's endless supply of relics. No one knew if this was actually true, but to have Tooky hold the relic over the signed insurance policy was a hell of an inducement. At least three people claimed the relic and its accompanying policy had cured them of hemorrhoids, TB, and a recurring rash in the groin area.

During the prayer Tooky shut his eyes only partially, being ever on the lookout for customers. He spotted Sport Baudoin, who'd had an unsuccessful tryout with the New Orleans Pelicans baseball team. Reportedly the Pelicans coach had told him, "Give it up. You can't catch, throw, or hit," which was astonishing because Sport had been the best athlete, majoring in four sports, ever to graduate from Richelieu High. So far as Tooky knew, Sport had no insurance.

Catfish François was on his knees in the kitchen, not getting too far from his gumbo. He didn't want anybody messing with it, and every one of these bastards thought himself or herself a cook. As far as he was concerned, they couldn't cook shit! He closed his eyes tightly, pleased that he could smell the wonderful aroma of the gumbo in the big black pot. Near him was Richelieu High's principal, and Ti Boy's teacher, Mr. Suire. Half starved on what the parish paid its teachers, Mr. Suire never ventured far from where there was food.

Hot Dog Hebert helped Nonc Doucet down to the floor. He was 101 and the parish's oldest citizen. Father Justin had told him it wasn't necessary for him to kneel anymore. It took at least two men, with Nonc groaning the entire time to get him up, but Nonc had said, "No, ah'm gonna pray the right way until I die."

"Then you'll pray forever," Father Justin had kindly said, always encouraging. Now he prayed in that wondrous voice that God had given him.

He led them in four Hail Marys and five Our Fathers, then motioned everyone to stand.

Hot Dog and Coon Soileau helped Nonc up. This time he not only groaned but yelped. Most people there secretly wished the old man would die, especially Big Shot Fontenot's ninety-five-year-old father, Li'l Shot, who would then be the parish's oldest citizen. As automobile dealer and bank president, Big Shot knew that patience was maybe the greatest virtue, although secretly he wished both men would die. Guiltily, he kissed the old man's bald head, which elicited the response "Ah wish you'd kiss my ass."

Father Justin was speaking melodiously but quietly. "Ti Boy wasn't your ordinary child. He loved his mother and his father, and he loved the holy Church. I know all of you are wondering why this little boy accidentally killed himself. Well it wasn't an accident. You see, Jesus and Mary, his divine mother, couldn't wait another moment to have this angel by their side, so they called him home. Come home, Ti Boy, they said, and ten thousand angels lifted their voices in song at this act of love. And Ti Boy went home. It is to a home that we'd all like to go. Some of us will make it. Ti Boy will be waiting there with a child's sweetness. Some of us won't make it. You know who you are. You know exactly who you are. Sinners. And now comes a joke. You believe yourselves to be secret sinners. Do you really believe that you could play your foolish games with God? Well? Whoever put the Octagon coupon in the collection plate Sunday, was that some kind of sick joke? God doesn't need to wash His hands! You need to wash your souls. And whoever lights a candle religiously without putting so much as a penny in the box, aren't you the wise one? When you stand there before our Lord, don't you know the first thing He'll ask you? Why? Why honor Me by lighting a candle even as you dishonor my Church by giving nothing? Oh, you'll reach into your pocket, into your shroud, and pull out some dirty greenbacks, but guess what? Sorry. Our Lord won't want it then. Too late! Take those green-backs with you into the flames. Burn with them throughout eternity."

Gradually his volume had risen, and now his voice wasn't sweet but instead had become a roaring, avenging angel. "There are no secret sinners! Amen!" he screamed.

Everybody sighed "Amen," and many an eye was cast about—who were those sinners? Each had his or her own suspicion. The guilty were frightened, and some made a promise to God to straighten up. You couldn't be too careful. They had simply no idea that anyone, not even God, knew.

The mood lifted. It was time for some of Catfish François's gumbo, and as they drank it out of the spoon or bit into a tender morsel of chicken meat or sausage, they wondered, Could the food in Heaven be better than this? They knew God must have some wonderful cooks, but better than Catfish? It was almost impossible to imagine.

They complimented Catfish profusely. "Woowee! Can you cook for sure!" Or "If you had a pussy I'd marry you tonight, Catfish." Senator Papoot Gaspard said it best: "Catfish, you're a national treasure, for sure, better than how you call it, Statue of Liberty. Hee, hee!"

Even as he laughed with Papoot, Catfish wondered if he ought to tell him that he wasn't nearly as popular as he thought. Everyone in Richelieu eventually ended up in Coon's place having a beer, playing bourrée, or eating some of Catfish's gumbo, and from what Catfish could tell, a hell of a lot of people felt that the Senator had been in there long enough, and that it was time for somebody else. He started to say something, but Papoot had moved on to someone else who was complimenting. And besides, Catfish reminded himself, it wasn't any of his business. Maybe he'd tell the Sheriff, although Catfish wasn't any too sure the Sheriff would give a shit.

Sheriff Boudreaux brought up the end of the gumbo line. He always stood in line and always at the back. You couldn't say he had the bighead for sure. Just like he passed the collection plate at Mass every Sunday, in his own quiet way, the man was a politician, a good one. He'd die in office.

Bobby was back of a woman, a stranger, with jet-black hair tied back in a red bow. A lot of men were looking at her. She had a body that they wouldn't mind tasting along with the gumbo.

Bobby said, "Excuse me, aren't you . . ."

She turned to him, eyes big like marbles, and blue with a little fringe of gray about them. "Yes, Ruth Ann, Zeke's daughter." She extended a hand, which he took.

"I'm sorry I didn't recognize Zeke's little girl grown up," he said, smiling. She stood self-consciously until he realized he was still holding her hand. He let it go and stepped back. "I'm sorry about your daddy. I know he's sick."

She nodded. "I guess you could call it that. Doc Mouton can't even give it a name. He can't remember anything. Not even me."

They took their gumbo and some hot French bread and stood together.

From across the room BeBe saw them but thought nothing of it. As her daddy had told her, Bobby's a politician, and he's got to be nice to everybody. Still she carried them plates of her potato salad, and

Bobby introduced her to Ruth Ann. BeBe got to the point: "What brings you back to Richelieu? Weren't you in New Orleans?"

"Yes. I was a reporter for the *The Times-Picayune.*"

"What a strange job for a lady," BeBe said. (BeBe wasn't a politician.)

"You don't know the half of it. I was the police reporter covering the jails, the courts."

"Aw go on," Bobby said.

"It mus' have been horrible," BeBe added.

"No, it was wonderful!" Ruth Ann's pouty lips were painted fire engine red, like her nails. "Coming home, that's horrible." She read the shock on their faces and quickly added, "I mean I never thought I'd end up back home in Richelieu. Not part of my plans. But somebody's got to put the *Gazette* out. Zeke gave his life to it."

"He's not dead," BeBe corrected her.

"Except that he is. I dress him every day and he sits in a chair. Just sits there. Either I or the colored girl has to feed him. Somebody's got to be with him all the time."

"I'm sorry," Bobby said, and BeBe said she'd bring some potato salad over one day real soon. Then she moved off to make sure that everybody had some.

"You have to forgive BeBe," Bobby said. "Sometimes she talks without thinking," he said and felt ashamed that he'd spoken to a stranger about her.

"I like it," Ruth Ann said. "People here just don't do it that much. In Richelieu everybody protects everybody about everything. It takes a dentist's pliers to get the truth sometimes, even about the simplest thing."

Her remark offended Bobby. He thought she was demeaning one of Richelieu's best qualities. "Anything wrong with kindness?"

"Oh no," she said. "But sometimes, once in a while, you need to hear things the way they really are. I mean all those kindnesses, well they're not really life." Then she looked at him. "Are they?"

"I don't know," he said honestly, not holding her gaze. "I guess I've never thought about it. Been here too long."

"Maybe that's what's the matter with me. I've been someplace else too long."

"Can we start over?" he asked. He didn't want her to go.

"You're right! May I ask you a question?" Now she didn't sound like Zeke's daughter. She sounded like one of those damn New Orleans reporters that from time to time plagued him about Misty's Paradise Inn.

"Go ahead," he said, but his voice was cold.

"What do you think about Ti Boy's death?"

"About what?" He didn't understand her, thought he'd misheard her. Yet he felt threatened, though he couldn't have said why.

"Ti Boy's death. You know," she said and she extended a blood-red-tipped finger in his direction. "Bang!"

"It's so sad."

"Yes, of course, that too. But what else?"

He smiled. "You looking for a mystery?"

"Maybe." Her gorgeous face was a mask. He didn't like it that way.

"You know Richelieu isn't New Orleans."

She persisted. "But people are people."

Fuck her! "No, they really aren't. People here are"—he paused for a moment, searching for the right word—"decent," he finally said. He felt foolish using the word, which he never used. But she'd forced him. Looks or no looks—and she had them—he didn't like her.

"There's some decent people in New Orleans," she said. "And there are some bad people. Maybe here too. I'm not sure the locale has anything to do with it."

He'd had enough. "Got to go," he said.

"I'll need to talk to you."

"I keep regular office hours," he said, which was a damn lie. He went to his office when he absolutely had to. When somebody had to see him.

"I'll be calling," she said, but she had to speak to his back as he'd turned away and found BeBe. "What's the matter?" she asked. She could always tell when her husband was angry.

"She's a horse's ass."

BeBe was pleased. Once her husband formed an opinion of someone, that was it, he never changed. "How you mean?" she asked him.

"Asking about Ti Boy's death."

"She's a horse's ass for sure," BeBe agreed.

"And a troublemaker," he added.

She saw the stress on his face. How she adored that beautiful face, even the mashed nose, which she kissed every night. He never told her it hurt when she did.

Suddenly there was a loud scream. Bobby turned and rushed to find its source. Across the room, Marie Brouliette had broken away from Father Justin and Aristede and was clawing at Ti Boy's coffin.

"My baby, my little Ti Boy, just let me kiss him good-bye. He's my baby. For God's sake!" she moaned.

Undertaker Watch Out Naquin whispered to the Sheriff, "She don't want to see that. I done my best but . . ."

Bobby caught Doc Mouton's eyes. The physician nodded and opened his black bag, which went with him everyplace, took out a hypodermic needle, and with Father Justin rolling up Marie's black sleeve, quickly gave her a shot. Her eyes snapped shut so suddenly that the Sheriff hoped Doc hadn't killed her. Bad Ass Thibodeaux looked up from his gumbo and said, "He mussa' gave her a double for sure."

BeBe and some of the other women carried Marie into a bedroom. Her husband, who was looking as old as Nonc, stood helplessly by, his big cotton picker's hands clenching and unclenching.

Ruth Ann Daigle edged toward the bedroom. Bobby caught her by the arm. "This is no time for an interview."

"Bastard," she hissed. "I just wanted to see if I could help."

"You can help," Bobby whispered. "Leave people here alone."

She wrenched free from his grasp, her pointed breasts heaving with emotion. "Just what are you afraid of?" she asked him.

"I dunno," he answered honestly, and the fire went out of her. "Look. Let's start over. Please."

"Yeah. Sure. Let's do that. But I still need to talk to you," she said.

"Don't you ever give it up?" he asked.

"No. Never."

He turned away, patted Aristede on the back, and left, closing the screen door quietly behind him.

He walked to his car on unsteady legs, his heart pounding. Chief Deputy Slo' Down Angelle held up a hand to stop nonexistent traffic as the Sheriff backed out of the driveway. Goddamn Slo' Down, such bullshit! Bobby thought. And then felt embarrassed that he was taking out his—what was it: anger? frustration?—on Slo' Down.

He slammed a hand on the dashboard. Get hold of yourself, Bobby, he said aloud. What in God's name was the matter with him? How'd he let some girl upset him so? Ti Boy had killed himself cleaning his .410 shotgun. An accident. Someone died that way almost every year, either cleaning a gun or in a duck blind where someone shot him by accident, or on a deer hunt. Ti Boy was a terrific little boy, helping on the farm, delivering the *Gazette,* and finding time to be an altar boy.

That damn girl bringing her New Orleans trash to Richelieu! She was nothing like her father. Zeke was a gentle, courtly man, one who espoused the philosophy of live and let live. Zeke didn't even like to print bad news—but then Zeke hadn't been corrupted by the big city either.

Still . . . what could she possibly be talking about? Doc Mouton, not only the parish coroner but a top-notch physician, first in his class at the LSU Medical School in New Orleans (that town again!), said Ti Boy died by accidental shooting.

He was cleaning his .410, must have forgotten there was a single shell in the chamber, pulled the trigger and blew his head to pieces. The Sheriff knew he had taken the call. It was gruesome, blood and bone and gray pieces of brain all over his room, so much blood for such a little boy. The Sheriff made the sign of the cross. What could she be thinking?

Again he slammed his fist on the dashboard. Damn her! And why was it getting to him? He shook his head and drove still farther out into the country.

Chapter 2

The sun had set, and the moon was making its first appearance of the evening. It was a full moon, its mountains not yet delineated. He came to a tall wooden fence with big wooden gates that stood open. Above the gates was a pink neon sign:

MISTY'S PARADISE INN

It had undergone a name change only the year before. Up until then it was MISTY'S PUSSYCAT, with PUSSY in hot pink and CAT in baby blue. Father Justin had told Misty in no uncertain terms, "That name's got to come down."

"Why?" she asked. She was seventy and beyond caring what people said about her, though her white hair was long and died a shiny platinum blond.

"Why?" he asked from the other side of the confessional. Misty was a devout Catholic and often sneaked into the last row at church after everybody else had gone in. She left first, too, and had never heard the last "amen." Nor did she ever miss confession, which is where she handed the priest a substantial donation "for the poor." She really didn't care where the money went. She was certain that Jesus saw her give it, and that was all that mattered. Misty was afraid to die because she had the feeling she was headed straight to Hell, given her life and all. She often envisioned a scene at the Pearly Gates with her asking Jesus, "How 'bout all that money I gave you?" In her scene, Jesus relented and let her into Purgatory, which wasn't all that good, but beat the hell out of Hell. The dream sustained her for a day or two, and then the fear took over again. "Why?" Father Justin asked again, his voice raised like she was crazy. "Because of the youth, that's why!"

"How's a sign gonna hurt, Father? Besides, the youth know all about pussy."

"Stop!" Father Justin squawked. "You're sinning in the confessional!"

Another damn sin to confess.

Father was adamant. "The sign's got to go."

"What I'm gon' call it?"

Father had to think about that. "How about 'The Gates'? You do have those big gates."

"They already using that in Opelousas."

There was silence as each considered an appropriate name that wouldn't do injury to the youth.

"I've got it!" the priest exclaimed, and she could hear his fingers snap on the other side of the grille. "Misty's Inn. That seems most appropriate."

"But dull."

The priest sighed. It was true. "You'll just have to think about it. You'll come up with something appropriate. You're not dumb."

"But definitely not pussy, huh?"

"There you've done it again. No, not Pu——. Now say ten Hail Marys and twenty Our Fathers."

She did think about it, even discussed it with Ballou Sinistere, her pimp, driver, bartender, cook, and bouncer. Ballou was intrigued. "Lemme see," he mused, his big face wrinkled in the effort of thought.

Ballou, who had been with Misty for twenty-five years, was famous in his own right. He had brought a girl named Red from Ogden, Utah, to Richelieu, where she introduced oral sex. It caught on immediately and became the rage. Na Na Duhon liked to say, "Can you imagine, our own Ballou, father of the blow job?" It gave the pimp status. Even Nonc Doucet agreed that he'd never heard of it before, and that went back 101 years!

"Now why do mens come to Misty's?" Ballou asked.

"Now what kind of stupid question is that?" Misty answered. "For pussy!"

"But you can't say that. There's got to be another way. Where do a man go when he comes?" Ballou asked. His forearms were the size of big hams.

"Where? To Heaven that's where."

"But you sure can't say that, Father would have a stroke. That's worse than pussy in his eyes." Ballou was no dummy, and he had the second biggest dick in the parish, the biggest belonging to Papa Sotile, who led the Richelieu Gents band.

"I got it!" he said. "Misty's Paradise Inn." And so it became.

"You're something else, Ballou," Misty said, love in her eyes. They didn't fuck anymore, but they were in love. If Ballou knocked off an occasional piece from one of the girls, maybe trying out a new one so he could evaluate her for Misty, she didn't mind. He loved her. As long as he was there, she wasn't alone. Ballou was a little younger than her and she was terrified of dying before him. That's why she kept a little pearl-handled pistol hidden away. Right before she died, she was going to kill Ballou so he would be waiting for her on the other side. They would always be together, and those flames wouldn't be so bad with Ballou frying next to her. Maybe the devil would let them hold charred hands. At least it was a plan.

After passing through the gates, Bobby parked his car next to Ballou's gold Cadillac, a pimp's car, he thought. There were other cars there too, and he knew who they belonged to. A regular crowd ended every evening at Misty's Paradise Inn. He could hear the jukebox playing inside.

In front was a big room with a bar running its length. Girls lounged about in see-through nightgowns and short shorts that showed their dimpled asses, though several were fat because Misty had found out a long time ago that some men liked fat girls. Behind the bar was Ballou's kitchen, where there was always a courtbouillon or some barbecue or a fish stew cooking for the girls to eat after work, which was usually about 4:00 A.M.

There was a dance floor and a big jukebox that cost a nickel to play.

Out back was another long building, reached by a little door to the left of the bar and covered in red cloth parted in the middle. It was discreet. Some men didn't mind being seen having a beer or even dancing—hell, everybody did that—but they weren't too hot on their neighbors and friends seeing them leave with a girl. Naturally every eye stayed glued on those red curtains.

The long building was divided into little rooms, where Misty's girls did their business.

The Sheriff entered to greetings from about the room. It was a dark place because, as Ballou said, "It makes the little girls look better." In the middle of the dance floor was a concrete pipe, which contained a revolving light purchased in New Orleans that sent little starbursts of light to the ceiling, which was painted dark blue. It was said to be the newest thing.

All the regulars were there. At one beer-filled table sat Big Shot Fontenot and his ever-present father, Li'l Shot, who was asleep in the chair. Next to him was Hurphy Perrault, then Sport Baudoin, who was talking about LSU football, which he predicted would win the national championship either next year or two years down the road ("If they get rid of that fuckin' coach. Thass all they need."). Sport was the acknowledged authority on the subject, and everybody drank to "a new coach." Also at the table was Mayor Big Head Arceneaux, whose little legs swung back and forth like those of a child in a high chair; Doc Mouton, who always put up with a lot of teasing because every Saturday afternoon at 4:00 he examined all the little girls to make sure that they didn't have clap or worse; Tooky Trahan, who was whispering a sales pitch for burial insurance to One Lung Savoy, who'd been turned down by every insurance company in the

United States and one in Europe but who Tooky was certain he could "fix up"; Watch Out Naquin, who looked professionally glum and who felt as an undertaker he'd taken a professional vow against smiling; and of course, President Prejean, who called for another round ("The drinks are on me!"). And Short Change St. Pierre, who was describing Sunday's brand-new feature at the Palace, a Randolph Scott Western, promising, "You gon' love it, Scott's the best there is. I ought to know!"

Over in a corner in whispered conversation were Na Na Duhon and his papoon, a tough little redhead with an ass that would stop a clock. She went by the name Lucky and claimed she hailed from Bossier City, in conservative North Louisiana. Na Na, dressed in a bright yellow checked sport coat, and easily forty years older than Lucky, was out to make an impression and nervously brushed back his pompadour, in which he took great pride.

Bobby stepped up to the bar. Someone had brought Nonc Doucet, who was drinking shots of V.O. chased with "a little Coke." Bobby said, "Someone's gonna have to take Nonc home."

Ballou Sinistere opened a Jax beer for the Sheriff and said, "Ah'll do it." He knew Bobby Boudreaux would nurse his beer for as long as he sat and still probably not finish it. "He's not a drinker," Ballou often noted to Misty, who responded, "Tell you the truth, Ballou, I'm not sure what he is." "Not no lady's man neither," said Ballou, "not like his papa." "Definitely not like him," Misty said. And she knew, since she used to fuck the old Sheriff Gaston Boudreaux two or three times a week. For free. And that wasn't all she'd given him either.

"How you doing, Nonc?" the Sheriff asked. It was his standard greeting, and tonight there was even less enthusiasm in it.

"It's all bullshit," Nonc said. It was more than a routine answer. In his 101 years that was how he'd found it to be.

"That was sad today," Ballou said. "Misty's got something for you to give the Brouliettes."

Bobby nodded and wondered just how far Na Na was gonna go

with the whore. He was kissing her hand, and she was brushing her hand through his pompadour like it was a thrill.

Misty came through the red curtains, and she and the Sheriff shook hands like they always did. She passed him a folded hundred, which he took without comment and put in the pocket of his khakis. "Tell 'em I'm sorry, or better, don't tell 'em nothing. They ain't got to know it's from me. Just as long as Jesus knows."

"He knows," Ballou said with certainty. He'd never seen a man or woman care so damn much about Jesus' opinion.

Misty turned to her pimp, who that very afternoon had tried out a new girl on the circuit from New Orleans. "How was she?"

"Good at the bottom, no great shakes at the top," he said.

Misty nodded. "She can learn. That don't take no scientist."

Bobby wished they would discuss their business someplace else. Somehow it was wrong for a sheriff to be part of that kind of talk. It was like he was letting someone, anyone down. It wasn't how he'd planned life to be.

"Say, Bobby," Misty said—only she, Papoot, and BeBe called him that—"I was thinking about your daddy." He hated that and knew what was coming, another story about the legendary Sheriff, a story that he'd have to laugh at but that actually made him feel ashamed. He faked a smile.

"About thirty-five years ago, this gal sped through Richelieu in a big car with a California license."

Bobby groaned inside. This would be the thousandth time he'd heard this particular story. The room had gotten quiet. Misty was a great storyteller, and everyone knew that anything she said about Gaston Boudreaux had to be funny as hell.

"So someone arrested this woman and took her to jail. The Sheriff made a little tour that night like he always did, and this gal says, 'Sheriff, I'm gonna need some Kotex,' and Gaston says, 'Hell no, you gonna eat what all the other prisoners eat!' "

Laughter exploded all over the place, and Big Head Arceneaux got so excited that he bounced up and down in his chair and exclaimed, "Whoop, whoop!" Bobby faked a big grin and shook his head. "That Gaston," he muttered, because he was expected to say something.

President Prejean waved the Sheriff over for a drink. He joined the table of men, carrying his beer with him. "That's not good politics, turning down a beer," President Prejean said. Bobby was saved from making a reply when all eyes turned to Na Na and Lucky going through the red curtains. Right before he disappeared, Na Na threw them a look of triumph. "Now ain't that some accomplishment," Possum the barber said, "a whore has agreed to take his money!" Everyone laughed and wondered how Possum had kept from being murdered all those years. He was so mean and so deadly accurate in his observations. He'd've made one hell of a detective, Bobby thought.

Doc Mouton leaned forward, his voice a whisper which was louder than any shout because everyone knew he was going to tell some medical confidence, which he never did unless he had two beers. "Would you believe he's eating her?"

"Bullshit!" Sport said. "Nobody's that low. How you know?"

Doc said, looking to the right and left to make sure that only a dozen or so people could hear him, "She told me Saturday when she came for her little examination."

Now they really laughed. The midget Mayor leaped to his tiny feet, jumped up and down, and bleated, "Whoop! Whoop! Whoop!"

This awakened Li'l Shot Fontenot, who said, "Sit down, Mayor Jackass, before you bus' a gut!"

From the bar, Misty defended her girl. "An' what's the matter with that, Doc? My girls are clean, and what about you? You ain't ever eaten a little bit?"

Doc blushed, and Nonc said in a quivering and frail voice, "It's all bullshit."

The doors opened, and Senator Papoot Gaspard and his driver, Moose Thibodeaux, entered like lightning bolts. His "Hee hee!" preceded him. It was a laugh, yet not quite a laugh, an expression of something short of merriment, more a kickoff, a start-up sound to whatever would follow, which was pretty much whatever Papoot Gaspard wanted.

He was seventy, but not a white hair in his full head of wavy hair, carefully combed and held in place by brilliantine. His skin was pink, and his face contained two big dimples. He looked like an aged, happy baby. Gold-rimmed glasses perched on his nose, and when he was serious he peered over the rims. He had been State Senator for more than thirty years, and a power in the state capital in Baton Rouge the whole time. He was the acknowledged leader and spokesman for what he called his "little people," as well as the father of Louisiana's old age pension, which along with Social Security, helped thousands of old people keep body and soul together.

Most important, he was a chief floor leader for Governor Richard W. Cole, which meant that he not only did pretty much what he wanted, but got whatever he wanted as well. What he wanted was state buildings in Richelieu, blacktopped roads in Richelieu, and jobs—a lot of state jobs for people who for the most part couldn't have qualified for work anyplace else, people who hadn't finished high school, or had a criminal record, like maybe murdering an in-law or something else not too important. He was also able to get paroles from the state prison at Angola. Some said the going price was five thousand dollars. One thing was obvious, there were a lot of murderers running loose in the parish, but as the Senator liked to say to an occasional critic, "Didn't our Lord pardon Mary how-you-call-her?" or "Everybody deserves a second chance." And to just about everybody, that made sense.

Zeke Daigle occasionally blasted him in the *Gazette,* but while everyone liked to read it, they really didn't much give a damn. There was too much else to think about, like a barbecue at somebody's camp. Maybe Possum Aucoin best summed up the local attitude about the Senator. He'd say, usually while giving someone a bad hair-cut, "He's not worth a shit, but who's gon' do better? Huh?"

Thus far no one had come up with an answer to that one. But there were rumblings, particularly at the Rotary Club—of which Papoot was disdainful, dismissing it with "a bunch of do-gooders," about the worst thing that could be said about anyone, because as most people knew, do-gooders wanted to tell other people how to live their lives and were always looking out for themselves and certainly not for "the little people."

Papoot's driver, Moose Thibodeaux, a hulking six foot five inches, was not without local fame himself. He had been the owner of a car wash which burned down one night, some people said mysteriously. Zeke Daigle had written on the front page, "How the hell can a car wash burn?" That brought the state fire marshal to town and ended with an indictment of Moose, who served six months in the parish jail, where he gained more than fifty pounds eating Trustee Herman "Thank You Please" Washington's boudin and hog's head cheese. Moose told the Senator it was the best six months of his life and he didn't like the car wash business anyway because he was always wet. "You can't control the sprinkle!"

Moose had one quality that made him a very desirable assistant. He was kin to just about everybody in Richelieu, and could usually deliver more than 250 votes. The day he got out of jail, the Senator hired him. Moose was dumb and curious. "Why you hirin' me, a jail-bird?"

"Who knows," Papoot said, "maybe I need something burned down. Hee, hee!"

Bobby nodded a greeting to his father-in-law, who reminded him that BeBe and him were coming to dinner that very Sunday. His cook Motile was preparing her specialty, "an old-time chicken stew and some fresh green beans cooked with bits of ham."

Bobby said, "We'll be there," and Papoot wondered what was eating him. He'd have to ask BeBe. She'd tell him. He hoped it was nothing serious, like BeBe's extra fifty pounds. He could kick her big ass. She'd never been a small woman, but recently she'd let herself go. He had to go easy, though. Whenever he tried discussing her weight, she'd burst out crying and run from the room. At least the run might do her good, he thought.

One thing for sure, he wasn't gon' let anybody hurt his BeBe, be it Bobby Boudreaux or anybody else. He'd see them dead first. Death wasn't no big deal to him, particularly someone else's. Papoot looked about the room, then went over to the end of the bar, where Misty was waiting.

Silently they watched some of the men dance with Misty's girls. Attorney Hurphy Perrault, clubfoot and all, was dancing with Patot, who must have weighed three hundred pounds but was amazingly agile on her feet. Hurphy let her do all the moving. Patot was very popular and made the most money of any of Misty's girls. "She's got her specialty," Misty said with pride. Patot was a genius at spanking bad boys with a Ping-Pong paddle. And while Misty didn't get that particular pleasure herself, she had to admit that it sure brought in the money, which made her think of Papoot.

On the dance floor, Hurphy whispered, "Patot, you dance like a dream. A big dream."

Patot answered, "Because I'm dancin' with a good-lookin' man." Actually, she was thinking about the fish stew bubbling on Ballou's stove. He made a red gravy that made her mouth water. This excited her so much she licked Hurphy's ear.

"Watch it," he warned, "I'm a Knight of St. Gregory."

"Baby," she said, "I don't care if you're a bull dyke, you make me sooo hot."

"Behave yourself, girl," he said and playfully slapped her on the rump.

Misty, taking it all in, shook her head. She's the best, she thought.

"She's wasting her time on Hurphy, that's one slick lawyer," Papoot said.

"Everybody's slick," Misty noted, "until they get a hard-on."

Papoot drank to that. Misty refilled his glass until he held up a hand signaling "enough." His finger contained a three-carat diamond ring. It flashed in the shadows and competed with the starbursts on the blue ceiling.

Misty was unimpressed. She had three rings like that, plus a yellow diamond that Ballou estimated was about ten carats.

Papoot was studying her over his glasses. Oh-oh, she thought. Here it comes. She smiled warmly. Papoot had years before gotten Ballou out of a knifing scrap which left twin brothers dead. Ballou hadn't served a day! That's how powerful Papoot was. It had cost her twenty-five thousand in cold cash, a lot of money back then, and she remembered Papoot counting it, every single bill, whistling under his breath. "All that's going to the poor," Papoot told her at the time, though he owed her no explanation. Yeah, *poor* Papoot, she had thought, patting his hand and saying, "You're a saint." Remembering that now, she wished she had the guts to stab him in one of those dimples. Maybe carve a new one on his healthy pink baby face.

Papoot said, "A week from today I'm going to Baton Rouge."

"Aw yeah," she said innocently, thinking, Oh, shit.

"The man himself called me to come. Said, 'Papoot, come on up here, I miss you an' we got to talk about the next session.' He tole me some of them Baptist do-gooders and some preachers from North Louisiana was pressin' him on prostitution. They want a bill to outlaw it. They want it to be an administration bill."

"Why don't they mind their own business? Leave us alone like we leave North Louisiana alone. Besides, if they outlaw prostitution, New Orleans is gonna fold up like an accordion. What the hell else they got but workin' girls and fancy restaurants that give you the stomachache with those sauces. Alfredo! Bolognese! Phooey!"

A few feet away, Bobby watched the two whispering and thought, God help us all. Ballou watched too and wondered how much this particular conversation was gonna cost Misty.

"Preachers can't leave nothin' alone," Papoot said sadly.

Then they sat in silence. He sipped his Scotch slowly. She watched his tongue in the glass and thought about cutting it off. Then no more "hee, hees!" It'd be her who'd say, "Ha, ha!" He smiled warmly, like he was about to give her good news.

"Ah better not go empty-handed," Papoot said, as if he was fixing to put up some money.

"That's true," she agreed. It was time to get down to facts. This wasn't no checker game.

"You don't look like you enjoyin' our little chat," Papoot said sadly. "Maybe you don't want to have the only place in Richelieu Parish. Maybe you need some competition. If it wasn't for me, there'd be a hundred whorehouses right on this street. Our mens do like to fuck."

"No, no! I didn't mean to look that way, sometimes I just get blue."

"I don't care what color you get, jus' don't give me no crap! I make myself clear?"

His dimples had vanished, perhaps in shame. She wondered how he did it. "Don't get mad at old Misty," she pleaded, "me and you always been together, and always will be." She patted his hand. The dimples had returned, his white Panama hat was pushed back on his head. He looked like Santa Claus without the beard.

"Fifty thousand."

"Jesus! How many preachers they got?"

She felt the bile in her throat. She wanted to protest. It's never been that much! Instead, she asked, "When you need it?"

"Sen' Ballou in the mornin' about seven a week from today. An' Misty, don't be no late, and don't pull no shortchange, 'cause I'm gon' count every penny."

"Of course not," she said and laughed gaily.

Papoot signaled Moose with a twist of his head. "Let's go!" On the way out, he waved expansively to everyone.

Misty moved down the bar to the Sheriff, who was now standing. It was getting late, and he had one more stop to make before he went home.

"You all right?" he asked. She was pale and breathing heavily.

"Fine, baby, Misty's just fine! You leavin'?"

"Good night," he said and waved to everyone. Some waved back.

Ballou moved to her. "You better sit down, you look like you been through a hurricane." He poured her a glass of French red wine from under the bar. She drank a big swallow-full. He waited for her color to return. "He wants fifty thousand," she said. Ballou's face was impassive. He survived by being whatever she wanted him to be. He was like her mirror, reflecting her, nothing else. If he had other emotions, he never volunteered them.

"I wish I could let you kill him," she said, and she wasn't joking. They never joked.

"I sure can do it."

"Maybe one day," she said. "Down the road."

"Jus' like you want," he said. He really wouldn't mind doing it. Papoot Gaspard had become a hog.

He went to check on his fish stew. Stirred it a little bit. It smelled just right.

Chapter 3

Crickets making their brittle night sounds and fireflies burning in the darkness along the bayou made the night look like Pontchartrain Beach, the big amusement park in New Orleans, with its strange and frightening noises, and thousands of tiny lights.

The bayou looked like a line of black ribbon laid down to set out boundaries, and sometimes something—a nutria, an alligator, or a turtle—splashed loudly in the water. The white egrets, with pencil-thin black legs and yellow beaks, fed quietly along its shore, and in the air was the smell of azaleas, which grew in profusion everyplace.

Bobby turned on his radio to WWL, and it brought him Leon Kelner's big orchestra live from the Blue Room in the Roosevelt Hotel in New Orleans. The announcer said people were dancing, and Bobby shivered as an involuntary tremor passed through him. He felt so damn alone.

Well, he was alone, and he told himself he liked it that way. Being alone was his secret, especially from BeBe, who would have been hurt and wouldn't have really understood. He couldn't hurt her, this gentle and decent woman who lived only to take care of him. The thing was, he didn't really want to be taken care of, and making like he did was an increasingly difficult chore. A burden. He spent a lot of time groaning inside; his pain was particularly secret, and he wondered how in his lifetime he'd accumulated so many secrets, accompanying deceptions.

And there was something else, out there in the far edges of his mind's reach. Some other gnawing, bothersome something. A fly, no bigger than a fly, buzzing about. Fear perhaps? But fear about what? His life was set, his world secure. He would live out the remaining days without the slightest change, exactly as he'd lived the ones that had come before. And wasn't that what he wanted, ultimate security against . . . what? There were no threats out there, no shadowy figure off in the distance daring him to follow. In the distance was more of the same—more of nothing.

And yet . . . there *was* something. As of this dying day, there was something. Something had dropped in unannounced and most definitely unwanted. Something not sought, not called for or conjured up. But it was a presence. It had now taken its seat at the table and had begun making its as yet unspoken demands.

Something brought in from New Orleans like bananas off a Lykes ship in the harbor. But unloaded in Richelieu.

By a woman. No, she was more than just a woman. She was . . . the dare, the unattainable, the face on the screen at the Palace Theater, the vanishing loveliness at the end of a wet dream, right before you knew it was just a dream and felt the damp stickiness of the sheets.

Impossible, he told himself. He was no schoolboy! The son of Gaston Boudreaux had never been a schoolboy. More was expected of him. Like how it used to be when he said some stupid thing and everyone laughed, a laugh of admiration, because his daddy had been so screamingly funny, and he figured he must be funny too. Until people eventually came to realize that he wasn't funny at all, just clumsy and stupid.

Papoot had once advised, "Bobby, you should be more like your old man used to be." And he said, "I tried," putting past tense on it, so the Senator would know that he wasn't going to try anymore.

"Ruth Ann . . ." He said the name aloud, holding his breath until he needed air. And the thought of the devil, because she was the devil, bringing sensual loveliness into a world that had forever locked itself against it.

She'd sneaked in through the cracks, coming on a tide of evil words. He heard them in his head: "What do you think about Ti Boy's death?" And later, she'd pointed her finger and fired, *Bang!* Ti Boy's

.410 firing; Ti Boy's face and head scattering about the ceiling and the floor. And him wanting to scream the obvious but only saying it: It's so sad. And she wouldn't leave that be but pressed on. Shocked, he'd asked her with a fake smile if she was looking for a mystery. Her god-damn answer, not yes, not no, "Maybe." Maybe what? And she'd talked about people in New Orleans and a world away, about folks in Richelieu, and her police reporter cynicism. People are people, she'd said.

Like hell they were. New Orleans and its French Quarter was a big, smelly whorehouse where sex and food were the two commodities that people came for, came there because they didn't want their little desires known in their hometowns.

Richelieu was . . . well, it was a soft and gentle place. Not perfect, of course, not no such thing, Bobby knew that, but my God, it was no New Orleans!

And then her threats: "I'll need to talk to you." And finally, "I'll be calling." Telling him that her ugly intrusions weren't just going away, and that she'd be around, and that she had things she wanted to know.

"There's nothing to know," he said aloud, back in his car.

He was on Main Street, the stoplight frozen in place, a light or two on over darkened windows, One Lung Savoy's poolroom and of course the naked bulb on all night over Moe Weiss's notions store. He stopped the car, killed the engine, and got out. He stretched, working the cramps out of his body, a lone man who seemed to be reaching to Heaven.

Inside he could hear the chanting of Moe's prayer. It was a strange combination of sounds foreign to his ears, but he didn't mind them. They seemed so ancient that there was a comfort in something that endured. Moe Weiss, too, had endured.

He had told Bobby the story of how he had lost his parents and the Düsseldorf department store they owned, and how he had survived the concentration camp by working as the commandant's accountant.

When he finally escaped and got to America, he opted to try life in Louisiana over New York, seeing Louisiana as the end of the earth. It was a story Moe had told Bobby a year after they became friendly; he never alluded to it again.

The subject was like his yesterdays—quite dead.

Now there was silence from inside the store, and Bobby tapped three times on the glass on the door. Moe shuffled out, the skullcap on his head, the BVD's hanging out over his baggy trousers. His face was grizzled with the day's growth of beard. He said nothing, nor did Bobby, who followed him into the small room behind the store in which he lived. There was a bed, unmade, a small cabinet on which his prayer book lay open, a bigger open cabinet, which contained his meager clothes, a refrigerator, a hot plate, on which he prepared his simple meals, and a rickety chair. Water was brewing for what had become their nightly tea—tea so bad that sometimes Bobby didn't even attempt to sip it but left it in his cup untouched. Moe never questioned this, or anything else. He accepted, making neither comments nor judgments. In fact, Moe never responded unless he was asked, and often Bobby felt he might as well be talking to himself, for even when Moe replied, he answered many questions with questions.

Moe poured their tea into two coffee mugs; it was always too hot to drink initially. He went into the tiny store and got himself a Keep Moving cigar, then sat on the bed, his skullcap slightly askew. He looked like he was either drunk or an idiot, yet Bobby knew that he did not drink and that he was a very wise man. The wisest he had ever met.

Moe Weiss had moved to Richelieu five years before, a refugee from something, maybe a hurricane, the kind that threatened Louisiana every year and that occasionally delivered destruction and devastation. All the townspeople knew for sure was that he had come from someplace terrible, and they didn't like that he made them somehow uncomfortable, as though he'd brought the terrible place with him.

One Saturday morning in Possum Aucoin's barbershop, they saw him walk past, and someone said, "There goes the old Jew." "He ought to go back to where he came from," someone else said. Bobby sat up in the barber chair and asked, "Now why would you say that?" And someone said, "They killed Jesus Christ, didn't they?" And Bobby said, "I don't know, I was working on another case that day." For a moment, there was dead silence, and then the shop exploded in laughter and that was the last time anyone ever mentioned Moe Weiss's religion.

The second year that Moe was in Richelieu, Zeke Daigle offered to do a story on him. Moe turned ashen. A band of sweat broke out on his forehead, and he asked the editor please not to. When Zeke seemed reluctant to hold off profiling this rare and exotic old man, Moe blurted out, "How are your books? What kind of shape are they in?"

"They're awful," Zeke acknowledged, "and I'm no good at keeping them. In fact, I don't. Every year I just guess, and then hope that the government will accept it."

Moe said, "Mr. Daigle, let us make a bargain. You leave me out of your splendid newspaper and I will keep your books."

Zeke extended a hand. "You just made yourself a deal!"

In a week, Zeke's books were perfect, and Moe even found four or five places where he could save money. Zeke couldn't resist. He was so impressed that he told everybody, "The man's a genius. First time the IRS ever apologized to me, like they were afraid I was gonna sue them or take my business someplace else. He's a treasure, our Moe Weiss. Wish I could print that, but he's got my word." That he made this statement on a Saturday morning at both Possum Aucoin's barbershop and One Lung Savoy's poolroom gave the story a much wider circulation than it would have received in the *Gazette,* and now everybody in Richelieu wanted Moe Weiss's financial services.

Moe declared, however, he wanted only to putter around in his notions store. Whatever ambitions he had had long ago fled him.

However, Moe Weiss could not completely escape local attention, and when there was an opening on the board of Richelieu State Bank, Big Shot Fontenot called on Moe and told him he had been elected by acclamation. Moe demurred, saying that his health was not all that good. It wasn't. To which Big Shot responded, "You don't have to do a damn thing. I mean it's not like we're asking you to run a marathon or lift weights. We want your brain."

Moe finally accepted and at meetings never said a word but sat silently, like he was in some other place or time. They did not want him for his personality. "He don' have none," someone noted. But when loans were discussed, when a decision was required on finances, President Big Shot Fontenot always called on Moe for his vote first, and however Moe voted was how the Board voted. Thus, in his own silent way, he became very powerful, though he didn't care. And the fact that he didn't care also made him attractive to the community. He was unique.

Thus did his conversation contain a purity unencumbered by anything. Bobby had never seen him react with any emotion to anything except a threat to his anonymity and privacy. And on those days when he visited Moe Weiss's room, Bobby would peer at him, wondering what was beyond that shrunken wall.

"It was a strange day," the Sheriff began, stirring his tea. "An uncomfortable day." Moe stared back with watery blue eyes that looked like they had been bleached by the sun. "Zeke's daughter, her name is . . ." Suddenly he couldn't remember, although he remembered her face and her words.

"Ruth Ann," Moe offered, and Bobby thought, Of course he knows her, he keeps their books.

"Yes, Ruth Ann," he managed. Why was he having trouble saying her name? "She had questions about Ti Boy's death. Nothing specific, at least I don't think so. I kind of cut her off. I guess I was a horse's ass, and BeBe came up and made it worse. Questions!" He spit the word out like it was a major sin. "We don't need questions in Richelieu. Everything's settled here. We have peace." Moe's expected silence suddenly irritated him. "Don't we? Is there a spot more peaceful than Richelieu?"

Moe agreed and nodded his head saying so.

"The thing is, once a question like that gets asked, it takes on a life of its own. You know? I can't shove it back in the bottle. This make sense?"

Moe nodded, poured himself more tea, lit his Keep Moving, and took a deep drag, locking the smoke in his mouth. It seemed to Bobby that he could hold it there forever.

"It's all I've thought about, and it makes me mad at her for saying what she did and mad at me too, because I can't dismiss it. I can actually hear her in here." He pointed to his head. More softly he added, "She's very beautiful."

Moe's face was impassive. At last he released the smoke through his nostrils. He supported his weight on his flattened palms outspread on his bed.

"So, suddenly, I find myself confronted; it's how she is and *confronted* is the right word. There's this line in the dust, and she's there and I'm here and she wants to know! Wants to know what? So now I've got to make a choice, one I don't want to deal with: let it be, go about my business, in other words, fuck it, or . . . God almighty, start looking, asking questions myself."

Moe sat impassively, still smoking. Did he hear him? Did he give a damn? Suddenly Bobby found himself infuriated with the man. "Well goddamnit, say something!"

Moe puffed on his cigar, little short puffs like he was trying to revive its dead ash. And the whole time he was staring, his face expressionless. Suddenly it dawned on Bobby that Moe was staring at his badge.

He sighed and stood. He was tired and wound up and sorry that he had lost his temper at this strange and damaged little man. "Hey, it's late and we're both tired. You do get tired, huh, Moe?" The little man smiled, and Bobby wished that he could reach out and touch his shoulder.

He fingered his badge, his fingers traversing the points of the star. "It's just some metal."

Moe stood and followed him through the dark store. "The tea was good and I thank you." He stood at the door. "The badge. Oath of office. Duty. That kind of stuff, huh?"

"Yes," said Moe distinctly. The Sheriff stared at him and left the store. He climbed into his car, started up the engine, and glided silently down Main Street, moving slowly, like he was afraid of waking someone up. But there was no one.

Richelieu was asleep.

Chapter 4

Bobby Boudreaux lived in the house in which he was born. Slept in the bedroom in which he had come into the world, and in which his mother had died giving him birth. Gaston Boudreaux's house. The old Sheriff's house. His father's house. It was a modest home because, his father had told him, "You don't want people getting jealous, you know." So Gaston had built a home in the part of Richelieu known as Elmhurst, a place filled with elms and azaleas and camellias. And now there were also BeBe's roses. She tended them like she cooked, with perfection and enthusiasm. She had a hundred books on both subjects, and she read them at night while waiting for him to come home. Sometimes, though, he was so late that she went to sleep on the big screened-in side porch in which they slept in the summer, a weak effort to escape the punishing heat. Gaston had planted bamboo along the side of the porch for privacy, and now every day at sundown hundreds of blackbirds found refuge there, staying until dawn, when they flew out like they all had the same important appointment. Bobby loved the sounds of chirping and wings beating, and the bamboo reeds had made great blowguns when he was a boy.

He got out of his car and walked to the swing that hung from a big elm branch in the front yard. He sat in it, remembering when his feet didn't touch the ground, Gaston stopping for a moment on his way to someone's camp, giving him a halfhearted push, the swing racing up to Heaven, and by the time it came down, he could see only Gaston's departing car lights.

The crickets were a loud chorus calling back and forth in the darkness—they always had so much to say. Lightning bugs danced above the roses—he remembered catching the bugs when he was a child, trying to gather enough to create a lantern.

He had always been a man given to introspection, but lately it had become acute. Everything reminded him of something from the past, a past he'd just as soon forget. It was over and done with, he'd say, but he was basically a ferociously honest man and knew that nothing was over, nothing was ever done with; that everything was standing there at the door waiting to come in, wanted or not.

He climbed the front stairs and went into the small entrance hall, where there was an antique umbrella stand that held several Stetsons. Then he went into the parlor, Gaston's parlor. Gaston was for him immortal; the man would never die, he was too strong to die. Bobby grimaced at the memories of his father.

The room was decorated in red velvet, Gaston's favorite color. The chairs and couch were plush red velvet, as were the heavy drapes. BeBe had tried to get some light into the room. "It looks like a damn whorehouse," she had said, but the changes she was able to make were minor. In the end, the past won out, his past.

Why did yesterday awe them so, frighten them so? Outside of his mother's death—and he had never known her—Bobby's life contained no traumas or, as he put it, no big deals. He had figured out early on, in grammar school, that in order not to be beaten up every day—because he was the Sheriff's son, because they had a big car and a nice house and nice clothes—he'd better learn to lay low. So he did. He wore old clothes, T-shirts and khakis, and tennis shoes with holes in the bottom; he walked everyplace, and said damn little. Gradually who he was diminished in importance, and he even became popular. He was not elected class president because he chose not to run, and at Richelieu High's annual Christmas dance, presided over by an elected king and queen, he turned down the honor. Except for membership in the Future Business Leaders of America, he managed to be almost invisible, and life for him became livable and quiet.

The parlor was dominated by a big photograph of Gaston that

hung over the fireplace. Gaston wore his Stetson, tilted to a jaunty angle, a Camel cigarette burning between his fingers like a magic wand. There was a diamond stickpin on his silk necktie, and his badge was surrounded by tiny diamonds. He had a pencil-thin mustache, the effect of which was to make him look slightly Latin.

Gaston had started out as a state trooper, a unique one. He arrested no one, never even wrote a ticket. He was, in fact, a kind of saint, doing favors for everyone, taking old folks who were ill to Big Charity in New Orleans, collecting food for destitute people, even pitching in to help someone build a barn. Children loved him, old folks revered him, this trooper who recognized no laws save the Golden Rule. You talk about a good man, they said. They all said it!

When he ran for Sheriff, he was elected with 85 percent of the vote! When told that he had six months to live, that he was dying of prostate cancer, he swore the doctor to secrecy, made possible only because he went to a doctor at Ochsner Clinic in New Orleans. There was no way to keep a secret like that in Richelieu.

He told only his son, and then only after the evidence was too obvious to ignore or laugh off. They had been sitting in the parlor on a wet Sunday afternoon, the big Philco in the corner giving soft dance music.

"Ah'm goin' die soon, cher. No use to talk big about it, it's one of them things. You. You wanna be Sheriff? Come on, Bobby, don't give me that bullshit of looking into space, there ain't no answer there. How you feel?"

"Shocked."

"Well, be unshocked, that don't mean nothin' either. Ah got me a plan. Ah'm gon' qualify to run again. There won't be no opposition, nobody's crazy, ah'd still be elected if ah was dead, you know?"

"Yes."

"Now at about five minutes to five, you go qualify. There won't be no one around the Clerk of Court office that late on a Friday, they'll all be at Coon's startin' off the weekend with some Jax. Comprende?"

"I do."

"At one minute to five ah'm gon' pull out. You'll be the Sheriff, no opposition, no nothin'. What you say? Come on, Bobby, don't sit there with you thumb up you ass. Say yes or say no, but say something. Goddamn you hard to deal with."

"I'll do what you say."

"Uh-uh. Thass some more bullshit. You gon' do what you want to do. This is one time you gotta do something, you know?"

"All right."

"Uh-uh. All right what? Say it, man! Say it." He grimaced in pain and squeezed himself between his legs. His boots were highly polished, his cigarette glowed in the red velvet gloom. A roar of thunder made its way across Heaven. Then the rain came down with vengeance.

"I'll qualify for Sheriff."

"That's what you wanna do, Bobby?"

"Yes. I want to be Sheriff. I won't be the Sheriff you are, but . . ."

"You sure as hell won't! You too . . . ah don' know what you are. Ain't that something? I got one son, so far as I know, ha-ha, and I don' know him at all. Who you reckon you are, Bobby?"

Bobby looked him in the eyes. "I'm your son, didn't you know?"

Gaston stood, extended a hand. "Ah'll have a few other personal things to tell you, but there ain't no rush." They shook hands. "Now one thing, don' tell your wife nothin'. Not a damn word. She'll tell Papoot, and that son of a bitch'll put up a candidate as sure as hell. Not a word, Bobby. Comprende?"

"I do."

"Well, thass that. Now I'm goin' to a sauce piquant. You goin'?"

"Sure. We can go together."

"Now that is a big surprise. Me an' you. Ha!"

On one side of Gaston's photograph was a painting of a smiling Christ. On the other was a portrait of Franklin D. Roosevelt, also smiling. The triumvirate above the mantel were happy. The room was exactly as Gaston had left it.

Bobby went into the bathroom, stripped, and put his clothes away in a hamper. Hanging on a hook on the door were his clothes for the next day, and below them another pair of shined boots.

He fell to the bathroom floor and began doing push-ups. He did this every night as an absolute necessity. There were at least five suppers at camps all over the parish every single evening. As Sheriff he was expected to "make the rounds," visiting each one, if only for a few minutes. They didn't care when he arrived or departed, what they cared about was that he try the food and comment on it. The next day what he said would be repeated all over the parish. "Bobby said Sport's chicken stew was the bes' he ever tasted." He could easily have weighted three hundred pounds, as did many of the men in town. There was so much food, and all of it was marvelous. Amazingly, there were very few heart attacks! Thus Bobby's exercise every evening before bed.

He counted aloud as sweat covered his body. When he reached fifty (he could have done a hundred), he stopped and slid into the big old bathtub, laying back in the ice-cold water. By the time the water had warmed slightly, he stepped from the tub and toweled with a big blue towel laid out for him on a chair along with blue-and-white-striped pajamas.

Then he went out onto the side porch. The ceiling fan turned slowly over BeBe's still form. He got into bed as quietly as he could. He didn't want to wake her. He didn't want to talk. He lay on his back, his head resting on his wrist on the big pillow.

He tried to sleep, but couldn't. His head was filled with trouble, and he recognized dread circulating through him like water through a pipe.

He tried dissipating his thoughts, punching holes in them in an effort to drift off, but it was a no go. His eyes were wide open, and he stared up at the fan's blades. He heard a blackbird stir in the bamboo, thought he could hear his own heartbeat. He began to count heartbeats as some count sheep.

BeBe stirred by his side and suddenly got up from the bed and disappeared into the house. He closed his eyes more tightly. In a few moments he felt her presence; she was standing by his side of the bed, wearing a white cotton robe. "Take this," she said, "you've got to get some sleep." She handed him a glass of warm milk, which he took and drank without comment. Then he lay back down as she got into the bed on her side facing him.

"It's that damn bitch, isn't it?" she asked softly. Now the blackbird was silent. It had found sleep.

"Yes," he admitted. It was no use to lie to BeBe. She knew him too well, better than he knew himself.

"She's beautiful."

"It's not that!" he said. He was angry like she had touched a nerve. "I think she's going to make trouble."

"For us?" Lately, she was not that secure in her marriage and wished that she could rid herself of fifty or so pounds. "I'll kill her."

He sat up. "No! Not just us. For Richelieu. She's a troublemaker. She's going to make trouble."

"About Ti Boy?"

"Yes."

"I don't understand."

"I do. Goddamnit."

She kissed his forehead, and he pursed his lips and made a kissing sound.

"You'll handle it," she said, and in moments he could hear her soft snore.

Mercifully he also drifted off.

Ruth Ann Daigle checked on her father one final time. There were so many things to be careful of. Maybe the pillow would be on his face and he would smother because he would not know, would not remember how to remove it. God, he didn't remember anything! She groaned aloud and was then afraid that she had awakened him. But no, he slept his silent sleep, lying there as if he were dead. He *is* dead, she thought. She could have cried, but she knew that would accomplish nothing. For a moment she wished him truly dead, and then she felt overwhelming guilt over that feeling. "I'm sorry," she said aloud.

She went down the hall and into her bedroom. It was ridiculously "little girlish," frilly and decorated in pink and white. She sat on her bed, legs crossed before her, polished her nails. When she was through she blew on them. They weren't perfect, but they would do. She stared at herself in the mirror. She thought, I am beautiful. She stood and let her pink robe drop and looked at herself in the mirror.

Her pink-tipped breasts were perfect. All her life men had stared at either them or her buttocks, which she turned to study. They were alabaster, with a blush of pink only slightly lighter than her nipples. Her triangle was full and curly. She smiled, made her full lips into a pout, and kissed at her image.

Then she got into bed. She slept naked, lying on her side, a pillow under her head, another pillow between her legs. She'd forgotten to say her prayers and promised herself that she'd say them twice tomorrow. She was too sleepy now. The last conscious thought she had before drifting off was that of a man's somber face. Bobby Boudreaux's face. She smiled. She slept.

Chapter 5

The shutters of his eyelids snapped open. It was 4:00 A.M., and he was wide awake. It was like that every day of his life, and it didn't matter what time he went to sleep, nor did he have to check his wristwatch. It was 4:00. It was always 4:00. He couldn't remember the origin of this habit. He did remember as a boy sitting alone in the kitchen waiting for Gaston to get up so they could drink coffee milk together. He knew how many red squares and how many white squares the kitchen oilcloth contained, but he often counted them anyway, out of boredom. His father would enter the kitchen about 7:30, dressed in shorts and a T-shirt, his face grizzled, even his little mustache seeming somehow unkempt. His greeting was always the same, "An' you, what you say?" and sometimes he ran a hand through Bobby's hair, which always made him tense up, something Gaston not only always noticed but always commented on too. "Goddamn, Bobby, I'm your daddy," he'd say, and then he'd pause, waiting for Bobby to reply. When he didn't, Gaston grunted. Bobby never knew what that grunt meant either.

Gaston would ask, "How's school?"

Bobby would say, "Fine."

"You gon' make all A's?"

Bobby, ever truthful, said, "Maybe one B."

"In what?" Gaston asked, though he knew.

"Math."

"Thass all a bunch of shit anyway. You don' need no math. In fact you don' need nothin'. Me, I had to quit school in the fifth grade to help with the farm. It didn't seem to hurt me none." He waited for Bobby to agree, and when the boy was silent, an irritated Gaston would demand, "Did it?" Bobby nodded his head in agreement. "You gon' be one stubborn man, Bobby, jes' like your poor mama. She was a saint, but as stubborn as a mule. Me, I'm not like that. No matter how stupid the other person is, I don' argue. Hell, I go along, thinkin' to myself, You fuckin' idiot, you ain't nothin' and I'm the Sheriff. Like I let them win all the little elections, you know? Long as I win the big one." Then he'd throw back his head and laugh until he had to wipe his eyes.

Next he'd asked what he always asked: "You need anything?" He meant money. Bobby always shook his head. "You never seem to need nothin', Bobby. Ah hope yo' life stays that way. Comprende?" He didn't wait for an answer.

Bobby went into the kitchen to drip his coffee in the white pot. BeBe was a late sleeper. He went out on the front porch, stretched, and breathed in the sweet morning air. He heard the birds stirring in the bamboo. Whenever the sun came up they'd be on their way. He loved to watch this ritual. A little part of the sky would grow black with them, like a sudden eclipse. Then he remembered. For a few hours, sleep had been a big eraser, but thoughts didn't stay erased. He dressed and then had one more cup of coffee, sitting on the front steps.

The sun had come fully up, and with a sudden whir the birds departed. To where he didn't know, though he often wondered. Then the bamboo stood still and silent.

As he drove away he saw roses in his rearview mirror. BeBe had the touch; that girl could make things grow. Everything but love, he thought and felt ashamed. Her marriage was more secure than any he could think of. He would never leave her. She had been so slender and pretty when he married her, and he felt guilty about that too. He thought that worry and insecurity had made her fat. He promised himself to take her to the Palace Theater Sunday night to see that new Randolph Scott film.

As he drove, he didn't have to think. The car knew the way. On Saturday morning the day officially began at Possum Aucoin's barbershop. All the regulars would be there for sure, hungry for Possum's jokes. He always had them; nobody knew where they came from, but the supply seemed endless. They were there for Possum's outrageous gossip too. Everybody was his target, and staying away from the barbershop just meant that you didn't get to hear what was known about you. Possum's gossip was good and bad, but mostly bad. He wasn't much on good things. He wasn't a bitter man, though—just a mean one, and a gossip.

He stood five feet, two inches tall and wore slippers. His bow tie was always red, his shirt white, with sleeves rolled up to the elbows. He was almost bald, with just a fringe of hair about his skull. He reigned over the shop, and while some tried to pay him back for his evil talk, there was no way to beat him. He was a pro. His haircuts, on the other hand, were less successful. He talked too damn much, and he didn't think about what he was doing.

This morning Big Shot Fontenot occupied the single chair. The regulars sat about waiting for things to begin. There was Hot Dog Hebert, Hurphy Perrault, Nonc Doucet, asleep in his chair, Sport Baudoin, Tooky Trahan, hustling him for insurance, President Prejean, and Watch Out Naquin. They greeted the Sheriff, who took a chair. It was a good place to politick, to get the lay of the land, to find out who was glad and who wasn't.

Big Shot, who had dreams about evicting Possum—and he could because the bank owned the building and Possum was never on time with the mortgage payments—braced himself. Possum was calling him "dickdo," and as yet no one had asked for an explanation. The tiny radio was playing too. Na Na Duhon was spinning a few records and sending sweet messages back home to his De De.

Hurphy couldn't resist. He was often Possum's straight man, even when he was the butt of the venom. "Possum, what the hell's a dickdo?"

Possum clipped Big Shot's sideburns, realized he'd made one side longer than the other, and said, "Big Shot's belly sticks out more than his dickdo!" Now that was a good one, and even those who owed the bank money laughed, some more softly, their eyes sending little messages of apology to Big Shot, who laughed because he had no choice and wanted to be a good sport. He could buy and sell all those cocksuckers, so what did he care?

Possum wasn't finished, of course. "When old man Gossen was dying, his little grandson stood by his bed. Gossen could smell some gumbo cooking in the kitchen, so he sent the kid to get him a little bowl. 'Lord, that's good,' Gossen said. He was so weak he could hardly sip. He told his grandson, 'Go get me one more little bowl from Grandma.' The kid went in the kitchen and asked Grandma, but she said, 'No, tell him that's for the wake!'" They laughed so hard Nonc woke up and asked, "What bullshit did I miss?"

Tooky told the joke again, but Nonc had gone back to sleep. They all listened to Na Na. "Ah'm goin' to go fishin' and bring my De De some perfect catfish, which she can cook better than anybody in the world." The men shook their heads in disgust. If he wanted to lie to his wife, that was okay, but he should do it in private.

Sport Baudoin shouted in his gravelly voice, "Play some music, fool!"

Then Mayor Big Head Arceneaux came in. His crew cut needed a little touching up.

Possum said, "Say, Big Head, somebody told me in Abbeville they got a good-lookin' midget girl, about nineteen, and she can play the saxophone."

Big Head was intrigued but tried not to show it. His eyes, which were surprisingly large, showed great interest. Still, there was a dilemma. How could he possibly get more information from Possum without it being told all over the parish?

Hot Dog Hebert interrupted his thoughts. "When the city gon' fix that red light? It's been stuck for a month."

"We're working on that," the midget Mayor assured him. He wished Hot Dog would die of leprosy.

Hurphy said, "That's what you said last month."

Big Head defended himself. "Truth is, we're waiting for a ladder from the highway department in Baton Rouge. We don't have one tall enough."

Tooky then asked, "Well, how the hell did the light get up there?" He knew the answer that was coming, they all did.

"That was done under the previous administration," Big Head said. He liked to show off his two years of college with big words. With that, he departed, little legs taking him across the street to the poolroom, everybody's next stop on Saturday morning.

President Prejean asked, "How big you reckon Big Head's dick is?" They often pondered this question because no one had ever seen it. When they happened to share a urinal with the Mayor, he very carefully held a hand over his privates and looked straight ahead like he was considering Richelieu's future.

"When he dies ah'm goin' tell you all," Watch Out Naquin promised for the hundredth time. "You got my word on that there."

This didn't satisfy them, and they stirred restlessly. Possum, now working on the Sheriff, had an idea: "Some night at the camp we ought to hold him down and measure it." The howls that greeted this woke Nonc, who laughed too, spittle from his toothless mouth hitting Hot Dog Hebert, who was sitting next to him. "Watch yourself, you old bastid!" Hot Dog said to Nonc, who was again fast asleep.

Now Na Na was playing everybody's favorite, "Jolie Blanc." They listened quietly, and President began to dance about the shop. He did this gracefully; he was easily the best dancer in Richelieu.

Sport said, "Goddamn, look at that man dance."

Prejean's eyes were shut, lost in the music of fiddle and accordion. *Oh, mais jolie blanc, tu m'as quiter.*

Possum said, "President might be thinkin' about dancin' to Baton Rouge. Huh, Prejean?"

Then President stopped dancing, his eyes wide open. "We could use some representation." They knew what he meant. There had been a rumor that he would love to kick Senator Papoot Gaspard's ass right out of office. And he wasn't the only one. Word at the Rotary was the old man had lost touch with the people.

Possum couldn't resist and asked the Senator's son-in-law, "What you say, Bobby?"

"It's a free country," Bobby said. Goddamn Possum! He wished he carried a gun so he could shoot the bastard. Asking him that in front of everybody.

"How'd you vote?" Possum asked, every eye in the place (except Nonc's) on Bobby.

"I'd vote for the best man."

Everybody laughed. He'd answered the barber good, for sure.

Bobby wondered if Papoot had any idea that a revolution was brewing. The Senator wasn't as popular as he thought he was. He was so darn powerful in Baton Rouge as Chairman of the Senate Ways and Means Committee, and had brought so much pork home and had been in power so long that he obviously thought he was once again a shoo-in. Well, he wasn't. Take this crowd in the barbershop. Papoot would have trouble getting votes from any of them other than Bobby and Nonc, who he had on the state payroll as a building inspector, with the official title Clerk of the Works. As Papoot liked to say, "Hell, man, it's a honor! We got the only hundred-and-one-year-old inspector, maybe in the whole world. Hee, hee!"

Not that anybody begrudged the old man a few extra bucks. They'd all like to be on the state payroll. But Papoot was pretty much looking after Papoot. Bobby's feelings were a mixture of loyalty to him because of BeBe and a sense that Papoot ought to call it a day. He'd been at the trough long enough. Too long, actually.

He'd tried discussing it with BeBe, who'd looked at him like he was crazy. "Daddy's gonna die in office," she'd said.

Given half a chance, President Prejean, with the backing of the Rotary, would be serious opposition. Damn serious. There were a couple of deals President had to put together, the main one with

Hurphy Perrault, who talked to Bishop Peter Paul Dupuis over in Lafayette a couple of times a week. If the Church went with President, who was keeping his head up Hurphy's ass, look out! The Senator claimed to be a big friend of the Bishop. God knows the Church got whatever it wanted in Baton Rouge. Governor Richard W. Cole, a thirty-second-degree Mason, knew where his bread was buttered too. He needed to secure some South Louisiana Catholic votes for sure.

Bobby thought that maybe he'd bring up the subject with Papoot on Sunday, when they gathered for the weekly meal. But that wasn't so easy either. Lately, Papoot had become a non-listener, changing any subject he didn't like or just getting downright silent, a quality BeBe had inherited from him. Still, Bobby had to tell him. Or maybe he'd tell it to Father Brother-in-law Justin. He was a good listener. Intense, like he was gulping down your every word, which always made Bobby feel threatened, though he couldn't say why exactly.

He and the priest got along okay, though Bobby didn't understand the man. He felt oddly uncomfortable in his presence. He had the feeling the priest could read his mind, especially his feelings about his marriage. He wondered if Justin was alluding to them when he gave that little lecture on the sanctity of marriage. There was no reason for it. He had never cheated on BeBe, hadn't even . . . He killed this thought, suddenly feeling guilty. That bitch from New Orleans was driving him a little crazy. It wasn't because of her sexiness, which Jesus Christ knew she had in abundance. Instead Bobby preferred to think it was what she had said. And who the hell was he gonna discuss that with? he wondered. Moe Weiss was pretty unsatisfactory, with his silence and haunted eyes. The guy needed to try and lighten up a little bit.

He got out of the barber's chair and paid Possum, who asked, "You not gonna even check how you look in the mirror?"

Tooky said, "He don't have to. He knows you made him look like shit!" Everybody laughed.

He crossed Main Street, looking up at the stuck stoplight and shaking his head. Then he went into One Lung Savoy's poolroom.

One Lung claimed to have been gassed in World War I. Possum had expressed some doubts: "How did a cook get gassed unless he put his head in the oven?" Still, he and Cap'n Eddie Sonnier, the school crossing guard who'd taken a bullet in the back on Iwo Jima (and even Possum couldn't question this because under his shirt Cap'n Eddie had a scar running down his back), were Richelieu's bona fide war heroes. Sadly, neither chose to join either the American Legion or Veterans of Foreign Wars, which led Possum to speculate that both might have Communist leanings.

Not that either veterans' organization was anxious to count Cap'n Eddie in its membership, with his little ways of giving teenage boys a quarter to see their weenies, or for that matter One Lung, who not only coughed a lot but sprayed spittle in copious amounts when he did.

Both veterans' groups hoped that someday there'd be another war and some decent hero would come out of it they could honor. In the meantime, they had to make do with Sergeant York and Audie Murphy. Possum (who'd spent the war cutting hair at Fort Polk in central Louisiana) was none too sure. He'd heard some rumors about York and Murphy too. People just shook their heads. Was anybody okay?

One Lung's poolroom was always dark, with what little light there was coming from the naked bulbs hanging down over the green felt-covered pool tables, and the neon signs back of the counter, advertising beer. It was a tough place to breathe in, with smoke and chalk dust clogging nostrils the moment you entered.

The place had one positive attribute, though—it made the best coffee in town, jet-black and served in little white demitasse cups, along with pretty good biscuits from Hot Dog Hebert's.

Bobby sat at the counter, and One Lung served the Sheriff himself. Both men watched the ebony brew go into the cup. One Lung coughed in greeting, and the Sheriff didn't flinch at the spittle that came his way, some of it settling on the rim of his cup.

Hurphy Perrault had once suggested to the proprietor that he charge extra for the spit. "Where else are they gonna get it?" One Lung cackled and coughed a hearty laugh. Hurphy wiped his face and wished that the Kaiser had gotten One Lung between the eyes instead of in the chest.

Tooky Trahan, half-carrying Nonc Doucet, entered. The insurance man wore a bright green sport coat, like he'd just won the Masters. Bobby helped him prop Nonc against the wall. One Lung served the newcomers, who each had two biscuits. No one in Richelieu charged Nonc for anything, and Tooky considered that maybe he'd be included in the largesse, but One Lung held out a palm. Tooky paid with a sigh.

Bobby sipped the boiling hot coffee and felt awake for the first time that morning. He'd gotten so little sleep the night before. "How's the insurance business?" he asked.

"Couldn't be better!" Tooky said. It was what he always said, and Bobby thought, With most of the diocese's insurance, how could it be anything else?

"When you have Jesus Christ on your team, life is wonderful!" Tooky said in a loud voice, causing those about to attempt tricky pool shots to look up and consider poling the insurance man between the eyes with their cues. But they were afraid of Tooky, with him having that saint's bone in his wallet. Jesus wouldn't stand for that for sure!

Tooky had a lot of state business too, thanks to the Senator, but word was he wasn't that happy with it, having to split with his bene-factor, or sponsor, as it was called. It was just a rumor, true, but still, there was less than burning admiration from Tooky when Papoot's name was brought up.

"Is President serious about running?" Bobby asked. And the insur-ance man studied him for a moment like he was deciding whether or not to tell the truth. "Who knows?" he replied diplomatically. But Bobby wasn't buying that. Tooky also had the sheriff's department insurance—vehicles, equipment, everything. "Don't give me any bullshit, Tooky," Bobby said softly.

Tooky studied the Sheriff briefly. The man had the coldest eyes he'd ever seen. "He's considering it," he finally responded.

"How much?"

"Says he's getting a lot of encouragement," Tooky answered.

"And how about Bishop Dupuis, think he'd let President oppose Papoot? Papoot's practically given the state to the diocese. What could President do for him, huh?"

Tooky got up to wipe Nonc's chin with a napkin, biscuit crumbs clinging to his mouth. Nonc held his face up for this service; he expected it, and always got it.

Bobby asked, "Tooky, what do you hear about Zeke's daughter, Mary Ann or whatever her name is?"

Tooky smiled with relief at having moved on to another subject. "Name's Ruth Ann, and have you ever seen an ass like that?"

Bobby shook his head. He hadn't. "What else?"

"Got a reputation for toughness, I mean a real bitch. Didn't give a damn who she went after, either. Kind of devoted herself to sending people to Angola. Politicians in New Orleans absolutely despised her. Damn lucky no one killed her, she was that tough. Know what her nickname was? Pit Bull. Why you asking, Bobby? In addition to her ass, I mean."

"She's got some questions."

"'Bout what?"

"Ti Boy. Specifically his death. Did the Brouliettes have any insurance?"

There was a long, long pause. "No. Thank God! Most tenant farmers don't. Can't afford it. Papoot picked up the funeral tab anyway. Ti Boy's not the first or the last to kill himself cleaning a shotgun. Hell, it happens once a year."

"I know. Still, something's made Zeke's girl want to know more," Bobby said somberly.

"What are you gonna do about it?" Tooky asked.

"Nothing. Open and shut as far as I can tell."

"Good," Tooky said, and this piqued the Sheriff's interest. Why would Tooky care? Why would anyone but the Brouliettes care, really?

"No one wants any trouble," Tooky said, and Bobby was more curious: who was "no one"?

Tooky saw the Sheriff studying him. "What I mean is, everything's fine in Richelieu. You know what I mean, Bobby."

"I guess so."

"Don't pay Zeke's daughter no mind, that's the best way."

"And it'll go away and I'm not even sure I know what 'it' is. I'd like to believe that, Tooky, but like you say, she's a tough one. When you've been in law enforcement awhile, they're something you can spot, the tough ones."

Tooky looked around. Conspiratorially he said, "And it sure wouldn't help Papoot none if you were to . . ."

"Yes?" Bobby asked. He was pissed. He did not take well to implied pressure.

"You know, get involved in some kind of investigation."

"Jesus, Tooky, that's my job!" Bobby said.

"Yeah, in a way. But that's not your main job. Keeping everything peaceful, that's what folks want out of you, Bobby. And you always do it."

Bobby nodded. Richelieu wasn't looking for trouble. "I agree, but I'm not sure about her, and she's not running for office. In other words, why should she give a damn?"

Bobby left some change on the counter. He paid for everything. It was the exact opposite of his father. Gaston paid for very little. More than once he'd expressed to his son his theory about this: "If the Sheriff pays, people gon' think he's a goddamn fool. It makes 'em proud to treat you. Then they can come to you for little favors without low-rating themselves. Even Stephen, like they say. You disagree, I can tell. Well, that ain't nothin' new. If your mother hadn't been a saint, Bobby, I'd swear you wasn't my son. Don' know where I got you, neither. You somethin' else."

• • •

Tooky watched Bobby leave the poolroom. He was a strange one all right. If Gaston and him hadn't faked that election, he wouldn't be Sheriff. Tooky laughed. It was a hell of a trick! Bobby would probably be running a Dairy Queen somewhere between Richelieu and Lafayette. Tooky laughed at his own humor, made his way to the door, and turned back. He'd forgotten Nonc.

"Come on, you old bastard!"

But Nonc wasn't quite ready to leave. "We got time for a little more coffee, Tooky?"

Tooky sat back down. "Okay, one cup."

Hurphy Perrault joined them. The attorney was curious. "What's up, Tooky? Hey, One Lung, give Nonc a couple more biscuits!"

"He's already had four," One Lung said and coughed. Everyone but Nonc ducked. "Give him his biscuits before I sue you," Hurphy threatened. One Lung laughed and put two biscuits before Nonc, who dove right in, his toothless mouth chewing away. Hurphy and Tooky watched the old man eat.

"Like a goddamn horse," One Lung said.

"At least he doesn't spit on nobody," Tooky noted.

One Lung moved off.

"So?" Hurphy asked. "And don't lie, I can see it in your face."

"It's Zeke's daughter."

"My God, what tits! I could drown in them," Hurphy said.

"The rest of her's all right too," Tooky answered. "She's not satisfied about Ti Boy's death."

"Says who?"

"She mentioned it to Bobby Boudreaux at the wake. I can tell he's concerned," Tooky said. Nonc choked on a biscuit, and Tooky hit him gently on the back until he caught his breath.

"Lord," said Hurphy, "my biscuit almost got Nonc. Can you imagine, I would have had to sue myself?"

They laughed. "Who'd have won?" Tooky asked.

"Me." Hurphy was confident, but he had a right to be. He was one smart lawyer, consistently kicking the asses of those big New Orleans law firms. "So, what do you think, Tooky?"

"Nothing. I don't think nothing. The kid killed himself in an accident, end of story, huh?"

When Hurphy didn't answer, Tooky pressed. "Well, isn't it?"

"Oh sure," Hurphy said, but he said it so lightly Tooky had the feeling the lawyer wasn't telling all.

"Are you gonna do anything, Hurphy?" Tooky whispered.

"Yeah. I'm gonna make a little ride to Lafayette."

"Talk to P.P.D., huh?"

"Kiss his ring first."

Tooky wiped Nonc's face with a paper napkin, and the three men left One Lung's.

Coon's parking lot was jammed, mostly with pickup trucks. From air conditioners that dotted the cinder-block walls came the sweet music of Papa Sotile and the Richelieu Gents. They were playing a classic, Nathan Abshire's "La Valse de Bélisaire." Bobby loved that song and hummed along as he got out of his car and entered the building.

Everybody was there, old people and young people, even babies in parents' and grandparents' arms, and everybody who could dance was doing so. Age and sex made no difference; girls danced together, old maids danced with married men, and those too old to dance clapped or tapped their feet in time to the music.

Papa Sotile and the Richelieu Gents consisted of accordion and fiddle that took the lead while guitar and triangle provided the rhythm. Papa was a giant of a man with wavy black hair and a big belly straining his white shirt and black string tie.

He whooped into the microphone, "Now we got with us Bobby Boudreaux, high Sheriff of Richelieu Parish. Come dance, Bobby, I know you love this waltz!"

On a table covered with beer bottles and whiskey glasses was CAJN's microphone, and back of it sat Na Na Duhon doing his live Saturday broadcast from Coon's. It was legendary.

Na Na reported to his listeners on the Sheriff's activities. "He's goin' right on the dance floor and dancin' with Grandma Pasqua. They make a handsome couple for sure. Dance, Bobby, dance!"

Now an eight-year-old girl took Grandma Pasqua's place, and Bobby never missed a step. She was replaced by a lady with a baby in her arms, and after a kiss, Bobby, mama, and baby were dancing up a storm.

Just off the lounge were four bourrée tables, with old rawhide-seat Cajun chairs. Lampshades, taped and patched together and suspended from the ceiling with old rope, were above each table, and the game was loud and vigorous as the players competed with the music. "You cheatin' for sure, you old bastid!" "Ooooo la la!"

Back in the long tin bar was a small kitchen presided over by Catfish François, sitting a big black pot of fish stew that would be served free to one and all. You could already smell it, and some bragged, "Ah'm goin' eat my share, an your share too!" or "Leave some for me, you piggy pig!"

Somebody handed Bobby a Jax beer, and he took a big swallow while he danced, this time with two old maid sisters. It was so hot in there! The air-conditioning didn't help much at all.

When "La Valse de Bélisaire" ended, people clapped and Bobby made the rounds, shaking hands with the men and giving the women a big kiss. He didn't miss any babies either, commenting to proud parents and grandparents on how big they were getting. No baby was crying; they were having a wonderful time too! Diapers were being changed and bottles were being given in between swallows of cold, delicious beer. They would remain there all day, and all cares and worries would vanish to the sweet music of Papa Sotile and the Richelieu Gents.

Suddenly the beer got to Bobby, and he headed for the men's room.

The smell of beer and piss was overwhelming as he urinated on the big blocks of ice. Then he went to the bar, where a place was made for him, and Coon put a fresh beer before him.

"You gon' stay for Catfish's stew? He says he really hit it today."

"I'm not going to be able to," Bobby said.

"Well, ah'm gon' get you a little taste," Coon said and returned with a bowl of stew. It was red like tomatoes, and Bobby could smell the onions and garlic, parsley and celery, and above all, the liberal dollop of hot sauce. "Oooooweeeee!"

Standing by was the chef, eyebrows raised, waiting for the Sheriff's opinion. Nothing was more important than how people felt about the food. Nothing. Bobby blew into his spoon, eyes on Catfish, tasted, swallowed, paused for effect. Catfish stirred restlessly. Finally he could stand it no more. "Well?" Everybody at the bar was listening, watching. Maybe Catfish had failed this time. Too much this, too much that. The news would make the parish in hours. Catfish would have to move to Texas. Competitive cooks, everyone in Richelieu, stood by, because one thing about Bobby Boudreaux, he couldn't tell no lie for nobody. Coon was sweating, the band was playing "Hip et Taiaut," and folks were two-stepping with the electric guitar. Na Na saw what was going on and told the world into the mike, "The high Sheriff had the first taste of Catfish's stew. How he like it, huh?"

Bobby didn't let the world down. "Make a bulldog break his chain!"

Coon slapped him on the back in appreciation and handed him a fresh Jax. Catfish said nothing, made like he personally wasn't involved. Na Na said, "It hit the mark, and ah'm gon' bring my little De De some for sure. Hip et Taiaut, cher!"

Bobby could feel her presence before he saw her. He didn't have to look into the long mirror behind the bar. She didn't smell of perfume. She smelled of her.

Her arm reached over his shoulder and took a cold Jax. She wore one of Zeke's old long-sleeved shirts over some trousers. She drank quietly, saying nothing, but he could hear her humming to the music. He didn't turn around to acknowledge her.

Papa Sotile said into his mike, "An' now, everybody's favorite, I know it's mine and yours too, 'Jolie Blanc!' "

She said, "I love it. Will you dance with me?"

He felt the muscles in his shoulders bunch up. Thank God nobody sitting by had heard her. But she just stood there, beer tilted to those full red lips, and waited. He didn't know what to do. He knew that in a couple of ways she meant trouble and wondered how best to handle it. Should he ignore it, or meet it head-on?

He didn't say anything but stood and made his way to the dance floor, stopping at one of the card tables because somebody wanted him to look at his bourrée hand. He studied it, face expressionless. She waited on the dance floor, arms at her sides. He looked at her neck, not wanting to look at her face. And he thought, God help me. And thought of BeBe and felt guilt about what, he didn't know—he hadn't done anything, but the potential was there. Could you be guilty of uncommitted sins? he wondered. He wished he could ask Father Brother-in-law. But he couldn't. He could always go to the confession in Lafayette. It was terrible having the only priest around be not only a saintly man—that was how he thought of Justin—but your brother-in-law too. Not that Justin would say anything to BeBe, but goddamn the man was judgmental. Then Bobby laughed. Wasn't that what a priest was supposed to be?

Almost unaware, they were moving to the music about the pretty blonde.

"Share it with me," she said over the music. He had no idea what she meant, but he found himself blushing. "You just laughed," she said. "What was funny? I just couldn't picture you laughing."

"I don't even remember," he lied, and she half-stopped, causing his body to be right up against hers. "Were you laughing at me?"

"Definitely not," he said. "I don't find you funny at all." And he wanted to lay down there on the dance floor and die, or at least vanish. He had an erection. He backed off. Had she felt it? What must she think? He looked into her face. Those big blue eyes with the gray borders around them, like they needed something to call attention to them. He read amusement in them. Was it his erection? His lack of self-control?

"Actually," she said, "I do have a good sense of humor."

"Sorry. I don't know any jokes."

She laughed. "That was quite funny. A little insulting, like I'm some kind of idiot, but funny."

People he knew, particularly women, just didn't talk like she did. It was to him like some kind of foreign language. "Maybe you stayed in New Orleans too long," he blurted out.

"Not long enough. I loved it!"

"But you came back," he said and felt foolish. He was sounding like a petulant child blaming another child for something.

"I had no choice. My father . . ."

He said nothing, danced, holding her at arm's length, breathed a sigh of relief when President Prejean cut in. She clung to his fingers a little longer than was necessary. "Got to dance with the press, 'specially when she's so damned beautiful!" Prejean said.

"Don't go too far," she ordered. "We have to talk."

Bobby went back to the bar for a Jax, took a big swallow. He was sweating and rubbed at his face with a paper napkin. Coon observed him and said, "I got the air-conditioning as high as it'll go."

Bobby said, "It's fine."

Coon replied, "She makes me sweat too."

Bobby said, "Who?"

They laughed. She was a blowtorch, even all covered up like she was. You could just tell that under that man's clothing there was ripe, voluptuous woman. He sniffed, but her smell was gone. Too much Jax and sweat. He watched President dance with her. The guy was campaigning for something, any fool could see that. But could Papoot? No fool, but getting on in years, not noticing the little things that a politician had to notice to survive. He heard her laugh, and he envied President. There was sweat under her arms, and he wondered how her sweat would taste.

Another grandma wanted to dance, and with a smile he followed her to the floor. "Hope I can keep up with you," he said. His seventy-five-year-old partner was delighted.

As he danced, he became aware that there were a lot of eyes on her, including his own. Truth was, she totally dominated the room. And there were plenty of pretty women there. But no one like Ruth Ann Daigle. She was almost too much. She looked at him over President's shoulders, and their eyes locked. He wanted to look away, but he couldn't; she was like a magnet.

Tottering onto the floor, barely able to walk, was Nonc Doucet. No one found anything unusual about a 101-year-old man wanting to dance. Hell, they all wanted to dance! Bobby loved it as with trembling hand Nonc tapped President on the shoulder. Without missing a beat she was in Nonc's arms, head back, laughing a throaty laugh. And Nonc was one good dancer, with wonderful rhythm. President watched the couple and fervently wished that Nonc would fall to the floor, dead of a heart attack. Shit! The old man was indestructible.

A crowd gathered about the couple, and people clapped their hands to urge them on. President joined Bobby at the bar. Coon brought each man a bowl of stew with some of Hot Dog Hebert's hot French bread. They dipped it in the stew and smacked their lips in appreciation.

President liked Bobby, had always supported him politically, and hoped what he was thinking about doing wouldn't ruin their friendship. He and Bobby had taken basic training at Fort Polk, then Bobby had gone into the M.P.'s while President entered the infantry. He was the only Private President in the country. His fellow soldiers called him Prez.

"Say, Bobby, I was thinking about the old days. You know it wasn't so bad, huh?"

Bobby said, "We've both had a dozen Jax beers, so nothing looks too bad."

President laughed. "Man, I never been so relieved as when I got to Fort Polk and found there was somebody from Richelieu."

"Yeah. It was a relief all right. Wonder whatever happened to those guys. What was his name, that little Italian from Brooklyn?"

"Abruzzi. Now he was a pistol!"

"Was?" Bobby asked.

"Yeah. He got killed at Anzio. Stepped on a land mine."

"I swear to God I didn't know."

They lifted their beer in a toast to Abruzzi.

"You lucky you came back, huh, President?"

"Damn lucky. Half my outfit didn't make it."

"I was lucky," Bobby said.

They watched Nonc and Zeke's little girl. The beer made them mellow. Honest too.

"You know, Bobby, no matter what happens, I hope me and you can always be friends."

Bobby asked innocently, "What's gonna happen?"

President laughed. "You never know!"

Bobby said, "I hope you won't run against him."

"He's been in there forever," President replied.

"He just wants one more term," Bobby lied. Papoot Gaspard wanted to stay in office until he died.

"It might be time for some new blood, Bobby. A lot of people are saying that. I'm getting a lot of encouragement."

"Well, I hate to fight you."

"But you will, huh?"

"With everything I've got."

"Nothing personal, huh?" President asked.

"Aw hell no."

President nodded and moved off to the dance floor. Nonc was dancing with Li'l Shot Fontenot, his heir apparent, as Richelieu's oldest citizen. Li'l Shot had gained that name only a few years before, when it
became apparent that his son Big Shot would never marry again. There
would be no Li'l Shot unless his poppa took on the name. Big Shot's wife
had fled from him on their wedding night and become a Carmelite nun.
It was Possum who gave Big Shot an heir. His father became Li'l Shot.

Ruth Ann moved back to Bobby's side. "Nonc is amazing. You know
he asked me for a date? He said all he could do is smooch, but he was
the very best!" They laughed.

"Did you accept?"

"I told him I couldn't. Said I had a boyfriend."

His heart dropped from his chest. He felt hollow, empty. Then he
thought, Good! Let her get married and move to Iowa or Alaska. But
he had given himself away, his face had darkened like he was about to
faint. She studied him closely and waited for him to ask her the
details. He swallowed his Jax. Not him. He wasn't going to ask questions and he wasn't going to answer any. Everything about him was
off-limits to this girl who in twenty-four hours had managed to dis-
rupt his quiet and semi-happy life.

"You know what I'm in the mood for?" she asked innocently.

Dear God! He thought.

"A ride. I want to take a ride in the country. Clear my head. You
look like you could use it too." She turned and headed for the door.
He just sat there, willing himself not to follow her. He could sense her
rump moving beneath her shirt, swaying to the rhythm of a tom-tom.
It called to him too, and hating himself, he followed.

She was sitting in his car, and he got in without speaking.

The road out of Richelieu was lined with cotton fields. There were a
few clumps of trees around farmhouses, some cattle grazing. Only
coulees broke the bleak landscape.

"I wonder why we love it," she said aloud, but the question was to herself.

Bobby had never been asked anything like that, didn't know what to respond.

"In New Orleans I used to dream about Richelieu, but I never thought I'd come back. It was just a lovely place to think about. Tell me about you, Sheriff."

"Bobby," he said, and she said, "Okay." The cab of his car seemed to have become mysteriously smaller, like the walls had closed in. He could smell her again. The scent reminded him of something. He searched for it in his memory.

"Please tell me," she said and touched his arm. Her touch shocked him like a cattle prod, and he gripped the wheel tightly not to jerk away. She seemed amused. "Should I apologize?"

"I've got a wife."

"Oh I know that," she said like it didn't matter, but he couldn't let her off that easily.

"I'm happily married," he said and added, "Like you've got a boyfriend."

"Oh that."

He wanted to scream, Goddamnit, tell me! Mr. Happily Married Man wanted to know.

"I was lying."

"Why?"

"Wanted to see if I could get a reaction. I did."

"There is no boyfriend?"

"Do you care?"

"Of course not, why should I?"

She shrugged like she didn't know. He waited. He was prepared to wait all day. No way was he going to ask again. He was angry for being so weak as to ask at all.

"There's no one."

His lips formed an *oh*, but he said nothing.

She was smiling with her own big red lips, and dimples appeared in her perfect face. He'd never noticed them before, and he swallowed like a man who'd witnessed a sighting of the Blessed Mother. The tip of his tongue tingled. He wanted to touch those dimples with it. Mercifully, they disappeared as she blew a dark curl back from her forehead. "So tell me about you. I know you're a happily married man, but surely there's more."

"I don't know what it is you're asking!"

"You have a history. Everybody has one."

"Oh that!" he said, relieved. That was safe ground. "When I was fifteen my father made me an auxiliary deputy, mostly directing traffic in front of the church. That's a good place to politick. I guess he had already made plans for me way back then."

"Would you have done something different?" she asked.

"Do you always look for the negative?" he answered.

"Touché!" she said. "Go on."

"I went to Richelieu High, of course. Played center in football. I was okay, but not too hot at getting the ball back there on deep punts." He laughed at the memory. "It had a way of going over the kicker's head or falling six feet from his outstretched hands. I wasn't worth a damn, but we didn't have that many players where the coach could afford to be choosy. That's when I started to go with Clara, BeBe. She wore my letter jacket. We were *the* couple, Mr. and Mrs. FBLA!"

"What's an FBLA?" she asked innocently.

"Mr. and Mrs. Future Business Leaders of America. It was an honor, I guess. Then BeBe went to SLI in Lafayette to major in home ec, and I went to LSU, the 'Old War Skule,' in general studies. See I was thinking about taking prelaw. Gaston had this fantasy about me being the only sheriff in Louisiana with a degree in law! I lived on the fifth floor of the stadium, where I spent most of my time playing bourrée. I think they housed all us Cajuns together. We played day and night. I met this gal Patsy in my library science class and started going out with her. She was smarter than me. One night I went to get her at her dormitory, and she stood me up for some fraternity guy. She didn't look like you . . ."

"What does that mean? How do I look?"

"Well to tell you the truth like nobody I've ever seen. But she was smart like you. Damn but she hurt my feelings! Anyway, about that time I got called into the Dean of Men's office. I was on scholastic probation. He told me I was the least motivated student he'd ever met. How do you like that?"

"Were you?"

"It's hard to be motivated when your life's laid out in advance. I mean, get motivated about what? So I switched to SLI, and I was with BeBe again."

"Then what?"

"The Japs didn't consult me, and bombed Pearl Harbor." He laughed. "My daddy insisted I join immediately. Funny, he never served in any army, but he wanted me to be a war hero. What bullshit!"

"And you did what he said."

"Of course. I joined and was first sent to Fort Polk and then to Fort Benning, Georgia. Red clay. That's what I remember about Fort Benning, red clay. At least it wasn't so far away. I stayed there the whole war as an M.P. My daddy liked that. I came home on leave, and BeBe and I married. We went to the Edgewater Hotel in Biloxi on a weekend honeymoon. Gaston had given me a pocketful of hundreds, but there wasn't time to spend it. We just stayed in the room."

"After that?" she said quickly.

He wasn't quite through. "I'll be happy to tell you what we did."

"Fuck you," she said, although he wasn't sure he'd heard her right. Outside of whores at Misty's, he had never hear a woman use that word. "Is that what you learned in New Orleans?" he asked.

"You just might be a son of a bitch," she said, and her bottom lip quivered.

He suddenly felt terrible, and he muttered, "I'm sorry." She shrugged. He'd noticed that she shrugged a lot. It saved a lot of words, and what the shrug meant was in the eye of the beholder. It was safe.

"After the war I came back. Your daddy ran my picture on the front page. I was a lowly M.P., but he made me sound like a war hero. Zeke always did right by the Boudreaux family. I'm so sorry about him. For you, and for him."

"Thank you. We'll be okay."

"One Sunday—damn, it looks like everything happens on a Sunday—one Sunday afternoon, Gaston and I were alone in the living room, him looking at his picture, me looking at him. We never had that much to say. He told me two things." He turned to look at her. "Say, you're not going to put any of this in the *Gazette*?"

"No. We're off the record. I'll tell you when I'm asking questions professionally."

"I hate that."

"Me being a professional? Well let's get something straight. I've worked like a dog to be one, and no one and nothing, repeat, no one and nothing, is going to take that from me. Do you understand?"

"I do. But I still hate it." She was even more beautiful when she was angry.

"So it's Sunday and you're sitting there with your dad . . ."

"First he softened me up, like we were in some kind of prizefight, not aiming for a knockout; you know, body blows to set me up. He told me the reason I stayed at Fort Benning the entire war was because he'd arranged it with Senator Odile in Washington. It was strange. I must have been so stupid . . ."

"Innocent," she said.

"Everybody but me at Fort Benning was leaving for real action. I stayed right there. I didn't even think about it at the time. So goddamn stupid! When I realized what had happened, I was shocked. Ashamed, too. A lot of my friends were killed. But not me. The worst thing that could have happened to me was getting hit on the head in Columbus, Georgia! So now, I'm softened up, breathing heavy, heart racing. Feeling miserable. Then he tells me I'm gonna be Sheriff and how we're going to do it. A trick."

"Even Zeke was shocked. He sent me the paper. He laughed. It was so typically Louisiana. Anything goes. What a disgrace! He could at least have written an editorial about it. *The Times-Picayune* did! But who in Richelieu Parish gives a shit about what those big shots in New Orleans felt about anything? I'd have written one."

"I'm glad you didn't, I felt miserable enough. And that's about it for me. Funny, you know?"

"What's so funny?" she said.

"Never in all my life have I talked with anybody about what I just told you."

"Not even BeBe?"

"She probably knows, but no, I've never talked about it. You have a way of making people tell their private business. I guess that's what being a professional is."

"On the other hand, maybe you needed to tell it."

"To a stranger?"

"Ever hear of psychiatrists?"

"And that's you?"

"Sometimes we act as each other's psychiatrists. You can't always keep everything stuffed inside. Sometimes it's good to let it out."

"Well I don't feel better," he said. But in truth he had no regrets about telling her. Then he felt uncertain. "You're sure all that was . . . how'd you say? Off the record?"

"My word of honor. And I do have honor, so forget it. It's dead."

"Even if we're on opposite sides?"

"No matter what. Are we on opposite sides? Aren't we both looking for the same thing? The truth."

"That *is* my job, I guess. But I'm different from you. I don't just go off half-cocked, stirring up dirt. Like what you said yesterday."

"A child is dead, you know. A child with all his years in front of him."

"Yes. But look, accidents like that happen every single year."

"Tell me, when's hunting season?" she asked.

"October, November."

"He was cleaning that rifle in June?"

"I better get you back to Coon's. I gotta go."

"Where? It's Saturday afternoon. Where does the Sheriff go on Saturday afternoon?"

"Well, to tell you the truth, after about a case of Jax, the Sheriff goes to take a nap. And remember, I got a whole night ahead of me."

"All the camps, huh?"

"Five of them tonight. I'll have to eat at least a little at every one of them, and of course you can't just sit there without a beer."

"Damn I wish I was a man! I'd love to make the rounds with you."

He blushed. He would have liked that too. He would have liked to see the world, his world, through her eyes. She saw things differently. It occurred to him for the first time that his life had gotten old. That his life was deeply embedded in a rut of his own making, and for a moment, he tasted bitterness. How had he let go? Why did he give up even without the semblance of a fight? But who would he have fought? His daddy, who called every shot? Gaston was long dead. And it sure wasn't BeBe—she went along with whatever he said. He was the Sheriff, he called the shots. But that was it. He had stopped calling them. It was easy to keep walking on the same path. No surprises. And why did he hate surprises so? Because in a surprise nobody called the shots. That's what a surprise is.

She had turned in the seat and was studying him. She had been in grammar school when he graduated from Richelieu High, and had no memory of him. When she saw him, the only thing that registered was, There goes the Sheriff's son, the Sheriff's handsome son.

"I like the way you look," she said. "Even your nose."

"I used to be self-conscious about my nose. I used to think everybody was staring at it."

"Ever consider getting it fixed?"

"No. I never did. It wasn't important after a while, or maybe there were just other things that really were important." He was glad she didn't ask what, because he didn't have an answer. He couldn't think of anything important. Goddamn, he said to himself, and barely held back from hitting at the dashboard in frustration.

"Stop the car," she said suddenly.

He pulled over to the side of the road. They were by a coulee. Minnows swam. An egret sat on the bank waiting for them to leave so he could catch his supper. Overhead in a mossy oak, a squirrel chatted to something or someone they couldn't see. Neither of them said anything.

"Well?" he asked. "You said 'stop.' What did you . . . Why?"

"You're married, happily married, so it wouldn't be right for you to kiss me. Right?"

He turned to face her, felt like he was dropping off into some other world, and now was this last chance, this moment, to grab on to something, his last chance to save himself. "Right," he said. Could she hear his heart? It sounded to him like the bass drum at the Richelieu High football games, muffled, off in the distance.

"But I'm not married, so it wouldn't be that bad for me to kiss you."

He swallowed. His throat felt gorged, and there was a stirring like waves between his legs. Did he show? Could she see what she was doing to him?

She was on her knees and leaning into him. He could feel her breath, feel it too on the bridge of his nose, and on the flesh between nose and mouth. His lips parted involuntarily. The tip of her tongue was showing between her lips.

She turned her face to the side as she positioned herself, and he felt her fingertips on his face and wanted to shout, Watch out, you'll burn yourself, I'm on fire! He had the need to close his eyes, but he couldn't. He wanted to see her. Them. He wished he was standing above them looking down. He wanted to see everything!

Her face was inches from his; she massaged his clenched jaw with soft and cool fingers. But nothing happened. What in hell was this? She said, "I've met you more than halfway. But now it's up to you." Oh, but he wanted to wrap his hands around that ivory neck, where he could see a pulse beating ever so gently. He wanted to curse her and say, What is this, some kind of New Orleans bullshit! But none of that would come out, and instead he groaned and, like a snail feeling its way along the ground, touched, just touched, his lips to hers, applied no pressure, just felt them, and now she helped him. Her tongue licked his lips, then forced them open, then probed against his teeth, looking for an opening.

He parted his lips. He had to have that tongue, and she made her way inside, her tongue traveling everyplace. She was learning him, getting the taste of him, drinking his saliva like it was sweet nectar. He was like a dummy, a zombie, just sitting there, being taken, unable to participate. She drew back an inch and said, "Suck my tongue."

Then she fed it to him, and he suckled it, then with his own pushed hers away and probed her mouth, licking like a hungry kitten.

A kind of battle commenced as tongue pushed tongue away, fighting for territory to claim. Suddenly she sat up, and he was left with his tongue sticking out, like a child. "Put it away," she said. "You may lose it."

He wanted to cry, and he felt his erection pushing against his khakis, demanding something, anything. She stared down at it. "He'll have to wait," she said matter-of-factly.

In his head there were visions of revenge, visions of him plunging into her until she screamed her surrender.

She read his anger and said, "This isn't the time. You don't know me, and I sure don't know you, and I won't be had by someone I don't even know."

He made no reply, and she asked, "You're angry, huh? I'm sorry, but not sorry enough to change my mind."

He made one more try, his need still urgent. "Couldn't you just—"

"No. I won't jack you off, though I have no objections if you do it to yourself. I'll even watch, but I won't do anything."

"Why the hell did you start with me?"

"Do you really have to ask? From the moment we saw each other at that piteous wake, something happened. Can you deny it? Can you say nothing happened?"

"I don't know. Right now I don't know anything."

"I know, it's time for you to have beddy-bye. Rest up for tonight."

"I'm not sure I'll be able to sleep."

"Then fuck your wife."

He heard the slam of his open palm hitting her face before he saw what he was doing.

"Goddamn you!" The imprint was on her cheek.

"I'm sorry," he said. "I didn't know what I was doing, but you shouldn't have said what you did."

She had turned away, facing the windshield. She didn't speak as he started the car and drove back into town. He let her out at her car in Coon's parking lot.

BeBe looked up from her roses when he drove in, and she saw him half-stumble out of his car. She went to him and, with her arm about his waist, helped him onto the porch. "Too much Jax, huh, cher?"

He sat on the bed. The ceiling fan turned lazily overhead, and he could smell flowers. She was on the floor before him, pulling off his boots and socks. Then she stood and, leaning over him, released his belt buckle and kissed his nose. She looked down at him adoringly. In her entire life he was all that she had ever wanted. She had seen him the first day in grammar school, they were all sitting at the teacher's feet while she read them a story. She had looked about at this new world in which she found herself, and there he was, his hands on his knees, his blue-striped sport shirt all starchy. She had no way at the time to express what she felt, but inside her, she said, There's my boyfriend, my little boyfriend.

From then on they were paired, the Senator's daughter, the Sheriff's son. Their sophomore year in high school they talked about getting married one day. It was so natural. There was no one else. There never would be.

It's not perfect, she thought, but it's perfect enough for me, and she hoped that he felt that way and was uneasy at the hope. No, it was impossible. He was hers.

"Bobby," she whispered, "do you love me?"

His eyes opened. "Don't be silly," he said, half asleep.

His answer didn't satisfy her. They would have to talk. She said, "Daddy called. He's gonna pick you up at seven. Him and you and Justin are gonna make the rounds."

But he didn't hear her. He was asleep.

Chapter 6

He awakened to Papoot's laughter in the parlor. He lay there and wished the sound would go away, or that he could just vanish. Finally he stood, stretched, and went into the kitchen for ice water. He had a slight headache, a slight hangover.

Moose Thibodeaux, the Senator's bodyguard and driver, sat at the red-and-white oilcloth-covered breakfast table, stirring a cup of coffee. Next to him was a big slice of BeBe's pecan pie. Moose greeted the Sheriff the way he greeted every human being, man, woman, or child: "Mah man!" His main man was Papoot. Bobby nodded to him. That was more than Moose usually got; he was Papoot's man and that was all.

Bobby drank from a jelly glass. The water was cold and soothing. A couple of aspirin would finish the job. Moose was eating loudly, smacking his lips. "Nobody can make pecan pie like Miss BeBe," he said. Bobby didn't answer. No answer was expected. For all intents and purposes, Moose was invisible, despite the fact that he was six feet five and weighed 250 pounds. He wore a cheap suit and a solid black necktie. Papoot had told him, "I don't want our colors to clash! Hee, hee!" There was nothing Moose wouldn't do for Papoot. And very little that Papoot hadn't asked of him. Bobby was glad he didn't know what all that entailed.

Bobby padded into the bathroom, dropped his shorts, pulled his T-shirt over his head, and took a cold shower. He stepped out, toweled himself, combed his hair, and walked to his bedroom, where his clothes were laid out, boots shined. He took a couple of aspirin from the nightstand and swallowed them down without water. Then he went into the parlor. Please God, he prayed, don't let Papoot be telling another Gaston story. BeBe and her father sat on the couch, a little cup of coffee on Papoot's knee.

Papoot said, "Bobby, I was telling BeBe about when your daddy was giving a campaign speech in front of the courthouse. It was Sunday afternoon and cold as hell. Well Gaston says to the crowd, 'There's not a man, woman, or child in this crowd I haven't done somethin' for!' And one old man at the back of the crowd hollered, 'Me! What you done for me?' And Gaston hollered back, 'You, you son of a bitch, I made Pineville for you!' " Pineville was the state institution for the insane, and Papoot and BeBe laughed, and Bobby was forced to laugh too. All his life he had heard that story. All his life he had laughed. He looked up. Gaston was such a presence in that room. Staring down from his portrait, he seemed to be sitting with them. He could almost smell the smoke from his father's cigarette.

Papoot was in his white suit and red tie, and wore his white Panama pushed back on his head. That was his ensemble. His trade-mark. Bobby couldn't recall ever seeing him in anything else. Papoot stood, kissed his daughter, and shouted, "Moose, alons!"

Moose lumbered in, and BeBe handed him a banana cake to take to the supper. Her men never went empty-handed. They walked out to the big white Cadillac. Bobby was about to get into the front seat with Moose, but Papoot held his arm and said, "Ride in the back with me; we can talk."

Oh shit, thought Bobby. Papoot said, "We got to pick Justin up. That priest don't miss nothin'. I wonder what he prays! Hee, hee!"

Bobby could smell Papoot's cologne and the brilliantine in his hair, his amazingly black hair. The old man's eyes twinkled above the rims of his glasses. He began to speak softly. "Me and you don't get to talk like we use to, Bobby. You not mad at me?"

Bobby smiled weakly. "Oh hell no, Papoot. I've just been pretty busy."

Papoot didn't even dignify that lie with an answer. Instead he grunted. A grunt that said, Bullshit! "We got to be a little closer, Bobby. Talk more. Talk politics, talk about everything. Right?"

"Right," said Bobby.

"Ah got a campaign coming' up. Ah'm gon' need you."

"I'll be there."

"I don't doubt that. You like Gaston, loyalty. Gaston use to say, you got to stay by the flag! That's you, stay by the flag."

Bobby said, "You've got that right."

"You think ah'm gon' have opposition?"

"I do."

"That ignoramus President Prejean?"

"He wants to run, bad."

"What a jackass. He's got as much chance beatin' me as that tree there. Huh?"

"He's got his following."

Papoot nodded. "All them good Catholics. That's why every time I see him he's got his head halfway up Hurphy Perrault's ass. Sometimes I think they sissy boys!"

"That Rotary crowd's with him too."

"Jesus Christ, them! Not a success in the crowd. I can buy and sell the whole bunch of them and not check my bank account for overdrafts."

"They'll probably ask you to debate him. They do it every election."

"Debate about what? What in the hell we got to debate about? He's one of the do-gooders; me, ah'm for the little people. Those bastids don't even know the little people exist!"

"If you don't go, they'll set up an empty chair and let him debate it."

"I wish the Japs would have bombed the whole bunch of them!"

"That's not likely."

"Ah don' know, the Japs probably got a price too! Hee, hee!" Bobby laughed. In the front seat Moose laughed too. "Goddamnit, Moose, how many times I got to tell you not to lissen!"

"Ah didn't lissen, Papoot!"

"An' how many times ah got to tell you call me Senator! Jesus Christ, man, show some respeck."

He lowered his voice, his face right up against Bobby's ear. "You and BeBe's all right?"

"How do you mean?" Bobby blurted, which would only prolong a painful conversation. He cursed himself. Why didn't I say, "Sure!"

"Ah'm an old hand, Bobby, not much I haven't seen and a few things I've done personally. Comprende? BeBe's let herself go. Ah'm not blind. I told that girl, How come you want to look like an elephant? She can't help it. She said it ain't got nothin' to do with how much she eats, she's just that way. Me, I say bullshit! I see her eat, an' she likes the trough pretty good. I tole her, BeBe, that ain't no way to keep a man. She started cryin', Bobby, my BeBe started cryin'."

Bobby was certain that he could hear Moose grunt with sadness up in the front seat. Papoot issued a warning to him. "Watch yourself, or I'm gonna put this Florsheim right up your ass."

"I didn't hear nothin', Papoot," Moose swore. They could see him making the sign of the cross. It was official.

Papoot was whispering again. "Now if you want to get a little on the side, ah can understan' that. Me, I'm a man too. Misty got some cute girls from what I can see, an' you don' have to do nothin' there. Hell, use my camp."

Papoot droned on. He sounded like an aged pimp. Bobby thought about the first and only time he'd ever had a piece of ass at Misty's. He had been a seventeen-year-old boy, and him and some of his buddies went there, all drunk on beer. He'd ended up in the back room with a platinum blonde named Teena. He almost fainted when Teena stepped from her red shorts and he saw that she wasn't a blonde at all. In fact, she was a brunette!

He climbed on her and started pounding, and she was groaning and almost shouting and he thought, I'm some kind of stud for sure! But something made him raise up on his hands and look down at her. She looked bored as hell; in fact she was almost asleep. She even had a cigarette in her hand. His erection died just like that. He never did come, and a year later he tried it with another of Misty's girls, and then he couldn't even get it up. That was the last time he touched a woman until he and BeBe went to the Edgewater Hotel on their honeymoon. It was good, or at least he supposed it was. He had nothing to compare it with. Truth was, seeing her blood made him a little ill.

Papoot had mercifully switched the subject to himself. "Me, I couldn't raise a hard-on no more with a derrick. Doc Mouton done tried on me every kind of pill there is. I don't know if it's old age or that dose I got a few years ago from a goddamn woman lobbyist in Baton Rouge. She got her vote for the cosmetology bill, and me, I got the clap. Some trade out, huh, Bobby? Hee, hee!"

Up front, Moose couldn't quite squelch a laugh. "But," Papoot continued, "I guess I had enough for ten lifetimes. You know somethin'? I don' miss it at all. But you, you still a young man. I want you and BeBe to be happy. Thass very important to me. So do what you got to do, Bobby, jus' don' hurt my BeBe. 'Cause if you did, then I would be your enemy, and I am a bad enemy. Comprende?"

"I'll never hurt BeBe," Bobby said. "She's my wife."

"An' you love her."

"Sure. I married her."

Papoot wasn't finished. "That don' mean shit! A hard dick, that's what that mean! Hee, hee!"

They pulled up to a white stucco cottage, roses growing on trellises up the side. "Wait in the car," Papoot instructed Moose. "I don' know why I keep the bastid around," he said as he and Bobby made their way to the front door. "Sometime he come in handy. I guess that's why."

Justin opened the door before they could knock. A light behind him illuminated his golden hair. He looked like a saint in a church window. He wore a black sport shirt opened at the collar, and his muscles rippled beneath it. "Hello, Papa," he said and kissed Papoot on the cheek. He and Bobby shook hands. "Brother-in-law," he said in greeting.

The cottage inside belied its bright exterior. It was austere, Spanish, with dark beams overhead, only a little furniture, most of it priceless Spanish antiques given along with the cottage by Papoot upon Justin's return to Richelieu. In the living room was Justin's dark desk, with a floor lamp beaming down on the naked top. That was where he worked, wrote his sermons that Papoot thought were a little tough for the people of Richelieu. But he'd said nothing, except once. "Justin, don' you think once in a while you should lighten up, you know, maybe tell a little harmless joke, make 'em feel good! People don' like to hear about hellfire all the time, especially in this heat. Hee, hee!"

Justin had replied, "I'm God's messenger in this community, His representative, just like you're the people's representative in Baton Rouge. We are sinners, and I've no choice but to say it exactly that way until I join Him."

Papoot had never brought up the subject again. Truth was, Justin's sermons made him uncomfortable. He was guilty of so damn many things that he did not like to contemplate a pitchfork in his ass. But he couldn't miss Mass, that was for sure.

They were seated, and from the gloom of another room, Justin brought out a decanter of dark red liquid. "I want you to try some of this port. I got it in New Orleans." About once a month Justin took the long drive there. He loved the architecture of the French Quarter, the iron balconies just like he'd seen in Europe, where he'd been educated. He'd go to Solari's too and stock up on things you couldn't get anyplace else in Louisiana, like huge black olives and cheese of every kind, and of course exotic liquors, which he loved to sip in the evening while he read or wrote. Currently he was in the middle of a brand-new version of the lives of the saints, a thousand-page volume!

Justin and Papoot sipped tentatively. They were not liqueur men. Papoot smacked his lips. "Si bon!" Bobby nodded in agreement. The stuff was too sweet for him. It was like drinking sugar.

Justin sat opposite them, legs outspread. Outside of being father and son and brother-in-law, the men had very little in common, and even for Papoot, who said he could talk to a mule if he had to, "an' make him like me, hee, hee!" conversation was strained.

"Your sermon about Ti Boy was great," Papoot said. "Everybody was cryin', even that jackass Mayor Big Head."

"It sure was," Bobby said lamely.

The priest looked at him with a wan smile. "How about you, Bobby, were you weeping too?"

"No."

"Sometimes you have to let go," the priest admonished, the barest hint of a direct order in his tone.

"Do you?" Bobby asked. It chapped his ass to be lectured to by his brother-in-law.

"Do I what?"

"Let go."

Justin's smile vanished. "Oh yes. But I let go to my Lord."

Bobby was spoiling for a fight. Papoot looked from one man to the other like they were engaged in fisticuffs. He dearly loved other men's blood, even if it poured from his loved ones, except for BeBe. She was the one special thing in his life. Even more than being "the Senator." Beyond that, he really didn't care all that much, even for Father Justin.

"I tell him everything," the priest continued. "He knows everything anyway."

"You must bore Him, Justin, you ain't got all that many sins."

They all laughed, the tension vanquished. Then they headed out the door and Justin said, "One of these days, Bobby, we'll have to have a little chat."

Bobby said nothing, and Moose greeted Justin, "Mah man!"

"Shut up and drive," Papoot said. Bobby sat up front. Justin was in the back next to his father. Father and son held a whispered conversation. Bobby could make out only a word or two, so he tuned out, and thought about her.

He saw her face. He remembered her lips and her tongue. Nothing like that had ever happened to him before, or affected him that way. It was as if he was on fire and only she could put it out. He questioned his sanity. But tuning her out was a lot more difficult than switching that dial on the Philco in the living room. He lay his head back against the headrest, closed his eyes, and saw her eyes, blue with that tiny gray fringe, eyes that undressed him, made him naked, not just his body but inside him too. He felt exposed, and he hated it. As much as Gaston had loved publicity ("yo' can't get it enuff in this business!"), he hated it, loved privacy, locking himself away from everybody, giving just enough to get by. Just barely enough. And people seemed to understand this and forgave him. "That's just Bobby's ways." They didn't judge him, and he was grateful for that. It made him love them, if distantly. They were like his children, all of them, but children in some other town.

Big Shot Fontenot's camp was by far the most elaborate in the parish. Sloping down to a bayou was a long screened-in building topped by a rooster weather vane. A sign read "BIG SHOT'S CHATEAU . . . everybody's welcome but other car dealers." You could still see, despite a new paint job, where someone had scratched out SHOT and printed in SHIT. Big Shot had shrugged. "They all jealous!" It was true. Everybody was jealous. Wasn't he the richest man in Richelieu, president of the bank, with the biggest car, biggest house, and even a swimming pool that someone swore was heated! Jesus Christ, wasn't that enough to be jealous about? And even if they kissed his ass, they all hated him, and were quick to point out to each other that actually, Li'l Shot was the brains of the two. When they were with him, they paid him lavish compliments (all but Possum Aucoin, which Big Shot tolerated, so people would say he was a regular guy even though he and they knew he wasn't) and kissed his ass at every opportunity, mainly by keeping him supplied with fresh game, seafood, and even vegetables, like he couldn't afford them.

Bobby had often noticed it was that way with rich people—they didn't have to pay for much, as people fought for the privilege of giving them things. Like somehow it honored the giver.

Papoot, who would later be by for a big campaign donation, started the ball rolling, slapping Big Shot on the back and exclaiming for all to hear, "I swear to God, Big Shot, but you don' age. I don' know what you doin', but you ought to bottle it and sell it!"

Everyone laughed, and Moose shouted to no one in particular, "Mah man!"

Papoot wasn't through yet; after all, his Cadillac had been purchased at below cost. "You a big man, Big Shot, big heart. Nobody's better to my little people than you, except me! Hee, hee!"

Big Shot returned the compliment. Papoot had gotten him a tax exemption every year like clockwork. In fact, the state owed him money! Hee, hee! "We all imitate you, Papoot. You all heart."

Possum had had enough. "Not just heart but hand, don't forget Papoot's hand. It's in our pockets!"

Now they really laughed, and Mayor Big Head Arceneaux did his little jumping up and down dance, exclaiming, "Whoop! Whoop!"

Everyone stared at the midget in a green sport coat and green trousers. He truly was an amazing sight. His bodyguard-driver stood by, nodding happily. Hadn't Big Head hinted on the way over that he might kick the police chief out and give him the job? After all, he had the biggest family. With more on the way. Four of his aunts and three of his nieces were pregnant right now. They were a vote factory.

Bobby joined Moe Weiss at a big tub of iced Jax. He saw Moose hand Big Shot BeBe's cake and was relieved it was still intact. Moose was known occasionally to steal little tastes. Bobby handed each of them a beer. He was pleased. Moe was invited to every supper, mostly due to their friendship and of course his power on the bank board. Whatever the reason, it gave Bobby a good feeling. He wanted the strange little man to feel at home. And Moe was a good audience, too, covering his laughter with a hand over his mouth like he was violating a law. Nor did he eat too much. A bite or two, perhaps one beer. He had become a man who did everything halfway, except suffering, and this he did in silence.

The others couldn't tell what it was Bobby saw in the man's company. He didn't know a single joke, nor could he cook. Still, they accommodated him when they realized that it didn't matter if he was invited or not. Chances were Bobby would invite him, and nobody wanted to get on the Sheriff's bad side. And it wasn't that Moe was a nonentity. He was too strange to be that, with his baggy clown trousers and little beanie with just the propeller missing. There was a gravity to him, the man's entire presence was a cement block that weighed you down if you thought about it. He brings the rain with him, was the way Possum described him in one of his rare serious dissertations. He didn't even cut Moe's hair; the little man did it himself. "But I don' mind," Possum would say, "me, he gets me down. Bobby might be a weirdo to fuck with him all the time!" And they'd all laugh at the barber's courage. Only he could call the high Sheriff a weirdo!

Big Shot's camp was impressive. His repair shop had built him a five-foot-wide steel wok. The wok was about sixteen inches deep and fired by a big burner made from a floor furnace. He could cook thirty pounds of chicken with all the accompanying vegetables in half an hour! Then he had a huge pot in which he could boil a thousand pounds of crawfish at one time. And that wasn't all. He had this special pot in which he cooked his wild duck.

Tonight he was preparing wild ducks, and his old man, was chopping banana peppers, onion, garlic, green onions, and bell peppers. Li'l Shot could chop so fast and so unerringly that you could hardly see his hand or the knife he held. Chop, chop, chop, chop. With the other hand, he held his beer.

Li'l Shot said, "Oh shit," because in came Nonc, leaning on Doc Mouton's arm like they were a date. "Look what the dog drug in," Li'l Shot said crossly, narrowly missing his index finger with the butcher knife. Nonc, who could hear amazingly well despite his advanced years, said, "Ah hope you wash you han's, Li'l Shot!" Everybody laughed, Mayor Big Head the loudest. Tonight in his green ensemble he resembled a creature out of some Irish myth.

Possum, seeing the crowd slip away, told a joke. "This fellow over to Mamou had a big bruise on his forehead, and his friends asked him, 'May what happen' to you?' He say, 'My wife and me was in the backyard an' the day was beautiful. So we decided to fuck an' my wife got on all fours so we could do it dog style. Suddenly my wife took off and ran under the house, and when I tried to follow her, bam!' "

Everyone laughed but Nonc, who gave a weak cackle.

The Senator began to regale them with political stories, most of them about Huey P. Long. They'd all heard them a hundred times before, in fact all their lives, but never tired of hearing them again and again. Tonight he told them about when Ringling Brothers wanted to come to Baton Rouge the same night as an LSU football game, which was the most important thing in Huey's life. So Huey came up with this law that all animals entering Louisiana had to be dipped for disease. The Ringlings thought about that, how big a hole would they need to dip those elephants! So they put off their show!

What they really liked to hear about was Huey fucking those big companies, especially Esso Standard Oil. Papoot liked to say, "Me and Huey, we alike; he wanted every man to be a king, me, I want the little people to all be rich. Hee, hee!" Bobby noticed the laughter was a little weak on this observation. He didn't like the looks of things at all.

And there was President, running to get people a beer like he was a waiter and they were crippled. This fellow was serious. Damn serious.

Hurphy Parrault sidled up and in his professional, soft voice said so that just Bobby could hear him, "He's gonna give Papoot trouble, Bobby. Mark my words."

"Not with friends like you, Hurphy," Bobby said. Hurphy didn't reply.

Na Na Duhon stood in line balancing three paper plates in his hand, one for him, one for his sweet De De, and one for his little papoon. He took care of both his women equally, but everyone thought he was fucking his papoon more!

Coon and his ace cook Catfish were on their second plate, and Catfish had to admit, "This is one of the best, Big Shot." He, of course, owed Big Shot money because of his little bourrée habit. Big Shot wasn't satisfied. "How does it stack up to yours, Catfish? Come on, be hones'."

Catfish swallowed. He found it hard to lie about food, and he wondered how he could answer and satisfy Big Shot even while letting everyone know for sure that his ducks were indeed the best. He said, "You a fine cook, Big Shot." It was noticed that he didn't say "great." Then and there Big Shot decided to take a long look at just how much money Catfish owed the First National Bank. He would do that on Monday, checking out whether his debt was "fine" or "great."

President Prejean had cornered Papoot, something he'd been trying to do since the Senator arrived. He stood with his back to the crowd and held out a hand, which Papoot took without enthusiasm. He should have let it go at that, but he didn't.

"Papoot, I hope you know there's nothing personal in what I might have to do. It's just politics," President said softly.

Papoot, face beaming like he was paying President a compliment, said equally softly, "You cocksucker, your daddy was a liar and a thief, and I see you are too. Get your fucking ass away from me. Scat!"

President heeled and hurried away. This was observed by everyone. There was excitement in the room, and Moose was feeling inside his coat jacket. Bobby went to stand by the giant. "If you take that gun out, I'm gonna have to put you in jail, Moose. I don't want to, but I'll do my duty."

Moose looked perplexed, like he didn't know what to do. The only person who told him what to do was Papoot. He didn't get Bobby being on the other side. His small black eyes bore into Bobby's, then he said, "I ain't gonna do nothin', mah man, I swear to gawd," and he removed his hand from the jacket. Bobby smiled and clapped him on the back. "You're a good man, Moose," he said, and Moose thought about crushing Bobby's face, maybe with a car jack. But not without Papoot's permission, of course.

Through the screens Bobby saw Justin sitting on a tree stump in the moonlight, looking out on the bayou. Getting a couple of beers, he joined the priest.

Justin was so far away in his thoughts that he didn't hear Bobby approach. He handed the priest a beer, which Justin took, nodding his thanks. He read concern on Bobby's face. "What's the matter?"

"Your papa and President had a few words. Then Moose was about to go for his gun."

"That man's quite crazy. One day he'll do something. You won't always be there, Bobby."

"I know. It worries me more than you know."

"An' Papa's kind of crazy too. Would you believe what he asked me?"

"Nothing would surprise me," Bobby said.

"He asked me to share President's confession so he could use it to keep him from running!"

"Jesus!"

"Please don't use our Lord's name that way. I can't tell you how upsetting it is."

"I apologize, Justin. I'll watch it."

"Okay," the priest said. "Anyway, when Papa asked me, I thought he was joking, you know, a hee hee! So I laughed. But he wasn't joking at all. Just one little sin, he begged me. I told him never to ask me that again or I'd have to quit talking to him. I meant it."

Bobby believed him. His brother-in-law was fully capable of a lifetime of silence.

"Sad, isn't it, I mean the deterioration in a man as he ages."

Bobby didn't respond to that because he hadn't noticed Papoot to be any different.

"Losing that election would be like death to him. His whole life is having 'Senator' attached to his name. No chance he could lose, I'm sure."

When Bobby didn't reply, Justin said, "That was a question, Bobby."

"Oh, this race is going to present Papoot some problems he's never had before."

"In other words, he could lose."

Bobby wondered why Justin wasn't facing him but instead was staring out on the dark bayou. He was forced to speak to the priest's perfect profile. With anyone else it would be insulting, but Justin just didn't pay attention to things like that. Maybe it was because he'd lived alone for so long.

Suddenly Justin turned to him, and even in the dark Bobby thought, What strange eyes he has—they were dreamy, things were going on deep behind them, yet they told nothing. Bobby wondered what part of Justin was dead. He had no doubt something was. Could it be the result of being stationed in Richelieu? The Church had given him the finest education it had to give, postgraduate studies in Rome, earning doctorates in dogmatic theology and canon law, then at the Ecclesiastical Academy, the Vatican's diplomatic school. But then he'd come home. Many had felt he was headed for the Vatican itself, but instead he came back to Richelieu. It could be nothing or anything. Maybe he enjoyed being a big fish in a small pond, Papoot's son, the Sheriff's brother-in-law, loved and practically worshiped by his devout flock. Or maybe there was something else.

"Bobby, you mustn't let him lose." The tone was imperial. Bobby wondered if Justin was even aware that he spoke in commands.

"I'll do everything I can. We'll go all out."

The priest studied him quietly until the silence became a weight. "You know, Bobby, you somehow sound dispassionate. Like you'll go through the motions, but you really don't care."

"That's horseshit!"

Justin's full, sensual lips broke into a tiny smile. "Naughty, naughty."

"You know, you can be very insulting. Does that go with being a priest?"

"I didn't mean anything, brother-in-law."

Bobby said, "I'm sorry."

The priest was still smiling. "How is my sister?"

"BeBe?"

"I only have one sister."

"She's fine, or I guess she is. With people, even people you live with, you can never tell," Bobby said.

"That's true. It's like the confessional. I know all the people on the other side of the grille, but the things that come out of there! I can still be shocked. Man's capacity for evildoing is without boundaries." There was a touch of sadness in his voice.

"People are okay." That was how Bobby really felt. "You've just got to roll with them. Sometimes the water gets a little choppy, but . . ."

Justin smiled, a big smile that showed off his perfect white teeth. "*You've* got to roll with them. There's always another election coming up, isn't there? I, on the other hand, have to point out to them their wrongs, plenty of wrongs, and then tell them how to get right in the sight of God."

"Am I getting tomorrow's sermon?"

"Actually I will be speaking on that subject. Secrets. That's my subject. Dirty, filthy secrets. Corruption and stench." Justin wasn't smiling; the passion of his words could be felt like a physical force.

Bobby had had enough. "See you inside."

Justin stayed behind, silent again, staring out at the bayou.

Inside, Na Na Duhon was holding court, surrounded by Hot Dog Hebert, Sport Baudoin, Tooky Trahan, and Short Change St. Pierre. Na Na had their full attention because he was discussing his papoon. They were fascinated because Na Na told everything! The radio man was without shame; he treated the world as his confessional. According to him, his little papoon was "by far the bes' ever to hit Misty's. Jus' ask Misty or Ballou. Misty'll tell you so herself, there's no sweet pussy like that gal. Now look, to show I'm not jus' poppin' off, ask any man who's had some." He looked about the room for verification, but everyone looked away or up at the ceiling or out the window, where the priest's presence was a grim reminder of sins committed, and those to be committed.

Possum wanted to know more. "How you mean sweet pussy, sweet like little dahlin' or sweet like you took a taste?"

"Shhh," warned Bobby, who'd walked up. "You don't have to tell that."

Possum disagreed. "Hell, he's proud of it, huh, Na Na? Tell him you proud."

"Well, I'm sure not ashamed. The truth is—"

"Shhh," warned Bobby again. He liked the radio man and did not want to see him make a complete fool of himself, even for Possum, who somehow brought out the very worst in people.

Na Na stopped Bobby with an extended arm, palm outward, like a policeman directing traffic. "She's a li'l baby doll with her little ways. She's sugary, you know? And her taste . . . there's no way to tell it. It's like cotton candy. Pink cotton candy." He smacked his lips in memory, as did several others. Everybody liked cotton candy.

"You gon' marry her?" Possum asked.

"An leave my De De? You crazy, Possum? I'm a Catholic, same as you. Jesus Christ!"

Possum snapped his fingers. "I got it! Adopt her!"

Everybody laughed except Na Na. His face was serious. Truth was, it was one hell of an idea—although there was the little problem of selling it to De De. Still, she was the most understanding of wives, and they didn't have any children.

Possum wasn't quite through. "Of course, they got that thing called . . ." He searched for the word.

Bobby helped him: "Incest."

Na Na looked perplexed. "What the hell is that?"

Attorney Hurphy Perrault helped out. "Incest is about twenty years in Angola!"

Na Na began to understand. "I couldn't . . ."

"Not no more!" Possum said. "Maybe you could still look, but no kissin', if you get me."

Li'l Shot joined them. "They had a fellow in Gueydan when I was a boy. Him and his sister had four kids. All was crazy. But good at basketball."

"But we're not kin," Na Na protested.

"Legally you would be," Hurphy counseled. "She'd be your daughter, same as if she'd been born that way."

Short Change had a question. "Would Papoon marry you?"

That was easy. "Ah got a wife."

"Better leave things the way they are," Bobby said.

"Don't be so cold-blooded, Bobby. The man's in love," Big Shot said.

Na Na was sunk in gloom. The problem was insoluble. Funny, he hadn't even thought of it as a problem until Possum had introduced other possibilities.

The supper began to break up. Tomorrow was Sunday, and that meant Mass. And more cooking and a few beers, not all that many, because you had to get ready for Monday, although there were several suppers planned for Monday night. Some of the men had brought Father Justin little gifts. A bottle of strawberry wine from Hammond near Baton Rouge, or some boudin from a fresh-killed hog. The priest had a nice little thank-you for each, and Moose loaded everything in Papoot's trunk. Bobby got BeBe's cake plate, its contents long gone. Lord but she could bake.

When the four men were on their way, Father Justin turned in the seat, looked at his father, and said, "Papa, what exactly did you say to President?"

"What? We was reminiscing about his old daddy. That was one

sweet man," Papoot said, eyes peering over the gold rims of his glasses. His hat was pushed back on his forehead.

Moose put a big paw over his mouth, behind which you could hear him fighting down a laugh. "Mah main man!"

Justin said, "I wish you wouldn't do things like that. It's demeaning."

Papoot exploded, "That bastid's lucky nobody kills him!"

Bobby asked, "Like who?"

"Like who? Like one of the little people. You think they want to see someone run against the best friend they ever had? Would you? Of course not! No, President or whatever his jack-off name is, is askin' for trouble!"

"Watch your language," Justin said.

"I'd hate to have to arrest one of the little people for murder, but I would," Bobby said.

"But gettin' 'em sentenced wouldn't be all that easy, Bobby boy," Papoot said. "Hell, they might get a medal. Hee, hee! And they sure would get a pardon from the Governor. Besides, Prejean's a wife-beater."

"Says who?" Bobby asked. He knew it was a damn lie.

"I got a tip."

Justin groaned. He'd heard it all before.

"What's more, his wife's not a Catholic!" Papoot said.

"She is now. She converted," Justin said.

"Once a Methodist, always a Methodist," Papoot said. Moose was nodding. Vigorously.

"I'd leave it be, Papa."

"Justin, lemme tell you one thing. Stick to your preachin' 'cause you don't know nothin' about politickin'. An' Bobby, when did you become so damn straitlaced? My God, Gaston mus' be turnin' over in his grave hearin' you talk that way!"

They rode in silence, first dropping off Justin, who said nothing in the way of a farewell. Then they took Bobby home. He muttered, "Thank you."

When the Cadillac rolled out of Bobby's drive and went down the street, Papoot said, "Moose, stop right here an' kill your headlights."

"What we gon' do?"

"We gon' see if Bobby stays home. Me, ah got this suspicion."

Moose was puzzled. Papoot was a naturally suspicious man, but checking up on Bobby was a new one. "What you tink, boss?"

"I dunno, but after all these years, I got a feelin', and ah'm seldom wrong. Comprende?"

"You never wrong!"

"Shhh, here he comes. Put out that damn cigarette. Shhh."

Bobby's car proceeded slowly up the street.

Papoot said, "Uh-huh! He's sniffin', thass what li'l Bobby's doin'."

"Sniffin'?"

"Pussy. Okay, take me home, Moose. It's been a long day."

"I don't understand."

"You, you never understan'. Maybe thass why you so valuable. Your ignorance has a lot of appeal for me, Moose."

Moose was overcome. He could have cried. Papoot hadn't paid him all that many compliments. He wondered what Papoot wanted.

"I'm no fool, you know. We gon' be in the race of my life. A lot of people are gunnin' for old Papoot. We might have to do some things we never done before."

Moose understood that kind of talk. "Ah'm ready."

Bobby drove slowly past her house and felt foolish. What exactly was he doing, except acting like a schoolboy? I've got to get hold of myself, he told himself. And wondered if he could.

Chapter 7

At St. Ann's Catholic Church, on Sundays there were Masses at 7:00 A.M., 9:00 A.M., 11:00 A.M., and 7:00 in the evening. Five minutes before these Masses convened, the bells in the steeple atop the red-brick building tolled, summoning the people to pray.

Papoot favored the 9:00 A.M. Mass because "eleven's cutting it too close to lunch, and me, nobody's gonna rush how I spen' my Sundays." Bobby had not so innocently asked, "How about your little people, suppose they need you on a Sunday?" Papoot made his point directly and quietly: "Fuck the little people! Hee, hee!"

At church he liked to sit right up front, BeBe next to him and Bobby next to her. On the very last row sat Bad Ass, next to Slo' Down Angelle, who'd had to arrest him that very Saturday for drunk and disorderly. But naturally he couldn't keep him in jail for Mass. They were all devout. Near them sat Moose, muscles bulging beneath a tan summer suit, a good one he'd bought in the old days, when he still owned that damn car wash.

Hurphy Perrault, wearing a string tie, and his good-looking if slim wife, Anita, in a blue dress that showed off her blond hair, sat looking on, bursting with pride at Hurphy Jr. in his altar boy vestments. The couple silently hoped that the boy might one day enter the priesthood and even had discussed it with Father Justin, who'd cautioned not to push him: "These things have to come about because they're natural and right. In other words, let him find the way on his own."

Now, a year later, Hurphy wasn't all that certain he wanted his son to enter the priesthood. Anita whined, "Aw, Hurphy," but he cut her off: "Leave it be, Anita." In fact, he wasn't so hot on Hurphy Jr. being an altar boy. Ti Boy's death made him uncomfortable, though he couldn't exactly say why. "Let him concentrate on his schoolwork, then he can go to LSU law school. Let someone else's son be the altar boy." Naturally he'd said nothing about these wishes to anyone else. After all, the church was by far his biggest client.

Father Justin today wore a red chasuble, centered by a gold fili-greed cross. Red was worn in honor of a martyr, though no one could recall that this Sunday was a particular martyr's day. He gave the Mass in Latin with his back to the congregation, Hurphy Jr. responding in Latin. The choir in the loft above and to the rear sang. The organ played.

The priest went up tiny stairs to an elevated pulpit, which looked down on his flock as God looked down from Heaven. That was what they believed, and even those who didn't quite buy it hoped it was that way. Forgiving God, above all else, forgiving, looking down, probably in sadness, seeing them, seeing through them, and miracu-lously—and this was the true miracle—forgiving them. It was too much to hope for, but they did more than hope. They believed. They accepted. They were devout and simple.

The priest was not quite so forgiving as God. He knew their sins from their lips. They whispered them to him every week. He had to fight the urge to get up in his pulpit—it was his pulpit—and point them out one by one, expose every dirty, filthy transgression. How dare they believe that their whispers and a few prayers recited by rote would bring them forgiveness? This belief, against all church teach-ing, was his secret. He thought about it much of the time as he went through the motions, miserable. Sin was not so easily washed away. The blood of Christ was worth infinitely more than a dozen Hail Marys, a thousand Our Fathers. He believed in greater penance. He believed in the burning fires of Hell, and he fervently wished that they could be transported here to earth. He would like to walk among his parishioners' writhing, burning bodies and exclaim to this one and that one, "You see! You see! I tried to tell you. You see!"

He had always been a stern man. In his heart and mind there was right and there was wrong, and no comingling. Gray areas were the demarcation between Heaven and Hell. Still, he was a kind man, considered himself compassionate beyond his official right to be. He had never, not once, denied them forgiveness. The forgiveness of God. Personally, secretly, he didn't forgive them at all.

It was his compassion, this chink in his moral armor, that had opened the crack through which Satan crept. It was Satan's fault.

He looked down at them as they looked up at him. To him. And became aware that he had just stood there, leaving them waiting. He wondered how much time had elapsed. His father looked concerned. His sister smiled. She would smile through hurricanes and floods and crop blights. Her smile marked what others called her "good nature." He thought of it as her stupidity. Bobby's face was expressionless, as he would have expected. Bobby thought that sin meant letting others know how you felt. A check mark for old Gaston, Justin thought. You created an island, a rather isolated one, instead of a son.

He smiled at them, releasing the tension. He could tell what they were thinking: That's our Father Justin, so deep in thought he doesn't even know where he is or that we are here waiting.

"You all probably noticed that today I am clothed in a red chasuble, the color denoting a day dedicated to a martyr of our faith. The more studious among you, like Counselor Hurphy Perrault, Knight of St. Gregory, can't think of exactly which martyr we honor here today. And he is quite right. There is none in church history or doctrine."

Papoot, with a big smile and a twinkle in his eyes, thought, What kind of bullshit sermon is this? Bobby for the first time wondered if the priest was crazy. Bad Ass gently snored, and Slo' Down nudged him sharply in the ribs.

"Today I choose to define what a martyr is. You say, someone burning at the stake, someone with his innards ripped out for his love of Jesus Christ and our Catholic faith. Joan of Arc. She is. But today I choose to say to you, my beloved in Christ, a martyr is someone who takes something that he or she does not want, or gives up something that he or she wants most desperately. Thus are we all, even in our simple, humble lives, capable of martyrdom. Each of us most dearly wants something, eh? A new car. A better house. Another sweet child. Each of us has something that we definitely don't want. An unhappy marriage, a crooked business partner, an evil child. We secretly wish they'd go away! But we do not act upon these needs, these most desperate needs, and this is our martyrdom. This is what my red chasuble speaks to today. So you see? You just might be a martyr. You just might be turning from overwhelming temptation which each of you cries out for. And you are the martyr. Think about it. Pray over it. Thank God that you have turned away from what it is you want. Amen."

Na Na Duhon was positive that the priest was talking directly to him. Frightened, he squeezed his De De's hand. Her diamond ring cut into his palm, and he let go.

Only Mayor Big Head Arceneaux could not think of one thing he wanted or didn't want, beyond being Mayor of Richelieu. He felt vaguely disappointed that he didn't qualify as a martyr. Then he thought about a joke he'd heard and was dying to tell it.

Possum Aucoin figured the priest was letting him have it for the mean things he said about everyone. He vowed to try harder even as he studied the back of Anita Perrault's head and thought about her performing oral sex on him, though he knew this wouldn't happen. She was way above him. He really didn't know why he was so mean. His mama and papa, both still living, were loving parents. Ashamed, he recalled that that very morning he had told his Eunice they would live forever " 'cause Jesus didn't want them kind of dopes around."

Nonc Doucet couldn't hear a word of the sermon but sat alert, nodding like he agreed with every word. Li'l Shot Fontenot studied the older man and was overcome with guilt. It just didn't seem right, wishing that someone was dead. His son, Big Shot, wasn't thinking about the sermon at all. He was thinking politics, and that he'd be talking to President Prejean real soon.

Short Change St. Pierre hoped that he'd have a big afternoon at the Palace. Sunday, after everybody ate and maybe took a little nap, was usually excellent for business, and popcorn with a lot of butter would sell like hotcakes. Short Change was elated.

Watch Out Naquin thought about seeing Anita laid out on his embalming table. He would finally know if that yellow hair was for real. He swore to himself all he'd do was look. Was anything wrong with that?

President Prejean, with eyes tightly shut to show just how devout he was, but with hand tapping on the back of his pew to let everyone know that he wasn't asleep, just devout, thought about Baton Rouge. The Capitol. The power. Senator. Jesus! Jesus Christ!

Doc Mouton's mind was on an operation he'd botched. Thank God the patient hadn't died, but he wouldn't speak again. The tiniest slip of the scalpel and there went the larynx. But the man had always been the silent type anyway, so when you thought about it, the difference wouldn't mean all that much. Additionally, he'd convinced the family that he'd saved their loved one's life. As long as they didn't go to New Orleans and have one of those Ochsner Clinic's shysters give a second opinion, he'd be okay. Maybe he'd cut a little something off their bill. Maybe.

Sport Baudoin didn't understand the sermon, but he enjoyed it. He was a genuine martyr, that was for sure. He'd given up all athletics, turned his back on them. Time had helped him arrive at this comforting conclusion, as he totally forgot that the New Orleans Pelicans had not wanted him. He was convinced that he didn't want them. Why, he couldn't exactly say, but when queried about his giving up, he liked to imagine he'd said, I leave with no regrets! He often saw himself as Lou Gehrig telling the fans in Yankee Stadium good-bye—but without that disease, of course!

It was time for the offering. Bobby took one side of the church, President the other. They held long poles with wicker baskets attached at the ends. Some parishioners gave their donations in little white envelopes. Papoot put in his hundred with great flourish, holding it above his head and swooping down slowly on the basket like a bird of prey diving for the attack. Bobby hated when he did this, but like Papoot had explained, "Me, I want 'em to see I'm not no short change. I give till it hurts! Hee, hee!"

Big Shot Fontenot had his own method for giving. He always cleared his throat loudly as he made his offering. It was always 150 smackeroos.

Mayor Big Head, who lived on his $250 a month salary and nightly camp suppers, always folded his dollar bill into a tiny square so that people thought he was giving more, though of course they knew differently.

Possum was good for four bits. Doc Mouton, a twenty. Hurphy Perrault, who made big money on the church, gave a hundred. One Lung Savoy gave a ten spot that not even the priest wanted to touch, certain he would catch TB or whatever it was One Lung had.

Now people began filing down the aisle to the communion rail, where they knelt and awaited Christ's body on their tongues. They opened their mouths with enthusiasm and experienced great peace as the priest made a tiny sign of the cross over each one.

They were cleansed. It didn't matter what they'd done, by God! And by God's sweet generosity they were okay. Not a one of them got to his feet without feeling lighter, like on a drunk, but without headaches or dizziness.

Then Mass was over and they filed out of the church, shaking hands with Father Justin, exchanging little pleasantries. The priest was genial, as if a burden had been lifted from him too. The sun beat down.

As Papoot shook hands with his son, who bent down and kissed his cheek, he thought, Now I know I'm the smartest man in this parish. So if I didn't get that sermon, imagine what the rest of 'em understood. He wondered if he should speak to his son about this but decided not to. Justin didn't want no advice from nobody, especially about religion. Papoot would have liked to fill his ear just one time, say everything he had to say. But he hadn't gotten around to doing it, and doubted that he ever would. He knew he never would. He really didn't get his son. Not one bit. But he figured that Justin, being such a holy man, a man like Christ, surely was right, and he was wrong. After all, he wasn't any angel.

Papoot and BeBe got in the Cadillac with Moose at the wheel. Bobby got into his own car. He didn't want everybody seeing him riding in a Cadillac. Not that it bothered Papoot one bit. "They expeck it of me," Papoot said. "Hell, I'm their Senator!" Justin would be along much later, after the 11:00 A.M. Mass.

Papoot asked BeBe, "What you thought about your brother's sermon?" BeBe said, "It was beautiful! Didn't you think so?" Papoot replied, "Uh-huh." Then he asked Moose, "An' you, what you thought?" Moose, honored to be asked, said, "It was too high for me." BeBe snickered. What could you expect from a moron? Papoot said nothing.

"Bobby's all right?" Papoot asked his daughter casually.

"Bobby's wonderful" was her answer, which was about what he expected. If she caught Bobby in bed with a water moccasin, she wouldn't say nothin'. Pride. Just like Annabelle, her mother, all pride. Annabelle had left the world with a .38 to her head. Papoot, in the parlor, had heard the shot, raced up the stairs, and found her. No note. No nothing. There she was, clutching a silver cross in one hand, the .38 in the other. Justin had been studying in Europe at the Vatican, had flown home to be with Papoot and BeBe, and had never gone back. "This is where I belong," he'd said. And everyone had said, "What sacrifice! What a man!" And he was going to be high up in the Vatican too!

This sacrifice gave Papoot no pride. He really didn't understand his son. They had nothing in common. Papoot passed it off as too much education, and a mother's fanatic adoration. Justin, from the moment he made known his wish to enter the priesthood, could, in his mother's eyes, do no wrong. He was sinless. She sincerely felt that she was a kind of Mary, and somehow, in some miraculous (and she was more than deeply religious) way, had produced this near perfect human being. Sadly, all of this had conspired to separate a father and his only son. Plus there were a couple of other "little things" which Papoot chose not to think about.

Now they were approaching Blue Lady, Papoot's house named for Annabelle. She always wore blue, sky blue. She explained that when she was a teenage girl the Blessed Mother had appeared to her and promised that if she wore blue every day of her life, her firstborn would be a priest. She had been buried in a sky blue dress, holding her missal.

The driveway was covered with outstretched boughs of live oak that made the road shadowy and mysterious and romantic. A white board fence surrounded the property. A veranda stretched across the home's front under a second-story balcony.

Inside, the flooring was heart pine, the ceiling laced with boxed beams, and there were twelve-inch baseboards. It contained eight fireplaces, a screened-in side porch, and three large double-hung windows that looked out on the veranda and front yard.

All of it was formal and furnished in French antiques. It resembled more a museum than a place to live in. Annabelle had been a formal woman, interested in her perfect son and perfect home. She'd had little patience with her imperfect husband.

The backyard sloped down to a huge man-made lake filled with fish furnished by the state's Wildlife and Fisheries Department, and a family of geese. Papoot didn't feel at home here. After all he had made his way from a sharecropper's cabin with an outdoor privy. He spent as much time as he could in Baton Rouge, where he maintained a suite on the top floor of Heidelberg Hotel.

Papoot would have been just another sharecropper but for that privy. He wrote to Montgomery Ward asking them to send him a case of toilet tissue. They replied that there would be a delay in the shipment but that in the meantime they were sending him their big new catalog. Papoot wrote telling Montgomery Ward to keep the toilet tissue, their catalog would do just fine. Hee, hee!

Word of this incident spread like wildfire among the good Cajun people, and overnight Papoot became a kind of celebrity. The Cajuns loved to laugh like they loved food. And they loved a character. When he ran for the Senate, he was overwhelmingly elected. The guy had it! He was a rascal, sure! But he was their rascal. Tweaking Montgomery Ward's nose, tweaking Esso's big corporate nose. They loved it. Tweaking noses.

But Papoot had stayed too long at the fair. The people no longer found him amusing. They laughed less at his "little ways." And they found him rich. Too damn rich. Big house, big car, tailor-made suits (from New Orleans, no less).

Thus he had become to them a villain or, as Possum Aucoin put it, "a no good sorry son of a bitch." He had got too big for his britches. Many vowed to vote his ass right out of Baton Rouge the very next opportunity. Give another fool a chance, and any man named President had to be a fool for sure. So far as they knew, President was not yet a crook, but they acknowledged at his filling station, there wasn't that much opportunity. Also, they were prepared to accept a little stealing his first term or so. But they didn't want him rubbing their faces in it.

Possum was heard to say, "What we need is a new crook, a beginner, somebody just learning the ropes. That way it won't be too much. Papoot's a hog. He wants his share and my share, and your share too."

Papoot knew they felt this way. Hell, wasn't he one of them, only smarter? If the election's today, he thought, I'd be beat hands down. But the election wasn't today. It wouldn't be until November, and that was about six months away. A lot of things could happen in six months, a lot of things he could make happen. He had a little idea or two. He laughed inside his head. He was smarter than any of them, and most important, he knew their weaknesses. That was what he excelled in, knowing other men's hungers.

He looked forward to the war, loved the blood that would be spilled, even his own. In all probability it would be his last. He wasn't gonna take no prisoners, and God help anybody who got in his way.

He was delighted at these thoughts. His blood hadn't coursed this way in years. He felt like a man, the man he felt he was. A stud. A fucking stud—that was what he was.

Bobby followed them into the house. They went straight out into the backyard, where Motile, who was as old as Papoot and had been with him and Annabelle since she was a thirteen-year-old girl looking for work to help feed her family, had everything ready for Moose, who did the barbecuing. He made his own sauce, and it was as hot as hell, and you could smell it for a mile. Three-inch steaks and tender chicken, sausage, all of it marinated the night before, waited on the pit.

BeBe had prepared her rice dressing, potato salad, and a pineapple upside-down cake, Papoot's favorite. And they had big hot loaves of garlic bread from Hot Dog Hebert's.

A bar had been set up, and everybody had a drink. They toasted Papoot, who expected it, and tried for a show of humility but failed. "What the hell," he said, "ah'm the host. Hee, hee!"

Moose looked on with much satisfaction. He loved being a part of Papoot's family, not all the way, but a part. Even a little part, say, like an illegitimate child. And if Papoot was somehow abusive (Moose thought of it as tough), well, what the hell—that was his right. Where would Moose be without this man? Nobody was looking to hire no jailbird, for sure! But Papoot had. Moose couldn't think of anything he wouldn't do for his savoir. It was a wonderful job!

The suite in Baton Rouge was filled with bourbon and Scotch, cases of it, all gifts from the liquor lobby. In fact, there was hardly a place to sit down. Moose mixed many a drink in that suite and knew the likes and dislikes of every single legislator and lobbyist and big shot. Papoot did a lot of entertaining, especially during the sessions. Papoot's suite was the hangout for all the big shots, and most of them called Moose by name! Even the Governor, that cold fish, would say, "Shit, Moose, how about a good glass of orange juice?" That fake North Louisianian couldn't even admit the glass was filled with vodka with just enough orange juice to cover it. And he didn't seem to have a bottom, either. He could kill a fifth of vodka and not show it. Not one bit! You had to admire a guy who could hold it like that. And he always said thank you. Not like some who didn't even notice who was serving the food or mixing the drinks, and never once said thank you. They ain't got no class, Moose liked to say. To himself. To them he said, "Yessir, coming right up!" like he was colored or something.

Moose had a family of his own who he hadn't seen in years and almost never thought of. He'd abandoned them, Beryl and the three kids, in a trailer park in Slidell. He was sure they were doing okay. They didn't have nothing to do with him. Papoot was his family. He couldn't even mask the adoration he felt for the man. He liked Miss BeBe too. She was one sweet gal, even if she was fat as a hog. Goddamn but she could make potato salad, with a lot of eggs and celery and the onions and olives chopped so small you couldn't hardly see them. But you could sure taste them! Woowee! He eyed the big bowl of potato salad sitting on the table, covered with a big white linen napkin. His mouth watered. He'd like to stick his head in the bowl and eat his way to the bottom, till not one bite was left!

Miss BeBe could bake too. Her cakes stayed moist! That was a big mystery how even after two days the cake was moist as the day it was baked.

Moose wasn't sure about Father Justin, though he was careful to show him all the respect in the world. He had picked up on Papoot's ambivalence toward the priest, so he wasn't sure about his feelings either. He knew one thing for sure—Justin wasn't like the rest of them, and he felt uncomfortable around him. Maybe 'cause I'm so bad and he's so good, he thought. An' smart, too! Way, way, way above everybody else. He didn't even listen to the same music as other folks, but chose things in Italian with people screeching their guts out and shouting to one another. Like everybody in the damn place was deaf!

It was Bobby who caused Moose the most trouble. He would have liked to slap the shit-eating grin off Bobby's dark face. Like he knew something. He wished Papoot would give the word. He even fantasized this.

They would be alone in the Cadillac, and Papoot would push his hat back on his head and wipe his brow with one of them fine linen handkerchiefs he blew his nose in. Papoot wouldn't be saying nothing, deep in thought, maybe even his eyes closed. But Moose didn't believe for a minute he was sleeping! He honestly didn't know when Papoot slept. The man had trouble turning his mind off. That was why he was way ahead of everybody, why you couldn't fool him, never! And Papoot was a waiter too. Moose had seen people try to screw him out of a deal in Baton Rouge, and Papoot would act like he didn't even know it. He'd wait his time, and then kapow! They never knew what hit them. The word was out about Papoot, and not all that many tried it anymore.

Papoot would open his eyes, they were cold over his glasses rims, and he'd say, "Our little Bobby's getting' too big for his britches. Go get him, tiger!" That was what Papoot would call Moose when he wanted him to do something special, Tiger, like the Fighting Tigers football team of Louisiana State University! And Moose would good-naturedly growl jus' like a tiger, "Grwwwww," and Papoot would pat him on the shoulder, like a signature on a contract.

He would do it special to little Bobby. Slap him around for about half an hour till he fell to the ground and then mash his nuts with a big shoe. And let him lay there puking on himself and then wrap those big hands around his throat until his eyes bulged out and he went to Hell, which was where he was headed. Moose was certain about this. He was an authority on the final destinations of his victims. Not many made it to Jesus because they had done this or that to Papoot.

Bobby was looking at him, and for a moment Moose felt he might faint. Had he done something? Or spoken his thoughts aloud? Sweat broke out on his forehead, and inside he was trembling. But no, Bobby was just looking, although it wasn't no normal look—it was like he was investigatin'. Oh-oh, Bobby was headed his way. Moose got busy and turned the steaks and chicken and sausage over on the pit, and gave them a good swab of his sauce with a piece of rag on the end of a stick.

"I've been wanting to talk to you since last night."

Moose gave him a big smile. Brothers.

"President and anybody else who wants to has the right to run against Papoot. That means I don't want anybody threatened or, worse, something to happen to them. I mean it, Moose. This is not bullshit. We can win without that. Comprende?"

Moose gave a salute. He'd seen it done in all those war films at the Palace. Him, he'd been 4-F, both his eardrums were busted years earlier in a bar fight. But you should have seen them other guys! One of them was still in a wheelchair. Moose always regretted not killing all three of them.

Bobby wasn't satisfied with the salute. "Do you understand?" He waited. Moose had the feeling he'd wait forever. He was that kind of a prick. "Sure, mah man, sure! I hear you all the way," Moose said, and Bobby turned about and left.

And Moose thought, One day, little Bobby, one day.

BeBe stood at the lake's edge, where the tame geese climbed up the embankment to be fed bread crumbs. She turned at the sound of someone approaching. It was Justin, in black, his shirt short-sleeved, his white collar still in place. "They're spoiled brats," she said.

Justin pecked his sister's cheek. He adored her. She reminded him of Annabelle. Decent. Innocent. Not equipped to handle—what would you call it, sorrow? Yes, that was it, sorrow. "Your sermon was beautiful," she said. And feeling foolish, he inquired, How? He was intrigued. It hadn't been written. It had come from someplace within him, though where he didn't exactly know. It came out of a persistent ache, like a nagging toothache. He'd had no choice but to say it. What exactly he'd said he wasn't certain. He wished he had a copy of it, to study tonight with a good glass of port as he sat beneath the dark and naked beams of his parlor. But there was no copy. Only God had a copy, only God understood.

His sister's big, open face looked flustered. She didn't exactly know how to answer. She studied him, waiting for him to let her off the hook, but Justin wasn't much on letting anybody off the hook. A near perfect man in her eyes, he expected something just short of that from other people. And never found it. It was a lifelong quest.

In Rome he'd asked an old Cardinal, "If man is created in the image of God, why are we so utterly corrupt?" The old Cardinal had given some pat and totally unsatisfactory answer. He thought about it a lot. Another mystery. He smiled at BeBe to signal her that her lack of answer didn't matter.

She surprised him. "It was so . . . mysterious!"

He was delighted, and his eyebrows shot up. She had gotten something, picked up on something! He kissed her again, and she beamed with pleasure. To please Justin was something! He asked her, "Tell me, sister, how is life treating you?"

He was so direct, not given at all to small talk. He was at another level, higher, and he let you know it quick! Did he mean it to be so painful? Of course. How else could he teach these cretins, these sinners, whom God had chosen to bury him among? There were no cardinals in Richelieu, Louisiana.

"It's okay," she said, then added, "I guess." She looked nervously in

Bobby's direction, but he was talking with Papoot, or listening more like it. Justin pressed, "Don't you know?"

BeBe sighed. If she couldn't talk to a priest, as she had always been taught by the nuns at Grand Coteau school for girls all the way up until high school, who else could she talk to? Old Sister Electrima of Trinity used to always say, "Priests have God's ear. They listen for Him. They're His ears on earth, so if you want to have a conversation with our Lord, go to a priest."

The fact that this priest was also her brother was the only problem.

He helped her. "Bobby?"

She looked like she wanted to cry, her lips trembled. He approved. He wanted the truth. Demanded it. She was his sister, true, but more, she was a part of his flock and he was responsible for her immortal soul. And that was some weighty responsibility! He thought of himself as a beast of burden, carrying all those rotten human loads. It was not what he had envisioned for his priestly life. He wanted to be a racehorse, going to seminars, universities, world conferences. But.

"Well, he's not the same. Bobby's changing before my eyes, and I don't know why or what to do about it." She waited. He'd know. Justin was the wisest man she had ever known. Even smarter than Papoot or Bobby. They were smart in politics, but that was all. Justin knew everything. Especially about the human heart.

"When did it start?" he asked her.

"It's been coming on, but lately it's worse. At first I just thought it was one of Bobby's moods. They come and they go. But this one came, and won't go."

"You'll have to be more specific, sister."

"I know." Her head hung like she'd done something terrible.

"I'm your brother. You're my beloved sister. If I had a problem, I'd probably discuss it with you," he said with a straight face.

Her head lifted; she felt good about herself. That this wisest of men would confide in her! "You would?"

He nodded, not wanting to tell her two straight lies, and reminded himself to confess both when he went to confession in Lafayette to old Father Soulier, who was three quarters deaf as well as on the road to senility. And a horse's ass to boot!

"Well, we don't sleep together."

"I see," the priest said, and he did. Did she possibly believe that a man could desire her with all that weight? She was a cow. A beloved one, but a cow.

"Since when?"

"A long time. We did it less and less, Justin, and then we just stopped."

"Have you discussed it?"

She was shocked. Talk about such things with a man? "Of course not."

He nodded like it was the wisest choice. She was glad she had done the right thing. She made the sign of the cross to thank God. She would talk to God. She could talk to Justin. But not to Bobby. Married people didn't do such things. It was so personal. In some ways she thought of sex as a sin. At least she'd been taught that way. The nuns knew for sure. Don't go against God, they would always say, and she'd tried mightily to do exactly that. She sure didn't want to go to Hell. She believed that Heaven would be strewn with roses even more lovely than the ones she grew.

"Let me handle it," Justin said.

This frightened her. "What will you do, Justin?"

"I'll handle it," he said and patted her head like she was a child. She nodded as Papoot called, "Hey, come and get it!"

Chapter 8

On Monday morning the sun had not yet made its way up above the horizon when Bobby pulled out of his driveway. It was still five minutes too early to turn on CAJN. Na Na went on the air precisely at six, with Father Justin giving a sermonette he called Prayer of the Day. Bobby wondered why the priest's words were so meaningless to him, and while he wasn't certain, he had the feeling that so much the priest said was spoken in anger. In Bobby's opinion, the man had a hard-on for the world. And he wondered why.

On the other hand, he felt pretty good about Justin. Bobby didn't know what he had said to BeBe, but she seemed much relieved, and the rest of Sunday had turned out better than it had in a long time. After lunch he had napped, and then they went to the Palace, where they split a box of butter popcorn, with enough butter for a change. Apparently Short Change had finally been won over by all the complaints.

After the movie, in which Randolph Scott saved the widow's farm from a cattle baron, Bobby and BeBe had gone home, where she put together some of the leftover barbecue and fixings, along with the last two slices of her cake, which she'd saved just for him.

He did his exercise, took his bath, and lay out on the porch listening to the music that floated in from the Philco in the parlor. BeBe climbed into bed, kissed his ear, and said, "I love you, Bobby." Bobby said, "Me too." It wasn't much, but it was better than silence, and they slept. The birds slept too. There was not a sound, not a rustle from the bamboo. It had been a rare and restful day. Now, this morning, he would have to start all over again. Another week—new uncertainties.

He turned into Courthouse Street, where the parish seat of government had been constructed in 1910. It was a redbrick building topped by a green brass cupola that housed a bell which was rung right before court went into session.

The Sheriff's office, along with the jail, was in the basement. Other officials and court occupied the first and second floors. He went down the stairs, past the radio room, where deputies on the morning shift were arriving and the night shift was checking out. There were two twelve-hour shifts. He had too many deputies, and he knew it, but it seemed someone always needed a job, someone who couldn't find one anyplace else, someone with a relative or friend who had political clout. Someone whose family was hurting.

All of them had a high school education, but none had police training. The pay was terrible. They were given badges, clubs, and some handcuffs. They had to furnish their own weapons. For the first couple of weeks they traveled with an older, seasoned deputy, someone who knew a little something. But then they were on their own. Most did it okay, but just barely.

Slo' Down, who was Bobby's Chief Deputy had been on the force forever, greeted him in his office. "Mornin', Sheriff."

Bobby mumbled something back. He was studying a bulletin from the State Police in Baton Rouge exhorting them to increasingly be on the lookout for marijuana cigarettes. Bobby snickered. There were none in Richelieu. In fact, the only thing he knew about them he'd learned in his M.P. training, and from when that Hollywood movie star had been caught with one. He thought, Thank God they don't want me to look out for beer! There was plenty of that in Richelieu Parish.

He crumpled the bulletin and tossed it toward the wastebasket, which he missed. Just then, Thank You Please, the trustee, came in with his two fresh-made biscuits, each containing a pat of melting butter, covered with cane syrup, and a cup of hot black coffee.

Thank You Please said, "Thank you please," and Bobby asked him,

"You all right?" Thank you Please said, "Yassuh," and Bobby reminded him, "You know you can get out whenever you want?" Most folks had forgotten what Thank You Please was in jail for anyway. He had killed his wife, which whites didn't think was all that bad a crime, as long as it was among the Negroes. And done to each other. He had long served his sentence, but he wasn't going anyplace. He had forgotten what it was like to be out. Here, nobody bothered him. He stayed in place and cooked for the prisoners. Bobby slipped him a few bucks from time to time, but outside of cigarettes, he really had no place to spend it. There was nothing he wanted. He loved the Sheriff, who had always treated him with kindness, and what else would a man want? It was a lot better than his wife had treated him.

"What you got for lunch today?" Bobby asked.

"Hash, fresh tomato salad, and banana custard, thank you please."

Slo' Down said, "We got people tryin' to break into our jail with food like that."

Bobby smiled. "Save me a plate, Thank You Please."

"An' one for Miss BeBe," the trustee said, always delighted with these instructions. He didn't ask Bobby if he wanted some more biscuits because with the Sheriff it was always the same. No less. No extra. The trustee departed, backing out of the room.

Bobby picked up a baseball from his desk. It was allegedly autographed by Babe Ruth, but Bobby wasn't all that sure. The autograph looked familiar to him. Gaston had brought it to him from a sheriff's convention in New York City. Anyway, the autograph was fading. Bobby tossed the ball in the air and caught it, then put it down on the desktop.

"Where does Cap'n Eddie live these days?" he asked.

"Out on the old Pecan Switch Road," Slo' Down said. "You goin' pay him a call? I could go, Bobby."

"No. I'd rather do it. I've put it off long as I could, but he's got to stop. First of all, it's sick, and second of all—" He stopped, being unable to remember second of all.

"He's not right in the head for sure," Slo' Down noted, pointing to his own head as some kind of proof.

"You telling me! Did you know him before the war? Funny, I didn't."

"He was jus' a regular fellow, but he didn't come back that way for sure. They was tenant farmers. Everybody else in the family's dead. He los' another brother in a car accident. He was older."

Bobby nodded. Slo' Down knew everybody in Richelieu, and their histories. Sometimes it even came in handy.

"He got some medal in the war."

"I know," Bobby said. "I heard he was a hell of a soldier. Now he's a hell of a bother. I guess that's the way it goes."

Slo' Down didn't quite follow, and didn't know how to respond. So he lit up a Camel and took a long draw. Then, "I guess I better go tell the day shift what to do."

Pointing to the wastebasket, Bobby said, "Be sure to tell them to be on the lookout for marijuana cigarettes." Both men laughed, and Slo' Down went to the door. "What they gon' think of next! Marijuanas!"

"Slo' Down," Bobby said, and the Deputy turned to him. "There is something I want done, but I'd rather nobody shot his mouth off about it. I guess that's impossible, huh?"

"Jus' about," the Chief Deputy agreed. "You know how them boys like to talk."

"Well, if I find out someone shot off his big mouth, his ass is mine. I'm going to fire them on the spot, and I don't care who their paran or nan nan is. Comprende?"

"Loud and clear."

"You know Zeke's daughter?"

"The one with the beautiful ass?"

Bobby sighed, felt a stirring. "That's the one. I want to know where she goes. She's screwing around into Ti Boy's death. Tell the boys to be on the lookout and let me know pronto. Now I don't want anybody to bother her. You do and she'll write an editorial blasting us for being Nazis or something. But I want to know. Okay?"

Slo' Down nodded, barely suppressing a grin, thinking that Li'l Bobby mus' have a hard-on for sure. He killed the smile and said, "I'll make sure they understand. I'll say it in French and English."

Some deputies spoke only French.

"Try sign language, too. Most of 'em are deaf and dumb."

Slo' Down laughed aloud in agreement—most were pretty stupid. Then he smiled to himself, knowing this was not a bad assignment, following that big juicy ass around.

Bobby was in his car driving out into the country. CAJN was on, and Na Na was telling listeners how many days it was to his De De's birthday. He did this every day and had managed to turn her birthday into a major event, like the Fourth of July, or Columbus Day. Finally, mercifully, he played some music, and Bobby kept time by tapping on the steering wheel. The day was lovely except for a handful of clouds, and that probably meant they'd get their little afternoon shower. The weather was so predictable. The temperature hovered at ninety and was going up. Summers in Richelieu.

Oak trees and Spanish moss were everyplace. The gray moss hung almost to the road like a big thick cobweb. The brightly colored azaleas made everything seem like a Mardi Gras parade, and there were red birds, blue birds, and black crows flying about, swooping and calling out like they were celebrating De De's impending birthday.

He tried not to think about Ruth Ann Daigle's ass. No, that wasn't the truth. He was trying not to think of her, period. But it was not so easy. Jesus Christ, but that face, that creamy skin. And the way she tasted. He could still taste her, and he allowed his imagination to soar. He would like to pour her in a glass and drink her. He realized he had an erection. If he was a boy he'd jack off and get rid of it. But he wasn't, and besides, it would be a terrible waste. He thought about exploding in her, filling her belly, making her scream aloud. Kissing her belly, running his tongue around her button, then down, down to . . . Stop! he ordered himself. He was almost at the point of explosion. He rolled the windows down and stepped on the gas, hoping to make a breeze, to cool off. He began to recite the Rosary: "Glory be to the Father, and to the Son and to the Holy Spirit; as it was in the beginning, is now, and ever shall be, world without end. Amen."

That helped. Maybe he'd get Tooky Trahan to pass his religious relic over his groin, he thought and then immediately felt ashamed for having such impure, even sacrilegious thoughts. What in hell was he turning into? And all over . . . Stop! He ordered himself. Don't think about it. He turned the car into a path, at the end of which was a tiny silver trailer, resting on cinder blocks. It was shaped like an egg.

Cap'n Eddie Sonnier, shirtless, sat on its steps, his gray mottled Catahoula hound dog BeBo at his bare feet. In his hand was his coffee in a tin cup. It looked to Bobby to be Army issue. Like Cap'n Eddie.

Bobby got out of the car. Cap'n Eddie was smiling, but that didn't mean anything. Bobby wasn't even certain that he could see him. His watery blue eyes that looked like they'd taken too many rinsings stared off in the distance, at something or someone only he could see.

"It's me, Bobby," the Sheriff said, and the eyes focused on him and Cap'n Eddie started to rise. Bobby motioned him to keep his seat, and Cap'n Eddie gave a lazy salute.

"Me 'n' you got to talk. You know what about. You can't look at those kids that way. I don't understand why you want to anyway. Look at your own. Save those quarters."

Cap'n Eddie's face was expressionless. They could have been talking about the weather.

"How come you're that way? I know you wasn't raised like that, right?"

Perhaps Cap'n Eddie nodded. He did something with his head.

Bobby smiled. "The cat got your tongue?"

Cap'n Eddie purred, "Meow."

The Catahoula hound looked up, hopeful, saw nothing interesting, lowered its great head, and went back to sleep. Cap'n Eddie reached out and scratched it behind the ears. The dog replied in its sleep. Bobby could hear insects buzzing around. For a moment they were the only two people on earth, an earth moving in slow motion. Bobby felt sleepy.

"Thing is, if you don't stop I'm going to have to send you away. Pineville or the Veterans' Hospital in Biloxi. I know you don't do nothing but look, but that's definitely against the law. Public lewdness or something. Man, I don't want to have to do that. Jesus Christ, I'm a veteran too, I mean not like you, I mean I didn't do anything, but it doesn't matter! I got to do my duty. That's what they pay me for. Comprende?"

The veteran drank from his cup, then showed Bobby that it was empty, like he was doing a magic trick and the coffee had disappeared. He stood, turned to go back into the trailer.

Bobby sucked in his breath sharply like he had been struck. It looked like a fist the size of God's had punched a hole in Eddie's back, a deep hole, red and angry looking. White veins crisscrossed it. Bobby lowered his eyes. He felt ashamed but didn't know why. He just stood there watching the empty doorway until Cap'n Eddie returned with the tin cup filled with coffee and sat back down.

The Sheriff was angry. The silence, the horror that wars leave had gotten him down. It was a kind of disease you could catch. "Now goddamnit, you gonna answer me, promise me you won't do it again, or I'll take you in right now! I'm not bullshitting, Eddie, an' don't look over my shoulder like Jesus is there because nobody's here but you an' me."

Then Chief Deputy Slo' Down Angelle tapped him on the shoulder, and Bobby almost jumped three feet. He hadn't even heard the man drive up! Cap'n Eddie's face said nothing. What did he see? How had life vanished like that?

"What in hell you want?" Bobby sputtered, angry at everything, mostly himself.

"Jus' followin' orders, boss man," Slo' Down replied. On the surface his tone was servile, but beneath there was sarcasm.

"Get to the point!"

"Zeke's little girl . . ."

"Her name's Ruth Ann, what about her?"

"You tole me to keep up with her. Well one of the boys saw her headed for the Brouliettes'."

"You sure?"

"Hell, I can't read her mind, but it looks that-a-way."

Bobby turned back to Cap'n Eddie, but both man and dog had vanished inside the trailer. And the door was shut. He sighed in frustration. "Thanks, Slo' Down. I'm sorry. I'm just not used to dealing with . . . whatever the hell Cap'n Eddie's got."

"I understan'."

Bobby wanted to say more but didn't, went back to his car, and said through the window, "If you want me I'll be at the Brouliettes'."

Slo' Down nodded politely but inwardly thought, You prick! He and all his family couldn't wait for the chance to vote against Papoot, and then maybe one day against Mr. Bobby Boudreaux. He looked about and lit up a Camel.

Zeke's black Pontiac with the PRESS sticker on the windshield sat parked near the Brouliettes' cabin. Bobby noticed the bicycle was gone and someone had cut the grass. Only Beulah the cow seemed unchanged, as she stood having her morning snack, tail flipping from side to side, looking at Bobby as he stepped from his car.

He knocked on the front door, and Aristede answered. Strain was all over his face. Ruth Ann was in the tiny parlor, being served coffee by Marie, still in black. Ruth Ann was dressed in a red blouse with a white skirt, and she wore high heel shoes. A red purse was slung over her shoulder, and she had her notepad and pencil in her hands. One eyebrow raised when she saw him. She said, "Am I crazy, or do I see the Sheriff's deputies wherever I go?"

"You're crazy. There's a word for it, but I don't remember it."

Marie handed him coffee and motioned to a wicker chair, but he shook his head. He would remain standing, stirring his coffee.

"The word is *paranoid,* it means imagining things. So what brings you here?"

"It's none of your business, but I'm seeing if the Brouliettes are okay."

"We fine!" Aristede said with a little too much enthusiasm for Bobby's liking. What the hell was "fine"?

"May I begin?" Ruth Ann asked.

"You don't have to say anything," Bobby said to the couple, who were now seated. Aristede was dressed for the fields, a straw hat on his knee.

"We don' mind," Aristede said, and Bobby cursed himself for not being there first. But why? What was he afraid the couple might say?

"Well, that's settled. Tell me about Ti Boy."

"For God's sake. They've just buried him!"

"I'm very aware of that. If the Brouliettes want me to come back . . ."

"No. Get it over with," Bobby said, glowering at her.

"Was that four-ten his?" she asked.

"Mine," Aristede said.

"He cleaned it for you?"

"No! I clean . . . Yeah, sometimes. That time."

"Why?"

"They don't know," Bobby said.

Aristede said, "He was looking for something to do. That's all. Something to do."

"Didn't he help in the fields?" she asked.

Aristede nodded. "All the time. Ti Boy was a good boy."

"And didn't he have a paper route? My paper. Looks like those things would have kept him busy, in addition to being an altar boy."

"He loved that the most," Marie said, gripping a handkerchief in her chapped hands.

Aristede nodded proudly. "He was even thinkin' about being a priest!"

"When? When the accident happened, was he thinking about it then?"

"I don' understand . . . ," Aristede said. "We don't know what was on his mind."

Ruth Ann smiled an evil smile that made Bobby look away. He'd have loved to slap it off her face, would have liked seeing his finger marks on her ivory skin.

"Well, let me put it this way," she said. "Ti Boy wanted to be a priest, right? Okay, at the end of his life, was he still planing on that?"

"Sure!" Aristede said, even as Marie whispered, "No."

Ruth Ann looked from one to the other, pen poised over her tablet. "Well, which is it?"

Aristede said, "He wasn't talkin' about it no more, but I'm sure he was still thinkin' about it."

"When did he stop talking about it?'

The couple looked desperately at each other, confused, wanting to say the same thing. Bobby tried to help. "How can they remember that? They didn't write it down, for God's sake!"

Ruth Ann said nothing, just sat there waiting.

"About six months ago, he just stopped." It was Marie who spoke.

"Hell, maybe he got interested in girls! Boys that age do, you know," Bobby said.

Marie studied him out of the corner of her eye. Bobby didn't look at her.

"Do you all know?" the reporter asked.

"No, ma'am," Aristede said softly.

"And you never asked him about it?" she pressed.

The couple looked at each other miserably and shook their heads. They had never asked him.

"I believe you did," Ruth Ann persisted. "It must have made you proud, this wanting to be a priest."

"We lived jus' for that," Marie said.

"So what did he say when you asked him?"

"Don't answer that!" Bobby commanded. "She's trying to trick you. You've already told her you didn't ask him. Am I right? You didn't ask him."

They looked at each other and nodded.

Ruth Ann looked at Bobby. "What are you up to? I get the feeling that you don't want these people to talk to me, to say anything. I can do a story on that too, a front-page story, with the heading 'What's the Sheriff Afraid Of?' "

Bobby loomed over her, glaring down. "You wouldn't dare!"

She smiled, dimples at the corners of those ripe lips, those ripe red lips. "What would you do, arrest me?"

"I might."

"Sorry, that dog doesn't hunt. The press of this nation would come to my rescue. See, we don't like to see each other get muzzled. You'd be famous, Sheriff. Richelieu boasts Nazi Sheriff." She stood. "Obviously I can't talk with these people with you here. Thanks, folks, I'll be back." She left, and he could have sworn she did something to her buttocks to make them swing from side to side. He could see the ridge of her panties beneath her skirt.

When she went out the door, Bobby said, "I'm sorry you all had to be put through this."

They nodded, and he couldn't tell exactly how they felt. He was at the door and turned back to them. "Aristede, you said you all are fine. Something happened, I mean to make things, you know . . . better?"

Aristede blushed "I didn't mean nothin'."

Marie said, "Don' lie to Bobby, Aristede. Not to Bobby. Not for nobody. Somethin' happened all right. Las' night, Mr. Hurphy Perrault and Mr. Tooky Trahan brought us some money."

"They what?" Bobby asked, astounded.

Aristede said, "A tousan' dollars. In hundreds. Me, ah never seen no hundred before. Goddamn!"

Bobby's heart was beating, and he felt a chill in the small of his back. "This thousand, did they say what it was for?"

"I don't follow you, Bobby, I mean Sheriff."

"Why did they give you the money?"

"Oh that! Mr. Tooky said it was for Ti Boy's insurance."

"His what? Where did Ti Boy get insurance?"

"We don't know, but Mr. Hurphy made us sign some paper so it's— how you call it?— legal." Aristede's face wore a worried look. "We din' do wrong, huh, Bobby?"

Bobby quickly reassured them. "Oh no" He stood there looking at them. Marie refilled his cup, and he took a sip. "Did Tooky or Hurphy say where the policy came from?"

Marie said, "From Mr. Tooky, I'm sure."

Bobby nodded. "He was the agent, but what I'm wondering, who paid for the policy when it was pur—— . . . bought?"

Aristede shrugged. "We don' know that, and like I tol' Marie, we sure not fixin' to look no gift horse in his mouth. That's for sure!"

"No. Of course not. Anyone would have done the same thing," Bobby said quickly.

"We gon' go to New Orleans for a weekend. We never done that, an' we not getting' no younger," Aristede said.

Bobby smiled. "Go, have a good time, you deserve it. And thanks for the coffee. I've never had a better cup. What kind is it, Marie?"

"The bes'. Mello Joy."

Bobby left them, got into his car, wondered what to do. Who would have insured Ti boy, and why? And more important, when?

He looked at his wristwatch. He knew just where to go. He'd get to the bottom of this. But then he suddenly wondered why he was so intent on getting answers. He wasn't a reporter. His job didn't have anything to do with truth, whatever that was. His job was to keep the peace, and by God there was peace. So what was he doing? Were a pretty face and a knockout body changing him that much? It wasn't possible. "No way," he said aloud. So what was it? He had the feeling that he had stepped off into a deep and dark pool, and if he wasn't careful he would drown. He had absolutely no doubts about that.

Possum Aucoin was giving Catfish François a little trim. His sponsor and boss, Coon Soileau, looked on, making appropriate comments. "Cut it short, Possum. Cut it short. I can't have no hairs swimming in the courtbouillon, no matter how good it tastes."

Not too short," Catfish protested. "My hair and my cookin's what drives the ladies crazy."

Coon said, "Bullshit," and that ended the subject. It was midmorning, and many of the regulars sat around, including the Mayor, Hurphy, Tooky, and Nonc. The Mayor was antsy, moving about in his seat like a guilty schoolboy. He was desperate to tell that joke given to him the week before by the Tuf-Nut salesman. And he was anxious to tell it right. He wanted a big laugh, and for the story to be passed about Richelieu, and for people to say, "That Mayor, he's a crazy one." His problem was he kept forgetting the punch line. In desperation he had written it on the cuff of his shirt. "Heard a good one," he began, inching his arm up like he was fending off a robber. "It's a riddle."

There were groans from everyone, and Possum said, "Let him tell it. Let him tell it. Let him tell his little joke." Everyone laughed but the Mayor. He was taking one final look at the joke before he lowered his arm. "Here it is," he said, jumping down from his chair. "What's the loneliest bayou in Richelieu?" His eyes bulged with glee and anticipation.

Hurphy dutifully repeated the riddle like he was giving it legal consideration. "The loneliest bayou in Richelieu. Hmmm."

Big Head exploded "By-you-self!" and it didn't matter that no one else laughed as he pranced about the barbershop giving one victorious "Whoop! Whoop!" after another, like a demented train.

Tears ran down his face, and he couldn't resist telling his silent, stony-faced audience, "Go tell that one. I dare you! Whoop! Whoop!"

Tooky, who was trying to sell the Mayor a burial policy (for your beautiful little coffin), laughed dutifully and, knowing the Mayor, said, "I got to tell that one! Now that's a good one. Bayou-Self! Ha, ha, ha."

The little bell on the door tinkled, and Bobby Boudreaux entered. "Gents," he said.

Nonc opened a bleary eye and said, "Now the bullshit's over for sure," and went back to sleep, exhausted from his contribution.

Bobby sat down next to Hurphy, and while the others talked, said so softly that he might not have spoken at all, "I need to see you and Tooky. How about your office?"

Hurphy looked uncomfortable and moved about in his shirt collar. "Why?" he asked. He had also turned a little yellow.

"Because," Bobby said, then got up and left. He crossed Main Street and stood in front of Hurphy's office, leaning against the building, his arms crossed. They could see him through the barbershop window. About five minutes later, Hurphy and Tooky joined him, and they entered Hurphy's office, where pictures of Jesus, Bishop Peter Paul Dupuis (autographed!), and President Roosevelt looked down. Hurphy sat behind his expansive desk, motioned the other two to sit down, and said in his best lawyer voice, "Now, Sheriff, what's up?"

"Ti Boy Brouliette's thousand-dollar policy. Where the hell did that come from?"

Hurphy said, "You not working for *The Times-Picayune*, are you, Bobby?" He smiled to show that he was speaking in humor, but all present knew that he was not.

"No, Hurphy. I'm speaking for me. The Sheriff. I am, you know."

"Aw hell yes, I know. I voted for you. Gave you two thousand dollars for your campaign when you didn't need it. Never asked you where it went. So I know you're Sheriff."

Tooky joined in. "That was three thousand from me, Bobby. No questions asked."

Hurphy said, almost as an afterthought, "And that doesn't count what we've given Papoot. He's gotten a little greedy, Bobby."

Tooky sighed. "I'll say!"

Bobby sagged inside like his entrails had seeped out his pores. He felt miserable. Every word they had spoken was true. It had never mattered before. He realized, nothing much had mattered before.

Hurphy stood, went around the desk, and put his hand on Bobby's shoulder. He could see that the man was suffering. "And Bobby, there's a little more to it than that. The policy. You don't want to know. Believe me, Bobby. It's going to be fine. Everything's fine, and the Brouliettes have some extra money for the first time in their lives. Let's leave it be."

Bobby whispered. "But Ruth Ann . . ."

"That'll be okay, too," Tooky said.

Suddenly Hurphy's voice changed from intimacy to old-time camaraderie. "Come on, let's go to One Lung's and get some coffee. I feel good!"

Bobby stood, and the three men went out the door and across Main Street to the poolroom. They talked about the crops, which they agreed looked good. Bobby thought, All of a sudden, everything's good. I wonder why I feel so bad.

Night fell, and Bobby drove to Zeke Daigle's house, not knowing exactly why. He sure as hell didn't want to see Ruth Ann. He had nothing to say to her, absolutely nothing! He thought, I don't want to lie to her. It seemed that his life had become a big lie, both his personal life and his professional one. And he wondered how this had happened, because he was basically an honest man. He arrived at a single-word conclusion: choices. His platter had suddenly become filled with them, like pieces of barbecued chicken on a plate. And in the light of day, in the light of knowing exactly what he was doing (he was not hypocrite enough to rationalize), he had made choices. But why all the wrong ones? He had stepped away from what was right.

Damn. There she was sitting on the porch banister, smoking a cigarette. She saw him, recognized him, and waved lazily. He continued around the block. then stopped the car and sat there, the motor still running. Choices. That word again. He could go home. He should go home. BeBe would be waiting up with supper for him. He could go by Misty's and do a little politicking, shoot the breeze with the regulars, play a little bourrée, talk about LSU football, crops, Na Na and his papoon. Or he could see her. Talk with her. Smell her. Kiss her. Taste her. He groaned aloud, cursed the choice he was about to make, drove to the corner, turned the car about, and drove up to her house, where she sat, waiting, like she had no doubt that he would be back. He stayed in the car, staring, transfixed. She got down from the banister. Her slacks were white, her blouse was red and tied in a knot above the pooch of her belly. She walked slowly to him, leaned in the window.

"Am I just gonna stand here?"

He opened the door, and she got in. He smelled her perfume. She turned in the seat so she was facing him. He put his foot on the accelerator and drove.

"Trouble?" he asked.

"Yeah. Zeke. He's forgotten how to swallow. We're having to force his food down. God but I wish he'd go, that God would take him. That something would put both of us out of our misery. I swear if I had some kind of pill I'd end it for him. He's not living. I wish he'd forget how to breathe. Do I shock you? Am I some kind of monster?"

Her bottom lip trembled. "Can I come sit by you? Can I? I need to be held."

He extended an arm, and she collapsed against him, buried her head in his chest, and began to weep. He felt helpless, and he patted her like a baby until they were out in the country. A big oak hung over a bayou, a single oak; the moss almost touched the water, and he pulled in beneath it.

"I'm so sorry," he said. "What can I do? Is there something I can do?"

She covered his lips with a single finger and whispered, "Just hold me." He kissed her finger, and suddenly it was between his lips and he was gently suckling it.

"Like a puppy," she said and added, "my puppy?" She asked it like a question, and he decided not to lie. He'd lied enough that day. "Yes, I think so."

"Say it," she said.

"Like your puppy."

"Beloved," she said and held up her face for him to kiss her. He did. Their lips met gently. She drew back. "I've never felt this way."

"Me neither."

"I know it's wrong. And God knows I don't need any more trouble, and I know that goes double for you."

"Triple," he said.

"What shall we do?" she asked.

"Thanks," he said, "for leaving me to give an answer. What happened to you?"

"I want you. Do you want me, Bobby?" She reached out a hand and held his sex, squeezed it. "Oh my, yes you do."

He summoned all his strength. "Thing is, that's not gonna solve anything. Things'll still be the same."

"They really won't."

"No. Lord, I'm about to cum."

She reached for his zipper, tugged it down, felt inside his shorts, and pulled his sex out. It was gorged with blood. She ran a thumb over the head, over the hole where his pre-cum seeped out. She rubbed that, then lifted her finger to her lips and tasted him. "Oh, I love that!"

For no reason at all, words sprang into his head: I am a man. And he said, "I don't want to cum in your hand."

She sat on her haunches and studied him closely, then shrugged and unbuttoned her trousers, pulled them and her white panties down midthigh, and lay back against the armrest, her leg on the dashboard. He looked between her legs at her pink opening surrounded by all those dark curls.

"Kiss me there," she said.

He hesitated, looking at the wet vertical lips.

"You don't do that?" she asked.

"Well, I never have." It was true. He and BeBe made love the formal way, the old-fashioned way, him on top. It was satisfactory. Good, but if it was that good, why had they stopped?

"I want you to. I want to be your first." Her fingers were playing with his ears, going in them, twisting in his hair. He leaned forward. The scent of new-mown hay, and he thought, Goddamn! A tendril of hair tickled his nose, and he thought, Please Lord, don't make me sneeze. He gave her a peck, tasted his own lips, liked the taste, leaned into her, running his tongue up and down. Her hands were behind his head, and she was pulling him in. He had the feeling of drowning, drowning in Heaven! "See it? My little button. That's where I want you." He saw it nestled up in the top of her like a bird peeping from a nest. He gave it his tongue, round and round, felt her thighs contract; the muscles were doing a dance in her thighs and a million miles away he could hear "Yesssssssssssssssssss."

He drank for dear life. He drank like a man starved for soothing water in the desert, and she was mewing like a kitten, lost off in some private, unreachable place.

He lifted his head, looked up at her. Their eyes met, and she caressed his face.

"Was it okay?" she whispered, and he said, "Yes, but now me. For God's sake, me," and he got above her, his sex sticking out of his trousers, felt the wetness against it, was ready to plunge down and in and in and in until—

She took him in her hand and said, "There's something I've got to tell you."

Is she fucking crazy? he thought. The talking was over, by God!

"I never have. I just want you to know that."

"Bullshit!"

"I want you. I want you now. But I want you to know what you're getting."

If it was the truth or not, what did it matter Nothing mattered except that he fill her belly with him! Instead, he felt himself dying in her hand. He couldn't do it. He simply would not, could not take what she was offering him, because he had nothing to give in return.

She increased her hand's movements, and in a second he came all over them. There was nothing joyous about it; it was a compromise; it was jacking off, not what his sex demanded of her and him. It's a bomb, he thought. A damn bomb, and he hated her and he hated himself. He was in a burning white rage, frustrated, messy with his semen, like a schoolboy. And he felt as he did years ago when he'd gotten onto his hands and looked down at the whore faking orgasm while she smoked a cigarette. Christ, he could still smell the smoke.

He sat back behind the wheel, and she sat in the far corner. The car's interior had become a prison that they were trying to escape from. He hit the steering wheel with the flat of his hand and said, "Why? Why'd you lead me on? Don't you . . . don't you realize . . ."

"I didn't stop you!"

"You didn't? You didn't? The hell you didn't!"

"I told you the truth. The decision was yours. And you made it. So blame yourself. Go blame yourself."

"Yeah. The truth. That. Ha!"

"Sorry. It is the truth. I just never have. Looks like I never will. That's me, Ruth Ann Daigle, girl reporter and professional virgin."

"Can I ask you something?"

"Anything. At this moment I don't have too many secrets from you, Sheriff."

"Just how many poor bastards have you done that to?"

"Sorry, this is gonna be a big disappointment. None. Hear me? None."

"I do not believe you."

"I wish I could have bled on you. That would be your proof."

"You never have?" he said with awe.

She touched his face, and he jerked back like she had shocked him with a cattle prod. "Oh, Bobby, I never have."

"Will you ever?" He had to know, but each answer bred a new question. She was this whole bunch of questions. She was driving him crazy. More crazy.

"Yes. Of course. I'm normal. When I meet the man I love who loves me. That's not all that complicated, is it?"

At first he didn't hear her, and then he didn't think he had heard her right. "Me?" he said.

"I think so. I know so. I love you."

The anger dissipated at the enormity of what this beautiful woman had said. A feeling of goodness washed over him. It was cool and refreshing, like a tall drink of water going down his throat on a hot summer day. He reached out and put his hands over hers. She waited, saying nothing.

"I'm not sure what love is. But I think I love you too," he said finally.

She said, "I'm glad."

"The thing is, Ruth Ann."

She said, "Call me 'my love.' "

"The thing is, my love, my sweet little girl, I don't think I can do anything about it."

"BeBe?"

"Yes."

"Being Sheriff?"

"Yes. The good Catholics of Richelieu would railroad me out of town, much less let me stay in office, if I harmed a hair on her head. She's kind of Richelieu's patron saint. I can't even think of it."

"But do you love her?"

"I suppose so. I don't know. I mean I'm not sure. You know?"

"Yeah."

"Tell me."

"Oh, I'm no better at definitions than you, love. It's how I feel for you. I've felt that way since I turned around and there you were at the Brouliettes'. I knew instantly and said to myself, Well, well, I've found my love. You. You're love. Mine. It's gonna kill me. If it wasn't for Zeke, I'd get back to New Orleans tonight."

"It's funny, huh, we're out herein the middle of noplace, lot of grass, water, sky, and damned if we're not trapped. At least I feel that way. I'm runnin' into fences I didn't know were there."

"Help me," she said.

"Hell, I can't even help me."

"No, I don't mean about us. I know there's nothing you can do. With that Ti Boy business. I know I'm on to something. The Brouliettes were lying. They don't do it very well, poor dears."

Choices. Now, once and for all, now when they had their personal business straight, not going anyplace now. That was the time to shut the other thing down too. But he could say nothing. He should lie to her. Everything in him told him to, but this wasn't a mere woman, this was somebody ("Call me 'my love' ") who loved him, and whom he loved in return.

Choices.

He heard himself speaking and wasn't sure it was him. The voice, his voice, sounded strange, like it weas coming out of a tree, or on the bayou bank, like he was no longer its source. "Somebody gave the Brouliettes a thousand dollars, said it was for Ti Boy's insurance. Nobody's saying who's the donor. Santa Claus just doesn't want to be known."

She nodded gravely, eyes huge, bottomless. He knew he was going to drown in them. "Sometimes kindnesses are done that way, you know, anonymously," she said.

"That's true."

"But you don't think so."

"Not anymore. It wasn't kindness. All the stops were pulled out to shut me down. And they did."

"Who were they?"

"It doesn't matter," he said.

She took his hand and squeezed it. "Like hell it doesn't! Me and you. We're in this together. Don't shut me out."

She was right. They were. Suddenly, just like that, he was with her wherever she was, wherever she would take them. He felt resentful. Life wasn't so simple anymore. Had he been tricked? Was that bait there between her legs, the juices still on his tongue? No matter. It was too late to wonder.

"Hurphy and Tooky."

"The Church."

"Yes. Our church."

"I don't understand . . ."

"Me neither."

"Tomorrow I'm gonna see Hurphy Jr., he was Ti Boy's friend, altar boys together. Then I'm gonna see Mr. Suire, Ti Boy's principal, who also taught him."

"Be careful," he said and didn't know exactly why he'd felt a need to say it.

"Why? Afraid Mr. Suire will bite me?"

"The Church is very powerful."

"More powerful than the high Sheriff?"

"Than anybody, anything. I don't mean they use their power to do harm, they do good, but I've never seen them threatened either."

"For the life of me, I don't see how the death of a child, a child alone in a house, could threaten them. Do you?"

He shook his head. "No."

"I better get home. Check on Zeke. Can I sit close by you?"

He turned the key in the ignition, the car hummed to life.

"It's where you belong."

BeBe awakened long after he was home and asleep by her side. He was restless, turning this way and that, and she thought she heard him say something, but she couldn't make out what. She had fed him some freshly baked ham with sweet potato casserole covered with marshmallows. He had told her how good it was, but that was all he'd said. He wasn't the same, she was certain, had no doubts. He said all the same things, was the same nice Bobby, like always, but she had the feeling—no, it was more than a feeling—that at some point he had put on a Mardi Gras mask and was speaking from behind it. It definitely was not her Bobby lying next to her.

She got up and went through the dark house and into the bathroom, where she flicked on a light. His clothes—shorts, T-shirt, pants, shirt, and socks—lay in a puddle on the tile floor. She reached down to gather them up, put them in the dirty wash for tomorrow, when she saw that the front of his shorts stuck together.

She held them up to the light over the washstand. There were dark stains on the white material. She held them up to her nose and sniffed. Cum. Bobby had cum in his pants. Then she held up his trousers, and sure enough you could see the stains. Now she picked up his khaki shirt and found it immediately, lipstick, bright red lipstick; it wasn't hers, and she knew who it belonged to.

She sat on the toilet, shorts and trousers in either hand like the scales of justice, and wondered what she would do.

She was Papoot's daughter, and she would do something.

Whatever it took.

He was her Bobby. Nothing and no one was going to change that.

Chapter 9

In Baton Rouge on manicured grounds filled with azaleas and roses of every color and magnolia trees that always seemed to be bursting with white blossoms, is a tall white marble obelisk that is Huey Long's capitol.

He built it and was shot there, dying two days later. Tourists came regularly to stare at the bullet holes embedded in the walls. Tour guides said, "That's the exact spot where, in 1935, Dr. Weiss got him, then Huey's bodyguards got Dr. Weiss." If a tourist was curious and asked, "Why did Dr. Weiss kill him?" the guide dutifully answered. "Old Huey said Dr. Weiss was part nigger." Both guide and tourists nodded. In that age and time, that certainly seemed reason enough.

On that morning, Governor Richard W. Cole sat behind his big oak desk, the state symbol of a mother pelican feeding her young hand-carved into the rich brown wood. Before him was a white demitasse cup holding his morning coffee. Otherwise, the desk was empty.

He was a handsome man who looked the part. Six foot three with a shock of prematurely (he was forty-three) white hair, patrician features and hooded gray eyes, and woodchopper's hands. Some said he resembled Abraham Lincoln, a young Lincoln. His double-breasted pin-striped suit had been made for him in Hong Kong, a gift from admirers. His shirt was snowy white, and his dark tie carried tiny dots of red.

Like all of Louisiana's governors, he came from North Louisiana, was an attorney (graduate of LSU Law School), and had served in World War II on a destroyer in the North Atlantic, returned home to the small town in which he'd been born, been overwhelmingly elected to the senate and then to the Public Service Commission, which regulated Louisiana's utilities, pipelines, and truck lines, and from which an amazing number of Louisiana's governors (like Huey Long) had come.

He was married to his childhood sweetheart and had four sons. His wife was a pretty lady who'd have preferred being on their plantation rather than in Baton Rouge. Everybody liked her.

His voice was slightly hoarse and sounded like it was always sharing a joke with the listener. He made asking the time of day sound personal, as if that listener, of all the people on all the earth, had the answer. When he laughed, and it was a booming laugh, he threw back his great head as though he was sharing the humor with Heaven. Often when he was in conversation, he gripped his listener's arm or shoulder, so that talking to him about anything seemed personal. You felt you really had his attention, and when he squeezed your arm, you felt good. The Gov meant it.

Next to his office was a smaller one where Billy Simms, his executive assistant, ran things, took care of all the crap so that the Gov (that's what folks called him) could tend to the big things. Simms was a small, red-haired, blue-eyed man who'd been with Cole forever, and who knew him better than anyone else on earth. Some said Simms had made a fortune on this knowledge, but no one had proved it. He lived like a man of modest means. Simms had originally come from Arkansas, and perhaps this was why he was upset. Simms loved to tell Cajun jokes, which Cajuns didn't find all that funny, though they were a big hit in North Louisiana, where people found the Cajuns quaint and frankly backwards.

Simms was a man of tremendous energy (once a used car salesman), and on that morning he bounded into the Governor's office. Richard W. (the W stood for Wood) Cole saw his face and immediately knew that something was up, something unpleasant.

"Lay it on me," he said.

"Senator Gaspard . . ."

"Oh shit," said the Gov and opened his desk drawer and removed a big expensive Cuban cigar, which unlit, he stuck into his mouth. He didn't smoke; this was a nervous habit. Simms, who did smoke, and who loved good cigars, would get them out of the wastebasket later and smoke them when he was meeting with legislators, lobbyists, and politicians in the Hunt Room on Lafayette Street in downtown Baton Rouge.

"He's on the phone. Says he's got to talk with you."

"Tell him I'm in conference. I'm not ready for him."

Simms smiled grimly. "I told him that. Said if you weren't on the phone in twenty seconds he was gonna call a press conference and tell every last thing you done for him."

Cole seemed alarmed. "How much time have I got?"

Simms looked at his diamond-covered watch and said, "About three seconds."

The Gov reached for a phone on a table next to his desk and boomed into it, "Papoot, how's my friend?"

In his pocket Simms bent and unbent a big paper clip. It was his little nervous habit. He would bend the metal until it finally broke, and then he'd bend a new one. At night his pocket was filled with bits of paper clips.

The Governor was speaking loudly, like it was necessary for his voice to carry the distance to Richelieu. "Hell, man, you don't need an appointment with me, you come anytime. And you're one man who won't have to wait. Don't you know that? You're my man, Papoot."

Papoot must have given an equally flowery reply (it was all part of the game, and they were both veterans, skilled ones), because the Governor answered, "Uh-huh. Uh-huh. That's true. I agree. You're right. No way! No way. Not you. You know you're my man. Uh-huh, uh-huh. Yes indeed. No, we agree on everything. Now tell me a good Cajun joke. Uh-huh. A bull. Uh-huh. Uh-huh. Lord have mercy!" He threw back his head and roared with genuine laughter. Billy Simms smiled broadly like he could hear the joke too.

The Governor handed Simms the phone which he replaced in its cradle. The smile vanished from Richard W. Cole's face. "He's a tough old bird. We're in for a big-time headache."

"He coming?" Simms asked. He knew the answer.

"Day after tomorrow."

"Any special time? Your schedule's already jammed."

"Of course no special time. When he damn pleases, and for God's sake send him right in no matter who I'm seeing. We've got to play this just right. In our own time. Not his."

"It's always his time. So greedy."

"Yeah, but a lot of them are. At least he's got some charm. Want to hear his joke, minus the accent? Well there was this bull . . ."

The accent wasn't that bad. Governor Richard W. Cole was a better-than-average mimic. He could have been an actor. In fact, he *was* an actor. In Louisiana the Governor had to be. In South Louisiana he got down and rolled with the masses, a Jax beer in his hand, dancing with all the ladies, young and old, seeming to love it. When he got up to North Louisiana, he became most distant, austere, a Bible in his hand, and if he danced at all, it was square dancing, do-si-do.

New Orleans was the third world he had to charm and dominate. There he had to be a sophisticated city slicker, able to mix easily with that city's power structure, who belonged to the Boston Club and who tried mightily not to let anyone else in. On Mardi Gras day he had to toast the king of Mardi Gras, Rex, whose float stopped at the Boston Club reviewing stand. Had to do it like he had been born to nobility, knew just how to lift the slender champagne glass, hold it up like a scepter, bring it to his lips, swallow delicately. Boston Club members stood about observing. After all, he really wasn't one of them, but out of rural North Louisiana. They weren't sure about him, but he was the only governor they had and, as Governor of Louisiana, possessed all the power of a king, thanks to the

Napoleonic Code, under which Louisiana was governed, power particularly over the oil industry, which was where the real money was.

He had to cater to the other side of New Orleans too, downing muffuletta sandwiches from the Central Grocery Store (where they had been invented), a roast beef po'boy at Mother's, sugary beignets with milk and coffee at an outside table near the Mississippi River. He had to have a Sazerac in the bar named for it in the Roosevelt Hotel, knock down half a dozen old-fashioneds at the bar at Brennan's on Royal Street, and even drop in and listen to some jazz (which he didn't particularly like or understand) in a couple of the French Quarter's less disreputable nightspots. And of course he had to eat exquisite food at Arnaud's, Antoine's, Galatoire's.

Louisiana was a weird state to govern, but above all else—and surely this was the Governor's toughest task—he had to stay just popular enough to get reelected.

That wasn't only number one—it was everything.

In Richelieu, Papoot hung up the telephone gingerly, as if he was afraid it might shatter. He sat back of his simple desk in a small, nondescript office he maintained for seeing his "little people." No coffee was on the premises because, as he had explained to Bobby, if you give 'em coffee they gon' sit forever. Nor were the chairs opposite his desk comfortable. The idea was to get 'em in, get 'em out. Every one of them wanted something. Most of it illegal and impossible, a lot of it desperate. For these, he was the court of last resort. A son on death row at Angola. The trick was to give very little and make it seem a lot, a trick at which Papoot Gaspard was a master. All of them, every last one of them, left smiling, most with a couple of folded-up bucks to "go have a beer on Papoot! Hee, hee!"

The only regal thing in his office was the chair in which he sat. It was the Governor's chair, with the state symbol embossed in its brown leather back. Governor Richard W. Cole had given it to him when he had run out of anything else to give. Papoot had looked longingly at the Governor's hand-carved desk, but the Gov had made like he didn't notice.

Not that the Gov didn't owe Papoot Gaspard! The first time Cole ran for office, Papoot had delivered Richelieu Parish against over-whelming odds. In fact, Richelieu had put Cole over the top.

This particular debt had been repaid thousands of times, but still the payment would go on forever. There was no getting through with Papoot Gaspard. When you owed him, the debt lasted until one of you died. Richard W. Cole fervently hoped that it would be Papoot.

Moose sat opposite Papoot in one of those uncomfortable chairs. He was not there because he had anything to contribute but because Papoot loved an audience. And you had to give it to Moose, he didn't say anything unless asked, and Papoot almost never asked him any-thing. He was a wonderful mix of a live body and nothing—the per-fect audience. And even, upon Papoot's instructions, a deadly one.

Papoot pushed his Panama back on his pink baby face, sat back in Richard W. Cole's chair, and laced his fingers over his belly. "He's gon' try to fuck me. It was plain as your nose. I know that long-legged bas-tard like I know me, and there's a fuckin' in the air. Fuckin' old Papoot. You believe he's gonna get away with it?"

Moose knew better than to answer. Papoot was asking himself the question. And he answered it. "Hee, hee! Hee, hee!"

BeBe wasn't as sad as she thought she'd be. She knew the truth, and for her that was not only a relief but a starting point. She knew that she was not particularly bright. It seemed she always needed advice, and because she had no ego, she had never hesitated seeking it. Her first thought was to turn to her brother, but Justin was way too straitlaced for something as embarrassing as this. He'd tell her to make a novena, or say a hundred Hail Marys. She would do that too, of course. She believed in the rites of the Church, and she enjoyed a personal relationship with the Blessed Virgin, whom she looked upon as an older sister. But at this point, she veered from doctrine and found refuge in one of her oldest clichés: God helps those who help themselves.

She would talk to Motile, her daddy's old colored woman who had just about raised her and Justin; she believed in Motile too. Motile would never lie to her. BeBe called her Mama Motile, and loved to have the old woman hug her to her breast. There was as much comfort there as there was in Mass. The old woman smelt like Octagon soap and Evening in Paris face powder, and her white uniform was always crisp with starch. She called BeBe her "little bird." BeBe had been a baby when Annabelle had come up dry, and Motile had let her suckle along with her own Junius, long departed for Detroit. Junius wasn't at all like his mama or his daddy, and when he wrote a letter home he talked about "change." Nobody was exactly sure what he wanted to change, but the word frightened them. Change from what? Change to what? Things had always been a certain way, and they weren't going to change. Just the thought of it was scary. Motile wished Junius would write about his kinfolks he was living with while he worked at one of those big auto plants. But he never did. It was like they didn't exist. "Change." Junius had gone a little crazy over change. And for what? There was a peculiar security in the sameness of things continuing the way they had always been.

Motile worked seven days a week for Papoot. The work wasn't hard—not no more. She had three helpers, two maids and a yard man. It was like she was the boss, and indeed often when she was alone in the big house, she thought of herself in that way: the boss! She liked the word, even though she knew it was a big joke.

The Senator took wonderful care of her, and she knew that when she was too old to work (about a year off), she would go right on getting her paycheck as always! That, her Social Security, and old age pension would make her richer than she had ever been. She would tend her garden (the Senator said she was the best gardener in all

Louisiana). Her husband, Sylvester, would go right on playing domi-
noes with his buddies at the Chatter Box Café in colored town. They
would have no worries except for Junius and that word: *change*. It
was his word, because nobody else used it, or sure no other colored
person. They knew their place and did just fine. The good ones
(those who obeyed) were well treated, never abused. The few bad
ones (winos, loudmouths, would-be uppities) had a pretty rough go
of it, and spent a lot of time in jail. Bobby wasn't much on them being
slapped around, but most had received at least a couple of knots on
the head from a deputy's nightstick. They deserved it and didn't com-
plain, or else they got more of the same. Richelieu had never had a
lynching. The Cajuns weren't prepared to go that far.

BeBe took a bath, watched her big breasts float in the soapy water,
and thought they hadn't always been that way. Bobby used to not be
able to leave them alone, and she would slap his hands and playfully
say, "You greedy, yeah?" She couldn't remember when she had let herself go—that's how she thought of it—and started eating everything
in sight. She could eat a whole bowl of potato salad all by herself. She
could put away a pineapple upside-down cake all by herself, and had
done it, in shame. This she did before Bobby came home, so that
when they sat down at the table she didn't eat any more than he did.
Bobby had never said anything about her weight, though Papoot
used to. "Your ass is getting' bigger than the courthouse! How you
gon' keep a man?" he'd say. This kind of talk hurt her, but not enough
to make her stop. Thinking about it now made her hungry, and she
decided to make herself a bread pudding that very day, with day-old
stale bread. That was the best of all. She'd do that later. First, go see
Motile. She needed a hugging for sure.

And more.

Motile was watching the two maids clean the house, and outside the
yard man was mowing the huge yard. Motile gave BeBe a hug, and

they sat at the breakfast table, where Motile handed her a big cup of hot coffee with a lot of heavy cream and four teaspoons of sugar, just the way she liked it. "Wass the matter with my little bird?"

Suddenly BeBe was ashamed. This was not something you talked about—your husband making a mess in his pants! "Everythin's fine," she lied, but a tear made its way from her eyes. Motile went to her and hugged her tight. "Tell Motile, li'l bird."

She looked up into the black and ancient face. "Bobby's got a woman. A whore."

"Mr. Bobby with a whore? Now that don't sound like Mr. Bobby."

"Not a official one. Not from Misty's. Zeke Daigle's daughter."

"How she look?"

"All right," she began, then buried her face in her arms. "She's gorgeous! And young! Younger than me, for sure."

"You know that somethin's goin' on for a fack?"

"Lipstick, and oh, Motile, I'm so ashamed, he did bad in his pants."

"My God," the old woman exclaimed, confused.

"Uh-uh, the other. Through his pee-pee."

"Oh, Jesus."

"Maybe I ought to go tell Justin. What you think? He's a priest."

"What Justin knows about mens and womens?" replied Motile, who was a devout Baptist. "He ain't never married and never gon' be. No. Justin don't know no more than you and me. Justin just tell you to say your prayers, but Jesus ain't got time to think about mens and their pee-pees."

"Tell me what to do. I feel desperate, you know?"

Motile nodded and brought BeBe some more coffee. BeBe added a little cream, stirred it, and waited. Motile walked about the kitchen, wiping her hands on her white apron. She sat down, her hand covering BeBe's on the checkered tabletop.

"If it was me, I'd go see MaMa Seego."

BeBe was shocked. "A traiteur, Motile? I'm a Christian! I made my communion. You was there!"

Motile shook her head. "MaMa Seego's not no traiteur, she don' practice medicine. MaMa Seego be voodoo!"

"What would Justin say? Oh, Lord!"

"He don' have to know."

"Oh, yeah. I got to go to confession. I sure wouldn't want that on my soul. You think I want to burn in Hell for all times? Not me. Uh-uh."

"I know, sugar, but I know MaMa Seego has helped a lot of wom-ens whose men's stickin' it where it don't belong. A lot of white wom-ens."

"I'm desperate."

Motile made no response. She had given the best advice she had to offer. BeBe stood. "Okay. Let her know I'm comin', Motile. It seems to me I ain't got no choice."

Motile nodded. Both women were ashamed. They avoided each other's eyes.

Her high heels made a clicking sound on Richelieu High's polished floors. The school was now officially closed for the summer, and she and a janitor pushing a mop seemed its only occupants. She passed the lockers that lined the wall, found 93, hers so long ago, touched it, and walked to the frosted glass door that read PRINCIPAL.

Mr. Suire sat behind his same old desk, and she was shocked at his loss of hair; it was now a fringe about a much-wrinkled forehead. His eyebrows were bushy, and he wore his seersucker suit like always. That hadn't changed. There were gravy stains on his blue necktie, which had an inordinately big knot. His collar was frayed. Teachers rather than principals received most of the money in Richelieu Parish, and Mr. Suire supplemented his income by building little odds and ends tables, which he sold for five bucks apiece.

He had come to Richelieu from Elton, Louisiana, a young teacher with a degree in agriculture from Southwestern Louisiana Institute in

Lafayette. Teaching jobs were not that easy to get in those days, and once placed there, he never left. He was a better than average teacher and after forty years had been named principal. His life's ambition was realized, and he wished that his mama and papa had live to see how wonderfully he'd made it.

He stood and extended a hand, which she took between hers. "Why little Ruth Ann, look what a beauty you've become. I'm sorry about Zeke. A good and dear man. Well! Welcome back to Richelieu High. I used to go upstairs every day to the library to read *The Times-Picayune* just to keep up with your wonderful writing. You're our outstanding graduate. No doubt about that."

"I got a wonderful foundation here. This was, is, a good school, Mr. Suire."

He beamed. "We try, we try. Now, what brings you back to us? I'm much too modest to think that it could be to see 'old man Suire.' A little joke to be sure."

"It's wonderful seeing you, Mr. Suire, but no, that isn't it. I wanted to talk with you about Aristede Brouliette, Jr."

Mr. Suire blinked, then realized who she was referring to. "Ti Boy," he whispered. "I don't understand. It's a tragedy, a true tragedy. He was a sweet and good child. I don't know who loved him more, his little classmates or the faculty. He was good. Ti Boy was a gentle, good boy. We'll miss him. But . . ."

"Mr. Suire, I'm not satisfied how Ti Boy died."

"*You're* not?"

"As a reporter."

"Dear me."

"I am, you know. And the *Gazette* is a newspaper."

"I read it religiously, as does Mrs. Suire. Zeke always sent the school a copy free. After an appropriate time, I take it home. We read it from top to bottom. Mrs. Suire loves the recipes and patterns, and I must admit I find the sports coverage admirable. She made a doily."

"I beg your pardon?"

"From the patterns!"

"Oh."

He seemed frightened, like he was talking about anything that might delay what she wanted to ask. "I can't imagine how I could add anything to the tragedy, happens every year, every hunting season, either in a duck blind or . . ."

"But this wasn't. This was in the summer. There was no hunting season and none coming up for months."

"Oh."

"Mr. Suire, was Ti Boy a happy child?"

"Oh, yes! By all means. Always a big smile on his face, a happy word for everyone. I can still see him on his bicycle, wind blowing in his hair as he zoomed down the street to deliver his papers. It's so sad."

"May I see his records?"

Now his face was sad. "I'm afraid that's confidential."

"I beg your pardon?"

He looked afraid. "Not without his parents' permission. Oh yes. That's the school board's rules. Always has been."

"No one would have to know I saw them."

He was shocked. "Ruth Ann!"

"No way, huh?"

He was adamant. "Absolutely not."

She stood. "You haven't been much help, Mr. Suire. In fact, none."

"Don't get that haughty New Orleans attitude with me, young lady. You're in my office."

"I'm sorry. And mystified. It's not like I requested the plans for the Normandy Invasion. A dead child's records. Well . . ." She stood at the door.

"What will you do?" he asked.

I'm not sure it's any of your goddamn business, she was about to say, but he looked so worn and pitiful, she said instead, "I've no idea."

"We're very proud of you," he said.

"Sure," she answered and closed the door behind her.

She stood by the wall, off to the side of the frosted glass, and pressed her ear to it. She heard him pick up the phone and dial.

"Mr. Perrault, please. Hurphy? Suire. Ruth Ann Daigle was here. She just this minute left. Asking about Ti Boy. Of course I didn't. I'm not a fool, you know, I'm an educator. Apologies accepted. Just this an' that. Nothing specific. Oh, she wanted to see his records. Of course I didn't! That's against the law! Isn't it? I thought so. Hurphy, I hate this. I know you do. Burn his records? No. I won't do that. I won't violate the law, Hurphy, not for anyone. Sorry. The answer is no! Yes I will. Good-bye." She heard him hang up the phone as she tiptoed down the long and empty hall.

Chapter 10

He heard confessions. They were sad, amusing, a few even shocking, but mostly repetitious, particularly those of the old folks who'd forgotten their patron saints' day of celebration or had been cross with a well-meaning child or grandchild. On these, he could barely keep awake. True, they were endearing, and also quaint, as their sins hadn't kept up with modern times, but he noted, they were still sinning.

He heard a lot about temptation, and made silent bets with himself whether or not his parishioners would be able to withstand it. He usually won his bets; they almost always gave in. Then came shame—promises to Jesus (through him) that they would never do that again. Temptation was man's true spiritual downfall. God, the right way, almost never won.

Temptations of the flesh particularly fascinated him. During those confessions he would listen to the breathing on the other side of the tiny confessional. Some quite obviously even became aroused as they whispered that they'd spied on a nubile daughter in the bathroom or rubbed against the babysitter's tits, by accident, of course.

Others were regularly stealing from employers: "It was my boss's fault, all that cash sitting there day after day, what did he expect me to do?" These words would be shouted in anger at the employer's stupidity. The very idea!

Indignant people amused him most. They were always guilty, yet despised anyone who knew it or even hinted that he did. "He's no good, Father. Just no good." And jealous! They were indignant that someone had more of something than them, had gotten the best of a deal, made more money, got more loving. They smoldered inside the confessional, and he believed that if they did not have this weekly opportunity to let off steam, some would blow their heads off. In fact, a few had.

Maybe some should blow their heads off, he thought, or take too many sleeping pills or drive off a bridge or put cellophane bags over their heads. "Go away!" he'd like to have shouted through the grille.

He admitted it. The grind, over and over, repetition of the same stupid wrongs, committed with full knowledge that they were doing abominations, had worn him down, and he no longer felt pity. None. Compassion had seeped out of him on a river of evil. Did anyone have any idea how much evil there was out there? It still astounded him! Why, the world was awash in it.

Only little children were innocent. Very little children. Puberty was the gateway to Hell, that was a given. That they raced through that doorway still astonished him.

And when old age overtook them, and they could no longer dip into all that wet horror, they still talked about it, all but smacking their rubbery lips in memory of their foul deeds. It went with them to the grave, molded with them in the earth, with bugs feeding on them and worms crawling in and out their eye sockets.

The image was both horrible and delicious. It was something he would like to watch while sipping a good glass of port. Sit quietly and watch. He had little more to say to any of them. As a young priest he'd said a lot, stormed and railed, raged and blustered against their sins. Meanwhile the people on the other side sat quietly, waiting for him to assign their penitence. Of course, they hadn't heard a word.

"Say ten Hail Marys . . ."

"Ten?" they asked. They expected more, the sin must have been bigger.

"Every morning, ten at noon, and ten in the evening at bedtime. And do not touch alcohol for a month. You understand that? You must give something up for what you've done. Amen. Go with God."

He smiled. They had gagged at that little alcohol addition. He'd got 'em right on target there. It would do them good. They were all souses, winos, alcoholics, drunkards, stumbling into the confessional. He wished he could put into effect a parishwide ban on drinking. No drinking every other month. It wouldn't work, of course. Couldn't be enforced. They'd cheat, even think about lynching him, their priest. They didn't fool him.

After confession, he drove home for a supper left to him by BeBe, roast beef and gravy, eggplant casserole, and a green salad full of huge black and green pitted olives. BeBe knew food. And she was very thoughtful—she deserved more, she deserved better. With supper he drank half a bottle of Spanish port, wiped his mouth with a big linen napkin, and then got into his car, a simple blue Plymouth, befitting a parish priest. A humble parish priest, thank you!

The ride to Lafayette was an easy one, and he drove slowly, not turning on CAJN (in a mile or two he could pick up KVOL in Lafayette). He could not listen to Na Na, who at this very moment was desperately trying to work out a ménage à trois with his lawful wedded wife, De De, and a prostitute from the Paradise Inn. Good God almighty!

Na Na had carefully and intensely explained in the confessional, like he was selling radio spots, that the arrangement was not sexual, wouldn't be sexual. She would be their little girl. As he listened, the priest had felt bile coming up from his stomach, and he had to fight down vomiting. He had squeezed his hands until his nails dug into his palms, raising blood, as this imbecile talked on and on about how it would be wonderful, even spiritual.

Justin thought he'd take care of that: "You, your wife, and this woman will all burn in Hell, and all the prayers ever uttered won't save your wretched souls." Na Na had said, "Love can overcome anything." And the priest had roared, "Antichrist! Get out of here, this minute, and don't come back until you've gotten right with your Maker." He could still hear Na Na fleeing up the aisle. He would have liked to chase him, beating him when he caught him.

He turned on KVOL, tuning in soft dance music, which he hummed to. It relaxed him and somehow lessened the dread he felt. The clock on the dashboard said he was right on time as he drew up into the parking lot of St. John Cathedral and parked his car beneath a giant oak, whose extended arms made him think of God. There were a few horse-and-buggies parked there, old people from the country coming to town to make their novenas. All those prayers floating upward, he thought, like multicolored balloons, up, up, up. In his mind they burst as he went into church and, praise God, saw none of them to whom he had to speak. "Good evening, Father, blah, blah, blah."

Father Soulier was an elderly priest, a joke really, heading down the stretch, going deaf. For all of these reasons Justin had carefully selected him as his confessor. He certainly didn't need some wiseass full of pat answers, none of them applicable to someone at his level. That was how he thought of his position, intellectually and in life: a level, another one, beneath Heaven to be sure (I am a modest man), but definitely up beyond most men. For the life of him, he could not think of anyone else who shared that exalted place, and he did try. Alas, there were none. Oh, how he wished he could discover another, share language that no one else could understand. Oh yes! He would have liked to talk about what he thought of as his distinguishing characteristics. Modestly he thought of them as his "little ways" and recognized the quaintness of this description, still more proof when you came right down to it that he was a man who possessed no ego. None!

He never had had any. So unlike the dolts of his experience. As a mere child he had recognized his differences from them—them being everybody else. Not that this gave him any pleasure; he was too simple (his word) for that. It was not that he felt better than anyone, just different. Though in his youth, he could not have said how.

In Rome he had found his answer. And rather than look upon it with trepidation, he felt that he had been given a mighty cross, a glorious one, to bear all his life. Thus he secretly felt Godlike. He was being crucified every day of his life, and he took quiet pride in the fact that he bore this anguish without complaint. Bleeding, yes, bleeding, and pain beyond pain, but all of it borne without an utterance for pity.

And though he tried not to think about it, he knew that in some way he was even better than Christ. For had not Christ cried to Heaven to his Father, "Why has thou forsaken me?"

He had never made such a plea, such an accusation. Perhaps this was his true glory! To bear excruciating pain became thus not a punishment but a validation of how he saw himself. And he secretly wondered—did this make him a saint?

As Justin sat in the confessional, he could tell that Father Soulier had the sniffles, and this disgusted him. He did not need a summer cold.

"Forgive me, Father, for I have sinned."

Sniffle. Sniffle. God with a head cold!

"Yes, my son?" the old priest's voice quivered. Perhaps he was losing that too, along with his meager brain.

"I haven't done it again, if that's what you're wondering." He did not speak to old Soulier as a penitent but as a fellow professional, like a couple of surgeons discussing someone's gallbladder.

The priest wasn't helping him much and greeted this statement with silence.

"Probably never shall again. Oh no, that's quite behind me."

"How do you know?" stupid old Soulier asked.

"The desire has left me. Vanished. Perhaps, dare I say, a miracle?"

No answer from Soulier. Miracles had to be thousands of years old with all participants rotting in the ground to arouse this priest's interest. Really, he had been too long at the fair.

"How do you know?"

Oh, good God! He felt belligerent. "How do I know? Is that your question? Well, quite obviously I know because I know." It was a simple declaration and appealed to him immensely, and he made a mental note to remember it.

"Are there any . . . is there any temptation around you?"

"Temptation? You mean . . . Why, I've never thought about it. Hm, let me see. No, I don't believe there is."

"And if there was?"

"But there isn't!"

"But there will be. There will be other altar boys."

"I'm obviously not communicating! I'm through! Finis! Over! Done with!"

"My brother in Christ, you need help."

"Just what do you think I'm doing here now, Father?"

"It is beyond me. I am a simple man."

You can say that again, Justin thought.

"A child is dead." The old priest's voice was calm.

There it was. Out on the table. Spoken aloud.

"I did not kill him."

Silence.

"I was as shocked at his death as anyone. I had no idea."

"I believe that. But that's the problem. You are not looking at what you are doing and the consequences of your acts."

"It was a sudden thing. Don't you see, I didn't plan it, for heaven's sake!"

"But it happened more than once."

"I . . . yes."

"Many times."

"I suppose. But he liked it. Encouraged it. May I speak frankly?"

"If not here, where?"

Whispered: "He seduced me."

"He was a child and you are a man. He was a sheep and you were his shepherd."

"I was a man!"

"No! You are a priest."

Silence.

"Is that it?"

"That's it."

"No Hail Marys? No Our Fathers?"

"No."

"Will you pray for my forgiveness?"

"I can't."

"Well then . . ."

The old priest heard him leave the confessional and depart. He wiped his wet nose with a soiled handkerchief. He felt miserable. After all these years he had come face-to-face with something for which he had no preparation, and he had heard every sin. There were no new sins, just repetitions, although that made them no less. But a priest. The sins of a priest, resulting in a death. Did that make him a murderer? Suddenly Soulier felt older than he was. Experience had not prepared him for this. If he was younger, maybe, just maybe, he could cope, would know what to do. For the first time in his adult life, he felt dirty, like his handkerchief.

For several minutes he sat there hunched over, looking much like an old overcoat tossed into a closet corner. Finally he left the confessional, moved slowly to the font, dipped his fingers in consecrated water, and made the sign of the cross. For the first time in a very long time, however, he did not feel the sweet, soothing balm of healing. His spirits did not soar, lifting the ugliness from him and leaving him restored. Instead his burden only seemed to grow heavier.

Father Soulier knew what to do. He would make an appointment to see the Right Reverend Peter Paul Dupuis, Bishop of Richelieu.

He would have the answer.

Finally Father Soulier felt restored.

Chapter 11

The midday sun that could bake them in their own juices had not yet reached that intensity when she parked in front of Hurphy's offices. Inside were thick carpets, a huge photograph of Bishop Peter Paul Dupuis, and certificates attesting to Hurphy being a graduate of the LSU Law School as well as a special tax school in Chicago. There was also a certificate in Latin, with many filigrees, stating to all the world that Pope Pius himself had named Hurphy a Knight of St. Gregory. And there was a picture of Anita and Hurphy Jr., taken by a prominent photographer in Lafayette who specialized in baby pictures.

The furniture was rich and modern, further attestation to Hurphy's wealth. The current issue of *The Saturday Evening Post* lay on a coffee table next to a vase of fresh azaleas. A pretty receptionist sat behind a small desk, buffing her long pink fingernails.

"Is Mr. Perrault in?"

"Who shall I say wants to see him?"

"Ruth Ann Daigle, from the *Gazette.*"

Hurphy himself came out to greet her, took her hand between both of his, spoke warmly. "Ruth Ann, you're even more beautiful, if that's possible. Come in, come in. We'll sit in the library, more cozy."

The library was white, with rich blue drapes. Its walls were lined with books, and there was a big oak conference table surrounded by expensive chairs. Hurphy motioned her into one and sat next to her.

"Ruth Ann, how about some coffee? We grind our own beans. Colombian. Now if someone demands Mello Joy, why we have that too."

Ruth Ann thanked him but declined. He was still smiling when she removed pen and steno pad from her purse.

"An official visit?"

She nodded. He was so friendly and gracious. Before she could begin, he inquired about Zeke, expressed what appeared to be genuine sorrow at his sad state, and offered any help he could give. "Once in a while, we lawyers come in handy."

"I may need you, Hurphy. Zeke's got a note coming due at the First National."

"Just say the word," he said and patted her hand. "Zeke has been nothing but a positive influence in this community, and helping the Daigles will be my pleasure. I know Big Shot will work with us. Your situation is hardly normal."

Tears came into her eyes, and he handed her his snowy white handkerchief. "You're very kind," she said, then cleared her throat. "Hurphy, the reason I'm bothering you is that I'd like to speak with Hurphy Jr. He served with Ti Boy as an altar boy. I'm doing a little research into Ti Boy's death."

"That's what I heard," he said mildly, nodding.

"I won't disturb Hurphy Jr., just ask him about Ti Boy's frame of mind."

"Have you had any psychiatric training, Ruth Ann?"

"Have I what?"

"Well, it seems to me that only a trained clinician, say a social worker or psychologist, people trained in that very rigid discipline, as you've been educated in journalism, can make a determination about a person's mental state."

"You mean I don't have the right to ask if he was happy or unhappy? If his moods had changed? These questions hardly take a degree in psychology, Hurphy. They get asked all the time by reporters like me."

"Of course you have the right, Ruth Ann, of course. Dear me, I'm afraid I'm thinking like the fuddy duddy lawyer I am."

"This isn't a court of law."

He patted her hand, a gesture that was becoming annoying. "Of course not."

Then they sat there like chess players studying the board. Finally she asked, "Well, may I?"

Hurphy blinked but continued smiling. "May you what?"

"See Hurphy Jr.?"

"Of course you could. If he was here. But Hurphy Jr. is off to summer camp in Maine. Anita felt, and I must say I concurred that it was high time for that young man to see some of the outside world. Someplace other than dear old Richelieu."

"When will he return?"

"In September, for school. If he does."

"If he does?"

"Anita and I are considering letting him stay up there, at a very excellent boarding school. It's our dream that Hurphy Jr. will go to one of those Ivy League colleges. But we're realistic. He's going to need no small amount of preparation."

"So, he could be gone for . . ."

Hurphy looked sad. "We miss him already."

She stood, and he pointed to her chair. "Stay for just a moment, Ruth Ann." She sat back down. "Good. Can an old family friend speak with you frankly? I've been Zeke's attorney for, oh, twenty-five years. But more, I've been his friend. And that applies to you, too, Ruth Ann. I want you to feel free to lean on me. We do want to keep the *Gazette* in the Daigle family, where it belongs."

"My father trusted you."

"And you, Ruth Ann?"

She hesitated, thought, What the hell, and said, "I'm no longer sure, Hurphy."

"And all over a tragic gun accident?"

"I'm not convinced it was. The more doors get slammed in my face, school records I can't see, witnesses out of town for a year, the more I feel I may be on to something. That's how reporters feel, Hurphy."

"Something?"

"Ti Boy may have taken his own life."

"Back to psychiatry, Ruth Ann." He shook his head sadly.

"Intuition."

He sighed. His face was tired and troubled. "As your lawyer . . . I am your lawyer?"

"Of course."

"And as your friend, I do qualify?"

"Oh don't be ridiculous, Hurphy. My father swore by you."

"Just checking. I'm going to give you some advice. Now when a lawyer gives that, and doesn't charge you for it, you have every right to question it. Free things usually aren't, are they? But this is from the heart, as a friend, and from the brain, as a lawyer, and isn't that a combination? Ruth Ann, leave it be."

"Leave it be?" she asked, wanting to goad him into being explicit.

"Drop this investigation."

"Why?"

"You're going to hurt our little community. Our sweet and lovely Richelieu. And Ruth Ann, you're going to hurt yourself."

"Exactly how? I'm a reporter. I do have constitutional rights. And I'm afraid I have a kind of moral imperative. Does that sound presumptuous?"

"Indeed you do have constitutional rights. The moral imperative, your driving force, is a little abstract."

"I don't think I can stop, Hurphy."

"Oh dear me. I'm so sorry. I think you're making a big mistake. I believe you're going to change the fabric of all our lives, particularly your own, and I'm afraid we're all going to pay for it."

"Like Ti Boy did?"

For the first time, there was a little steel in his voice. He wasn't good old Hurphy. He was Hurphy Perrault, attorney at law. "So be it. My conscience is clear. I tried to protect you."

"And who else, Hurphy?"

"Good-bye, Ruth Ann."

Hurphy watched her depart, his face downcast. He felt sorry for her, she was carrying a terrible load. About once a week he visited Zeke, and it was like spending time alone. Hurphy stood, ran a hand along the fine bindings of some law books, sat back down, this time at the head of the conference table.

Anita had hated Hurphy Jr. leaving. "For what?" she asked in a voice that was always an introduction to hysteria. "Because I say so" had been his first ploy. Not too successful. "You," she said in that voice that said "You shit." Then the tears and screaming, a weak punch or two, an insult about his clubfoot. "Your mind is clubbed too!" Then she'd calmed down. He promised a new convertible when they came out. It ended up with them in bed, her on top, which he dearly loved.

Hurphy Jr. hadn't taken the news too well either. "Maine? What I got to do in Maine?" "Precisely for the kind of question you just asked, 'What I got to do in Maine?' It's illiterate and ignorant. Time you had some real education."

"At a camp? I'm gonna be educated at a camp?"

Hurphy folded his arms, which meant end of conversation. Hurphy Jr. went off to get sympathy from Anita, who was very practical and said, "It's for your own good." And that was that.

Until Ruth Ann Daigle came calling.

Hurphy drummed his fingers on the tabletop. Thinking. Ruth Ann wasn't going away, of this he had no doubt. She was forcing him into a corner, which he despised. After all, she was right! Not that it had a whole lot to do with things. There was always the real world, which didn't make allowances for abstractions like that, things like right and wrong. He reached for a legal pad and wrote on it:

Fact: If Ruth Ann got to the bottom of things (a pretty good word, *things*), she would hurt a lot of people, only one of whom was guilty. Thus, a lot of innocent people would be destroyed.

Fact: $600,000 (that was what the diocese business was worth to him a year).

Fact: All parties were looking to him to get rid of this mess. They would not be surprised that he would bill handsomely for these services. The invoice would simply read "Legal Services," and no further explanation would be forthcoming or expected. God forbid that Details were so messy.

Fact: He would be saving his beloved Church in this parish and God knows where else.

Then he wrote in capital letters:

CONCLUSION: Stop Ruth Ann.

He studied the page, didn't like what he had written. He was a thinking creature, perhaps even a good man, but he could find nothing he disagreed with. He tore the page into tiny fragments and threw them into a waste container. He stood, stretched, and reached for a telephone. "Big Shot? Hurphy. Can you meet me at One Lung's? We better have a quick cup of coffee. I'm going now."

He and the banker sat at a table. One Lung served them, wanted to have a big conversation about an upcoming supper ("They gon' have barbecued steaks an' rice dressing with eggplant"), but they discouraged him, so he moved off, leaving them with one hearty cough.

The banker had a deviated septum, and his breathing punctuated Hurphy's quiet but intense words. He listened, face impassive. When Hurphy finished, Big Shot said, "Jesus Christ, Hurphy!" Hurphy nodded. He felt exactly the same way. "What you gonna do?" Big Shot asked.

Hurphy got to the point. "What *we're* gonna do, Big Shot. Us. You and me. Good Catholics."

Big Shot nodded. "I'm a good Catholic, Hurphy, but I don't make money on the Church like you do. I know what you got in my bank, and I'm sure it's a lot less than what you got in the Guaranty in Lafayette."

Hurphy started to deny this, but he needed the other man. "A good bit less."

Big Shot whistled softly. "You a rich man, Hurphy."

"Not as rich as you, Big Shot."

"Thass true, but you gettin' there." And Big Shot sat. Waiting.

"Tell you what, Big Shot. I'll move my account to the First National, but I need your help."

"A little more, Hurphy, a little more."

"God, but you're tough, Big Shot!"

"Me? Why no, not at all. But I'm a businessman for sure."

"What do you want?"

"I want a little diocese money, and I want it in a noninterest-bearing account."

"You've already got—"

"More."

"How much more, Big Shot?"

"About half a million, and I want it left in there for three years."

"They won't do that!"

"Well, then let's talk about something else. Did you hear—"

"All right."

"When?"

"A week. I'll need a week."

Big Shot extended a hand, and they shook. "A week," he said.

"Now here's what I need. I want you to call Zeke's note."

"I should have asked for more," Big Shot said. "The guy's a dying vegetable."

"It doesn't give me any pleasure either, Big Shot. Zeke was my friend."

Big Shot was breathing heavy. "Okay. Deal."

"When?" Hurphy asked.

"A week, when we get that deposit."

"Don't you trust me, Big Shot?"

"Ah don' trust nobody."

"Okay." He started to get up when Big Shot put a hand on his arm, forcing him to sit back down. Behind the counter One Lung eyed them jealously. He could tell something big was up and wanted to be in on it, but nothing more was offered.

Big Shot said, "And what about that fellow, what gon' be done about him? You can't have no maniac runnin' around loose in Richelieu with our kids."

Hurphy said, "You're telling me? My son's an altar boy, for Christ's sake!"

Big Shot asked, "So what you gon' do, Hurphy? Shuttin' it up's just half the job."

"I don't know. I really don't. I'll have to talk to two people about that."

"His daddy?"

"Oh hell no. Papoot would flip out. He might die on me. Moose would shoot me for sure."

"You don't think he knows?"

"Absolutely not. Definitely not!"

"So who?"

Hurphy shielded his mouth from One Lung, who was leaning over the counter in an attempt to hear. "The Bishop and Bobby."

"Makes sense."

Hurphy stood and left the poolroom.

One Lung was quickly at the table. "Whew! That looked big for sure!"

"It is big. Can I trust you?"

One Lung lifted a paw in an oath. "I swear to living Gawd, Big Shot."

"The diocese is gon' build a TB hospital right here in Richelieu, and we gon' stick you ass in it!"

Alarm on his face, One Lung said, "Don' joke like that, Big Shot. Jesus Christ!"

"Then mind you own business, One Lung!"

Chapter 12

Governor Richard W. Cole's waiting room was a big receptacle, filled to the brim with citizens in various stages of desperation, or greed, wanting something. Some sat, some stood, occasionally someone slept on the floor. Babies wailed, people softly cursed, more than a few moaned, well-dressed bond salesmen from New York whispered quietly to a Senator who had gotten them the appointment (for a piece of the action). All despised the Governor in anticipation of not getting what they wanted (deserved!). In their own minds, they already had been let down by him; by Louisiana; by the United States of America; by their families (especially mates, but children were not excluded); by employers, co-workers, neighbors, state and federal agencies, God—but most of all by Richard W. Cole. Each felt, would take an oath, that he had personally lied to them, made them a promise unkept.

State policemen in their sharp blue uniforms stood about, lest someone start shooting or screaming hysterically. Regular screaming was acceptable. It was when the octave climbed and spittle flew that the Governor's security detail eased a person out into the hall with soothing words. Truth was these troopers also despised the Governor. They had been promised promotions, being stationed closer to home; a job for their daddy, perhaps on a road crew; a pay raise; more pension; better cruisers; better weapons.

There were a handful of unusual cases. Like the aged politico who had in fact been promised that a highway would be named after him, or "jus' a li'l piece of the road," and who had come to Cole's office every day since inauguration. No one had the nerve to tell the old gentleman that in Louisiana the law prohibited anything being named for a living person. He would just have to die, but how do you tell someone that?

A blowsy bleached blonde, her hair in pigtails, sat next to her mother; fat and grim, they looked like Buddhas, and they held twin babies. Her husband was on Angola's death row; all appeals had been exhausted, except for this final one, the Governor. How would he tell her that her husband would have to fry in the electric chair in exactly eight days for killing and raping two teenagers? Her appeal: "He's a good husband and father, he never beat us, but when he gets on that Four Roses, he can't help hisself."

A lot of contractors, big and small, sat with various state representatives and senators (their sponsors), eager to get in on state contracts which by law were supposed to be awarded to the lowest bidder, in public. But everyone knew that was a little inside joke. Them that paid, played. They wanted to sell shell, concrete, insurance, electric supplies; they wanted to sell everything, and oh, but the state was a good, a big buyer. And the state paid. No bullshitting around. And if your money was sometimes late in coming, your sponsor brought a little something to an appropriate official, and just like that, your money came in the mail the next day! Hell, you could go get it yourself that day!

Who you knew, that was what counted. You were in this invisible loop, or you might as well not exist. If you knew the right person, if you had the dough, nothing was impossible. No scheme was too far-fetched, no dream too bizarre to escape possibility.

Did Richard W. Cole participate in all these wheelings and dealings? No. He was basically a straight man. Did he know that they were going on? Absolutely. They were the way of life, and if you wanted to remain in office, you didn't get in the way.

Louisiana had tried a reform governor or two, and then couldn't wait to get rid of them. They were too dull. And they stopped commerce cold. The legislature, all those "sponsors," killed their programs; business, cut out of big contracts with little expected in the way of performance, hated these "do-gooders" because their costs went up and their profits went down, and someone was always checking on them, for God's sake. The average citizens wanted, and enjoyed, rascals.

Finally they were supported only by other do-gooders, their families, and the state's big newspaper, which wrote boring editorials about "finally, a good moral climate," like anybody gave a damn! Like anybody read the editorial page!

The Cajuns had said it best, "Laissez les bon temps roulez!"—let the good times roll!—and they did. Besides, Louisiana had oil, and the wells would never run dry. Big checks from Texaco would never stop rolling into the state coffers, and thus taxes would never go up. Louisianians did not believe in taxes, particularly on a man's home. No taxes on your home was called Homestead Exemption, and God help any politician foolish enough to suggest that perhaps citizens might consider a tiny tax. He was obviously a nut. Destined for nothingness.

It was into this brew that Papoot Gaspard, accompanied by Moose in a yellow sport coat that he always wore to Baton Rouge, and carrying a huge cardboard box, descended.

Papoot shook every hand in the waiting room. Even the hands of those who were screaming. Everybody knew him, and more than a few fantasized him as their Governor: Wasn't he for the little people? You could hear his laugh, his "Hee, hee!" bouncing off walls and ceiling; it was like Christmas had suddenly come as some whispered in his ear little favors they wanted, and they nudged each other at how he never took a note yet could remember every need, want, and desire.

Moose beamed and told a state trooper, "Thass mah main man!"

Inside the Governor's office, Billy Simms stood by Richard W. Cole's desk holding the day's schedule. The two men listened quietly to the moaning outside, the anger, barely contained.

Cole shook his head. "They're restless."

"Same old thing," Simms replied.

"The woman outside?" Cole asked.

Simms nodded. "I hate that. Can't do anything for her."

"He's guilty as all get out," Cole said.

Simms said, "She's brought the twins and mom."

"Oh, good God! Don't let the babies in. I can't handle that."

"Yessir."

Putting off the inevitable as long as he could, Cole asked Simms, who made every party, knew every scandal, was in on every so-called secret, "Anything new? Tell me something, Billy. Tell me something good. I need to laugh."

Simms said, "Matter of fact, there is. You know Wally? Old Wally runs the motor pool?"

"Sure I know Wally. Big ladies man."

"Well, Wally's been tapping his secretary for years. She's a looker, big-titted gal, and I don't believe I could turn that down myself, well . . ."

"Shame on you, Billy! You'd screw her?" Cole asked.

"No quicker than I could draw my ass back," Simms replied, and the two laughed. "Well, Wally's on top of her on top of his desk, going at it, and she begins to scream, I mean really scream; and Wally says to himself, I am the world's number-one lover, better than Errol Flynn. Then it dawns on him that this gal's really screaming, I mean shouting her guts out. Don't you know they'd broken the glass desktop and there's a big piece of glass sticking in her ass! The desk's covered with blood! Can you beat that?" The two roared with laughter, and the Governor had to wipe his eyes with a handkerchief.

Amid this merriment, the door burst open with a bang, and Simms thought, Oh my God, an assassination!

But it wasn't. Close, but not quite, as Papoot entered accompanied by Moose and the big cardboard box, all smiles. Moose placed the box on the Governor's desk, and Cole asked, "Not ticking, is it?" Everyone laughed, and Moose and Simms slipped from the room.

Cole and Papoot embraced warmly, like brothers just back from the war. "How's the best Governor I ever supported, when everybody said he didn't have no chance, an' served under as his mos' loyal floor leader?"

"Couldn't have won without you, Papoot, and I never fail to give you credit. I tell everyone who'll listen, 'Papoot elected Richard W. Cole Governor of Louisiana.' "

This was their standard greeting. Papoot said, "Open the box, Gov."

Richard W. Cole did as ordered, although he had grown clumsy from having so damn many assistants and convicts to do things for him over at the mansion. He never had to do anything that took physical effort.

Inside was a solid silver coffee set. It was worth a fortune, but Cole knew that Papoot hadn't paid a dime for it. Papoot didn't pay for anything. Cole would have bet his life that some lobbyist had to come up with the money. Papoot stood back anxiously to get the Governor's reaction. He expected a big one.

Cole didn't disappoint him. Both played the game to perfection, like actors who've performed their roles night after night for a year. Cole took out his handkerchief and dabbed at his eyes. From behind it he muttered in a teary voice, "I'm overwhelmed, Papoot. Never had anything like it. You are one in a million."

Papoot couldn't resist. "Cost ten thousand, worth every penny of it."

"Ten thousand," the Governor whispered, as if in all his life he'd never heard of a sum that large.

Papoot nodded. Both had done well. He felt good.

Cole said, "Let me get you some coffee." That was the finishing stroke, the Governor himself going into a small annex and bringing Papoot his demitasse. Then some sixth sense, developed over decades of politics, hit Papoot, and he realized Richard W. Cole was nervous. Oh-oh, he thought.

He was absolutely certain of it when Cole took the big Cuban cigar from his desk and bit down on it. Papoot sat back, his hands behind his head. It was up to the other man, and he wasn't gonna lift no finger to help him. Papoot felt like a cornered animal. The air in the office had changed from love and appreciation to tension. It hung about the room like heavy fog.

"Papoot," Cole began, and Papoot studied him, his face expressionless. "The Bible is all wise."

Oh shit, Papoot thought. Here we go with some North Louisiana bullshit.

"It tells us that there's a time to live and a time to die. A time to plant and a time to sow."

"I know the rest," Papoot said, his face cold. That was how the Bible left him, cold, except to quote from in speeches.

"You've got an election coming up in November."

"Same as always," Papoot said. To him it was just another season, except that it fell every four years. A season of triumph, decade after decade. Strutting, boasting, everybody-kiss-my-ass, rooster-crowing triumph! It was indescribably and absolutely addictive. Once you had tasted it, gotten used to it, there was no doing without it. It was like breathing, and it was that important. Only those who'd tasted it could understand. To everyone else it was a mystery. They were intrigued, but not enough so to take a plunge. Those waters were inky black and bitter cold. It was not a game for those who were afraid. It was a game for those who wanted, needed, full-time affirmation, applause. Lots of it. Papoot couldn't imagine life without it. Death was preferred.

"Papoot, you and me have got to talk."

"Ah'm listenin'."

"I speak with a lot of people. I listen. That goes with the job. People call me to curry favor. Usually I'm first to know what goes on in this state. It's not just me, you understand, any governor. And boy do I listen. I want to know things before they happen. That way I'm prepared. Hate surprises. That's how I've managed to stay ahead of the game."

Papoot sat impassively. He didn't need a lecture on what he already knew.

Cole shoved the cigar back in his mouth, bit down on it again, removed it, held it like a magician's wand, waved it as if he'd like to make Papoot disappear. "You might consider hanging them up."

"Bullshit!" Papoot exploded, his face red, little beads of sweat breaking out on his forehead.

Cole was grim. "No, Papoot. No bullshit. If you run again, you'll get your ass kicked, and I don't want to see that."

"Who's gonna whip me, huh?"

"Just about anybody young with no scars and fairly respectable."

"You believe that?"

"Yessir. I do. I hate it. God knows I hate it. But I do."

"I still don't believe it."

"Then let me be blunt. I haven't spoken to one person, not a single human being from Richelieu Parish, who's going to vote for you. Even those who love you have called me and said, 'Don't let Papoot run. He'll be humiliated.' "

Now Papoot sagged like all the air had been let out of his lungs. There was a gray pallor in his face, and his mouth was dry. He licked his lips, which suddenly felt parched.

Cole was alarmed. He stood and went to the older man. "Are you all right?"

"For a man who just attended his own funeral, yeah, I'm all right."

Cole sat back down. "I'm sorry. I'm terribly sorry."

Papoot turned palms upward to Heaven in a gesture of surrender. It was God's will. It was Cole's will. So be it.

The Governor was none too sure this was over. He had braced himself for a good cursing, which he was prepared to take, soothingly muttering all the while, "Now Papoot, you don't mean that." He had never seen Papoot surrender. Never! So he was a little more than nervous.

Papoot sat with his head lowered. His hat was on his lap.

"Er, don't you think we'll have to let folks know?" the Governor asked, like he was inquiring about the time.

"Whatever you say," Papoot mumbled without looking up. His glasses had slipped almost to the tip of his nose. The lenses were fogged up.

"Yes, well, how do you think we should do that?"

You son of a bitch, Papoot thought. He said, "How you want it?"

"How about the Fourth of July Kickoff at the courthouse? And folks could present you a plaque, I mean a great big plaque, which I'll pay for, maybe even a Cadillac. And I'll say all the things you did for me and for them. You're a great man, and the plaque'll say so. I want my signature engraved on it. That sound okay?"

"It don't matter," Papoot said, his voice without emotion.

The Governor clapped his hands together. The gesture was vintage Richard W. Cole, and it meant, "It's done! Well then, everything's settled."

Papoot stood on trembling legs; he slightly tumbled and caught himself on the chair's back. "Ah guess ah'll be getting' on home."

Cole grabbed his shoulder with a big paw. "I love you like a brother, Papoot."

Papoot wiped his eyes with a sleeve and nodded and turned for the door. There he stopped and returned to his chair. "One little thing, like they say, a last request."

I knew it, it was too good to be true! Cole thought. God help me. "Anything," he said with a warm smile, as he held his breath.

Papoot sank back into the chair. "Before I die," he choked.

I wish you would, Cole thought. He said, "Yes? Yes?"

"There's one thing ah always wanted to do."

"I'm listening, Papoot."

"I'd like to see the Holy Father."

"Say what?"

"The Pope."

"I wonder how . . ."

"You and the Archbishop in New Orleans still friends?"

"Yes, we are. Fine man."

"He could set it up."

Cole was strangely relieved. He thought all of this would cost him a fortune. Instead it would take a single phone call. The Archbishop wouldn't turn him down. The state purchased schoolbooks for the huge system of Louisiana's parochial schools. Paid for their buses, too. One third of Louisiana was Catholic, about a million voters.

"I'll call His Excellency tonight," Cole said, "an' I'll call you right after." He extended a big paw. "Deal?"

"Yes," Papoot whispered and shook his hand weakly.

He stood and left the office. Simms entered, red eyebrows up, eyes blue and strangely lit, like they were powered by neon. "How'd it go?"

"Wonderful!"

"What did you have to promise, the state treasury?"

"Get this. Not a dime. The old man wants to see the Pope before he dies. I'll call the Archbishop tonight. Papoot'll announce his retirement on July Fourth and that's that, and I gladly add, Amen!" He slapped Simms on the back.

Simms broke the paper clip in his pocket. This was truly too good to be true! He asked, "Governor, are you sure?"

"Want to hear the entire conversation, tears and all?"

Simms was delighted, did a little dance step. "You taped him!"

"I didn't want to, but you got to protect yourself with a man like Papoot. His record for word is not all that good."

"Congratulations, boss!"

"Now get me President Prejean on the phone. He's waiting for my call."

• • •

In Richelieu, in Hurphy Perrault's law library, a group of men sat crowded about the conference table, strangely silent, all eyes on the telephone.

They were Na Na Duhon, Big Shot Fontenot, Hot Dog Hebert, Hurphy Perrault, who sat at the head of the table, Sport Baudoin, Doc Mouton, Mayor Big Head Arceneaux, Tooky Trahan, Coon Soileau, Possum Aucoin, Short Change, and President Prejean, sitting at the other end of the table. They were all nervous as hell, sweating in the air-conditioning.

Hot Dog Hebert said, "I'm glad it's the Governor and not me. Papoot's gonna be some pissed!"

"Fuck the old crook," said Possum.

"Second the motion," Mayor Big Head said.

"Simmer down, gentlemen."

The phone rang. Hurphy answered. "Good morning, Your Honor. President's right here. We all are. I'll put him on."

President took the phone, voice quivering. "Good morning, sir. Yessir. Yessir."

"What the hell's he saying?" Possum demanded.

"Shhh," said Hurphy. "Jesus Christ, Possum!"

President said, "He did? He did? Well, I'll be damned. Yessir. I'll call Mr. Simms and set up an appointment for next week. You won't be disappointed, Governor. I'll be your man and I'll represent my people too. Thank you, sir." He hung up the phone.

The Mayor shouted, "Well?"

"Papoot's not only going, he's going quietly. He'll announce on the Fourth," President said.

"And so will you," Hurphy said. He was a natural leader, and the only reason he wasn't a candidate himself was that he couldn't afford it. He was making so much money on representing the diocese he couldn't spare even a minute.

"Whoop! Whoop!" said the Mayor and began to march about the

room like there was a mob behind him, cheering him on. "Whoop! Whoop!"

Now the room exploded, and men began to shake hands, hug, and slap each other on the back.

The king was dead. Long live the king.

Big Shot said, "Let's head out to Misty's, drinks are on me."

"Whoop! Whoop!"

Chapter 13

Bobby, BeBe, and Justin sat in Papoot's den. The old man was melancholy, and no one could recall seeing him that way since Annabelle's sudden death. He told them about his trip to Baton Rouge. BeBe cried softly, tears traveling down her plump cheeks. Justin drank port. Bobby listened, saying nothing.

"It's over," Papoot said. He smiled. "Well, ah had a good run."

"No recourse, huh?" Justin asked.

"No."

Bobby was studying them. He didn't know why he didn't quite believe it, even as he knew how unpopular Papoot had become, especially with the parish's leadership and business leaders. Bobby really couldn't think of anyone of note who supported the old man. He had neglected them all, and now they had turned on him. "How about your little people, out on the farms? They always go for you."

"Except when they're told not to by someone like Richard W. Cole," Papoot replied. "He's in the driver's seat. And he's popular as hell. Am I right, Bobby?"

Bobby said, "Yes."

BeBe said, "It's so unfair. I mean after all you've done for this parish."

"Forgotten," Papoot said.

"People are like that," Justin said. "On the other hand, it's not like you died."

"It's not?" Papoot answered.

Bobby was ashamed that he had doubted the old man. Papoot appeared to be depleted, wrung out like a shirt left in the dryer too many spins. Still, Papoot had had a hell of a career and was many times a millionaire. "You'll have time to do some things you always wanted to do," he said.

Papoot smiled wanly. "Like what? Me, nothin' else ever mattered but helpin' my little people."

And making a fortune, Bobby thought. Most of it land. Thousands of acres.

Papoot sounded like he was reading Bobby's mind. "Ah took care of my people, and Jesus Christ looked after me. That's how it goes, huh, Justin?"

The priest, sounding not too convinced, replied, "Sure."

Papoot said as an afterthought, "There is one thing I wanted, and my great friend, that traitorous son of a bitch Richard W. Cole, gon' do for me. One thing. You all want to guess?" They were silent. No one had any idea what Papoot could possibly want, except to stay in office, and now that was gone. "Ah'm goin' to have an audience with the Holy Father! What you say, Justin?"

"It's . . . it's magnificent. The Pope and Papoot. Now the Church has seen it all."

BeBe rushed to her father and hugged him, tears flowing. "Oh, Daddy, I'm so proud!"

Stunned, Bobby said, "It is something."

Papoot said, "Hee, hee!"

"Will you go alone?" Justin asked.

"No. Ah'm gon' take Moose, and I want him to snap a picture of me and the Pope."

"That yellow sport coat in the Vatican!" Justin said, and they all laughed.

"No way," Papoot said. "Ah'm gonna buy me a black suit, and one for Moose. We gon' do it right."

"This is the proudest day of my life," BeBe said, her face radiating with joy.

Bobby stood. "I've got to make the rounds."

"Take BeBe with you. Let her see law enforcement up close," Justin said.

For a moment BeBe's face lit up, but Bobby was gone. They heard his car start up. "He's in a hurry," Justin said with an evil smile.

Papoot said, "Leave it be, Justin."

BeBe looked from one to the other as if she was being pulled between the arms of a magnet. Both men studied her silently, pity on their faces. "It'll be all right," she said.

"Only if you make it all right," Justin said.

"Leave it be, Justin, leave it be," Papoot said.

"I am a priest and I am her brother!"

"Butt out!" Papoot said. "Let BeBe handle things. It'll do her good." Justin shrugged.

BeBe sat silently, a hand touching a pin curl on her broad forehead. "There's one thing you can do for me, Justin."

"I'll do anything."

"Pray for me."

Papoot groaned.

Bobby parked his car on a side street, went up to the door, and knocked. Outside, the crickets made their metallic music; inside, the house seemed like death. The curtains on the door parted, and she stared out at him. He heard the dead bolt clang back, and the door opened and she stood before him, loose black slacks and a white blouse tied above her belly button.

"Go away," she said.

"Please."

"It's been a long day. Zeke's taken a step backwards and I'm tired."

"I'll only stay for a little while."

She stepped back, and he entered. The parlor was small, the furniture old but comfortable. There was a framed copy of the front page of the very first *Gazette*. Fresh azaleas were on every table. The room smelled good. She motioned him onto the couch. "Want a drink?" She brought him a beer and a glass. She sat a couple of feet from him on the couch, legs folded under her.

"Tell me about Zeke."

"Doc Mouton says it won't be long now. It's the darndest disease. Kills your brain. I mean kills it dead. Then it kills you. Mercifully it kills you. We're force-feeding him now, but the doctor says we shouldn't. I don't know what to do. I know death would be merciful, best, but to just sit there and let someone you love die, well, it's a whole lot easier to say than to do."

"I don't know what I'd do. But if it was me laying there, I know what I'd want. Peace."

"Funny, I never thought of it that way. Zeke *would* want peace. Thank you, Bobby."

"I love to hear you say my name, although I always hated it. Bobby's a name that keeps you a teenager. Who ever heard of an adult named Bobby?" He drew a smile from her. "I could watch you smile all day. I could just sit there and watch you. Where do those dimples come from? Where do they go to? It's a magic trick."

She touched his hand. "Oh, Bobby." They leaned into each other and kissed gently, then withdrew a few inches, studying each other like children watching a butterfly. "I've done some thinking," she said.

"Me too."

"I'm gonna drop my looking into Ti Boy's death. I can't get any-place, and I'll soon have the community hating me. When Zeke dies, I'll sell the *Gazette* and this house. It'll pay almost all our debts. Then—"

He put his finger to her lips. "Don't say it!"

"I'll go."

"Go where?"

"New Orleans. The *Picayune* will take me back. I'll never come back here, Bobby. I don't ever want to see Richelieu again. Somehow, in some way, it defeated me, forced me to take a look at myself and at it. Me, I'm not so hot. Not as hot as I thought. I always took pride in my brains and my looks. Well, where did they take me? I fell in love with a married man, and I stirred up the community where I was born. I botched things bad."

"Precious love . . ."

"Shh. You don't have to say anything. It's not necessary, Bobby, and you didn't do anything wrong."

"I'm an adult too. So thanks, but I knew exactly what I was doing. I couldn't help it. Some excuse, huh? I couldn't help it!"

"One of those things," she said. "I'll get married. There's a lawyer in New Orleans. Senior partner in a big firm. He wanted to marry me. I'll see if the offer's still open."

"You're killing me."

"The truth's that way," she said.

His eyes were glassy, and he stared, seeing nothing. His heart was pounding furiously. It was the first time, the only time in his life, that he had been backed into a corner, where nothing, not cleverness or humor or experience, was of any value. It was a moment of truth. His mouth was dry. When he spoke, his voice sounded very old. "I don't want to live without you."

"Don't be silly," she said. She was trying to help him, make it seem less awesome.

"Shut up and listen to me. I'll leave BeBe. I'll marry you. We'll leave Richelieu. Never come back. Give me a month or two to work it out. And one other thing."

"Yes?"

"Don't stop your investigation. I think you've scratched the surface of something evil, and never in all my life do I recall using that word before. I believe it."

"Evil?" She hugged herself. Outside the crickets were quiet. "I don't understand."

"I think Ti Boy might have done it himself."

"Suicide?"

"Yeah. Hard to believe. But yes."

She got up, returned with another beer, coffee for herself. "I tried to talk to his best friend, Hurphy Jr."

"And?"

"Gone to camp for the summer, and after that he may remain in Maine for school."

"Strange. Anita and Hurphy adore that child; he's their only one. I've never known them to let him out of their sight except for an overnight camping trip," Bobby said.

"Camping? Boy Scout?" she said.

"No. From time to time Justin takes the boys out. It's how he rewards them for being good altar boys. And I gather he loves children."

"I'm glad. The few times I've talked with him, I had the feeling that he wasn't that hot on adults."

Bobby nodded. "He's a very complicated man."

"And more."

"What?" he asked, like he didn't know what she meant.

"He's the connecting link between those two kids."

"Now wait a minute! There're a lot of links. They go to the same school, are in the same class, they're the same age. Didn't they both deliver the *Gazette*?" Bobby asked.

"Yes, that's true."

"So Justin's just another, okay, call it a link. But one of many. Am I right?"

"Yes, but . . ."

"But what?"

"My intuition tells me . . ."

"Oh Christ! Women's intuition," he said.

"Well I am a woman. Do you mind?"

He laughed at himself. "No. I don't mind at all. Come to me."

"You come to me."

"What a tough woman," he said and wrapped his arms about her and kissed her, unbuttoning her blouse. He pushed her bra down, lowered his head, and took a nipple into his mouth. He suckled her gently while she ran her fingers through his hair. Their breathing grew heavy, and she unzipped his trousers and took out his sex. She peered down. "I want to look at it." He felt her breath on him. Her nipples were now hard like bullets, and he rolled them between his fingers, teased them.

"Can I kiss it? I want to kiss it."

He groaned, and she took him into her mouth, bobbed her head up and down, stopped and began again, bathing him with her tongue, driving him crazy.

He grabbed at her hair and said, "Stop, I'm gonna cum," but she wouldn't. He moaned, clenched his jaws to keep the scream inside, and shot into her. She swallowed like she was starving, and continued even when he thought he couldn't stand it anymore. Finally she stopped and looked up at him. Some of him coated her lips and had spilled down onto her breasts. "I wanted all of you. And I loved it! I loved it. You're mine. Goddamn them all, goddamn right and wrong, goddamn everything I ever believed. You. I want you for me. For me."

They kissed, and he tasted himself, licked himself off her breasts. His sex was still in her hand.

"What about you?" he asked.

"I'm okay. I came when you did. My panties are all wet. Want to see?"

"No!"

"Want to shower with me?"

"Oh hell yes. But I won't."

"A little morality? Kind of late for that, wouldn't you say?"

"When I fuck you, it's going to be as your husband. Call it crazy. Call it old-timey. It's me. I'm that way."

"Whatever you want," she said, caressing his face. She couldn't get enough of him. She wanted him in her and she wanted him forever.

"I don't think we ought to see each other until I get things worked out," he said.

"Oh no!"

"Think about it. It's best. Christ, it won't be easy on me either. I don't think about anyone but you, and I dream about you all night, wake up hard, hard for you. But we've got to do this the right way. Hah! That's a good one, there is no right way, so let's be honest, the easiest way. Okay?"

"Just so I'm your love."

"You are. I don't think you have any doubts about that."

"I don't," she said. "So let me get this straight, you want me to go on with my inquiries?"

"Yes, I do. I feel right about that."

"Any suggestions?" she asked.

"If someone else was involved, maybe you could smoke him out."

"Thanks for the easy assignment. How?"

"Front-page editorial in the *Gazette.*"

"About what?"

"Tease him, if there is a 'him.' Make him think you've got a lot more on him than you do."

"I've got nothing," she said, "but intuition."

"Right. But he doesn't know that."

"Any ideas, I mean about content?"

"You're the journalist."

"And you?"

"I'm gonna be doing some illegal looking. You and me, we're in this and everything else together. Afraid?"

"Yes, I am."

"Good. Me too!"

Chapter 14

Father Soulier waited in the Bishop's outer office. It was 11:00 at night, and an antique table lamp with a rose shade was lit where he sat. In the corner there was a marble statue of the Virgin Mary holding the crucified Christ, a tiny light bathing its beauty. On the wall was a huge color photograph of His Holiness. Outside in the hall he could hear the cleaning crew.

It had taken two weeks to get this appointment, but he understood and felt no bitterness. The Bishop was a great and busy man. An old priest, all good days behind him, virtually moments away from retirement, could hardly be very high on Excellency's agenda. Actually, he hated to bother the man. As long as he had been in the diocese, he could not recall ever requesting a private audience. But he had no choice. He simply didn't know what to do, but he knew most assuredly that something should be done. Had to be done.

Monsignor Bellot, the Bishop's Chancellor, came out and greeted him. "Father, don't take too long. Not only do I find the Bishop looking exhausted but I worry about his health."

"Oh no," the priest agreed eagerly.

"Father, you're quite sure you had to see Excellency? You could have spoken with me, and I could have . . ."

He shocked himself by interrupting Monsignor Bellot. "Him! It had to be him!"

"Shhh," the Chancellor commanded, "you're shouting. Not wearing our hearing aid, are we?"

Father Soulier was ashamed and lowered his head. He never wore it because it was big and ill-fitting (a gift from a devout audiologist), and it hurt. It had in fact belonged to someone else and been turned in for a better, smaller model.

That very morning he had pressed his clothes, found his least frayed collar, and carefully polished his black shoes, using more than a little spit. His white hair, freshly washed, was brushed. He had even cleaned under his fingernails, though he could not imagine why. It was his thumping heart about which he could do nothing. He tried breathing deeply, but this caused him to grow breathless, and he coughed carefully into his handkerchief, which God forgive him, he'd forgotten to wash. That was the problem, really. His memory was joining his hearing, vanishing as he looked on helplessly. And he had the beginning of a headache that would soon grow into an unbearable migraine. He would end up on the floor, biting down on something to keep from screaming. There was no cure, at least none that he knew. He had written some specialist that he had read about in *Life* magazine but had never gotten a reply. He had given up after a year, a year of checking the mailbox twice a day, though the mail was delivered only one time daily.

He was not a particularly introspective man, much more interested in, indeed curious about, others. And he did possess this strong feeling of right and wrong, in fact, this was one of the main driving forces in his having become a priest almost fifty years before. He felt great anger at wrongdoing but was very quick to forgive. He could not recall a time when he had not forgiven, until now. This was unforgivable! He touched the cross that hung about his neck and, as always, drew comfort in it. He had no regrets about being old. It was proper, the way that life was structured and ordained.

Additionally, his youth had not been all that good. Both parents, drunks. Sweet and kindly drunks, who caused him so much shame that he had no friends, stayed to himself, found church, found God, found the priesthood. A life.

He muttered thanks to God. He had had a good life. Nothing great or spectacular, but he was not that kind of man. His talents were limited, very limited. But he knew right from wrong. On this single issue, he was an expert. It gave him much pleasure to let people, suffering people, know that it was okay, that their Father was a sweet and loving Father. Indeed, he often envisioned Him as a Norman Rockwell face, white hair, a beaming smile, slightly bent. He spoke with Him often, always on his knees, hands clasped, face upturned. And took much pride (a sin, that) in never, not once, ever asking Him for anything for himself. He prayed for others. And that was why this case was different. He found himself unable to pray for this sinner's salvation. Because he could not forgive him himself, he assumed that God felt the same way.

He looked at the Chancellor, seated behind the receptionist's desk, busily writing. Such busy men. Such talent. And education. Rome. Rome! Soulier's face lit up with admiration, and for the moment he forgot his fears. The Chancellor looked at him, and Soulier smiled timidly. The Chancellor, his mind no doubt on great works, did not smile back.

"Father, must I shout? His Excellency will see you now."

Soulier was confused. Had the Chancellor spoken? Goodness, his mind had wandered and he hadn't heard him at all. What had he said? With great and obvious patience, to be expected from a personage, he said through tight lips, "Go in, Father. And do not tarry. It's late and Excellency is exhausted."

The priest nodded eagerly and tottered to the door, where he tapped. "Go in!" the Chancellor shouted. "Get on with it, man!"

Excellency sat quietly at his great desk, hands clasped before him. He rose. Oh, he was as straight as an arrow! Truth, truth was written on his countenance. His brown eyes blazed with truth. It was like standing before a giant spotlight, the kind used annually at the St. John Church Fair. It seared. Father Soulier felt the heat and could not decide whether to flee (his first choice) or fall to his knees in reverence. The problem was, he wasn't certain that he could get back up. The knees were going too. Excellency held out a hand, fingers long and tapering, palm down, so that Father Soulier could kiss his ring. It was almost too much. Surely this was the culmination of all those years doing God's work timidly but, nevertheless, doing it.

He lingered too long, kissing the ring like a lover, and the Bishop withdrew his hand abruptly. The Bishop motioned him to a high-backed chair, but he couldn't do that, sit in the presence of this august man! The Bishop insisted. In his soft, musical voice—it sounded like the Mass—he said so kindly, "Sit down, Father."

Soulier nodded eagerly, and the Bishop peered out at him like he was looking into a microscope. They sat there. Soulier could not find his voice. It floundered about in his throat; he could feel it, he just couldn't make it work.

"Let's have a little glass of wine, Father; it's the end of a long day, and surely we deserve it," the Bishop said and poured each of them a glass of dark, rich, red French wine from a crystal flagon.

Soulier's hand trembled, but the Bishop motioned him to drink. The wine, more an elixir, went down his throat almost imperceptibly, and he knew that he was now capable of speech. "Ah," he said. This pleased the Bishop. He was a kindly man, and he refilled the priest's glass.

"Now, Father. It's very late. And neither of us is a boy. What brings you to me?"

The priest was prepared. "Something has come to my attention, Excellency." The Bishop stared at him without expression. "Something in the confessional." The Bishop's eyebrows shot up, but he maintained his silence. Father Soulier suddenly realized that he was on his own. "It concerns a priest," he whispered and took a quick gulp from his glass, for courage.

"Concerns?" the Bishop asked.

"Well, yes and no."

"You've lost me, Father," the Bishop said.

"I am the confessor of a fellow priest."

"Oh."

"This priest has confessed to me a great crime."

The Bishop stood. "I'm not certain, Father, that you should be discussing matters under seal, even with me."

"But I must!" the priest squawked.

"Quiet, Father, you're shouting! At me!"

The priest got down on his knees and gripped his Bishop's hand between his own. "Oh, please forgive me, Your Excellency. I am an old and simple man unaccustomed to speaking to great—"

The Bishop said irritably, "Get up."

The priest looked up at him, eyes moist, and said, "I can't."

The Bishop looked at him like he'd taken leave of his senses.

"My knees . . ."

The Bishop leaned down, enfolded Soulier in his arms, and helped him into his chair. "Here, have some more wine. Are you all right?"

"Yes, Your Excellency."

"The matter of the seal is quite severe. It's not to be broken, not even to me."

"But I must tell someone, Excellency. I am afraid the sin may be repeated and may result in another death."

"Did you say *death*? You don't mean . . ."

Father Soulier nodded. "Murder, of a kind."

The Bishop sat back down, not behind the desk but in a chair next to Father Soulier's. "I don't want to hear it."

"Excellency . . ."

"When do you retire, Father, get your much deserved rest?"

"Three months, Excellency."

"Hmm. That's a long time."

"Not so long, Excellency. In a lifetime."

"You're adamant about telling me?"

"I must tell someone or I will die. I am filled with this burden," Soulier said.

"And if I will not hear you?"

"I will have to go elsewhere."

"Elsewhere? Elsewhere?"

"Well, I don't exactly know where. It should be to an august one like yourself, Excellency, because, you see, I need help."

"Perhaps to His Holiness," the Bishop said and quickly laughed to demonstrate that he was joking. "A little levity is sometimes helpful, Father."

The priest's face was solemn. "Not in this matter." He nodded. "I suppose I would have to go to the authorities," he said, thinking aloud.

"The what?" The Bishop gasped. It was indeed no longer a laughing matter. "Pray tell, what authorities do you have in mind, Father? I know of no Bureau of Broken Confession Seals. Not even the Vatican has that."

The priest didn't follow but felt that he had to say something. He felt like something important was slipping away and he couldn't get a hold. He blurted, "Why, law enforcement, I suppose."

Now the Bishop's face was ashen. "Surely you're joking!"

The priest felt better. He sensed that for the first time in this conversation he had made a point. And that the Bishop was listening. Instinct told him to press. "It has to do with a crime. I suppose only one so far. But the potential for more is very much at hand." Now he waited. At last the ball was in Excellency's court, and he allowed himself a rare moment of triumph. He stared directly into his Bishop's eyes. He was astounded. The man seemed very mortal! Even fragile.

The Bishop sat back in his chair, hands on the desktop, knuckles bent as his fingertips tapped slowly. To the priest, they sounded like drumbeats. "All right, Father, tell it all."

"There is little to tell, Excellency. It's all very simple and horrifying. A priest has been sodomizing an altar boy and God knows what else."

"Else?" the Bishop interrupted.

"Other perversities. I do not know how to say them."

"This is serious."

"There's more, Excellency."

"Go ahead, Father."

"The lad killed himself with a hunting weapon."

"Dear God," the Bishop said.

"And the priest feels no penitence."

"Stop! I do not believe you!"

"I cannot stop. I will never have this moment again. When I leave here I will be the old me. Tiptoeing about, waiting for three months to pass. Retiring. It was the way he described it, Excellency. He said . . . he said, 'I pleasured him, I could not help it.' I said, 'How do you know that?' and he said, 'Why, he made appropriate noises.' And I said, I demanded, 'Be more specific.' And he said, 'He screamed.' 'Pain!' I cried. 'Tut, tut, Father,' he said, 'you have quite obviously not experienced orgasm in some years.' "

"And how did he feel about the youth's death?"

"He felt nothing. He is a piece of ice in a priest's collar."

"His name?" the Bishop asked grimly.

"Justin Gaspard from over in Richelieu."

The Bishop's eyes closed, and he muttered, "Of course."

Then, long silence, and Father Soulier suddenly became aware that a grandfather clock was chiming. He counted the chimes. It was midnight. Afraid that the Bishop would say no more—his eyes were still shut—the priest asked, "What am I to do, Excellency?"

The Bishop's eyes opened. "Nothing."

"No!" the old man shouted.

"Calm yourself, Father. I will handle it. I am, after all, the shepherd and all of you are my flock. Be of good heart and conscience. The matter will be handled." He stood, extended his hand. The priest rose, knelt, and kissed his ring. He wanted to thank the Bishop, whose back was now to him.

When he reached the door, the Bishop spoke. "Listen carefully, Father. Say nothing about this to anyone. I will handle this. Do you understand?"

"Yes."

When Father Soulier was gone, the Chancellor entered. "Monsignor, when does Father Soulier retire?"

"Three months and a few days."

"He's old and I fear in poor health, both physically and mentally. I want him retired tomorrow."

"Yessir."

"And send him to the retirement home in Mississippi. Or someplace else, as long as it's not in Louisiana. Good night, Monsignor."

"Good night, Excellency." As the Chancellor departed, he saw the Bishop sit back down and reach for the flagon of dark, red wine.

Chapter 15

Papoot was asleep in his four-poster bed, the canopy over it silk. The bed was more than a hundred years old, as was all of the furniture in the room. Annabelle had loved antiques. He was sleeping a dreamless sleep, as he always did. God had blessed him with the ability to cut off everything, no matter what, and go to sleep immediately.

The telephone on the heavy nightstand by his head rang, and he wakened immediately. With eyes still closed, he reached for it. He felt immediate dread. A glance at his wristwatch told him it was almost 1:00 A.M., and he knew that only bad news came at such an hour. He would handle it. Always had. Bad news was a part of life, a big part. "Uh-huh," he said.

"Senator?" He did not recognize the voice. "This is Bishop Dupuis."

Papoot sat up in bed. This was the second time in all his years that the Bishop had called him. The first call had almost killed him. It had killed Annabelle. "Hello, Bishop. How can ah help you?"

"Senator, we need to talk. It's quite a serious matter."

"Like last time," Papoot said, all the wind knocked out of him.

"Yes. Exactly like the last time, but more."

"Justin," Papoot said, voice expressionless.

"I'm afraid so. When can you come?"

"Monday all right?"

"I suppose so. But no later. Come at night, say about ten."

"I'll be there."

He and the Bishop hung up at the same time. There was no more to say. Papoot replaced the receiver in its cradle and lay back down in the darkness. He was calm. His heart retained its normal beat. But he couldn't help remembering.

The Bishop's previous call had reached him in Baton Rouge. Justin was studying in Rome, well on his way to becoming a member of the Vatican's diplomatic corps. Everyone said he was brilliant, top of his class.

Moose had driven him to Lafayette that day. The Bishop had come to the point quickly and, Papoot could not help but note, cruelly.

"Your Justin's involved with a mess. Homosexuality, no less."

"Say what, your greatness?" Papoot asked, not understanding.

The Bishop sighed, a sigh of exasperation. "He raped a young boy about twenty feet from the Vatican."

"He raped him? I don't believe it!"

"He's part of a gang, a few clerics; most, praise God, wealthy young Romans. They have these parties."

"Parties?"

"Men and boys only. It seems one of the regulars, a nineteen-year-old boy—"

"That's not no child."

"—brought his younger brother, age twelve, who did not wish to participate in the obscenities. Justin, probably drunk on wine, went right ahead anyway. The family took the injured child to a physician, who confirmed the sexual attack. The police were called, and they immediately notified the Vatican. It was kept out of the newspapers, but the family wants vengeance. A lot of vengeance."

This was the kind of language Papoot could understand, had dealt with his entire life. "How much?" he asked coldly.

"Twenty-five thousand dollars and, of course, medical expenses and psychiatric sessions for the youth. He's quite disturbed."

"I'll have fifty thousand dollars here tomorrow."

"I will not accept a check."

"Cash. Okay!"

The Bishop nodded. Papoot stood to leave.

The Bishop said, "I'm afraid we're not through." Papoot sank back in his chair wondering, What next?

"There's the little matter of what do we do with Justin."

"You can't leave him be?"

"The Vatican wants him out of Rome. They want him out of the priesthood too, but that, of course, is my decision. Frankly, I don't know what to do. I'm open to suggestions."

"It would kill Annabelle if her baby weren't no priest. That's her life."

"Mrs. Gaspard is a saintly woman."

"State President of the Catholic Daughters."

"I know. That's why I'm not booting him out right now. But the man is sick."

"He's not no man."

"The law says he is, civil and church law. He should be put away. Treated. It's a disease."

"I got an idea."

"By all means; I have none. Priests do not do this sort of thing. It's the very first case in this diocese. Perhaps any diocese, though I've heard rumors from time to time."

"Ah, but it didn't happen in this diocese. Rome's a far piece off. And it ain't been in the papers."

"That's true. Your idea?"

"Send him back home to Richelieu."

"As a priest? Are you serious?"

"Sure! Justin'll behave hisself. I'll guarantee it."

"It's a calculated risk, one I'm not sure I'm prepared to take."

"When I get through talkin' to Justin, believe me, he's gon' behave hisself for all times. An' I'll make a little gift to this diocese. A little cash gift. Say twenty-five thousand. You can do a lot of good works with them smackeroos."

"Done."

"When's he gonna come home?"

"There's a lot of red tape with Roman authorities. I should say a week or two."

"Okay."

"And Senator . . ."

"Uh-huh?"

"Consider this a last chance. Remember, you accept full responsibility."

"I ain't scared of that."

The two men parted without another word.

On the ride back to Richelieu, Moose noticed that Papoot was deadly quiet. He kept staring at him out of the corners of his eyes. "Look at the road, you fool!" Papoot yelled. He was wondering what he'd tell Annabelle.

They arrived at sunset. Moose dropped him off, asking, "When you gon' need me, boss?" Papoot didn't answer. He entered the house, bathed in shadows. It was so quiet and he was filled with dread. Annabelle sat in the parlor, crocheting socks for the orphanage in Lafayette.

Papoot made himself a drink and brought her one. "Too early for me," she said as he bent to kiss her. She was the love of his life. "Drink it," he said, and she looked at him. He was gray, the sparkle in his eyes had gone out. She swallowed the whiskey, felt it burn as it made its way down her throat. She shuddered. He sat down by her and took her hand. Now her heart began to pound. She started to get up to turn on a lamp, but he pressed her hand for her to remain seated.

"Annabelle, ah got some bad news."

Horror washed over her face. "Justin!" she gasped and then screamed. "He's dead!"

I wish he was, Papoot thought, hating him. "No, no, Justin's not dead. Not even hurt." The thought, Just us, just us are hurt.

"Then what . . ."

"Justin got hisself in trouble. I don't know how to say this. He . . . he raped a little boy in Rome."

"Lies!" she screamed. Her face resembled a Halloween mask, a mask of someone being tortured.

"Ah'm afraid not. They got the goods on him. He's one of those sissy boys, Annabelle, we got to face it. Our son is a sissy boy. He stuck hisself in a little boy. That's what those sissy boys do. It's filthy. He's filthy."

"What will happen to him? You're not just going to sit there? You've helped every bum in this parish. Justin's your flesh and blood. You've got to help him."

"Ah already took care of it. In two weeks he'll be back here."

"Here? But . . ."

Papoot looked down. He was ashamed. "He's gon' be the pastor of St. Ann's."

Her voice was cold. "Not quite what I had in mind. In my prayers I wanted him to be a Cardinal. I prayed for that every day of my life. Did you know that?"

"Sure."

"You, of course, don't pray. Well? Do you?"

"Me? No, I jus' get my queer son out of a shameful scandal!"

She lashed out at him, slapping his face. His glasses fell to the floor. He reached around blindly for them. "It's your sins he's paying for. All your stealing, bribing. All the filth you've done, you do."

Papoot stared at her.

She stood. "I'm tired. Suddenly I'm very tired." She left him standing there and climbed up the long stairs.

Now the house was quite dark, and Papoot sat in the darkness, his mind a blank, his body cold. It was summertime, but he was cold. He did not know how to handle grief. There was no one to pay off, no deal to cut.

The pistol shot brought him to. He raced up the stairs. She had shot herself in the mouth with a small .38 he'd given her years before. Blood was spilling out from her all over the coverlet, and her eyes stared up at him, accusing, lifeless.

Justin returned home the next day to attend his mother's funeral, and Papoot never spoke to him about anything that had happened. He couldn't think of one thing to say. It was over. All over.

Chapter 16

Front-page editorial, the *Gazette*:

> A child is dead. We knew him well. He delivered this newspaper. He never missed a day and he was never late. His parents, Aristede and Marie Brouliette, grieve for him. He was their only child and the light of their life. His bicycle still rests against the side of his house. Some other child will ride it. He was a spiritual child, an altar boy. Never missed and never was late there either. This child had all the makings of a God-fearing, hardworking member of his society. According to the law and to the coroner, he died by accident while cleaning a rifle. The question is, Why? We have discovered that he did not hunt. Ti Boy Brouliette didn't want to kill anything. Why was he cleaning this weapon months before it would be used? His family received one thousand dollars from an insurance policy about which they knew nothing. Who paid for it? We can't find out. How was he doing in his schoolwork? We can't find out. A door has been firmly shut on Ti Boy Brouliette. Someone wants him to go away. But the truth must be inevitable, inescapable. The truth, whatever it is, must be told. Then Ti Boy can have a true rest. In the meantime we'll be looking, asking, pushing to find out what really happened. Please don't resent our efforts. That's what a reporter is supposed to do. Seek the truth.

The *Gazette* hit Richelieu like a bombshell. Never in anyone's experience had there been an editorial like this one. At Possum Aucoin's barbershop they discussed it. At One Lung Savoy's poolroom they talked about it. Even at Misty's it was the only subject. Nor did Na Na Duhon fail to comment on it on the radio.

He said, "Cher, I read the *Gazette* like the rest of y'all, and me, I don't get it. If the Sheriff and the Coroner say it was a accident, it's good enough for me. Me, I'm not no policeman or doctor. Like I was saying to my De De, let sleeping dogs lie. I didn't mean nobody was a dog or nothin' like that, I just mean leave it be. Richelieu don't need no mysteries."

Possum got more to the point. "She's a cunt. Why don't she go back to New Orleans with them other whores?"

Doc Mouton said, "I'm a professional man, and I stake my reputation, my career on my findings. How can a person without an ounce of medical training debate me? Huh?"

Mayor Big Head Arceneaux, relieved to have something else to occupy people instead of them constantly bugging him about the damn stuck stoplight, said, "The girl's trouble. You can look at her and tell that. An' a home breaker." He was very proud of these observations and felt certain they would give him a leg up in the election in November.

Hurphy Perrault was strangely grim about this foolishness. "Zeke would have never written anything like that. Ruth Ann ought to be ashamed. My, my, my."

Big Shot Fontenot was almost subtle. "She'll get hers," he said quietly.

Misty said to Ballou, "I hope the girl's careful. She's beggin' for trouble."

Ballou said, "I think she's on to something."

"We gon' keep quiet, Ballou, you hear me?"

Ballou nodded.

President Prejean said, "What this community needs is not to be pulled apart. The girl's not a part of us and never will be. It takes a stranger to divide us, if we let her. We won't let her!" There was applause. He was already beginning to sound like a Senator.

Papoot was the most succinct. "Oh shit!"

The Sheriff said nothing. When asked, and he was asked a lot, he replied, "The official investigation's closed." That didn't quite satisfy anyone. They wanted to know, What about the unofficial one? He shrugged. No one who spoke with him felt good or comfortable. Possum noted, "Him, he's got his personal reasons." The boys in the barbershop understood and admired Possum for having the guts to say what they were all thinking.

BeBe read the editorial three times. In some strange way it motivated her to do something she had been putting off.

Justin spoke about it at Sunday Mass. "We love each other. We respect each other. We are in every way one. But the devil is not a part of us, and sometimes he speaks through the lips of someone, through the pen of someone, and we say, 'Why are they doing this?' What we don't understand is, it isn't them. It's Satan. And that's how we must treat it. Pray for the sinner. Be compassionate. Say, 'They don't know what they're doing.' Even as we damn Satan back to his black Hell, where he resides. We can do this by prayer. Now is the time for the people of Richelieu to pray mightily. Pray for the sinner, for we are a compassionate people. And pray for the devil to go back where he belongs! Amen."

Chapter 17

BeBe got up and took her bath with grim determination. I'm not Papoot's daughter for nothing, she thought. No whore was gonna take her Bobby, that was for sure. She poured some more soap bubbles in the water to mask having to look at her body and thought about a new diet someone had told her about at the Sodality of the Blessed Virgin meeting, where she was recording secretary. The diet had to do with papaya juice. It had to be freshly squeezed every day, and that was the problem. Where could you find papaya in Richelieu? Still, she promised herself that on her very next trip to Lafayette she'd go by Heymann's store and see if they had fresh papaya. In a way she hated to go in there because they had the biggest soda fountain, with milk shakes for a dime! Suddenly she was hungry, and to make that feeling go away she thought of the whore.

It seemed so simple. Why didn't she get her own man? God knows she wouldn't have no trouble, not with that big ass and those big tits. But no, she didn't want her own man, that was too simple. She wanted someone else's. Shame on her. For a moment, just the briefest moment, BeBe thought of her in a coffin, but she quickly squelched this thought, let the water out of the tub, and dried herself.

First things first. Plan her supper for when Bobby got home. She decided to stuff some cabbage and maybe have a fresh fruit salad covered with pecans and bananas and marshmallows. And of course, some good hot French bread from Hot Dog Hebert. But she didn't like to go there, because Hot Dog also made big whipped cream–filled cream puffs. Once, when she had let go, she'd eaten half a dozen! Nobody saw her, but she was so ashamed.

She put on a tentlike dress with no belt and some saddle oxfords. And a big straw hat with a red ribbon about it.

The day was so beautiful, all yellow and blue with just a tiny blush of pink, but not a cloud. Her first stop was St. Ann's, where she dipped her fingers in the font, made the sign of the cross. This ritual always refreshed her. Jesus Christ was so kind. She wished she could hug him to her like he was a baby, like the baby she and Bobby didn't have. Would never have. Bobby was, how they say it, sterile. Sometimes in the all-Catholic world of Richelieu, she felt out of place because everybody but them had families, mostly five or six children. Really devout couples had a dozen, even though Doc Mouton warned them that one more and he couldn't guarantee the life of the mother. They didn't pay him no mind. Thy will be done.

Possum Aucoin saw it differently: "They fuck like rabbits!"

She would have loved a baby, a little boy who looked just like Bobby, except the nose, which she joked about but found admirable.

The church was empty, and with much labor she got to her knees, looked up at her Lord on his crucifix, and prayed. "Please help me to keep my man. I don't deserve him, I know. It happened to me so quick. One day I was a pretty girl, the prettiest in Richelieu High, the next I was a pig. A big pig. I don't know why! How I let myself go? It wasn't Bobby's fault, that's for sure. Bobby was a good husband and didn't say one word about it. But then . . . then Bobby stopped payin' me any mind . . . in our bed. Well, what could I expect? Nobody wants no fat person. Me, I don't blame him at all. And really it didn't matter all that much. We still had each other in more important ways. Our marriage was so good." She was weeping.

"And then, I'll never forget that day, at poor little Ti Boy's wake, we both saw her. She's . . . different. I don' mean just in the looks department. She's not like us around here. Oh, she's beautiful, I got to admit that, but there's some other beautiful women here too, and Bobby not once paid them no mind. She's . . . I don't know exactly how to say it, baby Jesus . . . she's like a girl and a man. Like she's both! She looks like a girl, but she acts like a man. Women don't make no trouble, they keep things together, they do their little jobs and leave the rest to the menfolks the way you planned it. Not her! She's got my marriage tore apart and the town too. Everything she touches is big trouble. I know you help those who help themselves, so what I need to know from you, what should I do?"

She stood, then sat in a pew, waiting for Jesus to answer. But the day was quiet. St. Ann's was quiet. There was no message that she could hear. She stood again, thinking, Well I tried. I sure tried. Then she left the church and got into her car and drove out into the country.

She saw some wildflowers by the side of the road, and she parked and picked a bouquet to put on the table when Bobby ate his supper. Bobby liked pretty things. She groaned aloud. She was no longer pretty. She glanced in the rearview mirror to see if there were any remnants of her beauty. She couldn't see one. Not only was she fat but it was like she had aged overnight, and her mouth was almost a straight line, and her dimples were like a joke in her big face.

She looked around. She knew this area well; it all belonged to Papoot, though she doubted that anybody but the parish Assessor knew that. Papoot owned just about everything, and one day it would be hers and Bobby's and Justin's. She wondered why this gave her no pleasure. It was not like caring what Santa Claus would bring you at Christmas. Surprises had gone out of her life. She smelled the wildflowers next to her on the seat, and this made her feel a little better. They were so fresh, not like her life, old and used. Fresh!

MaMa Seego lived on a dirt road, in the only house for miles. It was a small house, painted pink, with a little white fence and a gate. The trees out front were bare, and there were no flowers. It reminded BeBe of a cemetery, and she shivered.

MaMa Seego stood in the doorway holding a black cat. She was a Creole, a black of color with Spanish and Indian blood. She was a beautiful, light-skinned woman, with not a wrinkle in her face. Her jet-black hair was in a bun, and she was dressed severely—like an old-time schoolmarm. She was well into her eighties, though no one knew her exact age. They knew she was timeless, not subject to the ills of age that befell other mortals.

She was the parish's only traiteur, a treater or practitioner of folk medicine.

Both blacks and whites considered her a kind of doctor. She practiced a benign medicine that consisted of the laying on of hands, the sign of the cross, and recitation of secret passages from the Bible. People brought her their head colds, minor aches, and pains of all kinds.

BeBe followed the traiteur into her small parlor. On the wall was a primitive painting of Our Lady of Perpetual Help. A beaded curtain over a doorway separated the room from the rest of the house.

She charged nothing for her services. People left donations: money, a chicken, vegetables, whatever they chose.

When they were seated in rockers, she asked, "Now, little girl, how can MaMa Seego help?"

BeBe was biting down on her handkerchief, her eyes tearing up, her bottom lip trembling. "Oh, MaMa Seego, my husband took up with another woman."

MaMa Seego nodded. She'd heard that problem many times before. "Tell me all, little girl."

BeBe felt good. She loved to hear herself called "little" anything. "It's so sad," she said, her voice piteous and childlike. "This big-assed woman, like a New Orleans whore, took him, and I know they're doing it."

"Mens are something," MaMa Seego agreed. She had been celibate her entire life. It was one of two secrets about her. Only one of them was deadly.

"I don't know what to do."

"You love him?"

"Oh, yes, MaMa!"

"How much?"

"Huh?"

"Enough to die for him?"

"Oh yes. I would die for Bobby."

"Hmm," MaMa Seego mused, and they sat there.

The stillness made BeBe uncomfortable. "What I'm gon' do?" She held her pudgy hands out to her sides, palms upturned.

"Bow your head, little bird, MaMa Seego's going to pray over it."

BeBe shocked her. She did not lower her head but looked into the woman's eyes. "MaMa Seego, I believe that God helps those who help themselves. I don' want to just pray."

MaMa Seego leaned forward in her rocker and stared through BeBe. "More?"

"Yes, ma'am."

"Are you sure? You've got to be sure."

"I never been more sure in all my life."

MaMa Seego stood and went to the beaded door. "Come when I call you."

"Come?"

"Through this door," MaMa Seego said and disappeared.

BeBe sat there rocking, heart pounding. A long time ago Motile had told her MaMa Seego's other secret. Voodoo. What seemed to be a man's voice called from the other room, "Enter."

On trembling legs, BeBe lumbered through the curtains, the beads hitting her face like rain. The room was dark except for a candle burning in a human skull on a tabletop. Behind it, with a black cat in her arms, sat someone—someone with a face painted white and red, like a clown, but not funny at all. The figure's hair was long, down to the waist. Its eyes burned.

"Where is . . . ," began a confused and frightened BeBe.

"Silence!" the voice, a deep bass, commanded, and BeBe sank into a straight-backed chair. "I will ask you a question. You will answer and you will tell the truth or you will rot here on earth, not in Hell, but right here. You will smell your own flesh as it falls away piece by piece until you are nothing but a face with one eye, a face that can see what has happened to the rest of you. This I promise. You hear?"

"Yessir, I mean ma'am."

"What you want is this evil woman dead where she can no longer entice your man. Is that what you want?"

"Yes, ma'am."

"Say it!"

"That's what I want."

"Fool! Say what you want."

BeBe swallowed. In a little girl's voice she whispered, "I want her dead."

The black cat leaped straight up into the air, howled like a banshee, and ran from the room. Or maybe it wasn't a room. Maybe it was Hell. BeBe didn't know for certain.

The face smiled, the mouth a black hole with no teeth. Now the voice was jovial. "Then you must kill her."

"That's a mortal sin!"

"Taking your love is a mortal sin. Removing the taker is no sin but a blessing. Your God will approve."

BeBe was shaking. "I don't know. I never done nothin' like that."

"Then you will lose him. Look at you. Can you compete with her?"

"But I love him."

"Have you ever considered, she may love him too?"

BeBe spoke clearly, a rush of strength suddenly taking over her fear. "I'll kill her."

But MaMa Seego wasn't through. "And he may love her."

"I want her dead!"

"Go."

BeBe stumbled from the dark room, left a twenty in a fishbowl, and raced to her car. The black cat lay on the porch, enjoying the brilliant sun.

Chapter 18

The banner headline in the *Gazette* was the second largest in the newspaper's long history. The only larger one had been in the paper's only special edition when World War II ended. It had read: IT'S OVER. MERCI GOD!

This one was not so cataclysmic, except to the citizens of Richelieu Parish. It read: PAPOOT GONE? The story explained:

> Baton Rouge sources claim that Governor Richard W. Cole has pulled the plug on Senator Glenn "Papoot" Gaspard's efforts to win a tenth term in next November's statewide elections.
>
> The veteran lawmaker and father of Louisiana's old age pension and the leading administration floor leader was told by the Governor that it was all over.
>
> Word is that President Prejean, president of the local Rotary Club and owner-operator of Prejean's Esso Service Station, will be the administration's candidate, practically assuring him of the election.
>
> That same Baton Rouge source tells the *Gazette* that Papoot will bow out and Prejean will announce for office at the big Fourth of July political rally when candidates make their intentions known.
>
> Senator Gaspard could not be reached for comment.
>
> Prejean stated, "All of us love Papoot, but time marches on. I'll make my intentions known on July Fourth in front of the Richelieu Parish Courthouse."

Except for those in the know, the news hit the parish like a hand grenade exploding. People couldn't get over it. Just about everybody thought it was a good thing. Papoot had been at the trough for so long. Prejean was very popular, and people liked how he didn't bad-mouth the old man.

Possum Aucoin, a big Prejean supporter, commented, "Really, when you think about it, neither of them's worth a shit!"

Mayor Big Head Arceneaux marched up and down his office and in a booming voice proclaimed, "Time marches on!"

Bobby admitted to Moe Weiss, late one evening over bad tea, "I just can't believe the old man's going out so quietly. He's a fighter, especially for himself. And of course, his little people. It's just not like him. On the other hand, Governor Cole himself told me the old man didn't even put up a protest when he gave him the news. Still . . ."

The next morning Bobby was at his desk when Slo' Down Angelle informed him that he had a long-distance call. From Mississippi. This puzzled Bobby; outside of a few sheriffs, he didn't know any-body in the neighboring state. "A sheriff?" he asked.

Slo' Down said, "No, it's an old man. I can hardly hear him."

"Put him on," Bobby said, and when Slo' Down was gone, he lifted the phone. "Hello."

The voice was old and quivery, and sounded like it was coming from a neighboring planet. Bobby said, "Please speak up!" and pressed the phone against his ear.

"Is this the Sheriff of Richelieu?"

"Yessir."

"I want to report a murder. Is this the place to report a murder? You see, I don't know these things."

"In Mississippi?"

"No. There. In Richelieu."

"Yessir. This is the place. May I ask who this is?"

"Soulier, Jacque Soulier."

"Where are you calling from, Mr. Soulier?"

"Not mister, Sheriff. I'm a priest. Or at least I was."

"I'm sorry. Where are you, Father?"

"Right out of Jackson, Mississippi, about ten miles."

"May I ask what you're doing in Mississippi, Father?"

The voice became expressionless. "The Church maintains a retirement home here. I've been retired here because I knew."

"What did you know, Father?"

"About that murder."

"I'm not following you, Father, and could you please speak up?"

"I'm doing the best I can. The phone's in the hall, and I don't want to be overheard. No telling where they'd send me. Maine, I suspect, or Minnesota, where I'd freeze to death. I hate cold weather."

Bobby tried gently to steer him back on course. "What murder, Father? I don't know of any recent murders here."

"Technically, I don't suppose it is. But it is!"

Bobby sighed with exasperation and considered hanging up. "What murder?" he shouted, and hoped that Slo' Down, who he suspected was on the other side of the door listening, didn't hear him.

"Why, the altar boy, who else?"

Bobby felt like the bottom had fallen out of his chest, and his heart plummeted to the floor. Suddenly he was freezing.

"Hello? Hello? Are you there?" Soulier demanded.

Bobby swallowed. "I'm right here, Father. Tell me more."

"Not on the phone. I'm breaking my vows, you know. I'll go straight to Hell for this, but Dupuis did me in, and I've no choice."

"Your vows?"

"The confessional."

"Oh, I see. May I ask who's Dupuis?"

"Bishop Peter Paul Dupuis, who else?"

"When can I see you, Father?"

"Anytime. I'm not going anyplace. Except to my Maker, but only after I clear my conscience and my soul. Then it's up to the Almighty."

"I'll come one day next week."

"Be sure to bring identification. I won't talk to just anybody."

"Will my badge do?"

The phone went dead. Bobby sat back in his swivel chair, hands behind his head, gazing up at the ceiling. He was exhilarated and frightened at the same time. This was what police work was really about: not knowing, wanting to know, and then miraculously, very rarely, a bolt of lightning that illuminated all the dark corners. It was the consequence of this impending truth that he feared, and he didn't exactly know why. At another, deeper level, he had suspicions, and if they were what he thought they were, grief would inevitably follow.

He shook his head in awe. Things, life could be going along so smoothly, and then, bingo! Everything turned to crap. When had it begun? How? He knew the answer to both these questions: when Ruth Ann Daigle had returned to Richelieu and begun asking questions. And . . . and when he had fallen in love with her. She was the connecting link between all the pieces of trouble, and he didn't know if he could live without her. He called her at the *Gazette*.

"It's me," he said.

"I love 'me.' "

"I love you. Isn't that something? I'm in love. I suspect for the first time in my life," he said, astonishment in his voice.

"Her?" she asked diplomatically.

"I liked her. I liked her a lot. It was one of those things that was . . . natural, even expected. But it wasn't a blowtorch."

"Maybe that's all this is."

"Oh no. It's everything. You're my love in every way. Every way!"

"I need to hear you say that. Sometimes I get frightened. I feel like you . . . we are vanishing. It's the strangest feeling, like a negative fading. It scares the hell out of me."

"No way. I promise."

"And I need you. Bad."

"I've got something to discuss with you. Can I come by this evening about ten?"

"Oh yes!"

"How's Zeke?"

"Any time now. It's heartbreaking."

"I'm so sorry. Good-bye, my love."

The Richelieu Rotary Club met in a private room at Coon Soileau's. The meeting began with everyone singing "God Bless America" led by Hot Dog Hebert, who had a good baritone voice. The song was sung with much enthusiasm. Then there was the Pledge of Allegiance, this led by Mayor Big Head Arceneaux, who was a superpatriot and carried a small American flag in his lapel whenever he led the pledge. Once in a while he forgot the correct words and pronounced "United" "Newnited." Still, he led with great gusto and had never missed a Rotary meeting since becoming a member of the club twenty years before. He had a lapel pin for this too, which he wore right beneath Old Glory.

A couple of visiting out-of-town Rotarians were introduced. They were a Mr. Desomeaux from Erath in Vermilion Parish, a well-known plumber; and Mickey Simon, all the way from New Orleans, who had come to Richelieu to fix the stoplight. Simon's introduction was greeted with catcalls and shouts of "It's about time!" which the Mayor made like he didn't hear.

Then followed a traditional lunch, a cup of seafood gumbo, baked chicken, a green salad, and a big wedge of fresh apple pie topped with a scoop of ice cream. Catfish François never let them down. And you could have seconds, which everyone did.

Then President Prejean stood. "I'm afraid our speaker today isn't able to be with us. He has a twenty-four-hour flu. So rather than leave you without a speaker, I apologize by telling you that I would like to say a few words."

There was much applause, though nobody could say exactly why.

"Give 'em hell!" Possum shouted. And everybody laughed because Possum wanted everyone on earth to catch hell. Even Possum laughed, though softly, as his gaze lighted on Mayor Arceneaux, who had laughed the loudest, and who had shut up immediately under Possum's spiteful gaze.

"It's proper that I talk to you, my friends, before I go public on the Fourth. First, I'm deeply grateful to our great Governor, whose confidence I seem to have gained. The Governor is a man of integrity and dignity, and to gain his confidence is one of the nicest things that has ever happened to me. Secondly, I want to thank Papoot Gaspard . . ."

There was much booing. Possum shouted, "The old crook!" The Mayor, anxious to regain Possum's favor, gave two of his famous Whoop! Whoops.

President held out his hand to quieten them. "I know. I know how you feel. That's why I'm running. But let's let Papoot go his way in peace. After all, when he was a younger man, Papoot did much for this parish. Actually, we owe him a lot. I owe him a lot. He got me a scholarship to college. Come on, fellows, give Papoot a hand."

There was a little applause. Some more boos. Everyone was not so forgiving. Truth was, Papoot had looked down on the Rotary and in many a speech had referred to them as "those uptown big shots!" They liked being "big shots," and they bitterly resented his derision. Besides, he never returned their phone calls unless there was a buck involved. A lot of bucks.

"So, on the Fourth, I'll make it official. I hope nobody else runs. I'd like to go to Baton Rouge with a real mandate, a mandate for good government! And no more taxes! The business community has been taxed to death. I want to help the poor the same as any good Christian, but not at the expense of those who pay the freight."

Thunderous applause. More "whoops!"

"I see it's one-ten, so I'll wind up by asking you for your vote. But more, for your prayers."

They rushed to surround him, shake his hand, and clap him on the back. He would be their Senator. Their very first.

• • •

Misty wasn't exactly weeping either. She remarked to Ballou, "Praise be the lawd, ah'm gonna have that cancer off my back. Boy but he was greedy, huh, Ballou?" Ballou flexed his big muscles and quickly agreed. "The man was a hog for sure."

"How about President?" Misty asked. Whoever was Senator had to be their ambassador to Baton Rouge, entrusted with keeping them open. It hadn't always been that easy.

One time the Governor got a letter from a young fellow from Richelieu. It read,

Dear Governor, a ruined man is writing to you. I hopes that what happened to me can save others. I was engaged to my childhood sweetheart and a Christmas wedding was planned by both our families. I work offshore in Grand Isle and was on my way home on the weekend when I got hungry for a Moon Pie and a RC, my favorite snacks all my life.

I happened to stop at the Paradise Inn, where I had never been before. I was greeted by a half-naked girl, who asked me what I wanted. I said, 'A Moon Pie and a RC, please, ma'am.' And then, Governor, she started fooling with me in my private area. Well, I am a young man (and a fool) and I had relations with this bad girl.

I had been gone from home for three weeks, and when I got there that very night I had relations with my bride-to-be. You can guess what happened. I had the clapp and gave it to her. Now her family wants to kill me and the wedding has been called off. My own Mama had to be taken to Big Charity in New Orleans for her nerves. She don't do nothing but groan.

It's too late for me, and all I ask is that you close that awful place down and don't let what happened to me happen to some other poor soul who only wants a Moon Pie and a RC.

Governor Cole had not stopped laughing for two days. Then he'd called Papoot to come to Baton Rouge on an important matter. Papoot was much pleased. Important matters inevitably translated to cash in his pocket. Cole had a solution.

"Senator, we just can't have this kind of thing happen," he said, barely suppressing his laughter and biting down on his unlit cigar.

Papoot was not so sympathetic. "Why didn't the fool wear a rubber?"

"That's beside the point. Here's what I want you to do. Go tell what's her name . . ."

"Misty."

"Go tell Misty I want the Paradise moved, say two hundred feet off the road."

Papoot loved it and rushed back to Richelieu and to Misty's Paradise Inn. He told her the grim story.

"Impossible," she said. "Doc Mouton checks my girls once a week. There's no pussy in Richelieu safer than my girls." She sighed, knowing it was a losing battle. "What's it gon' cost me, Papoot?"

"The Governor mentioned twenty-five thousand and—"

"Jesus Christ! More?"

"You got to move two hundred feet off the road."

"Bullshit!"

"Maybe I ought to tell him you said that. The State Police would be here that night and you and Ballou would go straight to Angola for white slavery and God knows what else."

She wasn't convinced. Her jaw was firmly set.

Papoot said, "Ain't Ballou still got that little charge on him in Mississippi? Pimping."

Misty said, "Send Moose for it, but ah'm gon' need a day or two."

Papoot didn't even answer and was on his way out the door.

Misty told Ballou about it.

"Why don't you let me cut his throat?" he asked.

"Hold your horses," she cautioned. "We don' need no more trouble. Besides, hogs like Papoot always ruin themselves. Every time."

Ballou was not convinced. "I could run over him, back an' forth over his head."

"Let's wait, cher."

Chapter 19

BeBe wanted to be the last person at confession. She waited outside St. Ann's in the darkness until she was sure they would be alone. She was right. The church was deserted and Justin was just leaving the confessional. He saw her, went to her, and kissed her on the cheek. "Hello, sister. Good to see my favorite person in the world."

"Just—— I mean, Father, this is not a social call. I have to confess."

"Let's sit down and—"

"No. Please! I want to do it right."

"As you wish," he said, genuinely curious. Outside of overeating, sister's confessions were laughable. They entered the confessional.

"Forgive me Just—— Father, for I have sinned."

He thought, Get to the point! And he said, "Yes, my child?"

"Oh, Father, ah'm so ashamed."

"Yes?" What on earth had this fool done?

"I can't hardly say it."

"Dear child. Do you think there is any sin that our Lord and Savior Jesus Christ has not heard and forgiven?"

"No, I don't guess so."

"Then don't insult Him. You wouldn't want to slap our gracious Lord in the face, would you?"

"Justin!"

He took a deep breath. She really was trying. How had anyone maintained such innocence for so many years? Now there was a miracle! "Tell me, BeBe, tell your brother in Christ your little sin."

"I went to see MaMa Seego."

"Yes?"

"About Bobby and you know . . ."

"Mary Magdalene."

"What?" She was confused.

"The harlot."

"Justin, you shouldn't talk that way in church!"

"*Harlot* is a word in the Bible. I'm quite within spiritual bounds."

"You' so wise, Justin. I wonder how I came out the other way?"

"It's all evened out, little sister. God gave you a great heart."

"You didn't get one?"

"Mine comes and goes. I have it and am full of love, even for the stupid and the blind, and oh, but there are lots of those, but then it seems to leave me and I see them for what they are. Utensils."

"What?"

"Another time. We're not here to discuss my shortcomings but your adorable little-girl sins. You went to see MaMa Seego about Bobby and that woman."

"Uh-huh. And she wanted to pray on me. But"—she lowered her voice and began whispering—"that's not what I wanted. I asked for the other, Justin."

"Voodoo?"

"I'm so ashamed, Justin."

"Go on."

"It was my fault, Justin. I can't blame MaMa Seego. I told her I wanted more than prayer. And she, I guess it was her, but it didn't favor her at all, and it talked low like a man, she said the truth—that I wanted that woman dead—'cause that's what I want."

Justin sat up, intrigued. It was Miss Ruth Ann Daigle causing all their trouble, stirring things up, wrecking people's lies. He despised her, but until now there hadn't been anything he could do about it. "Go on, little sister."

"I said it, Justin. I said I wanted her dead. And then . . ."

Justin was imagining torturing Ruth Ann. If only Zeke was a

Catholic, he could deny him the last sacrament. That would take care of Miss Cunt. "Go on," he said gently.

"Oh, Justin," she wailed, and he waited until she regained her composure.

"What did MaMa Seego say?"

Her voice was clear like an autumn day. "She said I should kill her. I came in to ask God's forgiveness."

"But you haven't, I mean you didn't do it?"

"No, but I thought it. I can't deny that."

Now, he thought. Now. "Then do it."

"What, Justin?"

"She's not a person. She's the devil. Only the devil would destroy a sacred marriage and break an angel's heart. So do it. God will love you for it. He wants the devil dead. They struggle all the time, and God doesn't always win. You must be His instrument. Do it. Do it soon, then come to me, and you and I will explain to our Lord and He will show His approval. Maybe even a miracle. I wouldn't be surprised at all if He doesn't show you a miracle for your good work."

"A miracle? What kind of miracle?"

"Oh, maybe the sun will spin in the heavens, or no, wait, I've got it, you'll see Our Lady."

"Like at Fatima?"

"Exactly that way. You'll be a saint. You are a saint."

"You really think it's okay? I wouldn't want to get caught."

"God will shield you."

"I never thought of that!"

"Not a word to anyone else about this, you understand? They're not pure and spiritual like you and I. You understand, BeBe?"

"Yes, Justin."

"I've never been so proud of you, ever! Oh, and BeBe . . ."

"Yes?"

"Do it soon. Don't wait. God can hardly wait."

"I feel good for the first time in a long time."

"Bless you, my child. Now come, let's say an Our Father together."

She sat by Zeke's bed with the sitter. His breath was ragged, and Doc Mouton told her it would probably be tomorrow. "I wish he was in peace," she said. The sitter comforted her. "He's not suffering. He doesn't know." Ruth Ann hugged the old black woman. She stood and went out to the front porch, trying to catch a breeze. There was none. The night was still and solemn. Death was in the air. The leaves in the oaks were frozen in place. She almost wept with joy when she heard him park and walk around to the front of the house. God, he was beautiful. A prince. Her prince.

He followed her inside, and she held a finger to her lips when they crept past the door to Zeke's room, where the sitter sat, her back to them, reading her missal. When they reached her room, he took her into his arms. Before he kissed her he looked down at her face. She made him feel religious—all that glory, all that beauty—surely she proved more than anyone he knew or had ever known that man was made in God's image. Then he crushed her to him and all thoughts of religion faded as her breasts and groin pressed into him and he responded. He held her hair in his hands, bent her head back, and kissed her throat, kissed the heartbeat that was there in a pale lavender line like a sliver of flower. They fell to the bed, pressed against each other, and their hands found each other's sex and squeezed and probed until both found release.

She rose from the bed and went into the bathroom, returned with a washcloth with which she washed him and kissed him, and he her, until they were dry and at peace. He lay back, his head on her pillow; she sat looking down at him.

"You know," she said, "unlike you Catholics, I thought miracles were humbug. But I'd never had a miracle before. It makes a believer of you."

"I love converting a sinner," he said, and they laughed.

"Bobby, I hate to ask you this, but does she know? Does BeBe know about us?"

"No! Absolutely not. How could she? Besides, I could tell. BeBe's as easy to read as the funny papers, and I've seen no sign. None. Relax, huh?"

She wasn't so sure. A woman could tell. She certainly could, in a heartbeat. Did Bobby know BeBe at all? Did they ever talk about anything but food? She doubted it.

"Now, tell me the news!"

He told her about the priest's call from Mississippi. She listened intently, asking only a single question. "Do you believe him?"

"I don't honestly know. He sounds very old and a little eccentric."

"But you're going to see him?"

"Oh, hell yes. I'd do that or die."

"I'm not going to say what I think."

"You don't have to. I'm thinking the same thing."

"It's scary," she said. "Shocking, too."

"Yeah. I didn't think I could be shocked anymore."

"Bobby, in the *Gazette,* can I write that there's a rumor that you may have a break in the case?"

"I don't know . . ."

"Please," she said and grabbed him between the legs.

"God, but the press is persuasive. Sure, as long as it's just a rumor. Shake some people up, huh?"

Before she could answer him there was rap on the door. Both jumped, and she motioned him into the bathroom. It was the sitter, her face heavy with sadness. "Miss Ruth Ann, I believe he's gone."

Bobby stepped into the room. The black woman didn't look at him. He put his arms about Ruth Ann. She wept softly against his chest, and he patted her back soothingly. Then they went into Zeke's room. Bobby felt his pulse. He shook his head and closed Zeke's watery, lifeless eyes. "Better call Watch Out Naquin at home."

"And you better go," she said.

"I'll come with the rest. Ruth Ann?"

"Yes?"

"You're not by yourself. You have me. I love you."

"I love you," she said.

Zeke's funeral from the small Methodist church was well attended. Reverend Soames summed him up. "He was a good man. Stubborn. Fiercely honest. Zeke was a newspaperman. He tried never to hurt anyone, and at the same time he called things exactly as he saw them. That must have been a very trying balancing act, but I do believe he carried it off with grace and dignity. In Richelieu, we never saw him fall from the wire. We never did. Good-bye, Zeke. Maybe the Lord can use a good journalist. What a lovely way for you to spend eternity."

The pallbearers were all community leaders: Big Shot Fontenot, President Prejean, Hurphy Perrault, Na Na Duhon, Moe Weiss, Tooky Trahan, and Hot Dog Hebert. Bobby and BeBe attended together, and even Father Justin Gaspard and Papoot were there. People said they'd never seen Papoot look worse. He was so unanimated, and many said, "In a way, it's sad." Prejean went out of his way to shake every hand, and even to pat Papoot on the back in a kind of commiseration.

The small Methodist cemetery was filled with mourners, and Slo' Down Angelle had to direct traffic.

Ruth Ann Daigle stood alone when the coffin was lowered into the earth. Hurphy and Big Shot put their arms about her for support. Bobby watched from a distance, and BeBe cried. Actually, she loved funerals and tried to attend every one, even those of people she didn't know. Black or white. She told Bobby, "It's good politics." Actually, it wasn't that at all. She just loved funerals, the finality, the lack of loose threads. It was to her a bookend that solved at least one of life's ongo-ing mysteries. It was the in-between that bothered her.

The next day Ruth Ann received a registered letter from the First National Bank of Richelieu, signed by its president, Big Shot Fontenot. The letter informed her that Zeke's note, now hers, was being called. Now.

Chapter 20

On Monday morning, three events occurred. Ruth Ann Daigle set out for the First National Bank and a meeting with Big Shot Fontenot, bank president; Sheriff Bobby Boudreaux, accompanied by Moe Weiss, departed for Jackson, Mississippi; and Senator Glenn "Papoot" Gaspard, who had all but dropped out of sight, not even showing up for the nightly suppers, held a mysterious meeting with Papa Sotile, leader of the Richelieu Gents. At this meeting, a respectable sum of money changed hands.

That week's issue of the *Gazette* carried a small article on the front page:

> Senator Glenn "Papoot" Gaspard will depart next week for a visit to Rome and a possible private visitation with His Excellency the Pope. The meeting was arranged by Governor Richard W. Cole. Capitol insiders speculated that this is Cole's "going away" gift to the veteran senator and floor leader, who is expected to announce his retirement at the July Fourth political rally at the Richelieu Courthouse. Papoot refused comment on the pending journey, saying only, "I'm sorry, but that's deeply personal."

People couldn't get over it! What could Papoot possibly say to the Holy Father, or the Holy Father to Papoot?

Possum Aucoin told the boys at the barbershop, "He sure as hell ain't gonna forgive the old bastard!"

President Prejean noted, "He's an old man, and I don't blame him for getting straight with his maker."

Only Bobby Boudreaux was suspicious, but he kept his own counsel.

Bishop Peter Paul Dupuis shook his head but, of course, did not question higher holy authority. Privately, he thought, Sacrilege!

Every male eye in the First National Bank was glued on Ruth Ann's remarkable figure. She was dressed in a conservative blue dress and wore a tiny string of white pearls, which only seemed to heighten her blazing beauty. Big Shot stood when she entered his glass-enclosed office right off the bank's lobby. He took her hands in both of his and planted a kiss on her cheek, thinking, Goddamn but she smells good!

She sat opposite his desk and refused his offer of coffee. Ruth Ann got right to the point. "How could you? Zeke wasn't even cold in the ground!"

He held both hands up in supplication. Yellow diamonds glittered from two huge rings. "Ruth Ann, you don't know how I hated to do that! I've seen you raised, you're like my own. But it's not my decision."

"It's not?"

"The bank examiners from Baton Rouge just finished our annual audit. They said your loan was too old and we had to act on it or else."

"Or else, what?"

"The bank could have big trouble. They could even pull our license."

She snickered.

Big Shot looked hurt. "It's true! You don't think I'd lie to you, for goodness' sakes?"

"I don't know what I think."

Big Shot said, "I understand, you're upset."

"Wouldn't you be?" she shot back.

"Sure."

"So that's it, huh?"

"I'm sorry, but that's it."

"How much time have I got?"

He studied the calendar on his desk. "A week from today."

"And then?"

"Why we'll have to seize the *Gazette*."

"Just like that, huh?"

"It's the law."

"Any suggestions? This must be a common problem."

"Not all that common," he said. "If you could get the money someplace else."

"Who's going to loan me ten thousand dollars? Who's got that much but you and Hurphy? I don't suppose you'd make me a personal loan?"

He sighed. "Ruth Ann, I hate to say this, and please understand it's got nothing to do with your financial problems, but . . ."

She watched him search for the right words. She knew what was coming.

"You've stirred up a lot of trouble in Richelieu. I'm afraid people don't quite feel about you like they did about Zeke."

"And if I promised to stop?"

He studied her closely. "We'd take a second look."

"I'm sorry, Big Shot, I can't do that."

He was losing patience. "May I ask why?"

"You wouldn't understand."

"Try me."

"A newspaper has a soul just like we do. Its soul is Truth. If I compromised that, my paper would be dead and I would have killed it."

"It is dead, Ruth Ann. The funeral's Monday." He stood. The meeting was over. He held out his hand, which she refused to take. She turned and departed, and as Big Shot watched her, he said under his breath, "What an ass!"

Mississippi was hilly, the soil red clay. They had ridden in silence. Finally Bobby spoke. "Life's funny, huh, Moe?" The little man nodded, and Bobby said, "Look, if you don't talk, I'm going to pull over and let you out right here!"

Moe laughed and said, "Okay. Yes. Life's funny, that's as good a word as any. It's our plans that are the jokes. We make them, and along comes the Almighty with a surprise we didn't plan on. So yes, it's funny."

Bobby nodded. He desperately needed to talk to someone, and Moe was his only choice. "My life's kind of screwed up. No, it's damned screwed up." He took a big breath and spoke aloud for the first time what he'd said only to Ruth Ann. "I've gone and fallen in love with another woman. Ruth Ann Daigle. I really love her, Moe. It's what I think about and what I dream about. I guess you could say I'm consumed. At first I thought it was middle age or a hard dick. But it's not."

"Does your wife know?"

"No way. Absolutely not."

"So?"

"I want to marry her. No, I'm *gonna* marry her."

"You won't be able to stay in Richelieu."

"I know that and I hate it. I love Richelieu. Is that crazy?"

"No. There's much to love. And I would know."

"You've become one of the boys!"

"Thanks to you, Robert."

They returned to silence for several miles.

"Any suggestions, Moe?"

"About?"

"God, but I hate when you're that way! About Ruth Ann and me."

"If you're prepared to take the consequences for your actions . . . there will probably be many . . ."

"Many and then some."

"How will your wife be affected?"

"Horribly. She may even try suicide. I love her, you know. But it's not the same. BeBe's a quiet, comfortable fire. Ruth Ann's a blowtorch! Either way, I'm gonna get consumed. Huh?"

"Either way."

"You're not much help, you know?"

"I do know."

"I was hoping you'd have a miracle to offer."

"My God is not without miracles. He can part the Red Sea! He can also let many people be gassed to death for no obvious reason. I'm sorry. My God has no answers in this matter. Only you do."

"What'd you say?"

"Only you."

"That's what I thought you said." And they laughed.

The retirement home was an old house that someone had halfheartedly painted white, and now it had gone to gray. Bobby pressed a button, and they heard what sounded like a fire bell clanging inside. After a lengthy wait, an old priest bent over a walker opened the door. He saw Bobby's badge, asked, "Am I under arrest?" and chuckled at his little joke.

The interior was musty and ill lit, and it smelled of death.

They asked for Father Soulier, and the old priest motioned them to follow him, which they did as he crept through the house and out a screen door at the back. There was a single sycamore tree in the yard, and Father Soulier sat beneath it on a lawn chair.

They motioned him not to stand, and Bobby said, "Father Soulier, I'm Sheriff Bob Boudreaux of Richelieu Parish, and this is my friend, Moe Weiss."

The priest's brown eyes sparkled as he said, "Why I do believe this is a first, two firsts. A badge and a yarmulke. We've had neither here. I hope you do not shock anyone into an early grave."

"We're quite harmless," Bobby reassured the priest, who then asked to see his badge.

Bobby removed it and handed it to Father Soulier; he studied it closely. "When I was a boy, several million years ago, that's what I wanted most," he said.

Bobby took it from him and pinned it to the old man's lapel. "Well, it's a little late in coming, but it's yours."

Soulier delightedly clapped his hands. "Am I an officer of the law?" he asked.

"If I swear you in."

"By all means, do it. I'm lost without official capacity. It was taken from me. One moment I had meaning, the next . . . Well, you see me in exile, waiting to die. That's grim for a priest, isn't it? But you see, I don't feel like one anymore." He tottered to his feet; Moe grabbed his arm before he fell.

"It's so strange, so very strange. I've a million new ailments now that I'm nobody. My legs were fine. Now, well, somebody has to help me move about. Not that I do that much. To Mass. To my knees. To meals, and out here. I like it here." He raised his right arm as Moe held on.

Bobby swore him in. "You're a deputy now." Soulier sank back into his chair. Bobby and Moe sat at his side on a small wooden bench with no back.

"I have a problem. What I heard was in the confessional. That means I cannot testify in any court of law."

"We may need that testimony, Father."

"It's out of the question. I am breaking my vows by this meeting. Do not ask me to do it publicly."

"I respect your wishes, Father."

"So what I will give you is what I learned in the confessional. You must use your ingenuity and brains to do something with it. And you must protect my identity. Do we agree?"

"Yes, Father."

"You see, it wasn't your garden variety confession, nor was it to a single session or even two. It went on for several weeks. Without remorse. I think that's what got to me—no remorse. I don't think this person is capable of it. Additionally . . ."

"Go on, Father."

The priest swallowed. "He's a priest. Like I am."

Moe and Bobby looked up sharply, then at each other. The old man's words rang out to Bobby like a pistol shot. For a minute Soulier just sat there, though they could hear him breathing as he fingered the sharp edge of his badge.

Finally he spoke again. "I was his confessor. He came to me regularly. We began almost with—what you would call it?—shoptalk! Yes, the little thises and thats of the priesthood. And then one evening—he always came after sunset—he told me that he had been a bad boy!" The priest raised his right hand to Heaven. "So help me God, that's what he said. My hearing is no longer good, and I asked, 'What?' He said that he had had sex . . . it's so ghastly . . . with an altar boy. One of *his*. I was too shocked to respond, and then he went into a description. He simply could not stop. He had sodomized the child, introduced him to oral sex. I asked, no, demanded that he cease this abomination. He responded that that would not be so easy. I became physically ill, and while I vomited into my handkerchief, he departed. I think I even heard him chuckling."

The old man had begun weeping, and Moe patted his back while Bobby looked on stunned.

"We should stop," Moe said, and Bobby said, "Father, we can come back . . ."

The priest looked frightened, his voice now a wail. "No! I don't have much time." He pointed to his chest, on which the badge was pinned. "Angina." He reached into his pocket, removed a bottle, from which he took a small white tablet, and swallowed the pill. His complexion was gray. "It's all right. I'm all right now.

"He continued coming to confession, but it was no longer confession—it was as if he was taunting me. And then . . . he told me the lad was dead. He called it suicide, but I knew it was cold-blooded murder. The boy couldn't carry the burden of what had happened to him. I'm not a psychiatrist, mind you, but I'm also no fool. It was too much and something broke. Death."

"That son of a bitch," Bobby said and quickly added, "I'm sorry, Father."

"No, that's what he is. Shall I go on? What was I to do with this information? Fifty years as a priest told me to pray for sinners, do nothing else. But I couldn't! Had it been anyone but my own kind, had it been a postman or a lawyer, I believe I would have prayed and done nothing. But a cancer in my church, *on* my church, I could not dismiss. I could not sit by and perhaps let it happen again! Or maybe even if he had shown the slightest remorse, sorrow, shame, but of this there was nothing. So I went to my Bishop. I took the matter to Peter Paul Dupuis."

Bobby leaned forward, fascinated, anxious to know how this legendary cleric, this great and good man, had handled such a mess. "And . . ."

"He told me—no, promised me—that he would take care of this matter. And then he retired me, buried me alive here outside Jackson, Mississippi. Thank God it won't be for long. And that, gentlemen, is my tale. I've done my duty. I am confident that God approves. At least I hope so. It would be terrible to burn in Hell after all those years of doing His work. I think about it."

"I too have thought about God," Moe said suddenly. "Have questioned Him. Have watched His handiwork with shock and dismay. It's not unusual to wonder about . . . about things, to question. I believe that it is this journey, us seeking not only Him but his handiwork, that enables us to understand."

"And do you? Understand?" Soulier asked.

"No. But I keep trying. Sometimes I think I've inched forward, but it's an illusion. I've stayed in place. The thing is, though, I keep on trying. Maybe that's all that God wants of us, expects from us. That we keep on."

"Thank you," Soulier said. "And now I'm tired. If you gentlemen will help me inside, I will be in your debt."

They helped him to his feet. He turned to Bobby. "Am I truly a deputy?"

"Father, you're the Sheriff of Richelieu Parish."

They laughed.

On the way home, Moe turned to Bobby. "What will you do?"

"Go see the Bishop."

"And the priest?"

"Yes, him. I don't know what I'll do. Any ideas?"

They rode the rest of the way in silence.

Chapter 21

The call came to her at the *Gazette,* where she was just finishing up. It was Papoot Gaspard, asking if he could see her. She said of course, and he asked that she drive out to his home that evening. He sounded glum and old. Of course, he *was* old, but it was more. The bombast and fire had gone out of him. Zeke had thought of him as a lovable scoundrel and had feared the people of Richelieu electing a scoundrel who was not lovable. He had told Ruth Ann, "Even as we grit our teeth in rage at his shenanigans, we laugh." Zeke had believed that was as much as the people of Richelieu could expect. "After all, we're not perfect, either." Ruth Ann had responded, "Pop, you've been in Richelieu too long. The gumbo's gotten to you."

Papoot opened the door before Ruth Ann had rung the doorbell; he suggested that they sit out on the back lawn. She followed him and said, "It's beautiful." Papoot asked, "Your first time here?" She nodded, and he said, "Zeke and I killed many a bottle of port right here. He didn't exactly approve of me, but we were good friends. Did you know that?" She said yes and studied him.

His white suit was wrinkled, his necktie askew, his usually pink face was gray, and that indescribable sparkle in his eyes—that sparkle that seemed to say, "Relax, relax, it's all a joke!" had gone. Now his eyes were wary, and there were new little lines about his mouth, more prominent than his dimples. He poured a glass of sherry for each of them. Lifting his glass in a toast, he said, "To Zeke."

When they were seated he said, "You are one beautiful young lady. You could go to Hollywood!" His remark was pure Papoot, but she had to admit to herself that it delighted her.

"You've got my vote!" she said, and they laughed. He was charming, and she found him easy to be with. It was like sitting with your grandfather, a storybook grandfather with pockets full of candy.

Suddenly his face darkened. "Ruth Ann, I heard about what the bank did to you. Ah can't say ah was shocked, because Big Shot turned on me as soon as he saw me weak. Banks is bastards."

She drank in agreement, and he refilled her glass.

"May I ask what you gon' do?"

"May I ask why you want to know?" she answered.

He gave her a little toast and smiled. "Maybe ah got an answer."

"I'm all ears. God knows I don't have one."

"Suppose, just suppose, ah gave you what you owe to pay that note."

"And what would I give you in return? It will be at least five years before I could repay you."

"Ruth Ann, Ruth Ann," he said sadly. "Ah don' want no repayment. It's just money. Me, ah got plenty of money."

She thought to herself, Dear God, is he going to proposition me?

Reading the look on her face, Papoot threw back his head and laughed. "I know what you're thinking, and ten years ago you'da been right!" They both laughed. She couldn't help but love the man.

"Surely you want something?" she said as calmly as possible, trying to fight down the excitement she felt. She'd stride into the First National Bank and throw that cash in Big Shot's face! She could taste the moment. She almost didn't hear Papoot's next words.

"There's one little thing, small, won't cost you nuthin'."

Her excitement died. Here it comes, she thought.

"Lay off your investigation."

"About Ti Boy?"

"Yeah. Poor little fellow. Let him rest in peace." He wiped a tear from his eye, only one of them. "It would be best for all concerned."

"Who's 'all concerned'?"

"Why, Ruth Ann, ah'm surprised! Everybody in our li'l community. The peoples."

"What's it to you, Papoot?"

"These are mah people. Of course ah care! An' it don' matter if ah'm in office or out, they are mah people."

This was said with so much sincerity that for a moment, only a moment, she believed him. Then she stood to go.

He remained seated, his eyes narrowing. "You know you ain't exactly no saint yo'self."

She felt relieved. Now she was seeing the real Glenn "Papoot" Gaspard. She felt a kind of release. She decided to press him. "Meaning?"

"Runnin' with a married man, an' don' deny it, ah seen you all myself."

"What's it to you, Papoot?" As soon as she spit this out she wished she could reach into the air, gather up her words.

"Hell, sugar, it's mah daughter's husban'."

She tried bluffing. "That's a lie!"

"You think we all fools? There ain't nobody in Richelieu who don't know you're Bobby's pussy."

"You bastard!"

"Better be careful, li'l Ruth Ann, one of these Sundays everybody's gonna come out of Mass and find on their cars a circular telling all about you an' Bobby. All about you all. Might even have a photo taken in your bedroom."

"You wouldn't!"

"What ah got to lose? Me, ask anybody. Papoot's finished."

"And what about your daughter? You'd put her through that?"

"Ah'd do what ah got to do."

"You're a mean old man."

"You know, ah think you right. An' would you believe ah didn't plan it that way."

"Who are you really protecting, Papoot?"

"You better go."

"Who?"

"Bitch! Get out!" he roared, and she fled.

She was suddenly genuinely frightened, felt that she had been in the presence of real and ancient evil. It was a terrible feeling, and as she drove, she found herself keeping an eye on her rearview mirror, but the road behind was pitch-black. She locked both her doors. What was she afraid of? At what level had she been touched with bone-chilling fear? This was a new experience, and one that she hoped she'd never have again.

Reaching home, she rushed into the house like a frightened child, bolting the door behind her. She leaned against the wall in the small front hall, breathing heavily and trying to regain her composure. Wait! What was that sound? Had there been a sound? Surely it was her imagination, her wildly overcharged imagination. Get hold of yourself, Ruth Ann, she commanded, but she was only giving orders, not taking them, and she felt her pulse course, her heart pound. She went to the front window, raised it and peered out. Nothing stirred. She heard the sound of crickets, like always, saw the half moon, a few clouds in the sky. Nothing more. Nothing threatening.

Then *crack!* And a bullet came hurtling through the darkness. She screamed once, then moaned. After that, there was only silence. Even the crickets were still.

Chapter 22

Bobby got back to Richelieu at midnight. He and Moe had had a steak at Mike & Tony's on the Scenic Highway in Baton Rouge, where he shook hands with politicians and lobbyists. Then he dropped Moe off at the store on Main Street. Because he had been gone all day, he went to his office to check for messages in the in-box. There was nothing of importance—there never was. He checked on the night dispatcher to make sure that he was sober; he was. Then he sat at his desk, thinking. He began with a conclusion: Justin had to be put away. If Father Soulier's story was true, and he had no reason to doubt it, the community—its children—had to be protected. He had no idea how to go about this, and given that Justin was his brother-in-law, he needed counsel. Actually, he needed more; he needed someone who could help. He made a note to call Bishop Peter Paul Dupuis first thing in the morning. Christ, it *was* morning, 1:00 A.M. He had promised to call Ruth Ann, no matter what time he returned to Richelieu. He dialed her number.

He let it ring—four, five, six, seven times. He hung up and redialed. Same result. He replaced the phone in its cradle, concerned. She had to be there. He pictured her with someone else. No! He was flooded with rage. He'd kill her, kill them both. Then the rage passed and he got hold of himself. It was ridiculous! She would never do that. He decided to go see for himself.

Her house was in darkness. There was not a sound. He stood staring at it. Everything was the same . . . No! No, the front window was open. He rushed up the front steps and climbed in through the window. Her face, looking like a beautiful mask, was framed in a pool of black. She lay on the floor. He went to her, dropped to his knees, felt for a pulse. He couldn't tell. If there was one, it was flickering, like a lightbulb that was dying. He stood and searched for a light switch—there had to be one. He found it, and suddenly the room was flooded with light. Blood was bubbling from a wound between her arm and her chest. He tore her blouse off and pressed it to her wound, then cried out, "Hold on!" He found a phone and called Doc Mouton.

"Doc? Bobby. Come quick to Ruth Ann Daigle's, she's been shot. Looks bad."

Then he knelt by her and begged her again to hold on. It seemed like an hour, but it was only minutes before he heard a squad car and an ambulance roar up. Now the house was bathed in flashing red lights, almost like a scene from Misty's Paradise Inn. It took no imagination to see Na Na and his papoon dancing in their lurid glow.

Doc Mouton burst through the door and told Bobby to get out of the way. He opened his bag and gave Ruth Ann an injection. An ambulance crew stood by, their gurney ready for her. Outside, neighbors drawn to the scene stood about in pajamas and nightgowns, peering anxiously across the street. Slo' Down Angelle stood between them and the house, motioning them back.

"How is she?" Bobby asked.

Doc looked up, his face grim. "Not good, Bobby. She's lost a lot of blood. I'm gonna have to operate." He motioned the ambulance attendants to take her. They lifted her onto the gurney; moments later the ambulance was a red light and a horrifying bleating sound, rushing away.

Bobby wandered about the house. He had no idea what he was looking for. He went into her bedroom; a registered letter leaned against a table lamp. He opened it and read. "Bastards! Dirty bastards."

Leaving Slo' Down to watch the house, he went to the hospital, where Ruth Ann was already in surgery. Soon the waiting room was filled. Hurphy Perrault, face unshaven, shook his head in shock and sadness. President Prejean arrived and squeezed Bobby's arm, saying, "If there's anything I can do, anything! Maybe blood." Bobby nodded.

Bobby groaned as Watch Out Naquin entered. "I'm not here offi-cially, just as a friend," he explained. Being an undertaker required a lot of explanations in Richelieu.

Bobby looked over his shoulder as Big Shot Fontenot entered. He was about to speak when Bobby interrupted. "You dirty son of a bitch," he said softly. "I saw your fucking letter. What in the hell are you doing here?"

"Bobby," Big Shot protested, "I got to do my job, same as you."

"You motherfucker," Bobby hissed and was about to slap the man's face when he felt a hand grip his arm.

"Calm down, Bobby," Moe said.

Bobby looked at Big Shot with pure hatred and walked away. He heard Big Shot say, "Let his Jew tend him."

Mayor Big Head Arceneaux entered, looking confused, wanting to say the right thing, not able to find the proper words. He turned to the others and said, "The light's fixed." No one responded.

Hurphy went to Bobby and said, "You've got to get hold of your-self. You're the Sheriff, Bobby. You've got to find out who did it."

For a moment Bobby was stunned; he hadn't even considered that. "Me? No, I'm not up to it. I'm calling in the State Police."

"Good thinking," Hurphy said, and then they grew silent. All of them. All eyes were glued to the swinging doors behind which was the operating room. There was a big clock on the wall. Bobby watched the second hands go by, one by one.

Father Justin entered. He put his arm about Bobby, who moved away. Justin said, "Folks, let's pray." Everyone dropped to their knees, everyone but Bobby, who stood, open-mouthed, horrified at the cha-rade being played out while Ruth Ann . . . It was unthinkable. He watched Justin down on his knees. Bobby saw Ti Boy standing before him, then shut his eyes against the horror of his vision. When he opened them, Justin was again at his side. "This is terrible," he said. "Who on earth could do such a thing?"

Bobby could not resist. "You know, Justin, I could have done it, or even you. Lately I find that people, all people, are capable of any-thing. Anything. No horror is beyond us."

Justin's eyes locked into his. He knew. He smiled and turned away.

Moe whispered, "Not here. Not now."

They sat with the others. Waiting. Bobby looked at the clock. It was as if time had stopped. He buried his face in his hands, looked up when he heard the swinging doors open. It was a nurse; she shook her head, and for a moment Bobby thought that meant Ruth Ann was dead. He stood, the blood leaving his face. The nurse said, "Doc will be right out. He'll tell you." Bobby groaned. No one looked at him.

Big Shot, face still ashen, whispered to Hurphy, "Jesus, Hurphy, what have we gone an' done?"

Hurphy, eyes blinking rapidly, replied, "I didn't shoot her, did you?"

Bit Shot was shocked. "Man, don't talk that way!"

Again the swinging doors opened, and Doc Mouton, in a bloody green surgical gown, entered. "She's gonna be okay. The bullet missed her heart by exactly two inches. She's a lucky girl. Does anybody know if there's any family?"

Bobby uttered a silent prayer of thanks. Justin did it aloud, "Praised be God. He is a merciful God." There were "Amens." Big Shot said, "No, Zeke didn't have no family. His brother died last year in California."

Doc said, "Somebody's going to have to sit with her, tend her."

Bobby blurted, "BeBe will do it." Justin gave him a long look, face impassive. Hurphy said, "Count on Anita, too." Everybody chimed in with offers of help.

Bobby asked, "Can I see her?"

"She's still under, Bobby. Wait awhile," Doc Mouton said.

It was still dark as Bobby returned to his office and placed a call for Colonel Harrison, who commanded the Louisiana State Police in Baton Rouge. He explained the attempted murder and asked for help. The Colonel promised to send out his top investigative team that morning and reminded Bobby to keep the crime scene off-limits. The crime lab would be there too. Bobby thanked him and hung up. Then he got in his car for the drive home.

BeBe lay on her side. She appeared to be in a deep sleep. He touched her. "BeBe, wake up. I need you." She turned over immediately, thrilled that he needed her. She covered his hand with hers and waited.

He sat on the side of the bed. "Someone tried to kill Zeke's daughter."

"Aw no!"

"Yes."

"Did they do it?"

"Huh?"

"Is she dead?"

"No. They missed. But close. Almost got her in the heart."

"That's terrible."

"She's at the clinic. There's no family. I was wondering if you'd go sit with her?"

She jumped up. "Of course! Poor thing." She sounded sincere. He could not meet her eyes.

She went into the bathroom, and he sat slumped over, looking down at the floor. What was he going to do? His world was spinning out of control. He had lost the handle. He thought of the old priest and shuddered. BeBe returned, dressed, and Bobby said, "I'll take you."

When they were on their way, Bobby said, "BeBe, I appreciate this."

"I'm a good Catholic," she said.

To that he had no answer.

"Who do you think did it, Bobby?"

"I've no idea. It could be a lot of people. She'd stirred up trouble, the town was upset with her. It could have been anybody. I've got the State Police coming to investigate."

"I never heard of you doing that. Couldn't you do it, Bobby?"

He didn't know how to answer. He said, "No."

"You never told me where you went today, Bobby."

"Just business," he said, then, to reassure her that he hadn't been with Ruth Ann he added, "I took Moe with me."

"You closer to Moe than your own kind, Bobby."

He answered honestly, "Right now I don't exactly know who my own kind is."

"You must be mixed up."

"Yes. I am."

"Maybe you ought to have a talk with Justin."

"I plan on doing exactly that."

BeBe smiled and squeezed his arm.

Chapter 23

For Ruth Ann it was a long and disturbing sleep. She saw the bullet, saw it coming at her, spread her arms and waited. When it smacked against her (there was no sound in these dreams), she felt it enter her, a liquid feeling, like something dropping through yellow-gold oil, then passing through her. She felt a breeze pass through the hole, cold and foreboding, like a cube of ice melting inside her. She saw it slowly blend like blue water and then pink and finally a crimson red. The red was a throw rug, and she was in its center, arms and legs out-stretched symmetrically, a pattern. Then sound. A woman's voice coming from someplace else, over a hill, off in the distance.

"She's coming out of it."

Her eyes fluttered open, then closed, then opened wide. She believed she was dead and in Hell; it was payback time for her sins. She felt guilt and mumbled, "S-sorry."

BeBe and Bobby stood over her, BeBe, leaning over her, tenderly wiping her brow with a cool cloth, Bobby behind, looking over his wife's shoulder, dark, like BeBe's shadow.

She muttered, "I'm hurt. I hurt."

He said, "Ruth Ann, you were shot, but it missed your heart. Doc Mouton says you're gonna be okay."

She saw the tube leading from her arm to a bottle suspended over where she lay. Was she on the rug or in a bed? And what did it mat-ter? What did anything matter? She sobbed, because at that moment, nothing did.

"It's all right, it's all right," BeBe said and squeezed her hand.

Bobby said, "BeBe, Anita, and a lot of the ladies, are looking after you. You're not alone."

Now she was wide awake. "Who did it?"

"We don't know that. The State Police are investigating. They'll catch him."

BeBe nodded. They were so sure. Ruth Ann wasn't. "It could be anybody," she said.

A nurse entered the room. "Sheriff, there's a phone call for you."

Bobby went to the phone at the small nurses' station. "Sheriff? Oubre here with the State Police. Better come down to your office. We've got a confession."

Stunned, Bobby hung up slowly, for a moment unable to fit the receiver into its cradle. He returned to Ruth Ann's room, where BeBe was supporting her head while she drank water through a blue straw.

"That was the State Police. They think they've got someone."

BeBe dropped the glass. Water splattered over the blanket. "Look a' me. I'm so clumsy," she said. BeBe and the nurse were changing Ruth Ann's bedding when Bobby went out to his car.

The radio was on, and Na Na was offering his expertise. "Me, I never thought such a thing could happen in this town. I was tellin' my De De, 'What's this world comin' to?' No matter what Ruth Ann Daigle did, she didn't deserve nothin' like that! Ah'm gon' play a tune for that little girl." And he put on a scratchy recording of a choir singing "The Lord's Prayer."

Bobby angrily flicked off the radio. What did the Lord have to do with this? Or anything! he thought. Anything!

In the barbershop, the shooting was the single topic. Possum had a theory: "How they know she didn't do it to herself?"

Hurphy looked exasperated. "They didn't find the gun! What the hell you think she did with it, ate it?"

Big Shot said, "The bank's gon' offer a reward. Five hundred dollars for anyone who knows anything. It's a disgrace!"

Nonc Doucet awakened from his slumber and said, "For that much money, I'll confess!" Then he went back to sleep while everyone laughed.

Tooky Trahan said, "Me, ah been prayin' for her since it happened. She wasn't no angel, but she didn't deserve nothin' like that."

One Lung Savoy coughed as the others eyed him with distaste and tried to duck his spittle. "Two to one they don't catch him."

Coon Soileau agreed. "Naw, not a chance. Me, ah got Catfish makin' a big gumbo to bring to the poor little thing."

Watch Out Naquin said, "Whoever it was, wasn't no good shot. They wouldn't have missed."

Hurphy considered this and said, "Maybe they wanted to miss. Maybe they were a damn good shot."

Possum said, "Why the hell would they do that? You kill or you don' kill."

Hurphy shook his head. "It could have just been a warning."

Hot Dog Hebert liked the theory. ". . . to stop askin' all them questions and leave the dead rest."

Possum added, "Or to stay away from a married man."

Moe, in a corner, waiting his turn in the barber's chair, said nothing.

As he got out of his car, Bobby wondered what he would do. Could he control himself? Or would he choke Justin there and then? He felt rage building inside him.

Detective Oubre greeted him in the hall. "We put him in your office."

Bobby said, "Mind if I question him alone?"

"It's your courthouse," Oubre said as Bobby turned the doorknob.

Cap'n Eddie Sonnier, in khakis with his crossing guard hat, stood quietly looking out a window. When Bobby entered, he turned, a winsome smile on his face. Bobby didn't know what he felt. It was some combination of anger and relief. The trouble was, it didn't make any sense. He motioned Cap'n Eddie into a chair, and he sat on the corner of his desk, wondering where to begin, how to begin.

"You confessed?"

Cap'n Eddie said, "Yessir."

"Why?"

"I did it."

"But why'd you confess?"

"I want to leave the earth."

"I don't follow you."

"I'll get the chair."

"No. She didn't die. If you really did it, you'll go to . . . I don't know, Angola or a hospital. Now why did you do it?"

"Remember our little talk?"

"I remember."

"I didn't stop. I couldn't stop."

"Did you do anything with Ti Boy?"

"Who?"

"Ti Boy!" Bobby shouted, then felt ashamed. It was shouting at an oak tree. "Little Brouliette."

"Him. Yes."

"You looked at him?"

"Yes. Yes I did."

"More?"

"Yes. More."

"What?"

"With my mouth."

"Oh shit. How many times?"

"Many. Lots of times."

"And he went along with it?"

"He didn't want to. I kept on."

"Okay. You forced him. I'm not gonna ask you why; I don't guess you know."

"I don't know."

"Well, let's get to the shooting. Your rifle? Okay. What did you do with it?"

"I don't know."

"Man, cut out the bullshit."

"I threw it in the bayou."

"Okay, which bayou?"

"I don't remember. It was dark. Night is dark."

"Why?"

"Huh?"

"Why'd you shoot Ruth Ann?"

"I don't know."

"You read the *Gazette*?"

"No. Not anymore."

"Eddie, look at me. Why do you want to die?"

"I am so alone."

Bobby wanted to cry. Never in all his life had he heard anyone say that. It was the saddest thing he'd ever heard anyone say. He stared at Cap'n Eddie, standing there with that ridiculous cap. And Cap'n Eddie stared back at him, his face a solemn mask.

Bobby stood. "I'm gonna put you in jail. You need to be protected from yourself. I'll get Doc Mouton to have a talk with you. We'll send you someplace, someplace nice. The Veterans have a place in Biloxi. It's near the beach; you'll see the sand. But, Eddie . . . you didn't kill anybody. It was you that got killed."

"And I won't be alone?"

"No, cher, you won't be alone."

Word spread like floodwaters when the dam breaks. Ruth Ann had been right: Cap'n Eddie Sonnier, a crazy man, a war hero, was responsible for Ti Boy's suicide (it was a suicide), and for trying to kill Ruth Ann for digging it up.

Sport Baudoin told the boys in the barbershop, "I'd like to throw my fastball right at his head."

The American Legion quickly took down the plaque displaying Cap'n Eddie's name.

Hot Dog Hebert said, "I'd like to shove him in my big oven. That'd fix him."

Possum Aucoin took the philosophic approach: "A cocksucker's a cocksucker."

Papoot, suddenly religious, said, "The Lord works in strange ways." He no longer spoke to Justin. Not a word. What he wanted to say he could not say, so he said nothing. The two men stared at each other, a dare on both their faces—who would speak first? BeBe didn't even notice, because she was so busy with Ruth Ann.

It was the best period of BeBe's life since her early years with her beloved Bobby. She spent all her time at the hospital, bathing the other woman, combing her glorious hair (the shine was returning, BeBe noted excitedly). She gave her alcohol rubdowns and even took out the bedpan. She loved feeding her, careful not to spill a drop.

Ruth Ann said, "You're so good to me."

BeBe kissed her cheek and said, "You're my little girl." And both women wept. Bobby came for a visit once a day and made small talk. Never, not once, was he alone with Ruth Ann, and their eyes stopped meeting, sending messages. There might as well have been a stone wall between them. BeBe's love and attention were so strong, so powerful, they were impossible to penetrate. BeBe clucked about Ruth Ann like a mother hen. "Look how pretty my Ruth Ann looks today. See, her color's coming back!" Bobby nodded dumbly.

The other women stopped visiting—BeBe didn't want them. Ruth Ann was hers! And when, after ten days had passed, Doc Mouton said Ruth Ann could go home, BeBe took her to their house, hers and Bobby's.

Maybelle insisted on coming out and giving Ruth Ann the latest Parisian haircut, at absolutely no cost. And when she was finished and gone, BeBe and Ruth Ann had a good laugh as BeBe combed the hair, back to the way it had been. "Nobody can improve on that," BeBe said, and Ruth Ann squeezed her hand.

That night Bobby drove to Lafayette for his appointment with Bishop Dupuis. He couldn't recall ever having a 10:00 P.M. appointment before.

It struck him that the Bishop's red cap looked exactly like Moe's little black cap. The Bishop extended his hand, and Bobby kissed his ring. When the Sheriff was seated, the Bishop offered no help. He waited, his hands clasped in a temple before him. Bobby noticed the nails were buffed. The Bishop saw him staring, collapsed the temple, and folded his hands in his lap.

"About Ti Boy Brouliette . . ."

The Bishop smiled. "I was so relieved to hear you've got the guilty party."

Bobby was astonished. It was like the Bishop had socked him in the solar plexus. He didn't know what to say. Should he leave it be? Let the guilty go unpunished? He was suddenly conscious, in a way that he had never been before, of the badge on his chest. That was what it was about! The law. It was just that simple. It was tangible. Something had to stay in place. Faith was okay, but you couldn't see it—it was inside you. But the law . . .

"Bishop, that won't do."

The Bishop was incredulous. No one, no one, disagreed with him, not to his face. It was as if the other man had slapped him. "What did you say?"

"I said it won't do. I know, and you know, who's responsible for Ti Boy."

"Oh? And where pray tell did we learn this?"

"From Father Soulier. His confessor."

"He's senile. Don't you know? Crazy as . . . as . . ." He unsuccessfully searched for a word.

"A loon," Bobby helped out. "No, sir. He's old and buried—you buried him. But crazy? No sir. He's as sane as you or me. And probably a lot more honest."

"Are you aware who you're talking to, young man?"

"Yessir. The Bishop. My Bishop. But I'm somebody too. Sheriff of Richelieu Parish, elected by the people. I guess you've got a duty, but I've got one for sure."

The Bishop's handsome face broke into a smile. "Tell me, Sheriff, have you discussed this with your father-in-law? Oh yes," the Bishop said, and it sounded like he was suddenly enjoying their conversation, "he knows, he knows it all."

"I don't understand."

"Better understand. I told him, of course. We were talking about his son, his only son. I don't believe he wanted anything done to that son. Tell me, Sheriff, have you a son?"

"Have you?"

The Bishop studied him steadily. He was not used to a verbal battle in his own office. How strange, he thought; in their past dealings he had found Bobby Boudreaux easygoing, pliable, wanting to be liked. Even innocuous. But no more. Something had changed in the man; the pliability was gone, and in its place was a sense of duty. The Bishop removed his red cap. From here on the discussion would be man-to-man. How seldom that opportunity came to him; he rather enjoyed the prospect. He was a man. And, obviously, so was Boudreaux. His tone changed.

"Sheriff, let's start over. There's no need for enmity between us. We both have a job to perform, an unpleasant one. Perhaps if we put our heads together—and only perhaps, because it won't be easy—we can arrive at a solution mutually satisfactory. Shall we give it a try?"

Bobby sensed the Bishop was sincere. He said, "I'd like that."

"Would you like some port? It's good." Bobby nodded, and the Bishop poured two glasses. He said, lifting his glass to Bobby, "To the right decision." Bobby's glass touched his, and they both drank. The walls were down.

"You see, there's a precedent, an ugly one, for what happened in Richelieu. You remember when Father Justin came home from Europe?"

"When Miss Annabelle killed herself."

"He was coming home anyway. He had been caught in a rather ugly homosexual matter in Rome. With a young boy. I called Papoot. We talked and I erred, perhaps we both did. Papoot said if I sent Justin to Richelieu, he would be responsible for his son's actions. Now a child is dead. Sorry to say I have not heard one word from Papoot. It's like our agreement never happened."

"That's him all right."

"It's my intention to send Justin someplace else. Perhaps to a diocese in Montana. Maybe on an Indian reservation. It'll be over."

"Maybe your job will be done. Mine won't. In a way, Justin killed that kid, just the same as if he had shot him himself. I'm the Sheriff, I can't sweep murder under the rug. I'd like to, it's my natural instinct, sweep it under the rug, try to forget about it. Especially in this case. A year ago, a few months ago, I could have done it." His voice lowered. "I've changed. I have no explanation for it, but I have."

"Maturity. Some of us mature late. Some of us never do. Some of us have selective maturity, depending on the occasion." The Bishop sighed. "Some of us do things because we must. That's me I'm referring to. I can't have this diocese destroyed. I love it. It is my life. Can you understand that? I love them. All of them. I'm one of them. I know them as a father knows his young, their good and their bad, and like all human beings, they possess the potential for both. That attitude does me no great honor. I also seem to have lost a sense of right and wrong. You, on the other hand, seem to have found it. I envy you."

"Don't. Believe me, I'm nobody to envy."

"Want to tell your Bishop about it?"

"No. But I will. I've fallen in love with another woman. A beautiful young woman. I want to leave with her."

"Leave?"

"Richelieu. My job. My . . ." He hesitated. "My wife, who is a very good woman."

"I see."

"I doubt it. How could you?"

"You also are one of my children, Bobby."

They drank their port, and they followed it with another glass.

"Well, aren't you going to say something?" Bobby asked.

"You mean, am I going to tell you what to do?"

"I guess that's what I wanted to hear."

"I'm sorry. I won't do that. Surprised?"

"Yes."

"I have a feeling, as I sometimes do, and I've learned to trust these feelings, probably because they're based on nothing. I have one now—that whatever you do, you'll do the right thing. I find you a good man, and good men almost always do the right thing."

"That's not much help," Bobby said.

The Bishop laughed. "I think it is. Now, what about Justin?"

"I'll handle it."

"Will you arrest him?"

"No."

"What about Montana?"

"No. There's kids there too." Bobby stood, as did the Bishop, who extended a hand, but Bobby asked, "May I kiss your ring?"

Bishop Peter Paul Dupuis's eyebrows shot up. "Why?"

"I believe you're a good man too."

Bobby knelt and kissed the Bishop's ring.

Chapter 24

Papoot sat back of his desk, Moose opposite him. "You gon' take me to Rome?" Moose asked.

"Are you crazy? You ain't lost nothin' in Rome. Besides, I got somethin' for you to do right here."

Moose tried to mask his disappointment. He had been to Rome, Georgia, but never to the one overseas, and he sure would have liked to say he'd been to both. "What's that?"

Papoot smiled. "I want you to grow a beard. A big black one."

"A what?"

"A beard, you know, hair on your face."

"I ain't never had one of those."

"Well, you gon' have one now."

"How I do that, Papoot?"

"Don' shave. Not one time while I'm gone. In fac', lay low. I don't want nobody to know."

"To know what?"

"Fool! That you got a beard." Papoot sat up, taking his white shoes off his desk. "Now, is Papa Sotile out there?"

"With his fiddle."

"Sen' him in. You wait outside. An' don' listen at the door. This is private. Comprende?"

"Yes, chief," the giant said and lumbered out.

Papa Sotile entered, cased fiddle in his hand. He was a short, rotund man, with wavy black hair and a carbuncle on his nose.

"You got it, Papa?"

The fiddler nodded. "Perfeck."

"Well let's hear it."

"It wasn't easy, no, Papoot."

"You bastard, you charged me enough! Now play!"

Papa Sotile opened the case, removed the fiddle and bow, put the instrument under his chin, and began to play.

Moose, ear pressed against the door, was confused. The tune was sad, and he'd never heard it before. And for the very first time since Papoot had saved his ass, he wondered if his main man was going crazy. And how 'bout askin' him to grow that hair on his face? What the hell was going on?

Inside the office, Papoot wiped away a tear and said, "You got it!"

Papa Sotile touched his carbuncle for luck and said, "Enough for a little bonus? Say another twenty-five?"

Papoot reached into his wallet, took out three twenties, and extended them across the desk. "Sixty-dollar bonus. You done it, Papa, you done it!"

Now Moose was certain that Papoot was crazy—usually he didn't pay no debt and then dared the other person to do something about it. "Sue me! Hee, hee!" he would say. And here he was givin' a sixty-dollar bonus! Moose wondered if he could get a little extra—all them li'l hairs he had to grow on his face had to be worth something.

Big Shot Fontenot jumped to his feet as BeBe waddled in, noting that she was getting as big as a house. He wondered if she had any idea just how rich she was. For years Papoot had been depositing big money in her account but putting nothing in Justin's. Families were funny. Big Shot gave her a big kiss and watched her settle in the chair, looking, he thought, like one of them hot-air balloons setting down on earth.

He poured her a cup of coffee from a silver urn and opened a box of Danish butter cookies he kept for special customers. He got them every month from Solari's in New Orleans. Regular folks got coffee in paper cups, if they were lucky. Big Shot wasn't all that big on giving away much to anybody. That was not the way to accumulate a for-tune, which he had done. It was okay to talk charity, but be damn sure you kept it just to talk. He'd known many fools who'd charitied themselves to the poorhouse. That wouldn't happen to him.

"Now, sweet girl, what brings you out in all this heat?" he asked with a smile. The heat had to be terrible on her, he reckoned, carrying all that fat. His office was actually cold. "It's not too cool in here, is it, BeBe?" But she didn't hear him as her fingers traveled over the butter cookies, choosing just the right one. She'll never get to it, he thought. Taking the tin from her, he closed it and extended it back to her. "Take this home, cher, you and Bobby will enjoy it."

She hugged the can to her. He said, "Yes?"

"Big Shot, I want to pay off what Ruth Ann owes."

He wasn't certain that he'd heard her right. "You what?"

"What she owes on the paper. Do I have enough money in the bank?"

"Why, yes," he said, like the sum wasn't so huge. "You could do it."

"Well, let's do it now."

"BeBe, you know, to me you're like my own daughter, and I got to ask you this: Are you sure you know what you're doing?"

"Sure, I'm sure."

"May I ask why?"

"Me and Bobby never had no kids, and Ruth Ann, well, she's like my little girl."

Big Shot sagged in his chair and thought, You idiot! He asked, "And Bobby?"

"I'm the mama and Bobby's the daddy."

Big Shot collapsed in the chair. "I see," he said, like she made sense. Fool, fat fool! he thought, his face beaming all the while. BeBe was busy prying open the tin and removing a butter cookie. It disap-peared into her mouth even as her fingers located another.

"Er, BeBe, have you thought about what you'll do with the *Gazette*?"

"Me?" she said, swallowing her third cookie.

"Why yes. You'll own it."

She stood, chewing. "We'll see. Me, ah don't know nothin' about no newspaper."

"That makes sense," he said.

Ruth Ann was cutting up vegetables for a salad when BeBe returned. BeBe watched her with great satisfaction. She was teaching Ruth Ann to cook, and she already was able to make a pretty good potato salad and a better than average banana pie, both among Bobby's favorites. BeBe wanted to offer her some of the butter cookies, but there were none left. Not even a crumb.

They sat opposite each other at the breakfast table. Ruth Ann poured the coffee. It was so cozy, and BeBe thought, It's sure nice not to be by yourself.

BeBe said, "Ruth Ann, you don't have no more worries."

"I don't?"

"I went to the First National and paid that bill you owed."

"No!"

"Aw yeah. Look, here's the papers."

Ruth Ann's eyes glistened. "I don't know how I can ever repay you. You've saved my life. Nobody, not even Zeke, has shown me the love you have. And you didn't owe me anything." She wanted to say, You owe me a kick in the head, but she couldn't bring herself to say it. She was confused. She had been confused since the bullet knocked her to the floor. How could someone as simple as BeBe confuse her so?

"The only thing is, it won't be your paper no more. Big Shot says, Me, I own it now."

"I'm glad. Anybody but the First National. I guess it never was mine. They owned it. They just didn't own me. I like you being the boss! And I'm ready to go back to work, if I'm still hired."

"Just like always," BeBe said. She poured them a second cup and wished she had saved a few cookies, but since they were gone she decided on the spot to make a banana pie, maybe two. "Ruth Ann, can I ask you a favor?"

Here it comes, thought Ruth Ann. She said, "Anything," and meant it.

"Can I come with you to the paper and do little odds and ends? I won't get in the way."

Ruth Ann laughed. "Can you? You're the boss! Of course you can!"

"You won't mind, Ruth Ann?"

"I love you, BeBe," she said, and she realized as she said it that she really did.

BeBe clapped her pudgy hands together, thrilled. She couldn't remember when anybody had said that to her. "And one more thing."

Ruth Ann looked her in the eyes and thought, If it's about Bobby, what'll I say?

"I'm ashamed to ask this," BeBe said. She was blushing and looking down at her coffee up.

"Go ahead."

She was whispering so softly Ruth Ann could hardly hear her. "Would you . . . do you think . . . once in a while, when we by ourself, could you . . ."

"Yes?"

"Call me Mama?"

Ruth Ann didn't hesitate. "Yes, Mama."

The two women wept and fell into each other's arms. Neither found it bizarre. Real love came so naturally.

Bobby sat parked in front of St. Ann's Catholic Church. A handful of cars dotted the parking lot. The sun had set, and clouds moved across the full moon. The night was dark and still. Bobby went inside, dipped his fingers in the font, and made the sign of the cross. He sat in the very last row, his eyes on the confessional. Candles flickered about him, throwing shadows across his face. A woman walked out of the booth and, without looking his way, proceeded down the aisle and outside. Bobby stood, went to the confessional, slipped inside and sat down. There was silence from the priest's compartment.

Bobby intoned, "Forgive me, Father, for I have sinned."

Justin sat up with a start. Bobby. Little Bobby. He had never heard his confession. "I'm glad you've come. God's patience was wearing a little thin."

"Yes, Father," Bobby said dutifully.

He's contrite! Justin thought. Mr. High and Mighty is contrite. Why dear me, the arrogance has vanished from his voice. Justin shifted about, making himself comfortable. Hearing this confession would be a pleasure, and there hadn't been that many lately. When Bobby remained quiet, Justin decided to wait him out. Let him stew in his own wretched juices, he thought.

"I am guilty of the sin of doing nothing," Bobby began.

Hardly, Justin thought, and wondered if Bobby was going to deny his adultery. Just let him try it! He and his slut wouldn't get off that easily. God wouldn't stand for it. And I won't, he thought. Justin often confused his and God's reactions to people's sins, the major difference being that he was a lot tougher than God. Not so forgiving. Pound of flesh time, he thought, pounds of flesh. Saw Bobby's naked skull, strips of bloody meat hanging off. It was a glorious sight.

He could have shouted, sent his voice echoing through the church! Instead he made his voice most pious, filled with charity, wisdom, yet not without mettle. "The sin of omission is as serious in His sight as commission."

"I know," Bobby said. "I know." He sounded deliciously guilty.

Spill it out, you bastard, Justin thought, rubbing his palms together in anticipation. "You may tell me."

"Oh, I must!"

Was there something ironic in that response? The finger of uneasiness tickled Justin, and now his hands locked in a clench. "Proceed," he said dully.

"I did nothing about the commission of a crime."

Justin did not want him to go any further. He had the need to scream Stop! He bit his bottom lip, drawing blood. He could taste himself. "Say ten Hail Marys . . ."

"Father, don't you want to know about the crime?"

"All right, but get on with it. It's late. It's been a long day and I am very weary." He was. His shoulders suddenly felt as if they were under a burden, and he experienced pain at the base of his spine.

"The crime was murder."

"Uh-huh."

"The murder of a child. An innocent child."

"We are none of us innocent! Corruption, decay, finality begin with birth."

"This child was innocent. Whatever corruption there was, whatever evil, was placed on him like a yoke. He couldn't bear it. So he took his life."

"A tragedy."

"An unfinished tragedy."

"God will finish it."

"I don't completely trust God."

"Blasphemy. You're in His house!"

"We're both in His house. I, who am not sure, and you . . ."

"Yes? What am I?"

"Don't you know?"

The priest's voice was louder, hysteria barely contained. "What am I?"

"Sick. Very, very sick."

"Oh? And are you a physician? A psychiatrist perhaps. I don't remember, did you ever finish high school?"

"Barely."

"A fool."

"But not sick. You see, Father, I don't find kids, little boys, sexually attractive."

"You, I believe, tend to go for whores. Is there a difference? Is there that much difference? We all break vows. Sometimes I believe that's what they're created for, to be broken, to put us in touch with our morality."

"I wonder when it began. In Rome? Probably before that."

Justin shrieked, "Who told you that?"

"Bishop Peter Paul Dupuis."

"It was never proven. It never went to court."

"No. They got you out of there just in time. But not in time enough to save Annabelle."

"You bastard! Leave my mother out of this. My mother was a saint!"

"A dead one. Another death on your record."

"*Liar!* Blasphemous liar!"

"She killed herself over you and your disgrace. You should have gone to jail then, but Papoot bought you out of it. But not this time. This time you're going to make the payment. This time you're gonna close the account, Justin."

"How sanctimonious and righteous you are! Oh, my God, mark the upright! If only you knew."

Now Bobby felt uneasy; the match had shifted subtly.

Justin felt himself becoming sexually aroused. Inflicting pain was a glorious high, had always been. Well, didn't God inflict pain? Wasn't God loving this? Sinners flaying each other to ribbons—the whole goddamn church was covered in blood. God didn't need to do the dirty work. God could stay majestic, off at a distance. Puny, stupid, weak men did the dirty work for him.

Justin's voice was calm now, normal. "Maybe you'd better talk to your wife."

"BeBe?"

"My fat sister."

"Don't talk that way! She's a better person than you or I will ever be."

"Is she? Is she now? Ha! Ask her if she has tried to kill anyone lately? Huh? Will you ask her that? Mister Righteous! Mister perfect man."

"What . . . ?" Bobby was dazed, sat limp. Had the walls of the tiny compartment moved? Suddenly there was less space, no space, and he had trouble breathing. He was gulping for air.

"She shot your pussy, tried to kill her, just missed. Go home, Bobby! Go home, make an arrest."

"Justin, listen to me. Listen very carefully. In a week I'm going to arrest you. You'll be put away. You're insane. Criminally insane."

Once more the game shifted. "No! No, you can't do that. I'll leave. I'll go someplace else. You'll never hear from me again. I'll be out of your life, gone from Richelieu. I swear. Do you hear me, Bobby? I *swear*!"

Bobby's voice was sad. "I can't do that, Justin. Wherever you go, there would be kids. I can't turn you loose on them."

"I'll stop. You have my word as a priest! My sacred oath—it's over. I don't need it anymore. I'm in full control. Can't you tell? I'm in control!"

"One week from today," Bobby said, calmness back in his voice. "That's seven days."

Justin was crying now, sobbing. To Bobby, he sounded like a baby. "Why are you doing this to me? Have I ever hurt you? Why, Bobby, why?"

"Because I am the Sheriff of Richelieu Parish." He stood on trembling legs. He felt vanquished, like his spine had left his body. He made his way down the dark aisle. A single candle still burned.

From the confessional came the sound of gut-wrenching sobs.

Chapter 25

BeBe loved working at the *Gazette* with Ruth Ann. She willingly became the errand girl, the coffee maker. She even enjoyed sweeping the always littered floors. Ruth Ann was still weak and could not have done without her.

She said, "BeBe, I have an idea. Why don't you write something?"

BeBe blushed. "Me? I can't hardly spell c-a-t."

"I'll do the spelling. But I know something you could really write, something people would love. Why don't you write a recipe column? We'll call it 'BeBe in the Kitchen.' What do you say?"

"I never did nothing like that in my life, Ruth Ann. I'd have to ask Bobby if it's okay."

"What does Bobby have to do with it?"

"He's my husband, Ruth Ann."

"But you're a person too."

"Me, I never thought of it that way. Still, ah'm gon' ask Bobby. But if he says no, ah'm gon' do it anyway!"

The two women laughed delightedly.

In the past few days, Bobby had become silent and morose. He spoke only when spoken to. He avoided eye contact with either woman.

They sat eating supper, the two women prattling away, Bobby quiet, looking down at his plate and the chicken stew it contained.

Ruth Ann said, "When we're finished eating, I need to talk to you."

BeBe said, "I'll go right now so you all can . . ."

Ruth Ann said, "No, I need to talk to both of you."

Bobby's chicken stew turned to ashes in his mouth, the taste leaden. He stirred the remaining food in the plate. BeBe stood and got the banana pie, three fourths of it whipped cream. She cut three huge slices. They ate it in silence, Bobby forcing every delicious morsel down his throat. He feared he would gag, throw up the contents of his stomach. He and Ruth Ann did not look at each other. BeBe said, "Thass gon' be my firs' recipe for my column. I made up this pie."

Ruth Ann nodded in agreement. Bobby hadn't even heard her—he was hearing only his own heartbeat, pounding as loudly as the bass drum at the Friday night football game.

Ruth Ann said, "Let's get this over with." Bobby looked directly at her for the first time, and BeBe looked from one to the other like she was watching a tennis match. "I'm leaving," Ruth Ann said. "As soon as I can pack. The paper's yours, BeBe, and I'll help you find someone to do what I did. It shouldn't be any trouble. Maybe we can get an LSU journalism grad."

"The paper's what?" Bobby asked incredulously.

"Now, don't be mad, Bobby. Ah was gon' tell you. Ah went to Big Shot and paid Ruth Ann's note," BeBe explained.

"Why?" He really wanted to know. He leaned forward, studying his wife, perhaps for the first time. He looked for evidence of the pretty girl she'd been, but it was buried in fat. Her eyes were still gentle, her mouth sweet, her dimples deeper. It was still a youthful face. But it just wasn't the same. He wondered for the first time if he knew her. Had he ever known her? Another goddamn mystery.

BeBe looked back at him with tenderness and love. Her Bobby! How could a woman be so lucky! What had she ever done to deserve such a beautiful man? "I didn't want Ruth Ann to have no worries. Me and her is close. She's like . . . Don't be mad, Bobby, I don't want to start cryin' but she's . . . like my own little girl."

"Jesus."

"We don' have no kids." She said it without emotion, but he could read her. Regret and sadness. How strange! He'd never even thought about it, didn't know it mattered. Obviously it did.

"If it had been any other woman than BeBe," Ruth Ann explained,

"I'd stay here. I'd stay here and fight for you, Bobby. But if I won you, it wouldn't really be a victory. I know that sounds, well, peculiar, but I'd win and lose. I . . . we couldn't build a life, not here, that way. If BeBe wasn't so loving, if she wasn't so decent, I'd go for it. To hell with the consequences! But she is. She's, well, I guess you could say she's the mama I never had. It was always just me and Zeke. Something very big and important was missing."

She tried to kill you, Bobby screamed in his head.

"Ruth Ann, I'm the one done it," BeBe said, tears welling in her eyes.

Ruth Ann turned to her and gently patted her hand. "I know. I guessed. But I'm not sure I wouldn't have done the same thing."

BeBe was crying. "You don' hate me?"

Ruth Ann squeezed her hand. "I love you. You too, Bobby. That's why I gotta go."

BeBe stood. "You all talk." She left them.

Ruth Ann spoke quietly. They could hear the crickets outside, and amazingly, a slight breeze blew through the open window. Perhaps it would rain later. "When I lay in the hospital, I hated myself for ever coming back here. I upset the balance in this tiny piece of the world. I got in the way of the natural rhythm of the way things went along. And the tragedy's not through, is it?"

"No."

"Justin?"

"Yes."

"Poor BeBe. She adores her brother."

"He's a real sick man. He gave her permission, his blessings, for what she did."

Her face was filled with horror. "My God!"

Bobby stared back. There were dark circles under his eyes. In only moments he had aged visibly, joy had fled him. It would, he knew, never be the same again.

"What will you do about him?"

"I've given him until July fifth, and then I'm going to have him put away. He should be locked up. He's quite mad and capable of any-thing. I believe he confuses himself with God."

"Why July fifth?"

"Oh, so he could see Papoot call it a day. Hell, I don't know why."

"You're lying, aren't you?"

"Yeah."

"You don't want to arrest him."

"No."

"You want him to—"

"Let's talk about something else. Please. We haven't much time."

"No time."

"Ruth Ann, in the name of God, why are you doing this to us? I told you I'd go with you. You knew it would take a little time. I had to finish the Justin business, but it's almost over now. Please. Please, Ruth Ann, I'm begging you, I love you."

"I know that. You are my love. But it wouldn't be any good . . ."

"You're killing me!"

"Me too, Bobby. Me too."

"BeBe. Is it possible that she planned . . . Naw, no way."

"No. I'm sure not. Conscience. She knew what she had done. She wanted to make it up to me. She's a good woman. She truly is. And a lonely, confused one. She had a great void in her life, a great need. I filled that need, and then it wasn't conscience anymore. It was, I believe, love."

"Love!" he spit out.

"Isn't it the damndest? Comes in so many varieties, shapes, sizes. It's like the wind. You can't see it, but Lord, what power."

"I'll never love again. I had a taste. One taste, and oh, but I loved it. I loved being in love. Jesus, that doesn't leave me much."

"We'll remember."

"Memories aren't what I had in mind."

"Sometimes they have to suffice."

"What'll you do in New Orleans?"

"The *Picayune* will take me back."

"And that guy?"

"I don't know if he's even there anymore. Had his eyes on Chicago."

"He'll be there. Nobody's dancing off from you unless he's got no choice. That's me. No choice. It's you doing the dancing. Me, I'm standing in place. Got noplace else to go. Alone. Goddamnit but I hate to be alone. It never bothered me before. I thought it was the way life was. I was alone with my old man, alone with my wife. Then you . . . and God but it was nice!"

"It was wonderful. Good-bye, Bobby. Good-bye, my love." They looked at each other, read each other's eyes, heard each other breathing, and heard each other's heartbeats.

He stood and went to her, wrapped his arms about her, looked down into her beautiful face. He lowered his lips to hers, but she had turned, and he kissed her on the cheek. Her cheek was wet with tears, and he tasted the salt. He released his hold on her and they parted.

BeBe sat outside on the swing. The first drops of rain fell.

Chapter 26

They lay in bed out on the porch and listened to the rain fall in the bamboo. She turned to face him, her hair spread out on her pillow. "Bobby," she began, "ah hope you not gon' hate me. Ah'll try to be better, to be more good, not ever again to try to hurt nobody. Ah never done that before. Ah jus' couldn't stand to lose you. Please, Bobby, say you don' hate me. You don' have to love me, ah don' expec' that, but I couldn' stand you hating me."

He wanted to say, We've wrecked our lives. My life is finished, and you helped kill me. But he couldn't. "I don't hate you, BeBe."

"But you don't like me neither, huh, Bobby?"

He turned over on his back, his arms behind his head. "BeBe, to tell you the truth, I don't know what happened. Maybe we just got too used to each other."

"I don't blame you none. I'm fat and ah don' even try to do nothin' about it. I used to try, but it looked like it didn' matter at all to you. So I stopped."

"So, I'm to blame for that too? Jesus, is there anything I'm not guilty of?"

"No, no, cher, ah'm not sayin' that at all. But if you had, you know, said somethin' to me, like 'BeBe leave the food alone,' I would have tried harder. But you didn' seem to care. That's what hurts the most, Bobby, when the one you love don' care."

He was guilty and refused to lie, so he said nothing.

"Bobby, will you do me a favor?"

"Uh-huh."

"Can I lay in your arms? Like when we was young. Lord but I used to like that. To be in your arms."

He extended an arm, and she lay in it.

"Bobby."

"Uh-huh?"

"You think in time, when time has pass', you might not be angry no more, and maybe you'd like me a little bit?"

"I'll try."

"You know, Bobby, I believe Jesus forgives me what I done to Ruth Ann. I'm not sufferin' about it like I did. Well, if He can forgive me, maybe you can. You gon' try?"

"Yes."

"You swear to God?"

"I do."

"Say it, Bobby, say . . ."

But he had drifted off to sleep.

In the bedroom, only feet away, Ruth Ann sat at a dresser and combed her hair. She studied herself in the mirror. She still liked what she saw, but she liked it less than she had just a few months before. The wear and tear of Richelieu, the strain of desperate love, had left little marks, sears that she hoped only she could see. Her big eyes didn't glow like they used to. An invisible film now covered them; what had smoldered now seemed veiled in smoke.

Her full, petulant lips were now enclosed by two tiny bookends, lines etched on either side of her mouth, the residue of shock and suffering.

The scar between breast and arm was angry and still ripe. Doc Mouton had assured her it would fade in time, although it would never disappear. It would always be there, a reminder of . . .

Oh, Bobby, she thought, I will always love you. The last thing I'll see at night will be your dark face. It is so unfair. Richelieu could have been so damn perfect. You the Sheriff, me the newspaper lady. Us, husband and wife. I want to cry out your name. I want you to come to me. I want to make the love we never made. I want . . . Now she spoke aloud: "I want peace."

She wondered if she'd ever regain it. It was not so easy to come by.

Of course, eventually she'd build a life, some kind of life. And if it really wasn't life as she'd known it, dreamed about, still she'd call it that. Find an apartment, ride the streetcar to work, eat beignets by the river, at night go listen to some jazz, sleep late on Sunday, have brunch with friends. It would be okay. I'm a survivor, she thought, and crawled into bed.

Her last thought was, This house is so quiet, and then she thought of him, and she slept.

Chapter 27

The front page of the *Gazette* carried a picture of a contrite-looking Papoot, standing, head bowed, before His Holiness Pope Pius XII. The Pope seemed dazed, and the boys at the barbershop, at Coon's, and even at Misty's Paradise Inn speculated as to why.

Possum's theory was that Papoot had tried to shake the Pope down "for his little people."

Big Shot roared, and Li'l Shot issued a warning: "He's up to no good."

Nonc said, "Maybe he's confessing! I hope the Pope got a lot of time!"

Misty offered, "Two to one he's makin' money on the deal!"

Ballou said, "Only a fool would take that bet."

Na Na commented on the air. "De De, my little sweetheart, said to me, 'You know, Na Na, Papoot looks holy.' And he do. Me, I believe Papoot's gettin' straight with his Maker. De De said, 'Na Na, have charity, he's an old man.' So I think my De De's right, and I say, Good luck, Papoot, whatever life has in store for you."

Someone even mentioned the fact that Moose had dropped out of sight. Possum said, "Maybe he's burning down someplace in Texas!"

President Prejean was charitable and told the boys at Rotary, "If he's found God, more power to him."

Mayor Big Head said the only clever thing he would ever speak in his lifetime, and didn't realize it. He said, "If I was God, I'd hide from him." But no one laughed, and the Mayor soon forgot what he'd said.

Justin sat at his desk in his white stucco cottage. Puccini arias were playing on his record player. He wept for Mimi and for Cio-Cio-San and he wept for Justin. He had stopped reading the *Gazette,* so he hadn't seen his father's photo.

They had a brief conversation before Papoot left for the airport in New Orleans. Papoot had dropped by at sunset, surprising Justin. He'd invited himself in, sat at Justin's desk, and just stared at his son.

Finally, he spoke: "Me, ah don' know how you got that way; little boys for God's sake. Me, ah don' even understan' what you all do. It makes me sick to the stomach. Everything ah ever done in my life, and believe me I've just about done it all, ah never touched no kid. It don' make no sense. That's two you killed, Justin. Two."

"The one in Rome did not die."

"Ah'm not talkin' about no Italian, ah'm talkin' about your mama."

"No!"

"Sit down, you bastard! Why you think she done it, huh? She couldn' stan' what her darlin' boy had become, thass why! As long as ah live, and thank God it won't be all that long, ah'll never forget that look on her face when ah told her. She blamed me. Me! Goddamn you, me! Ah'm gon' go to my grave with that. You killed her too. How you got so bad, Justin? You supposed to be God's man!"

Justin crossed one leg over the other and sat there, saying nothing.

"An don' look for me to proteck you, you fake priest. You ain't no more a priest than me, an' ah sure ain't one. But there's one big differ-ence—ah don' claim to be one. You, you stan' up there in them cos-tumes and tell people how to lead they life, and then I'll be goddamn if you don' have the nerve to listen to their secrets and tell them what they got to do to save their souls. What bullshit! You can't save yours! If you even got one. Ah don' know. Ah know somethin's missin'. You not whole, Justin. What the hell ah'm supposed to do, ah don' know. Even the Bishop don' know. You know where he wanted to send you that firs' time . . . a Indian reservation in Montana. How you like that, huh? I shoulda let him do it; at leas' that kid wouldn't be dead. But me, ah said, 'No,' ah said, 'it would kill Annabelle.' Well, that was a surprise for sure—it killed her anyway. How it feels to have your own mama's blood on your hands? I bet you never confess that! Ah can' pay no one this time; the Bishop would spit in my face, and he'd be right. You know what ah had to promise him? You wouldn' do no more bad. Me, ah'd look after you. I thought sure your own mama's death would make you change your filthy ways, but you can't change. Right? Answer me, you goddamn devil, answer me!"

"I have changed. You've got to believe me. I prayed to Jesus and to His mother Mary and they . . ."

"You cocksucker, you pullin' that shit on me? Ah invented bullshit. But you know somethin', Justin, ah sure didn' invent you. Ah swear before Christ ah don't know where you come from. Hell—thass where you come from, and thass where you goin'."

"He forgives. He is a forgiving God."

"You believe that, huh? Me, ah'm not so sure. If He forgives you then He's a fool, an' ah can' believe God's no fool. He got to be smarter than that."

"What am I going to do?"

"How the hell ah know? This is one time ah ain't got no answers, and there sure ain't enough cash to get your ass out of this mess."

"Then I'll be arrested. How would you like that? Papoot's son, his only son, arrested. Put away in a madhouse. Well? How does that sound?"

"Who gon' do the arrestin'?"

"Little Bobby."

"Bullshit. More bullshit."

"No. He came to church. He told me so. I have until July fifth to turn myself in. You can talk to Bobby. You all talk the same language. He's a member of this family. Tell him . . . tell him it would kill BeBe. No, better not tell him that, he might like that."

"At leas' he's fuckin' a woman. Not no little boy."

"We're all sinners, didn't you know? You too. All that wheeling and dealing, that fixing, skimming, grafting. Think that's okay just because you got by with it? I say *got* because it looks like that's over.

Even your boob followers have had enough. Can you imagine, those morons have had enough!"

"Ah wonder why Bobby didn' arrest you then and there? How come he gave you a deadline?"

"I'm sure I don't know. We are family."

"Not Bobby. Bobby ain't never been family. He been a big disappointment to me. When him and your sister married, ah thought for sure he'd be like Gaston. He wasn'. He ain't nothin' like Gaston."

They sat in silence. Their faces were white in the gloom; their eyes were locked in, unable to avoid looking at each other.

"Get me a lawyer. A good lawyer. Every lawyer in this parish owes you. I'll get off and I'll go away. You'll never hear from me again. Look, I swear it. I swear it. You can do it. You're still Papoot, you still run this parish."

Papoot didn't answer, his face was a blank.

Justin fell to his knees. "I'm begging you, Papa. Save Justin, save your little boy. I've been a bad boy, I admit it, do you hear? *I've been a bad boy!*"

Papoot spoke quietly, with no expression. He could have been reading a grocery list. "Justin, you know what ah hate the mos'? When your mama did what she did, ah was angry with her. You hear me? Ah wasn' all that sad, I was pissed. Her takin' off and leavin' me with a woman big as a house and a priest who sucks cocks. She lef' me holdin' a sack of shit. An' there wasn' no way to get rid of it. Me an' that sack was gon' be together until ah died. You made me hate my Annabelle."

"You'll see a lawyer? Say you will. It's my only chance, my only chance. See Hurphy, he's the best. Hurphy can do it. Say you will?"

Papoot stood. He was exhausted. "Yeah, all right. You mah sack of shit. Ah'll go see Hurphy."

"You'll call me? Say you'll call 'em!"

Papoot nodded. "If you don' hear from me, you know he turned me down."

"He won't turn you down. You're the best. Your tongue's made of gold. Hurphy'll do it, you'll see."

Papoot's back was to him. He stood at the door. He said, "Goodbye, Justin."

"Papa . . . Papa . . ."

Hurphy met Papoot at his law offices. Main Street was deserted. They sat in Hurphy's conference room, Papoot at the head of the table. Hurphy was dressed in a T-shirt and khakis. He took out a bottle of Jack Daniel's and two glasses. Papoot shook his head; he didn't want one. Hurphy poured half a glass of the whiskey and gulped it down. He refilled the glass.

"Bobby's gon' arres' Justin for Ti Boy. He gave him until the fifth. They gon' put him away."

"I know," Hurphy said.

"How you know?"

"The Bishop told me."

"Ah wan' you to defend him. He'll go away. For good."

"I'm sorry, Papoot. I owe you. When I came here after the War, you got me my first state contract. It kept us going for a year. So I owe you big time. But I can't."

"If ah did all that for you, Hurphy, how can you say no?"

"The Bishop told me to keep hands off. He said leave it to Bobby."

"When Bobby became such an expert on everything, huh? Me, ah must have been sleeping. Does the Bishop know about him and that woman?"

"I have no idea. I suppose so. He pretty much knows what's going on in the diocese. I do know he and Bobby met. And he sent for me and said to keep out of it. I had already given the Brouliettes a thousand dollars in a fake insurance policy."

"Tell the Bishop ah'll give him double what Bobby gave him. Ask him how he'd like a million dollars. In cash, Hurphy. All of it in cash."

"I don't believe Bobby gave him anything."

"When did the Bishop become a saint?"

"I'm sorry, Papoot. I really am."

"Thass my son, Hurphy. My only son."

"I can't do it."

Papoot stood. His face was red, and he was trembling with rage. "I should have let you starve, Hurphy, thass what I shoulda done."

Bobby sat at the bar at Misty's. He drank Coke. Misty stood near him. It was early, and the place was empty. Nat King Cole sang on the jukebox, and the lights danced overhead. Ballou stood in the kitchen. Bobby could smell red beans and rice simmering with big pieces of sausage.

"I want you to do something, Misty."

"Sure, Bobby," she said, wondering what it would cost her.

He smiled. "It won't cost you anything. At least no cash."

She smiled, her face a bunch of wrinkles and white powder. "Whatever you say, Bobby."

"I want you to get rid of Na Na's gal. I want her to go tonight. And I don't want anybody to know where she's gone to."

"Why?"

"Na Na's making a fool of himself on the radio. He's got a good wife . . ."

She thought to herself, You got a good wife too. So? But she kept quiet.

"He's gone off the deep end. He's not a bad man. Just a fool. I've got to protect him."

"That goes with bein' Sheriff too?"

Bobby smiled, but it was a grim smile. "To tell you the truth, Misty, I don't know what goes with being Sheriff. The law ought to be simple, you know, black or white, but it's not. Not by a long shot."

"I coulda told you that. Ain't nothin' to do with people is simple.

People! If you knew the things ah seen. What people want—Jesus. It still amazes, me, an' I seen it all."

"Me too."

"It's like we're in the same line of work, huh, Bobby? You an' me?"

He laughed. "Well, I never thought of it that way."

She touched his arm. "Bobby, do me a favor."

"What?"

"Let the li'l gal stay till the fifth. The Fourth is a big day for me. All them mens filled with patriotism and politics and all that bullshit. It goes straight to their balls. Please, Bobby."

"Okay."

"I won't forget you, Bobby. You can count on me."

"I do," he said.

"You ain't gon' have no competition anyway."

"Well, you never know."

"No. Poor Papoot."

He couldn't help grinning. He knew how much she hated Papoot.

She grinned too. He noticed for the first time a diamond in her teeth. "That's a tough man, yeah, Bobby. I seen some in my time, but he's the toughest."

He nodded. He knew.

She scratched her head gently with a single finger. "You know what I wonder, Bobby? I wonder if he's gon' get his. Ah don't just mean havin' to leave office; you know, really get his?"

He wanted to tell her, Yes, he's about to get his, but he just shrugged like he didn't know. He stood, put a dollar on the bar. She protested, but he walked out.

Ballou approached Misty with a big wooden spoon filled with red beans. She blew on the spoon and put it to her lips. "A li'l more red pepper, Ballou, jus' a li'l bit."

He nodded. "I think so too. What Bobby had on his mind?"

"We got to get rid of Na Na's papoon."

"Aw naw!"

"Ah hate it too. Me, ah was about to own me a radio station. How you reckon Bobby knew that? Huh?"

"He don' miss much, little Bobby."

"He's a funny one for sure. Ah believe he's gettin' his ass kicked some too."

"Over that girlfriend?"

"Yeah."

"Man, how would you like to have her workin' here for about a month? We could retire."

"Ballou, don't go thinkin' ah'm goin' queer on you, but ah believe ah could go for some of that too."

"Me too!"

"Ah'd cut your balls off, Ballou."

"Just jokin'. You ma one an' only."

"Make sure you remember that. Huh?"

"Yes, ma'am!" he said and saluted.

Chapter 28

Pink and blue flyers appeared on every telephone post and in almost every store window in the parish telling of the "Big Fourth of July Political Event!" There would be speeches, balloons, hot dogs, and Cokes for everybody, "All Free!!!" And there would be music by Papa Sotile and the Richelieu Gents! It would start at noon.

Na Na Duhon plugged the event with all his powers of persuasion. "CAJN will broadcast live, and me and my sweet De De gon' cover the scene from top to bottom. We'll be tellin' an old friend good-bye; no matter how you feel about him, you got to treat that person with respec'. He might have been bad a time or two, but you got to respec' his age. Besides, the Holy Father must have forgive him, so we can too! Then we gon' welcome a new leader. My De De says he's a new breed; me, ah don't know about that, but he's gon' be for all the people and the business community. You can' have one group in and one out. America don't work that-a-way. In the meantime, everybody who's anybody gon' be there, so if you wanna be somebody, you better be there too. And if you want to be interviewed, jus' give me and De De a signal and we'll put you on the air. We got a lotta time to kill."

Possum Aucoin, listening along with the other boys in the barbershop, said, "Na Na makes me feel edjicated!"

Li'l Shot Fontenot, responsible that day for his archrival, Nonc, said, "His daddy was a fool too."

Nonc Doucet said, "His grandfather wasn' no prize neither! Ah remember when he stole Poon's daddy's pig."

Possum observed, "Now Poon was a real fool!"

"How you know, Possum? He was before your time," Li'l Shot noted.

"Ah heard it from mah daddy, that ole son of a bitch," Possum said and spit on the floor. It was widely known that Possum despised his father.

Hurphy Perrault, sitting in a corner with the *Gazette,* decided to make trouble. "Now, Possum, I remember your father as a great man. Great!"

Possum accepted the challenge, made the sign of the cross in case his father was listening from Heaven, and said, "My father was a sack of shit."

"Shame on you, talkin' that way about you own flesh," Li'l Shot said.

Possum was thoroughly pissed. "That's it! Carry your ass from this shop, Li'l Shot, and take Nonc with you! It ain't no help to business for two old geezers who ain't got no more hair anyway to take up valuable space in my shop. No wonder ah'm a poor man."

Everyone laughed. Nonc opened an eye and said, "It's all bullshit anyway!"

One of President Prejean's two sound trucks passed, blaring an invitation to the rally to one and all, in French and in English. The trucks were painted red, white, and blue, and bore the slogan "Richelieu Needs a Great President!" In between announcements Cajun music was played over the loudspeakers. The sound was turned down only when the trucks passed St. Ann's.

The sound trucks had been loaned to the campaign by Big Shot Fontenot, who knew that once the campaign was over the trucks would vanish. They always did, with no one knowing what happened to them and certainly no one accepting responsibility for their disappearance. It was a tradition, one that made the job of sound truck driver much sought after. In fact, many a successful politician had started just that way.

Everyone seemed beyond happy. Politics was bigger than Christmas and was a constant topic from one election to the next. The desire to run for office beat in practically every man's heart, and many a political dream (most ending exactly that way, as dreams) began every third Fourth of July.

It was a beautiful day and not even too hot! The sun was shining, not blazing as it usually did, and crowds began collecting early that Sunday morning. People came in cars, on bicycles, and even in horse-and-buggies from the outreaches of the parish. They were there from all over, from Montaigne, from Bayou Blue, and even from the swamps.

In St. Ann's, Father Justin Gaspard, in white with a huge gold cross, stood before his congregation. He stared out at them, silent for an uncomfortably long time, like he was looking for something in the air directly over their heads.

Hurphy and Anita stirred nervously in their seats. He whispered, "I think he's gone completely crazy." Anita said, "Shhh," but Hurphy couldn't stop. "No, I mean really crazy! Look at his eyes, look at his eyes."

Finally, Justin lowered his gaze, like he hadn't found what he was seeking in the air above them. He smiled a wan, timid smile, and those who were close to the altar saw his Adam's apple bob up and down as he swallowed. There was a titter. When would he start? Would he ever start? Could he? What was the matter with their pastor? Doc Mouton felt for the bag on the floor between his feet.

Finally Father Justin spoke, softly, so softly that those in the rear had to lean forward to hear, and old people cupped their ears.

"I won't keep you long. Politics, not religion, is in the air. I want to talk with you about the very toughest of all things. Tougher than the worst illness, tougher than the worst tragedy. I want to talk with you"—he paused, his jaws clenched, and he seemed to choke the words out—"about forgiveness."

Possum thought, He's beggin' for his father. They gon' forgive him all right, election day.

"What is it, this toughest of all things to come by? It is a state of grace, the ultimate state of grace. It is more in God's image than anything we do, for He is a God of forgiving. The question is, Are we His children, children of forgiving?"

BeBe thought, He's talking about me. He's tellin' me ah can be forgiven. She wept into her handkerchief and wondered why her father hadn't accompanied her to Mass. But come to think of it, he hadn't come to Mass anytime lately. Surprisingly, Justin hadn't said one thing about it.

"Forgiving is not easy. I suspect it may even be difficult for God. You see, some of us are not that easy to forgive. We are—how shall I say it?—terrible. We do not conform because we cannot conform, and in not conforming we cross a line, we become monsters!"

BeBe thought, I knew it! Thass what I am. Like the Mummy, or Frankenstein.

Hurphy thought, If he confesses, here on the pulpit, he will destroy this church forever.

"But what are we to do with these line crossers? There are not that many choices. Spiritually we may leave them to Heaven, as they say. Alas, there is also a physical self, and that presents a problem. We can lock them away, keep them filled with chloral hydrate, watch them through peepholes in steel doors. And when they get out of line, we can shower them down with a fire hose. We have to watch them, for monsters have this urge to die. You see, they know what they are, even though the rest of us don't recognize them because, well, they look just like us. But they know what they are! And that is their personal horror. They know. It takes a long time to die when you're suffering. Moments seem to be lifetimes. Pain. It's all pain.

"And we who have suffered by them—shall we forgive them, or shall we also leave this to God? You do see, it's not that easy to forgive. I mean, look behind a monster and you will find the bodies fallen in its wake. These monsters are detestable creatures! So what would you do if a monster entered that back door, ran down that center aisle, threw himself at the foot of the altar, and looking up at the crucified Christ, screamed from a bloody soul, 'Give me sanctuary!'

"Hmmm? I submit we would flee this place, leave him to his Savior. He would be alone. But that would be nothing new for the monster. I will let you in on a little secret: Monsters are alone every day of their miserable existence. They even come into this world, your world, alone, and they know it. They have committed the ultimate sin, one which they will pay for so long as they breathe. The sin of *being different!*"

Justin looked out over the congregation and smiled a brilliant smile, full of perfect teeth. The light reflected off his golden hair, and he appeared to those before him to be more beautiful than any movie star. They did not see a monster.

And he was alone.

Now throngs surrounded the courthouse. The cupola had been polished by trustees and shown like the dome on some Eastern temple. Papa Sotile, fiddle in hand, led the Richelieu Gents in "Jolie Blanc," and people began dancing on Main Street, in pairs and by themselves, doing the two-step, lost in their own memories. Papa had a pint of Jim Beam in his back pocket and took frequent nips. He, above everyone else, had to get into the spirit of things because, he thought, I am the spirit! Jolie Blanc!

Then the band broke into "Allons a Lafayette," let's go to Lafayette, yeah, cher, le's go! Grandmas danced with babies in their arms, and grandpas, with saucy looks upon their faces danced with high school beauties. Football players swaggered about in their letter jackets despite the heat. It was a day to show out and show off.

Then Richelieu's fire engine slowly made its way through the crowd, its siren blaring. On it Mayor Big Head Arceneaux sat side by side with Bozo the Dalmatian. Possum muttered, "Bozo would make a better mayor." Big Head bowed and shook his clasped hands above his head, the champion's sign of victory. When he spotted people he knew, he gave the thumbs-up sign, and when they returned it, he was delighted. It had become the secret sign by which President Prejean supporters made themselves known to each other. It was as popular as the KC sign. Possum said, "Papoot used the finger, we might as well use the thumb."

The sound trucks circled the courthouse, music blaring, tributes to President Prejean interspersed in the music. Papa Sotile shouted to the driver, "Turn that goddamn thing down," but got a big laugh and the finger in return.

Ruth Ann and BeBe stood off to the side; both carried notebooks to cover the story. BeBe was thrilled. It was the first time in years that she was more than either Papoot's daughter or Bobby's wife—she was the *Gazette*'s owner, the *Gazette*'s reporter.

The courthouse was decorated with red, white, and blue bunting and flags. A dozen Old Glories framed a backdrop. At center was a microphone and behind it a wooden box—also decorated in patriotic crepe paper—for the Mayor to stand on. Big Head, in his glory, strutted to the mike and said, just the way he'd heard professionals like Na Na do it, "Testing, one two, testing, one two, testing . . ."

A voice from the crowd that sounded suspiciously familiar called out, "Fool, you done tested enough!"

The crowd roared with laughter, and the Mayor jumped down from his special box and broke into his famous "Whoop! Whoop!" jig, which was greeted by huge applause.

There was a noticeable division in the crowd. Just about everyone there stood in the center and to the right of the courthouse. Off to the left stood a handful of old-timers from the country—all that was left of Papoot Gaspard's "little people." They seemed bewildered, dazed, in mourning, and they spoke in whispers, being careful not to laugh. It was not a happy day for the little people.

Na Na and his De De made their way through the crowd carrying a microphone on a long extension cord, furnishing up-to-the-minute descriptions of the proceedings, never once stopping to realize that no one was left at home to listen.

It seemed that everyone had a balloon and a Coke. The free hot dogs wouldn't be served until after the speeches, to ensure everybody sticking around. Some would go home with fifty of them, food for two weeks. Free hot dogs! It was almost too much.

Na Na was eloquent. "History's in the air; you can feel it. Out with the old, in with the new! This here day will never be forgotten in Richelieu history."

The Mayor wiped the perspiration from his face, jumped aboard his box, and said in a voice that really required no amplification, "Ladies and gentlemen of Richelieu, welcome to the old-time political Fourth of July celebration! If there's anything we the officials of Richelieu can do to make you more comfortable, let us know."

That same familiar voice interrupted, "You can hurry up!"

The crowd laughed, as did the Mayor, who resisted the urge to dance.

"We celebrate today . . . ," the Mayor began, and Watch Out Naquin said to Short Change St. Pierre, "Oh shit, here he goes with his young American blood speech."

". . . the blood shed by young Americans," the Mayor intoned almost on signal. "What did they die for?"

A voice shouted back, "For you to get through!"

The Mayor, ever eager to be appealing to the voters, never answered his own question. Instead he began the introduction of speakers. "Our first speaker needs no introduction."

A voice called out, "Well, don' introduce him!" The crowd laughed. Even Bobby laughed.

"Our own popular Sheriff Bobby Boudreaux!"

Someone shouted, "Give 'em hell, Bobby!" and everybody had a good laugh because Bobby didn't give nobody hell.

Bobby, nervous, not a good public speaker, stepped atop the Mayor's box, where he towered over the microphone, and when he began speaking Hurphy called out, "We can't hear you!" Bobby blushed and stepped down from the box. "I want to welcome you to this special day. I hope everybody has a safe and good time. Please watch that the kids don't hurt themselves with fireworks. Some of these things are dangerous, and every year we have accidents. Anyway, I just want you to know I'll be a candidate for reelection in November; that's just a few months away, and I'd appreciate if you don't forget me on election day. I thank you."

There was more applause than the speech deserved. BeBe looked proudly at Ruth Ann. To BeBe, his words had been poetry. Ruth Ann smiled back.

The Mayor hopped back on his box as Bobby made his way through the crowd, stopping to shake hands, to thank everyone, to exchange little meaningless banter, at which he was very good. He kissed babies and every lady who seemed to want to be kissed. He shook every extended hand and even squeezed those that weren't offered. He joined Moe at the rear of the throng and said, "Now comes what they're really waiting for."

Mayor Arceneaux rose to new oratorical heights. "Every once in a while there comes a new leader of his people." You could feel the ripple of excitement through the crowd, the almost electric hum of anticipation. "Where these people come from, or even why, is a mystery. But they do. Thank God! Ladies and gentlemen, may I present President Prejean."

The band broke into "Happy Days Are Here Again," and Hurphy looked on like a proud father, arms folded across his chest. He had written the Mayor's speech, even rehearsed him in how to deliver it. He had offered the same service to President, who'd politely turned him down. "I want to speak from the heart," he said.

Now President looked out over the people. Shortly they would be his people, and he had to fight down the emotion he felt. "Citizens of Richelieu, I am honored to be here today. I wasn't sure that I would be. During the War there were moments, more than one, when I had doubts that I would even be alive. But I made it, and believe it or not,

I used to wonder why I did. So many good men, better than me, didn't come home. Yet I had. And I asked myself, why?

"One day, one Sunday, I was on my knees in Mass and the answer came to me. I don't mean I heard a voice, I didn't. But something inside said to me, 'You came home to serve, to serve the people.' "

A hush had fallen over the crowd, and several could be seen dabbing their eyes.

"So that's why I'm here with you, the people, today: to announce that I will be a candidate for State Senator in the November election!"

Bobby said, "You can't take it from him, the man can really talk." Moe nodded. He too had been touched.

BeBe wondered for a moment if MaMa Seego might have some little something for President, something that would put him out of commission, maybe make him lose his voice. But shame quickly settled over her, and she made another oath, to be different, to be better. Still, Papoot was her daddy, and to see him hurt so publicly broke her heart.

The fire engine's siren blew, car horns honked, fireworks went off, turning the air blue. The applause for President was deafening. But he wasn't through. "It wouldn't be right for me and for every one of you not to let Papoot know that we appreciate and will never forget his lifetime of service."

The crowd grew quiet, and a familiar voice called, "You mean, his years of stealing!" At first everyone was stunned, and they drew a collective breath, but then they erupted in hearty laughter, followed by hoots of derision. Coon Soileau turned to One Lung Savoy: "They jus' don' want no more of Papoot's bullshit." One Lung coughed in agreement, spraying those near him.

Posters carrying President Prejean's name and slogan had magically appeared in everyone's hands. They waved them frantically, like people wanting to surrender. Now the crowd began to chant, "Prejean, Prejean, Prejean." The candidate waved to them, then motioned for them to stop, as he stood aside and the Mayor mounted his box.

"And now here's Senator Glenn 'Papoot' Gaspard, who I'm sure wants to share a few thoughts with us. Let's give him a hand."

Except for his old-timers, the handful of his little people, the crowd didn't follow instructions. The lack of applause was embarrassing. Bobby said, "Jesus."

Papoot, in his familiar white suit, red tie, and white straw hat, stood before the microphone. His face was pink, his smile warm, and his eyes danced with expectation, excitement, even with joy.

"My friends," he began, and again that voice called out, "Not likely," and everybody, even Papoot, laughed.

"Well, you can't win 'em all," he said. For some reason this stopped the laughter, and one catcall rang out, but when nobody joined in, the shouter fell quiet.

"Ah jus' got back from Rome, an' that's a far piece for an old man like Papoot. Ah went there to seek the advice of the wisest man in all the world, the Holy Father. An' me, when ah finally stood before him, what you think happened? Old Papoot froze, he couldn't speak. The Holy Father looked at me, and he must have figured ah was deaf and dumb—a lot of cripples go for his blessings—but he smiled, not no big smile, jus' a little one, and he said, 'What can ah do for you, mah child?' It's been a long time since anybody call Papoot mah child, and I broke down and cried. The Holy Father spoke clear, and his English was better than mine."

Everyone laughed. Their English wasn't so hot either.

"Just like that, old Papoot was cryin', and you know somethin', it didn't make me feel ashame', not one bit. Tears felt—how they say?— natural, when the Holy Father called you 'mah child.' Me, I didn't know what to say, though a tousan' things went through my head. Ah thought about askin' him to pray for me a few more years, but I figured that would be a waste because that was up to the Lord. Ah know ah didn' have long to speak because other peoples were waitin' in line, like when a good show plays to the Palace."

Laughter, warmer laughter. Not outright friendship, but some of the ice had cracked.

"So I said to the Holy Father, 'Me, there's not much you can do for me, mah life's pretty well lived, but mah people, the people of Richelieu, you can do somethin' for them.'

"He didn' say nothin', but some of his Cardinals were lookin' nervous, like ah might tap him for a few bucks, you know, hee, hee!"

Now the crowd roared with laughter. This was vintage Papoot, letting them in on the tricks he was playing, with a little boy's wink, and the dimples dancing in his cheeks.

"Ah said, 'Holy Father, ah would like you to bless some crosses for every man, woman, and chile in Richelieu, crosses that they could wear pinned to their shirts and even on their pajamas when they went to bed, crosses that would proteck them from all harm, from hard times and even from sickness.' "

The crowd was so quiet now that you could hear a mosquito breathe, the heartbeat of a frog, a flower's petals unfolding in the swamp.

"The Holy Father touched my shoulder jus' with the tips of his fingers, and he said, 'Ah'm gon' do that because you love your peoples so, jus' like our Lord loved His peoples.' "

Almost imperceptibly, Papoot gave Papa Sotile a little signal, and the fiddler put his violin under his chin and began to play "Ave Maria." People listened in stunned silence; it was so beautiful, so touching, and almost everyone made the sign of the cross.

Suddenly there was a murmur at the rear of the throng, and people began looking over their shoulders to see what it was all about.

Bobby looked too and did not believe his eyes. Moe looked to Heaven, incredulity on his usually blank face.

Coming up the center of Main Street was a donkey pulling a cart and led by Moose Thibodeaux, dressed in a white choir robe and sporting a long, black beard.

There was a collective gasp. Right before their eyes was a miracle: their catechism come to life. And Papa Sotile played on.

People began making the sign of the cross another time, and many of the devout fell to their knees and started to pray. Senior citizens wept, and some surged forward to touch Moose, the cart, and even the donkey.

The crowd parted like the Red Sea to make room for the cart to be led up to the stage. A hush fell as people saw the cart's contents: three huge barrels containing something that glittered in the sunlight like a billion diamonds.

Papoot held up a hand, finger pointing to Heaven. "These barrels contain them crosses blessed by the Holy Father, and you don' have to push or rush, there's a cross for every one of you."

People began to cheer, and the cheer became "Papoot! Papoot! Papoot!" and President turned to Hurphy and said, "We've been fucked!"

Hurphy said, "Don't give up yet."

President said, "Thanks, but *you* run for the damn thing. It would be like opposing the Pope, or Jesus Christ himself."

Mayor Big Head Arceneaux, quick to read the direction of the wind, jumped up on his box and screamed at the firemen, "Blow the whistle, blow the whistle!" And from the box he embraced Papoot, hugging the man about the waist.

Firecrackers went off! Roman candles shot up into the air, and now, almost as if on signal, the bell of St. Ann's began to peal!

The grin on Bobby's face grew. The old man had pulled out all the stops. Fire engines, bands, thousands of voices screaming "Papoot! Papoot!" and now church bells!

BeBe was smiling at him when she saw his face change as if a cloud had come between him and the sun. He uttered, "Oh my God," turned, and began to run toward St. Ann's. BeBe was bewildered. What was Bobby doing? Then she saw. "Oh, God, oh, my God!" She waddled behind him. "Bobby, wait for me! Wait for me!"

The fire engine's siren blew a long, catlike yowl, and sirens on all the deputies' cars began to scream. And through this banshee chorus, you could still hear "Papoot! Papoot!" And beneath that Papa Sotile kept right on playing "Ave Maria."

Bobby threw open the heavy door of St. Ann's. The sanctuary was deserted. No candles burned, and the only light came through the stained-glass windows showing the Stations of the Cross.

Bobby called out, "Justin! Justin! Justin! Where are you, Justin?"

Outside the chant continued: "Papoot! Papoot!"

People formed an orderly line to get their tiny crosses that had been blessed by the Holy Father. Those who wanted two, got two, but that was the limit per family. President Prejean was nowhere to be seen, though Hurphy still looked on, glassy-eyed, stunned, watching a dream go down the toilet.

Even Possum couldn't hold back the enthusiasm. "You got to give it to the old crook. He kapowed President and all them would-be big shots for sure!"

"Justin! Justin!" Bobby called out again.

Then slowly he walked to the area behind the altar. There was a flight of wooden stairs, which he began to climb. Hearing someone behind him, he turned and saw BeBe. "Go back," he said, but she paid him no mind, though her face was covered with sweat and she was breathing heavily. The stairs were high, and when he reached the top (the floor beneath the cupola and the bell) hanging from the bell rope was Justin, his body now still, the bells no longer sounding.

He was dressed in his white surplice, and only the peculiar angle of his head gave evidence of his death.

"Aieeeeeeeeeee!" BeBe screamed, collapsing.

"Papoot! Papoot!" The chant continued outside.

And "Ave Maria" could be heard through it all.

Chapter 29

It was a cold and wintry night. Main Street was dark except for Moe Weiss's Notions and Tobacco. Rain pounded against the building's metal walls, and thunder sounded as lightning flashed across the sky.

Bobby, in a fur-collared police jacket, was helping Moe take inventory. It was necessary because Moe's eyesight was going fast. Bobby stood on a small ladder calling out items to Moe, who held a pencil stub over a notebook.

"Five packs, Gillette Blue Blades. Half a box, Keep Moving cigars and a full box of King Edwards. Here's three bottles of Lucky Tiger . . ."

"Enough for a while. Come, Bobby, we'll have our tea."

"It's the weather for it. I might even actually drink the damn stuff. But make it hot."

They went into the back room, and Bobby sat on Moe's bed, legs outstretched and crossed. His boots were wet. He needed a shave. It had been a busy day, as several of the parish's roads had washed out and at least one bridge was in structural trouble.

Handing him the steaming cup, Moe studied his friend's face. He had aged in the months since July Fourth. He had gone from "little Bobby" to a middle-aged man whose hair was now silver in many places.

Bobby tasted the tea. It was awful as usual, and he shook his head at Moe, who smiled. "It takes some getting used to," the little man said.

Bobby said, "In a hundred years I couldn't get used to this crap."

Moe sat on a chair opposite him, saying nothing.

Bobby sighed. "I went to New Orleans. It was strictly business. No.

That's a damn lie. I went to see her. I went into the Monteleone Hotel and called her at the *Picayune*. She was nice, but she wouldn't see me. Said she was engaged. I said I understood, and then we didn't have a whole lot more to say. Oh, she wanted to know how was BeBe. They don't communicate anymore. BeBe blames her for Justin. I guess that's a lot safer than blaming me."

He paused like he was making up his mind. "Oh, and I told her I loved her, that I always would. I had to say it, Moe. I swear I don't know why. And Moe, she said . . . she loved me too. I said, 'That's pretty goddamn unfair!' I think she laughed, like life's unfairness was funny. I didn't see one thing funny about it. In fact, if you want to know the truth, Moe, these days I don't find many funny things."

Moe nodded.

"So what do you do if you can't laugh?"

"You weep."

"You do?"

"Inside. Sorrow is very personal, private."

Bobby stood, put the cup of tea on a side table, and said, "Let's get through with the inventory. I've got a long night ahead, checking the roads and bridges, and some fool is sure to fall into the bayou."

"Yes, a long night ahead," Moe said.